Frisky Business

WITHDRAWN

TAWNA FENSKE

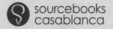
sourcebooks
casablanca

Published by Sourcebooks Casablanca, an imprint of Sourcebooks, Inc.
P.O. Box 4410, Naperville, Illinois 60567-4410
(630) 961-3900
Fax: (630) 961-2168
www.sourcebooks.com

Printed and bound in Canada.
MBP 10 9 8 7 6 5 4 3 2 1

For Craig.
If love and laughter make the world go 'round,
you are smack-dab in the center of mine.
That sounded filthier than I meant it to.

Chapter 1

EITHER MARLEY CARTMAN HAD STEPPED IN DOG DROPPINGS, or the makers of her new lotion had a weird concept of *sweet seduction*.

She dragged the toe of her Jimmy Choo peep-toe across the concrete floor of the Humane Society lobby, thinking it was absurd she'd dressed this nicely to drop paperwork at a business with a goat pen in the foyer.

The goat snorted and stretched its neck out to nibble the edge of Marley's overpriced skirt, so she stepped back, wincing as the shoes pinched her toes. Why on earth had she worn this?

You're a new professional in the community, she reminded herself. *Appearances are important.*

So is having circulation in my toes, she wanted to argue back, but she straightened her skirt and gave the receptionist a broad smile.

"A little loud in here," Marley shouted. Her voice vanished in a cacophony of barking and the metallic ping of kibble in dog dishes.

"What?"

"I said it's a little loud in here."

The receptionist shoved a surly gray cat into a wire kennel and turned to display her ample cleavage and a name tag that said *Tiff* and *Cascade Humane Society*. "What?"

"Nothing," Marley called as cheerfully as possible. "Um, do you think Ms. Peterson would mind if I waited outside until she's done phoning the mayor?"

"Virginia stopped boning the mayor three months ago," Tiff yelled with a smile. "Now she's boning one of the county commissioners."

"Okay," Marley said and looked back at the goat. It cocked its shaggy head to one side and bleated at her.

"Creepy, huh?" Tiff said. "I always feel like it's staring at me."

"It probably is," Marley replied, reaching out to scratch a spot between its two stubby horns. "Goats have rectangular pupils so they can survey broad areas for predators. Maybe he thinks you're plotting to eat him?"

Tiff laughed and shuffled a stack of papers to one side. "Are you a goat expert?"

"Not really. I've just been studying up on animal facts so I can be knowledgeable when I start my new job this Thursday at—"

"Marley Cartman?" Marley spun around to see a muscular brunette marching in with flushed cheeks and a pencil stabbed through her frizzy bun.

The woman thrust her hand out, not waiting for a response. "I'm Virginia. I'm so sorry to keep you waiting. We have a neutering clinic tomorrow and I've been inundated with calls from men wanting to know if they're eligible and whether we'd tell their wives and… well, anyway, I'm so glad you're here."

"It's great to finally meet you in person." Marley shook the woman's hand and dragged a toe across the concrete again. "I'm a little late getting here anyway. I hit some bad traffic getting out of Portland, and then I had to go extra slow over the mountains because of the U-Haul."

"U-Haul? Are you finally moving here?"

Marley nodded and beamed, pinched toes and dog doo

all but forgotten. "It took me a while to get my affairs in order and find a job here in Bend, and then my fiancé—well, ex-fiancé—made partner in his law firm, and since he didn't get any offers on his house anyway, he decided to stay in Portland, but it's all okay because I got this great job as the development director out at the wildlife sanctuary and, well, here I am."

Marley did an outward shrug and an inward forehead slap, annoyed as usual by her habit of over-sharing. But Virginia smiled like Marley hadn't just admitted her ex had chosen a corner office and granite countertops over pledging eternal devotion to Marley.

"Oh, that's just wonderful," Virginia gushed. "We've certainly appreciated all the pro bono fund-raising work you've been doing for us, but I always knew you wanted to leave the city and find a position over here where you can spend more time on your hobby."

"Hobby?"

"Photography, right?"

"Oh, right," Marley said, feeling her face redden. She'd forgotten she'd offered to take pictures for a grant proposal several months ago, hoping to endear herself further to the Humane Society board. It had worked, and Marley knew the director's reference was part of what had landed her the new job.

Still, she was hardly a photographer. The last picture she'd taken had been a cleavage shot she'd sent her fiancé—ex-fiancé—in hopes of adding sparks to their dying relationship. That might have gone better if she hadn't sent the photo to her father by mistake.

Marley cleared her throat. "So I have the paperwork here for you. If you'd like to take a look at—"

WHAM!

Marley staggered as a soggy cannonball slammed into the back of her knees. She made a frantic grab for the edge of the counter, sending a pile of papers flying through the slats of a kennel. The obese Persian inside gave the documents a halfhearted sniff and closed his eyes.

"Magoo, no!"

Marley gripped the counter and whirled around. She stared down at a dirty, wet mop on steroids and four legs. A pair of large hands circled the creature's chest and hoisted it off the ground, sending all four legs flailing and water dripping onto the concrete. The dog gave a startled grunt and farted.

"Sorry about that," called the dogcatcher. He clipped a leash to a red collar and deposited the squirming canine back on its feet. Then he stood up, blew a shock of red-brown hair off his forehead, and flashed a high-wattage grin that would've made Marley's toes curl if they weren't crunched in uncomfortable shoes. "Magoo gets a little excited when he's wet."

Marley stared at the man's eyes—one blue, one green—and tried not to fixate on the words "excited" and "wet."

"Right," she said, diverting her gaze from the mismatched eyes to a pair of broad shoulders and hair that glinted with hints of copper. She zeroed in on his T-shirt that read *Free Tibet (with purchase of second Tibet of equal or greater value)*. "It's okay, I'm fine," Marley said. "Just a little damp."

"Aren't we all," Tiff said, eyeing the dogcatcher's chest. The comment was probably supposed to be a suggestive murmur, but it came out more like a shout over the din of barking.

Marley felt her cheeks heat up. Virginia ignored them all and touched the man's elbow.

"Will, honey, I'm not sure the bath's really necessary. You know Magoo is next on the list."

Tiff grimaced and looked at the dog. "Sorry, Magoo. Overcrowding. Nothing personal."

The man stooped and gave the dog a scratch behind the ears. "Hey, he's got a few more hours to make a good first impression here. He can't do that smelling like lawn sausage."

Marley dragged her soiled shoe across the floor and looked at Tiff. "You mean Magoo's days are numbered?"

Tiff gave a sad shrug. "When the shelter's full, we have to start taking a closer look at some of the less-adoptable animals that are older or aggressive."

Marley stared down at Magoo, who was sniffing a potato bug. He didn't look aggressive, so he had to be old. With her father's happy thirty-sixth birthday card to her tucked in her purse, Marley could relate.

Never mind that she'd just turned thirty-five.

"You're getting up there, Marley," her father had said over dinner when he handed her the card and a check Marley knew she'd never cash. "Maybe it's time you had more financial security in your life so you don't end up in trouble like your mom did."

Maybe it's time I grew a pair and gave up my desperate quest for Daddy's approval, Marley wanted to reply, but she'd settled for, "Please pass the salt."

"Maybe Will can take Magoo home," Tiff said, jarring Marley back to the present. "Like the other three."

Magoo chose that moment to shake, sending a spray of muddy water into the nearby kennel and soaking both the Persian and Marley's papers. The cat didn't stir, and Marley looked at Magoo. His fur cleared his face for an instant, revealing one brown eye, one blue one.

"His eyes—they're two different colors," Marley gasped. "What is he?"

"Will?" Tiff asked. "He volunteers here every Thursday, but the rest of the time he's—"

"The dog," Will interrupted. "I think she meant the dog." He smiled at Marley, making her stomach do a funny little flip. His mismatched eyes glinted with amusement. "No one knows for sure, but probably some mix of Australian shepherd and cocker spaniel and maybe anteater."

"Anteater?"

"He has a bit of a licking problem."

Prompted to demonstrate, Magoo swiped his tongue over Marley's left calf. She knew she should probably discourage it, but she bent and scratched his ears instead. He looked up at her and wagged his stub-tail, and Marley's heart did a warm little squeeze in her chest.

"Hey, boy," she said.

Magoo sniffed her hand and licked that too.

"You have a dog?" Will asked.

"Nope. Always wanted one, but my mother hated dogs, and then I was traveling a lot for work and my fiancé—ex-fiancé—was allergic, which probably should have been a sign from the start, but—" Marley cleared her throat. "A simple no would have been better, huh?"

Will grinned. "Not really."

"I don't have a dog. Yet." Marley looked down at Magoo, who was stretching his neck to lick her elbow. She smiled, feeling warm and joyful about her new job, her fresh start, the chance to do whatever the hell she wanted now. She scratched Magoo's ear, and he leaned into her hand with a soft grunt of pleasure.

"He's a good dog," Will said. "A little too free with his affection, but I try not to hold that against anyone."

Marley scratched Magoo some more, focusing on the dog's mismatched eyes so she wouldn't be tempted to study Will's. "Are you really going to adopt him?" she asked.

"Can't. My other three would revolt."

Marley nodded and stood up, turning to Tiff. "I'll take him."

"Magoo or Will?"

Will laughed and pressed the leash into Marley's hand. His fingers were warm and solid, and Marley felt a current of heat pulse pleasantly up her arm. "The two-for-one special isn't 'til March," he said. "I'm sure you and Magoo will be very happy together. You can pick out a new leash from that rack over there or just take this one."

"It's free," Tiff added.

"Free bag of kibble, too," Will added. "I'll go grab it."

"You do have a home that allows pets, right?" Virginia asked.

Marley nodded and gripped the leash. "My dad owns a condo on the river. He's letting me stay there for as long as it takes me to find a place of my own."

"Free affection, free leash, free kibble, free condo," Virginia said with a smile. "Lucky girl."

Marley held the leash tighter, feeling the imaginary choke collar tightening around her own throat. "Free," she repeated. The word tasted bitter, and she knew it wasn't the stench of the kennel making her eyes water. She squelched the familiar sense of dread and instead looked down at her new pet.

Her heart gave a happy twist of gratitude, and Marley bent to pet him again. Magoo gave her shoe a suspicious sniff before raising his face to lick her knee.

—⁓—

Will retreated to the Humane Society's storage room, his mind still back in the lobby where the woman with the killer legs and sleek blond hair mistakenly believed she'd just saved a death row dog.

"Where the hell did you put Magoo?"

He turned to see his sister standing with hands on hips and a leash draped around her shoulders. There'd been a time Will might have enjoyed the thought of hooking it to a spiked collar and dragging Bethany behind his Volkswagen. Now he just shrugged.

"Magoo isn't moving to the Portland shelter after all," he told her. "You can still take the other transfers though."

"Remind me again why I let you talk me into volunteering as a dog chauffeur."

"Because it's the charitable thing to do."

"Uh-huh."

"Because you're a kind soul."

"Right."

"Because it's your penance for stealing my wife."

Bethany rolled her eyes. "You aren't bitter about that and you know it. Things weren't working with you and April long before she and I started playing kiss-the-bunny-on-the-nose."

"I've forgiven you for that, but not for the disturbing visuals."

Bethany laughed and tossed her long, auburn hair as she dropped the spare dog leash into a bin on the counter. "Just doing my part to keep things awkwardly friendly between all of us," she said, and Will had to admit he appreciated her for it. "You know, just because your wife turned out to like tits and ass as much as you do doesn't make you less of a man."

"No, but it does make this conversation disturbing. Is it almost over?"

"Yes." Bethany stood on tiptoe and gave Will a kiss on the cheek. "I missed you when you were out of town last week. Next time you want to go rafting, you're taking me. And April."

Will gave her a squeeze and thought for the hundredth time how grateful he was to have his sister as a best friend.

In spite of everything.

"I'd be too tempted to throw you overboard just to see if witches really sink," Will said. "Besides, April hates water."

"Minor detail. So are you coming to the charity dinner tomorrow night?"

"Will Aunt Nancy be there?"

"If I say yes, are you going to call at the last minute and tell me you can't come because of a sudden herpes outbreak?"

"Probably."

"Will—"

"The last time I attended a charity function with Aunt Nancy, she recited excerpts from *Integrated Treatment for Sexual Perversion* while stealing canapés off the host's plate."

"They were good canapés," Bethany pointed out. "Besides, you can't really blame her for wanting everyone to know she wrote a bestseller."

"Just like you can't blame me for not wanting to go to another charity dinner and hear her talk about it."

"Come on, Will. I need you," Bethany wheedled. "She won't stop talking about the goddamn figurines she donated and how much they'll be worth to the historic society *slash* wildlife sanctuary *slash* wealthy socialite's ego-boosting machine. Swear to God, she thinks they're going to rename the whole place after her."

"The Nancy Ursula Thomas-Smith Arts Center." Will frowned. "Have you pointed out the acronym is NUT SAC?"

"I try to minimize the amount of time I spend discussing testicles with our dead mother's sister."

"Absolutely. It frees you up to spend more time crafting awkward cunnilingus euphemisms for your brother."

Bethany grinned and slugged him on the shoulder. "Come on, Will. I need you there."

Will shrugged. "Fine. But I'm not changing clothes."

"Of course not," she said, stepping back to eye him. "Holey jeans smeared with mud and fur are the perfect choice for a formal dinner."

"I'm glad you understand."

Bethany shook her head. "At least wear shoes this time. Why are you still in your bedroom slippers?"

Will tipped up the toe of one slipper and admired the green plaid. "They're comfortable. And the duct tape was peeling off my sneakers."

Bethany grabbed the keys to the Humane Society's transfer van off the pegboard above the counter and gave Will's shin a playful kick. "Just bring wine. Expensive wine."

"That, I can handle."

"Love you."

"Drive safely."

Will watched his sister march toward the back room to collect the rest of her canine transports. He unlocked the door to the storage cabinet and thought about Magoo's new owner. Her blond hair had looked soft and touchable, and he felt dizzy again remembering the flashes of silver in her hazel eyes. She was petite, but not too skinny. Curvy in all the right spots. Her suit had definitely been Armani, which was an odd choice for an outing at the Humane Society. But Will wasn't one to judge someone's fashion choices.

He smiled a little, thinking of her scent. Not the smell of dog—he was used to that. When she'd bent to pet Magoo, Will was sure he'd smelled fresh blueberries. Weird, considering it was September in Central Oregon and fresh blueberries were way out of season. Weirder still, considering blueberries were Will's favorite treat in the whole world.

He opened the storage cupboard and grabbed the woman's free bag of kibble, hoisting it onto his shoulder. He trudged back to the lobby, surprised to feel his gut sink when he didn't see her there.

"Where's Magoo's new owner?" he asked.

Behind the desk, Tiff shrugged. "She filled out the forms, toweled off the dog, and headed out. Guess she didn't need the free kibble."

"Maybe she forgot."

Tiff grinned. "You offering to deliver it?"

Will opened his mouth to protest, but Tiff shoved a stack of papers at him. "Here. Take these with you if you do it."

"What is it?"

"Paperwork she forgot. A bunch of fund-raising stuff she was working on for Virginia, but her duplicates fell through Rex's kennel. She might need them."

Will knew it was ridiculous. The woman obviously didn't need free kibble, and even if she needed the paperwork, she knew where to find it. She certainly didn't need a strange guy showing up on her doorstep lugging a bag of dog food and looking like he might be casing the joint for valuables.

Dumb idea.

But dumb ideas had served Will pretty well in life. He shifted the dog food bag on his shoulder and reached for the paperwork.

"What's the address?"

Chapter 2

"DAD, I KNOW," MARLEY SAID INTO THE PHONE AS SHE filled Magoo's new water dish and set it on the floor. Fresh from the bath, Magoo wagged his tail and bounded toward the bowl, tripping over his feet en route. "I appreciate the offer, but I want to find my own place."

"I don't understand this, Marley," her dad said with a sigh. "I'm telling you to stay in the condo free, no strings attached, and you're refusing?"

Marley picked up her mug of blueberry tea and dropped heavily onto the plush leather sofa. *There are always strings*, she thought.

"What's that, dear?"

"Nothing," she said, annoyed to realize she'd spoken aloud. "Just telling Magoo not to eat my, um—my ring."

"Your engagement ring? I didn't know you kept it." He was quiet a moment. "If you kept the ring, does that mean you're getting back together with Curtis?"

"I'm not marrying Curtis, Dad."

"Why not?"

Because I don't love him seemed like the wrong answer, not just because she *had* agreed to marry him at one point. Marley wasn't sure her father saw love as an integral element in marital bliss.

"I know a really good couples counselor you two could see here in Portland," he said. "I could give you his card."

"The one you went to with Janine?"

"No, with Barbara. Or maybe Ellen."

Marley sighed. "Is that the therapist who told you to learn empathy by wearing each other's underwear for a month?"

"It was really silky."

Marley cringed and wished for a cranial Brillo pad to scrub the visual from her brain. "Look, Dad. I don't want to get back together with Curtis."

"Well, what *do* you want, Marley? You aren't getting any younger."

"Thanks for clarifying. I was confused about the role of time travel in the aging process."

Magoo took a final slurp of his water and trotted over to the sofa. He hesitated a moment, seeming to wait for permission. Marley patted the cushion beside her and the dog heaved himself onto the couch and curled up beside his new mistress. She scratched behind his ears, and Magoo gave a contented grunt, smearing viscous slobber on the back of her hand. She leaned down to squeeze him, thinking how warm and sweet and *necessary* he felt snuggled against her leg.

"I love you," Marley murmured to her new pet.

"I love you too, honey," her father said, and Marley jerked her attention back to the phone. "You know I just want what's best for you, baby. You know I'm not wrong to worry about you and money after the situation with your mom, and then with what happened when you—"

"Please, can we not talk about this now?" Marley ran her palm over her forearm, willing the little hairs there to lie back down. "I'm trying to make a fresh start here, and I'd rather not be reminded of… of *that*."

Her dad sighed. "I just don't want you to end up like your mom. Or like any other woman stuck in a bad situation because she didn't have financial security."

"I've dated a long string of wealthy jerks," Marley said, ignoring her cousin's voice in her head whispering *daddy issues*. "I don't think marrying a rich guy I don't love is my ticket to financial stability."

"I'm not saying that. I want you to find a good, supportive man with a stable future and a respectable means of supporting you both."

"You left out great pecs and multiple orgasms."

"What?"

"Nothing, Dad." Marley sighed. "If I'm dating a man based on the size of something, it's not going to be his wallet." She stopped scratching Magoo, an idea dawning. "Actually, Dad—maybe that's *exactly* what I need to be doing."

Her dad was quiet a moment. "Modern medicine has made a lot of advancements in that area, and I know there are pumps and penile implants and pills and—"

"Not *that*," Marley interrupted, already regretting her decision to bring up penises with her father. "I mean dating a guy based on the size of his wallet. That's what I need to be doing."

"It is?" Her father was quiet a moment. "Personality and chemistry should be a factor, but I agree that a man's net worth—"

"Should be low," Marley finished, hardly hearing him anymore. "The smaller the wealth, the smaller the ego. I think I like this idea."

"What?"

"I need to date a poor guy. Someone with holey jeans and dirt under his fingernails and a car that's at least twenty years old."

"Marley—"

"There are tons of guys like that in Bend," Marley interrupted, her mind swirling with images of the perfect, blue-collar man. "Rafting guides, construction workers, maybe even a handyman at the wildlife sanctuary."

"Marley—"

"I've gotta go, Dad. Someone's at the door."

She hung up before her dad could offer to buy her future husband a penile implant. The knock sounded at the door again, and Marley looked down at Magoo. He was asleep on the sofa beside her, his ears not even twitching at the sound of the doorbell.

"Aren't you supposed to bark or something?"

The dog opened his blue eye and looked at her. He licked the back of her hand and closed his eye again with a grunt.

Marley got up and padded to the heavy teak door. She stood on tiptoe to look through the peephole, expecting to see the moving van with the rest of her stuff or maybe a FedEx guy with paperwork for the new job.

Instead, she saw a big bag of dog food and a crop of coppery hair drifting across two mismatched eyes.

She flung the door open with more force than necessary, surprised to see him there. "William?"

He grinned and blew the hair off his forehead. "Just plain Will, actually," he corrected. "Kibble delivery for Ms. Marley Cartman." He slung the bag off his shoulder and set it on the doorstep. "Technically, I guess it's for Mr. Magoo Cartman. That's assuming he's taking your name. Or maybe you're taking his?"

Marley grinned in spite of herself. She hesitated a moment before stepping back and gesturing him inside. Surely a convicted murderer wouldn't be volunteering at the animal shelter?

She frowned. "Wait, this isn't community service, is it?"

Will gave her a puzzled look. "What?"

"You didn't just get out of prison?"

"Define *just*. It's been two weeks, so I really think I'm reformed now." He set the dog food bag in her foyer and turned around, studying the space. "Great place you've got here. River views?"

"From the back deck."

"Very nice." He pivoted, taking in the mountain views, the slate entry, the giant bronze statue Marley always thought looked like a pterodactyl with Tourette's syndrome.

"Are those teak floors?" he asked.

"Are you house hunting, Mr.—"

"Will," he said, turning back to face her. "Not William, not mister, just Will." He grinned broadly, softening his words and leaving Marley with the sense that someone had put her spleen in the washer on spin cycle. "I just wanted to bring the kibble and the paperwork you dropped."

Marley was so struck by the crazy, dual-colored eyes that it took her a moment to remember her manners. "Kibble," she repeated. "Paperwork. Right, I already bought kibble on my way home, but I was going to call about the paperwork. How much do I owe you for bringing this?"

"Fifty bucks, plus sales tax. Is that enough to buy myself a new pair of shoes?"

Marley frowned. "What?"

"I'm kidding. There's no sales tax in Oregon. Just the fifty bucks will be fine."

"Oh. Let me get my checkbook from—"

"Relax, Marley. I'm a volunteer. I don't need fifty bucks."

She looked down at his feet, which were encased in what looked like bedroom slippers. *Old* bedroom slippers. What was this guy's deal? "You *do* seem to need new shoes."

"These are antiques."

"Antique slippers?"

"Very valuable. Anyway, you were on my way home, so I offered to drop this stuff off. I was going to offer to finish his bath, but it looks like you already took care of that."

Marley tore her eyes off his slippers and returned her gaze to his face. *Mistake.* The dimple in his left cheek and those crazy, mismatched eyes sent her heart slamming against her rib cage.

Your first day in town, and you're panting over a dog-catcher, she told herself.

Maybe he's the blue-collar hottie you wanted, her conscience argued back.

Her conscience had a point.

"At least let me offer you something," she said. "A drink, maybe?"

Will stepped closer and inhaled deeply. Marley sniffed the air, pretty sure she smelled just fine after leaving her shoes on the back deck.

"Do I smell blueberries?" he asked.

She took a step back, sure he could hear her heart pounding in her ears. "It's my tea. Blueberry spice. I buy it by the case. Would you like some?"

"Yes, please. If it's not too much trouble."

"No trouble at all. Right this way."

She led him toward the kitchen, feeling oddly disconcerted. Magoo chose that moment to lift his head off the sofa. He looked at Will and thumped his stubby tail twice in acknowledgment. Then he put his head back down on the couch and closed his eyes.

"Quite a guard dog you have there," Will said.

"He's not sure yet if I'm worth guarding."

"Still in that getting-to-know-you stage?"

"I think we've progressed quickly beyond getting to know you and into the realm of sharing a bed and bodily fluids."

"Ah, one of *those* relationships. Well, when there's chemistry, sometimes you can't help it."

Marley laughed. "Seriously, thanks for introducing us. I love having a dog. I never realized there was this Magoo-shaped hole in my life, and now that he's here, everything just feels so... so..."

"Viscous? Slippery? Smeary?"

"Well, yes. There is a bit of slobber involved." She laughed again. "You weren't kidding about the licking issue. But it's a small price to pay for the best dog on the planet."

Magoo raised his head again and looked at Marley. His stub-tail thumped against the sofa, and Marley smiled with fondness. Taking his cue, Magoo jumped off the sofa and scrambled over to lick Marley's shin. She stooped down and scratched his head, feeling warm all over.

"Looks like the love is mutual," Will said. "In the interest of full disclosure, I should tell you Magoo wasn't on death row."

"He wasn't?"

"Nah, he was just being transferred to another shelter."

"Oh." Marley straightened up and shrugged. "That's better, actually. I get myself into trouble sometimes needing to rescue others. I like the story better if Magoo had other options, but fate brought us together anyway."

"That *is* a nice story."

Magoo thumped his tail on the ground again before

trotting back to the sofa. He jumped back up and curled himself into an O shape while Marley washed her hands at the kitchen sink. She turned and busied herself with the kettle, aware of Will's eyes on her back while she worked. She was also aware of the awkward silence filling the room, so she snatched the remote control off the edge of the counter where she'd left it. She aimed it at her father's expensive stereo and scrolled quickly through stations, considering her musical selection with more care than it probably required.

You're new to town with a reputation to build. What should the development director of a prestigious philanthropic organization listen to at home?

She settled on a classical music station and set down the remote before turning to finish preparing the tea. The scrape of something against the wood floor made her turn to see Will easing onto one of the ornate wooden barstools tucked against her father's granite island.

"So you're new to Bend?" he asked.

"More or less. I grew up in Portland, but my grandparents had a house over here. I spent a lot of time in Central Oregon in the summertime as a kid, so I always wanted to move here. Then I ended up working at a big corporation doing donor relations, which is a fancy way of saying *schmoozing rich people for money*, and pretty soon I got engaged to a guy who really didn't want to leave the city, or at least didn't want to be with me enough to leave the city and—" She stopped, her hand poised over the kettle as she frowned at Will. "A simple *yes* would have been better."

"Not really."

Marley shook her head. "I have a bad habit of

volunteering way too much information in response to basic questions."

"You'd make a terrible criminal."

"I'll cross that off my list of potential careers." Marley pulled the kettle off the heat and started to steep the tea. "How about you?"

"I'd actually be a pretty good criminal. You let me waltz right into your home after we just met."

"My vicious guard dog will protect me."

They both glanced over at Magoo, who was snoring on the sofa.

"Right," Will said. "Anyway, I was born and raised here. Third generation Bend-ite."

"No kidding?" Marley set the mug in front of him. "I didn't think many people were actually *from* here. Isn't most of the population comprised of transient ski bums and tourists who decide they want to live where they vacation?"

"Mostly. There's also a blend of wealthy investors and their trophy wives, semi-retired doctors and their boy-toys, underemployed river guides, suburban soccer moms, and a handful of socially awkward environmental activists. I think that sums up the Bend population in a nutshell."

Marley waited for him to elaborate on which category his family hailed from, but Will just stared into his mug with an unreadable expression.

"So what do you do when you're not washing dogs at the pound?" she asked at last.

Will shrugged and took a sip of tea. "A little of this, a little of that."

Unemployed, thought Marley, trying not to feel disappointed. She wanted blue-collar, not a collarless wife-beater tank top with a mustard stain. *Still, maybe he could get a job…*

"What's this we're listening to?" Will asked.

"Classical music."

"Thanks, I thought it was death metal. I meant who is it? Chopin? Bach? Hayden? Mozart?"

Marley squinted at the stereo, as though that would make her less clueless about classical music. It was a station her father had pre-programmed into the satellite radio, and Marley had no clue which dead white guy had composed the tune.

"Probably one of those," Marley finally answered.

Will laughed. "Not a classical music fan?"

"Sometimes. It just depends on my mood."

"And drinking blueberry tea with a stranger who brings you dog kibble is a classical music kinda mood?"

"Exactly." Marley took a sip of her tea. "What kind of music do you listen to?"

"Highly sophisticated musical arrangements characterized by soulful melodies and artistic lyrical nuances."

"Death metal?"

Will grinned. "Eighties bubblegum pop."

"Naturally." Marley couldn't tell if he was joking, but she wasn't sure what else to say. "Sugar?"

Will gave her a quizzical look. "I'm not sure we've known each other long enough for pet names, but okay... *Babycakes? Pookie-bear? Love-chicken*? Let me know when I hit the right one."

Marley shoved the sugar bowl at him. "In your tea. Do you like sugar, or maybe honey?"

"It's perfect just the way it is," he said, and took a big sip. "I'd love a little more if you have it."

"Absolutely." Marley took the box of tea out of the cupboard and set it in front of him. Then she turned and grabbed the teakettle off the stove. It was still warm, so she tipped it over Will's mug and poured carefully.

"Um, Marley?"

"Yes?"

"Is it possible your teakettle has a crack in it?"

"What?"

"Well, it's either that, or I just peed myself at your kitchen counter. I'm hoping it's not the latter, but I won't rule out the possibility."

Marley looked down and saw the dribbled splotch of water on Will's crotch. "Oh no!"

She dropped the kettle on the granite counter and whipped a dishtowel off the rack behind her. She scrambled around the island and began mopping at the front of his pants, dabbing frantically. "I'm so sorry, I had no idea. I hope I didn't burn you or—"

"Marley?"

"—I'm happy to pay for dry-cleaning or—"

"Marley?"

"—maybe my dad left something behind that you could change into while I put those in the dryer or—"

"Marley!"

His shout was more amusement than anger, but Marley froze anyway. "What?"

"As much as I'm enjoying the sponge bath, it's probably best if I do that myself."

Marley looked down at his lap. Her hand was poised right over his fly, with only a thin layer of dishtowel and denim separating her from—

"Oh, God!" Marley jerked her hand back. "I'm so sorry, Will."

"Don't be. This is the most action I've seen in

months, though it'd probably be better without the second-degree burns."

"I can't believe I... here, wait, let me get some ointment."

"Marley." Will grabbed her wrist and pulled her back. His mismatched eyes flashed with something Marley couldn't identify, and she shivered as a flood of heat surged up her arm.

"What?" Her voice was a strange little whisper.

"I'm not burned, and I'm not upset, but if you keep rubbing me with that towel or you start smearing me with ointment, I might be arrested for public indecency."

"This isn't public." It was an absurd thing to say, and Marley couldn't believe she blurted it out loud.

Will grinned. "In that case, rub all you want."

Marley looked down to see she'd twisted the dishtowel into a tight, damp knot around her hands. Will's fingers were still clasped around her wrist, big and strong and strangely possessive. Marley's fingers throbbed, aching with the tension and with the ridiculous urge to touch him again.

Will reached out and tugged the towel, releasing the pressure and drawing her closer. Marley looked up, scant inches from him now. She swallowed, searching hard for the right words to say.

"I shouldn't—"

Then she kissed him, forgetting all about *shouldn't* and embracing every *should* that pulsed through her veins. Will's mouth was warm from the tea, and he kissed her back with an urgency that made Marley drop the towel and twist her fingers in his hair. His hands slipped around her waist and came to rest just above her hips. She pressed herself against him, the dishtowel tangling around her ankles, the scent of blueberries making her dizzy.

Will pressed his fingertips into the small of her back and deepened the kiss. His lips were soft, and his hair was much too long. He tasted like summer berries and something darker, more mysterious.

In the distance, Marley heard a fuzzy vibration. She thought it might be her brain exploding and decided she didn't care. She just wanted to keep kissing him like this forever—

"Marley?"

"Mmm?"

Will drew back, his lips less than an inch from hers. "Normally I wouldn't interrupt something like this for a call, but it looks like your phone is about to vibrate itself right off the counter."

Marley jerked back and spun around, catching her iPhone just before it did the topple of death off the edge of the granite. She fumbled it to her face, not entirely sure which side was up or which button switched it on.

"Hello?" Marley breathed, pretty sure she sounded like a woman who'd just been ravished against the kitchen counter by a mysterious, blue-collar stranger.

"Marley, hon! I'm so sorry I'm late, but I'm just pulling up your driveway now, and—"

"Jane!" Marley blinked at the sound of her realtor's voice. "It's no problem at all. I'm ready to go see the properties right now. Just let me grab my purse and I'll meet you right out front."

"Thanks for understanding, sweetie. I've got some great places for you to take a look at. See you in just a sec."

Marley switched off the phone and stared at Will. She took a deep breath and one step back. "I'm so sorry. I forgot we set this meeting, and I really need to go."

Will grinned and nodded. "Actually, I'm the one who probably needs to go."

"What?"

"You live here. It seems logical I should be the one to vacate the premises."

"Right. Um, thank you for the kibble. And, um… everything."

"Everything." Will grinned wider. "Yes, thank you for *everything*. The tea was great too."

Marley took another step back, not sure whether to feel embarrassed, annoyed, or disappointed. As her doorbell rang, she decided it didn't matter.

"It was nice meeting you, Will."

"You too, Marley. I'll see you around."

Not likely, she thought as she stepped toward the door. *Pity, that.*

~~~

Thursday morning, Marley reported for duty at the Cascade Historical Society and Wildlife Sanctuary. It was the first time she'd prepped for a board meeting while watching an otter groom its nether region.

"Soothing, isn't it?"

Marley turned to see her new boss gazing fondly through the glass at Bridget the otter. For a moment, she wasn't sure if Susan meant the peacefulness of the water or the ability to chew one's own tail. Sensing her audience, Bridget the otter turned, ceased her grooming ritual, and did a belly flop into the tank.

Marley looked at her new boss, the director of the Cascade Historical Society and Wildlife Sanctuary. Forty-something and fit, Susan Reynolds wore a black pencil skirt, a green blouse, and a pouch of dead fish around her waist.

"Want one?" she asked, offering Marley a fish.

"Absolutely."

"Just toss it over there in the corner when she swims by. She'll grab it."

Marley did as ordered and was rewarded by the sight of Bridget's sleek little body streaking past to nab her breakfast.

"I always come here before big meetings," Susan said. "There's something calming about it. This is one of the wildlife sanctuary's most popular live exhibits."

"I can see why." Marley touched a finger to the glass and watched the otter bob closer to check it out. "I've read that otters can swim faster than any other four-legged animal and can consume up to twenty-five percent of their body weight per day."

Susan smiled. "You've been studying your animal facts."

"I figured a certain amount of animal expertise might help me fit in better in this job."

"That's one of the things the interview panel liked best about you. You've got a great ability to soak up new knowledge and really relate to people."

Marley beamed. "Thank you. I hope I can live up to your expectations."

"You'll do just fine." Susan tossed in another fish and looked at Marley. "I hope you're not too nervous about being thrown in the deep end like this." She glanced at the tank. "So to speak. We wouldn't normally start you off with a board meeting so soon, and I know you've got your hands full helping out with the charity event tonight and dealing with the appraisal on those antique figurines. But this is a special executive session, and we won't have all the trustees together again for another month."

"It's fine, really. A good chance to meet everyone."

"I'm glad you feel that way. And really, let me know if you want help dealing with the appraisal. I know it's a pain, but we can't have those figurines insured until the appraisal's done."

"I completely understand," Marley said. "I've been researching appraisers who specialize in… um… erotic art from the mid 1800s. The graphic nature of the figurines—"

"It's okay, Marley," Susan interrupted. "We'll call them figurines in front of the board, but in private we can call them what they are. Antique, Native American sex toys."

"Right," Marley said, regrouping. "There are a number of experts in the field, and I just need to identify the right person to do the appraisal. I realize everyone's on pins and needles with valuable antiques sitting around uninsured."

Susan smiled. "I'm glad you appreciate the delicacy of the situation. Nancy Thomas-Smith is one of our more *challenging* donors, so we're eager to have this dealt with quickly."

"*Challenging* how?"

"She's a retired sex therapist with an entitlement complex and a penchant for making inappropriate comments in public."

"Another one of those?" Marley turned back to the otter enclosure and peered through the blue-green water where Bridget was making laps underwater. "Why is there only one otter?"

"Bridget didn't take kindly to the young male we had in there with her last year," Susan said. "She's a rather dominant female, and Fritz kept trying to exert himself and take charge. We had to move him to another facility after Bridget chewed off the tip of his tail."

"Way to stick it to him, Bridget," Marley said.

"Many species of otters just aren't very social. She's fine on her own."

"Maybe I should take a lesson from Bridget."

"Pardon?"

"Nothing." Marley smiled brightly. "I got all the paperwork filled out this morning, so human resources should have what they need now."

"Wonderful. Did you sign the form allowing us to pull your credit report?"

Marley froze, her smile locked in place like a vise grip with teeth. "Credit report?"

"It's standard procedure for us to issue you a company credit card." Susan waved a dismissive hand and zipped up the fish pouch. "No worries, we'll take care of it later. Shall we get ready for the meeting?"

"Of course."

Susan smiled down at Marley's legs. "Thank you for wearing tights. I know it's an antiquated rule, but one of our board members is very insistent on a dress code for board meetings. Pantyhose or tights—no bare legs for women." She shrugged. "If it's any comfort, she makes all the men wear ties, too."

"It's no problem. I'm accustomed to dressing to impress in a professional environment."

"Still, it's a pain sometimes. Things have gotten a little stuffy here with the change in management a few years ago. I just hope we don't lose all the quirks that made this place so unique and appealing to community members." She turned and pushed open the door to a small washroom.

"Never mind. Let's get cleaned up. Can't go into the meeting stinking like dead fish."

Marley waited while Susan scrubbed up at the little sink. When it was her turn, Marley pumped the soap dispenser twice. The container sputtered and coughed up a disappointing teaspoon of foam.

"Damn," Susan said. "Harry was supposed to replace that."

"It's okay," Marley said, doing the best to de-fish her hands under the tepid water. "I'm fine as long as no one smells their hands after we shake."

Susan smiled again and pushed open the washroom door, holding it for Marley to pass. "Don't worry about the meeting. You'll do just fine. The board's going to love you."

"Any last-minute tips?"

"Speak loudly," Susan said. "At least half of them are over seventy. Oh, and don't be surprised if our chairman badgers you about the appraisal on the sex t—*the figurines*. The donor is his aunt, and the figurines have been in the family for quite some time."

"Thanks for the tip."

Susan stopped walking and lowered her voice. "You might as well know, our chairman can be a little… touchy."

"Touchy?" Marley frowned "Like he's a sensitive old guy prone to emotional outbursts, or like I should be careful not to bend over within grabbing distance?"

Susan laughed and shook her head. "Neither. He has some trust issues, that's all. Don't take it too personally."

"Got it. I appreciate the advice."

"On the upside, he keeps things interesting around here. Pretty much the opposite of stuffy."

"Good to know."

"Ready to head in?" Susan asked, nodding toward a pair of giant oak doors.

"Ready as I'll ever be."

They pushed through the doors together and stepped into the small, overheated boardroom. Marley surveyed the crowd of well-dressed, older citizens gripping coffee mugs emblazoned with the wildlife sanctuary's logo. Everyone turned to study her, and Marley resisted the urge to wipe her hands on her skirt.

"Marley, I'd like to introduce you to some of the board members you didn't meet during your interview," Susan announced. "Folks, this is Marley Cartman, our new director of development. She'll be taking charge of donor relations and financial management. Marley, this is Gladys Gainsworth, Bed Playman, Stan Martin, Peter Quon, and Martin Braylard. Oh, and here's our board chairman."

Marley turned as a man in a three-piece suit strode into the room, straightening a tie she was pretty sure cost more than her car. She stared at the suit, at the shoes that were surprisingly devoid of duct tape, at the eyes that were disturbingly mismatched, at the lips that were disconcertingly familiar.

Marley opened her mouth to speak but couldn't find any words at all.

"Marley, this is the chairman of our board of trustees, William Barclay the Fifth," Susan said. "Marley here is our new director of development."

Marley stuck out her hand like a trained dog. "William," she stammered.

"Just plain Will," he corrected, smiling down at her. "How's Magoo?"

"Fine, thank you." She glanced down at the floor, not

trusting herself to meet his eyes. "You aren't wearing the antique slippers."

"The duct tape clashed with the tie."

"You're… you're—" Marley stopped, not sure what she meant to say. *You're the guy I made out with* didn't seem right, nor did *you're the best kisser I've ever necked with in a kitchen.*

"You're here!" she finished brightly, wishing the ground would swallow her up.

"That I am," Will agreed, giving her the tiniest wink.

Susan clapped her hands together. "Okay, folks, shall we take our seats?"

Marley stumbled toward a chair at the far end of the conference table, still trying to wrap her brain around the volunteer dogcatcher in holey slippers masquerading as a wealthy trustee oozing old money. Or was it the other way around?

At the other end of the table, Will tapped a stack of papers with an expensive-looking pen. "Let's get things started, since I know everyone's time is valuable. Ms. Cartman, since this is your first board meeting, would you mind introducing yourself before we kick off the executive session?"

Marley stood and smoothed the front of her skirt with her fingers. *Be brief, be sincere, be seated,* she coached herself silently. She cleared her throat and smiled.

"I'm Marley Cartman, and I'm delighted to meet all of you and excited to be working with the Cascade Historical Society and Wildlife Sanctuary," Marley announced.

"Cheez Whiz," Will said.

Marley blinked. "I beg your pardon?"

"Cheez Whiz. It's the acronym for Cascade Historical

Society and Wildlife Sanctuary. Much easier to say." Will smiled, making his mismatched eyes sparkle, and Marley forgot her name for a moment.

"Oh, CHSWS." Marley nodded. "Okay then."

Susan cleared her throat. "Will's family has been volunteering here for many years. It's his chief goal to keep things… well, *lively* here."

"To keep it from being stuffy and dull so guests actually *want* to come here and learn things about wildlife and natural history instead of wanting to drown themselves in the otter pond out of sheer boredom," Will said, turning back to Marley. "Sorry to interrupt. You can keep going with your bio."

"Right." Marley cleared her throat. "I have a degree in economics, and I've worked in philanthropy and donor relations for twelve years now, most recently for Woolstein and Associates in Portland. I've done pro bono fundraising work for the Bend Humane Society for a couple years now, so I'm thrilled to finally make it to Bend on a more permanent basis."

She flashed her best smile at the assembled group, pleased she hadn't blurted what was really running through her mind. *My name is Marley and my hands smell like dead fish, Stan Martin's fly is down, and I've tongue-wrestled with the board chairman.*

"Do you golf, dear?" asked a woman at the end of the table wearing diamond earrings the size of small grapefruits. She smiled, but the expression didn't quite reach her eyes. "We have twenty-six courses in Central Oregon, and so many business deals happen out on the course, you know."

Marley smiled back as her palms began to perspire. "I've been known to pick up a club from time to time," she replied, trying to remember the last time she'd done that. Did visiting a driving range in college count?

A man with salt-and-pepper sideburns picked up his green-and-yellow coffee mug, and Marley tried to remember which Oregon sports team had those colors. "Are you a fan of the Oregon State Beavers or the U of O Ducks?"

A man across the table hooted and stroked his orange-and-black tie. "There's the million-dollar question! Which are you, Marley—a duck or a beaver?"

The group laughed, and Marley tried to join them as she fumbled for an answer that wouldn't alienate anyone. "I'm not really a fan of college sports," she replied slowly, wiping her palms on her skirt. "But I'm very excited to take advantage of all the outdoor recreation Central Oregon has to offer."

A frowning older woman cleared her throat. "You've been briefed on our dress code, correct?"

"Yes, ma'am," Marley squeaked, smoothing a hand over her tights.

"Good. And I trust you've been briefed on the reasons your predecessor is no longer employed with the organization. You're aware of our policies regarding fraternization between company executives, members of the board, and the employees we oversee?"

Marley tried not to let her surprise show. The rule was news to her, as were the reasons for her predecessor's departure. But there was no sense letting her ignorance show, and definitely no sense expressing dismay over an antiquated policy.

"Of course," Marley said. "Rules are important in any major organization."

She waited for more questions, hoping there wouldn't

be any. She hoped she'd given the best answers, that she'd made the right impression. After a few beats of silence, she took her seat again, ready to move on with the meeting. Two spots down, an elderly woman with a bushel of white hair sprouting from one ear peered at Marley. "You kept your last name, dear?"

"Pardon?"

The woman smiled, and Marley remembered her from the interview panel. Martha or Margaret or Margie?

"You mentioned a fiancé when you interviewed," the woman shouted. "Or did the wedding not happen yet?"

Margaret. Margaret Flowers. That was her name.

Marley cringed, recalling now the woman had a fondness for intrusive questions. Marley wasn't sure if she felt more like kicking herself for mentioning the engagement in the interview, or more like kicking Margaret for remembering. Marley pasted her smile back in place and folded her hands on the table.

"My fiancé—*ex*-fiancé—chose not to join me in the move to Bend," Marley said, struggling to keep her tone light and cheery.

Margaret frowned, apparently not getting the hint. "Does this mean you'll be returning to Portland for the wedding then?"

Marley clenched her fingers together and smiled so hard her jaw hurt. "No, there won't be a wedding."

"A courthouse ceremony?" Margaret made a *tsk-tsk* sound. "In my day, women didn't settle for things like that. We insisted on a proper wedding with attendants and flowers and—"

"I'm not getting married, Ms. Flowers." Marley interrupted. "My fiancé—*ex*-fiancé—decided not to move with me, and I decided I deserved better than a guy who'd choose his career over the woman he professed to love, so I moved by myself and got this great job and a dog and a new mountain bike and a plan to only date guys with simple jobs and small bank accounts and priorities in the right place."

The room fell silent, and Marley considered crawling under the conference table. All eyes were on her, unblinking. At least she hadn't cursed or cried or tucked her skirt into her panties. She'd been so careful, so good about biting her tongue until—

"Well, now," Will said. His expression was bland, but there was laughter in his mismatched eyes. One corner of his mouth quirked up as he looked at Marley—*was that a wink?*—before picking up a stack of papers and clearing his throat. "Thank you for that colorful introduction, Ms. Cartman. How about we use that as a segue into another challenging topic, the second quarter financials. If you'll all open your packets to page three, I'd like to review the numbers from—"

Marley resisted the urge to groan as she picked up her paperwork and the remaining shreds of her dignity.

It was going to be a very long meeting.

Chapter 3

"WE'VE BEEN OVER THIS SEVERAL TIMES, BED," SUSAN SAID, touching the older woman on the shoulder as the rest of the meeting attendees filed out of the boardroom. "The wildlife sanctuary does not currently have any pure white rabbits."

Will desperately wanted to avoid being dragged into the conversation between the sanctuary director and the kooky board member who'd donated millions to the organization over the years. He'd survived the board meeting without falling asleep, a feat he attributed more to the fact that he was leading the financial discussion as opposed to any real personal growth on his part.

Okay, the glimpses he stole down the front of Marley's blouse may have played a bigger role in keeping him alert. It was the end result that counted, right?

Now Will just wanted to go home, put on his slippers, fix himself a snack, and play fetch with his dogs.

But Susan grabbed the sleeve of his jacket, yanking him into the discussion and thwarting his escape plans. She gave him a stiff smile and kept a death grip on his arm.

"Will, so good to see you," Susan said. "Bed and I were just talking…"

Will's eyes landed on Marley Cartman, who was apparently part of the conversation. His urge to flee evaporated.

"Ladies," he said.

"Will." Marley folded her hands in front of her skirt and gave Will a smile even stiffer than Susan's.

A whole lot of stiff *for one conversation*, Will thought. He gave Marley a real smile and tried to get the word *stiff* out of his brain.

Susan cleared her throat. "Will, you've hosted one of our animal-centered charity events before—you know how this works."

Will nodded. "Of course. Don't let guests pet the porcupines."

"Well yes, but—"

"Make sure you ask if the skunk has been de-scented before you pick him up?"

The corners of Marley's mouth quirked, and she looked down at the floor to mask her smile.

Susan sighed. "Bed's charity dinner is tonight, and we'd arranged for the two badgers to be there."

"Floyd and Frank, sure," Will said.

"Wonderful animals," Marley chimed. She sent Will a nervous glance, and his pulse kicked up a notch. "The world's fastest diggers, if I'm not mistaken. They dig extensive tunnels and burrows known as *setts*." Marley flushed and looked down at her hands before looking back at Bed. "I'm sure you'll be very happy with them, Deb."

"*Bed*," the two women corrected, and Will watched Marley's expression turn to a frown.

"Bed?" she squeaked. "Oh… um, like you sleep in?"

"Among other things, yes," Will said, earning himself an eye roll from Susan and a *what's that, dear?* from Bed. Will cleared his throat. "Bed is short for Beddy, which is short for Bernadette."

"They've called me that since I was a little girl," Bed huffed, and everyone offered another round of stiff smiles.

"Of course," Marley said. "*Bed*. My mistake."

"Bed doesn't want the badgers at her charity event tonight," Susan said, giving Will a pointed look as she tried to steer the conversation back on track. "She's questioning their appeal to party guests."

"Big donors love the badgers," Will offered. "Ed Bainbrich had Frank and Floyd at his last cocktail party and raked in tons of donations for Cheez Whiz by letting guests have their photos taken with them. Sarah Wilcox donated three grand when Floyd chewed the toe off Carl Madley's shoe."

Susan frowned. "There was no damage to Carl's foot, and everyone at the party had a lovely time."

"I want *bunnies*," Bed snapped. "White bunnies. *Pure* white. Four of them. I plan to dye them mauve and green to match the drapes."

Susan sighed, and Marley kept her stiff smile pasted in place. Will tried very hard not to laugh.

"We don't have any white bunnies at CHSWS," Susan explained slowly. "And even if we did, you wouldn't be allowed to dye them for a dinner party. The wildlife sanctuary specializes in *native* species."

"As far as rabbits go, that's the Oregon cottontail or the black-tailed jackrabbit," Marley offered. "Both brownish gray in color."

"Can we dye those?" Bed asked.

"No!" everyone chorused.

Marley bit her lip, and Will wondered how often Marley'd had to deal with nutty donor demands in her previous job. Where had she said she'd worked? Woolstein and Associates in Portland. He should probably do some sleuthing into her background, just to be safe. It was never smart to assume you knew the important details about someone, only to discover you'd missed something ridiculously obvious. That a person wasn't who she pretended to be.

Like April.

Will focused his attention back on the conversation and on the soothing, pleasant hum of Marley's voice.

"I completely understand your need to have the animals match the furnishings, Mrs.—*Bed*," Marley said. "It makes perfect sense to me."

Will quirked an eyebrow. "It does?"

Marley ignored him and touched the old woman's arm. "How about this… I'll come take a look at your drapes before the party, and then I'll stop by the fabric store to buy some ribbon in complementary shades. We can weave the ribbon around the badgers' cages and maybe purchase leashes in the appropriate colors. If you like, we could even work some wildflowers into the display."

"*Native* wildflowers," Susan clarified.

"Of course."

Bed appeared to be mulling it over, and Will stole a glance at Marley. Clever thinking on her part. He wouldn't have pegged her as the crafty, Martha Stewart type, but the ribbon thing could work.

"Hmph," said Bed. "I wanted bunnies."

"I'll bring photographs of bunnies," Marley said. "We'll set up a display educating people on the rabbit species native to Central Oregon. Accented with frames to match the drapes, of course."

Bed frowned for a few more moments, tugging on her bottom lip as she considered the offer. "Can you Photoshop the pictures so the rabbits are mauve and green?"

Susan grimaced, and Marley offered another stiff smile. "That's a great idea. We'll see what we can do."

"In that case, I'll see you at my house in an hour," Bed said. "You can take a look at the drapes and make sure you get the colors just right."

"I've got your address on the forms," Marley said. "I'm sure I'll have no trouble finding it."

The old woman harrumphed and walked out of the room. Will turned and smiled at Marley.

"Nicely done, Ms. Cartman."

"Marley, please. And thank you."

"You certainly know how to handle donors."

"I've been handling donors for most of my adult life." Marley grimaced. "That sounded filthier than I meant it to."

Will laughed. "You're welcome to handle the donors however you see fit, as long as it gets the job done. You probably never imagined your skills with ribbon crafts and Photoshop would come in handy for this job."

"I have no skills with either of those things. I'm the least crafty person you've ever met." Marley shrugged. "I guess I have a couple hours to learn."

"Good luck with that," Will said. "You know, I wouldn't count on being able to find Bed's house easily. She lives on a big ranch several miles east of town. It's tricky to get to if you don't know where you're going."

"I'm sure I'll manage."

"I'm sure you would, but I'd be happy to take you out there if you like," Will said. "I have to go out there anyway to drop off a case of wine she'll be auctioning during the charity dinner."

"Is it the 2000 Mouton Rothschild?" Susan asked, eyes wide.

Will fought the urge to grimace. "It is."

Susan beamed. "Oh, thank you, Will. That should fetch a nice sum. $1,400 a bottle?"

Will kept his smile pasted in place, fighting the discomfort that surged when any conversation turned toward his net worth. "Something like that."

"That's very generous of you," Marley said. "Thank you for supporting the Cascade Historical Society and Wildlife Sanctuary."

"Cheez Whiz," Will corrected.

"Right."

Will glanced at his watch and gave a quick nod to the women. "Marley, I'll come find you in your office in thirty minutes, if that works for you?"

"Sounds just fine. Thanks again."

Will nodded again. "Ladies, if you'll excuse me a moment, I have some numbers to review with Ed."

He turned and strode away, reluctant to leave Marley, but pleased at the thought of spending an hour in the car alone with her.

Dumb idea, Barclay, he told himself. *You know the company policy about dating among board members and employees.*

Okay, so he wouldn't date Marley. But he needed to get to know the new development director, didn't he? That's all there was to it.

There you go—tell yourself more lies about a pretty girl, his subconscious scoffed. *You're good at that.*

The second Will was out of earshot, Susan turned to Marley and quirked an eyebrow. "You said something about his slippers when I introduced you earlier. I take it you two have met before?"

"At the Humane Society," Marley said. "And at my house. He was delivering dog food."

Susan laughed. "Sounds like something Will would do. He's the king of the volunteer circuit. Same with his sister, Bethany. I'm sure you'll get to know them both quite well as you settle into the job."

Marley nodded, resisting the urge to bombard Susan with questions about the mysterious millionaire with duct tape slippers and designer suits.

"Will's been on the board awhile?" Marley asked, keeping her expression neutral.

"A few years. He's very passionate about wildlife education and natural history. Very supportive of the organization's mission, even if he sometimes has an odd way of showing it."

"How do you mean?"

Susan smiled. "Will can seem a little… *irreverent* when it comes to the Cascade Historical Society and Wildlife Sanctuary."

"Like the Cheez Whiz thing?"

"Precisely. It's well-intentioned. He wants the organization to be accessible and welcoming and not to take itself so seriously that people stop showing up to learn."

"Sounds like a healthy approach."

"It can be." Susan hesitated and glanced back at Will before speaking again. "You know how eccentric a lot of wealthy donors can be?"

"Well—"

"Multiply that by one hundred, and you're just brushing the surface of William Barclay the Fifth."

Marley glanced nervously toward Will, who was on the other side of the room and well out of earshot. "I have to admit, I wouldn't have pegged him as a wealthy donor when we met yesterday. He seemed—"

"Bedraggled? Lazy? Unkempt? Impoverished?"

"I was going to say *from modest means,* but sure." Marley shot another glance at Will. He was having an animated discussion with a man she recognized as the accountant for the wildlife sanctuary. Will shook his head fiercely and pulled a ballpoint pen out of his pocket. Marley watched him scrawl something on a page of the financial report they'd been reviewing in the meeting. She admired his hands, large and steady, and the way his coppery hair flopped across his forehead as he bent forward. She remembered what his lips had felt like pressed warm against hers, his hands cupping the small of her back and sliding down, down—

"Don't you think so?" Susan asked, and Marley snapped her attention back to the conversation.

"I beg your pardon?"

Susan laughed. "You just answered my question. I asked if you found Will attractive."

"Oh, um—"

"It's okay. So does every other single female in Deschutes County." Susan smiled and lowered her voice. "Word of advice—don't get involved with board members."

"Of course," Marley said, her cheeks flushing. "Bed mentioned the rule in the board meeting."

"Right. Yes, well, there was an unfortunate incident with a former board member having relations with the previous development director. It turned out she was embezzling money and he was helping cover it up, and the whole thing created quite the local scandal."

"Oh dear."

"The fraternization policy is in place to prevent that from happening again in the future."

"And Bed has a personal interest?"

"You could say that." Susan grimaced. "The board member who had the affair was her daughter-in-law. I should say *ex*-daughter-in-law. Bed's son divorced her shortly after the news got out."

"Yikes," Marley said. "Sounds messy."

"It was. And we're hoping to avoid any future scandals."

Marley nodded and did her best not to look at Will. "I understand completely."

Susan smiled. "You're fine to date other employees if you like. But the board of directors supervises your position, so they're all off-limits. And even if the rule weren't in place, you'd want to steer clear of Will Barclay."

Marley flushed, dismayed to realize her interest was so obvious. "Married?"

"No. Not now, anyway. He was. His ex-wife ran off with his sister two or three years ago. Speaking of local scandals." Susan shrugged. "Everyone's on friendly terms now, and his ex-wife is just the nicest woman you can imagine."

"It must have been tough for Will."

"I suppose. It was actually a pretty amicable split. Well, as far as most lesbian-sister-runs-off-with-brother's-wife divorces go. She probably could have tried for alimony or some sort of huge settlement, but she didn't go there. Sweet girl. Just not the girl for Will."

Marley risked a quick glance at Will, hoping he couldn't hear their conversation. Susan had been right earlier when she'd remarked on Marley's natural interest in people giving her an edge in donor relations. She loved getting to know people, learning about their interests and what made them tick.

Still, she didn't like to gossip.

Gossip has nothing to do with why you're curious about Will Barclay.

Marley flushed and looked back at Susan. "Is it family money? The Barclays, I mean."

"There is family money, but Will avoids that. His aunt is Nancy Thomas-Smith—the donor of the figurines."

"That's his *aunt*?"

"The one and only. She raised Will and his sister from the time they were little, so she's really more like a mother to them. You'll meet her eventually."

"That's where the money comes from?"

Susan laughed and shook her head, leaning close to Marley and keeping her voice low. "No, Will's wealth isn't family money. On his twenty-first birthday, he went to a convenience store to buy his first legal beer. While he was there, he figured he'd buy a one-dollar lottery ticket."

"No!" Marley said. "He won millions from a scratch-off?"

"No, he won a few thousand. But he used the money to buy stock in some sort of pharmaceutical company and made millions that way."

"So the Cascade Historical Society and Wildlife Sanctuary is very lucky to have him. And the rest of his family, from the sounds of it."

"Absolutely." Susan shot a sidelong glance across the room, where Will was still deep in conversation with the accountant. "Word of advice: Will doesn't like to talk about his money. Barely likes to acknowledge it exists. Keep that in mind when you're dealing with donor relations."

"I'll do that."

Susan smiled and patted Marley's arm. "You did well in the meeting today. And nice job handling Bed. The thing with the ribbons and photo frames—that was great thinking. We made a good choice hiring you."

Marley flushed. "Thank you."

"You came very highly recommended, you know. The hiring committee was unanimous in its decision to offer you the job."

"I'm so glad," Marley said, and tried not to feel guilty about that. She hadn't done anything wrong. Not really.

You didn't tell them everything—

"I'm glad we were able to find a solution for Bed," Marley said. "I had visions of dead pink bunnies dancing in my head."

Susan laughed. "I'm heading back to my office. I'll talk to our wildlife specialist, Darin, about getting the bunny pictures ready. I'll text you the sizes when I know what we've got."

"Perfect. I'll grab the frames and ribbon while I'm out."

"If we don't cross paths this afternoon, I'll see you tonight at the dinner."

"See you there." Marley turned and began gathering coffee cups and pieces of scratch paper off the boardroom table, trying hard not to look like she was eavesdropping on Will's conversation with the accountant.

"I'm not sure it's fiscally responsible to include proceeds from the traveling exhibit in next year's budget when we don't have the appraisal yet," Will was saying, his voice steely. "I know you're getting a lot of pressure from my aunt on this, but we need to hold off."

Marley shot a sidelong glance at the accountant's face

and saw him sigh. "We're expecting the appraisal to come back in this range." He tapped his pen twice on a notepad. "If the numbers pan out and the exhibit generates the sort of income we're expecting, those figurines should end up being the largest donation Cheez Whiz has ever received. We could build the new education center."

"It seems premature," Will said. "I know Aunt Nancy thinks they're invaluable, but—" Will looked up and caught Marley staring. She flushed and grabbed his coffee cup. "You through with this?"

Will frowned. "You don't have to do that, Marley. You were hired to court big donors, not to be a busboy for the board of directors."

"Bus*boy*?" She quirked an eyebrow at him. "I know I wasn't required to disclose my gender during the application process, but I didn't realize there was any confusion."

Will grinned. "I can assure you, I'm not the least bit confused. Seriously, Marley, you aren't here to wait hand and foot on people."

"Waiting hand and foot on people is a crucial part of donor relations."

"Fine." Will handed her his empty coffee cup and tucked his pen back in his pocket. "I'm ready to head out to Bed's house whenever you are."

"Let me put these things down and grab my purse, and then I'll be ready to go."

Marley turned and scurried down the hall, not sure why she felt so out of sorts.

Because he's hot. Because you were eavesdropping on his conversation. Because you can't stop thinking about him ravishing you against the counter?

She loaded the cups into the dishwasher and the papers in

the recycle bin before hustling down the hallway to her office. She grabbed her purse and turned toward the mirror tacked above her desk. She paused long enough to slick on a fresh coat of lipstick, assuring herself it was her job to look professional and polished for any major donor or board member.

That's not why you want to look good.

"So do you want the badgers to dig?"

Marley turned at the sound of the man's voice. He stood in her doorway wearing khaki pants and a matching khaki shirt with dirt on the sleeves. His brown eyes were kind, his brown hair was tousled, and his expression was curious.

Marley blinked. "I beg your pardon?"

The man smiled, displaying a neat row of very white teeth. "I'm sorry. I guess I should introduce myself first." He stuck out his hand, and Marley shook it automatically. "Darin Temple, I'm one of the wildlife specialists here. I'll be in charge of the badgers tonight at the charity dinner."

"Darin, it's a pleasure to meet you."

He smiled again, and Marley opened her mental Rolodex to take notes. *Cute, unshaven, a little dirt on his sleeves. Definitely blue-collar dating material. Definitely a much better prospect than the absurdly wealthy board chairman with trust issues.*

Marley rubbed her lips together and tucked the tube of lipstick back in her purse. "I appreciate you helping us prepare for tonight's event. Did Susan talk to you about the rabbit photos?"

Darin grimaced. "Yes, I can do that. We have some existing displays I'll sort through in the storeroom, and I can send a few photo files to Costco within the hour for a quick print job. Do you think something like an eleven-by-seventeen would work?"

"That would be perfect, thanks. Just have Susan text me how many frames we'll need, and I'll grab some at the craft store." Marley hesitated, biting her lip. "I don't suppose you could use Photoshop to make the rabbits mauve and green?"

Darin raised an eyebrow, and Marley shook her head. "Never mind. Forget I asked. What were you saying about the badgers digging?"

"Right, of course. We have a program here at two o'clock every day where we put one of the badgers at the top of a big Plexiglas cube filled with dirt. There's an opening at the very bottom and the trainer stands there with a treat, which urges the badger to dig his way out." He gave her a sheepish smile. "Sounds corny, but guests love it. It's fun to watch, and it's a good way to educate people about the animal. Do you want me to bring the digging setup to the event tonight?"

"That would be wonderful. Badger digging. I wonder if we could use that for fund-raising."

Darin shrugged. "Probably. I'm bringing both badgers, so we could lead them in one at a time and let people place bets on which badger will dig fastest. Or maybe something about which badger can displace the most dirt?"

"Brilliant." Marley grinned and jotted another note in her mental Rolodex. *Clever, creative, helpful.* She glanced at his left hand for a wedding ring and was rewarded by the sight of a bare finger and a healthy bit of dirt under his nails.

Perfect.

She looked back at his face and suppressed a smile as she saw him studying her left ring finger, too. *The mating ritual of single thirty-somethings everywhere.*

"So, Marley," he said, shuffling his feet on the carpet. "I guess I'll see you tonight."

"Likewise. Here, let me give you my cell number in case you have any trouble with the photos."

She reached for a pad of sticky notes, smiling at the cartoon figure of Goofy on the top sheet. If Will Barclay was determined to keep the organization from taking itself too seriously, Marley was equipped to do her part.

She pushed thoughts of Will out of her mind as she scribbled her phone number on a sticky note. She peeled the note off the pad as Darin held out his hand.

"Here you go," Marley said, pressing the note into his palm and holding it there a second longer than necessary. She smiled and received a smile in return. "Thanks again for helping tonight."

"My pleasure. Look, if you need someone to show you around Bend sometime—"

Just then, Will rounded the corner into Marley's office and clapped his hands together. He grinned at Marley, and she felt her stomach flip pleasantly.

Darin withdrew his hand.

"Sorry I'm a little late," Will said. "Hey, Darin. How's it going?"

"Not bad, not bad. You?"

"Can't complain. You need a little more time here, Marley?"

"Oh, well, we were just wrapping up."

"Take your time. I'll wait out in the lobby."

He turned and walked away, and Marley fought the urge to check out his ass. She failed, though it was one of the more pleasant failures of her life. He had a fantastic ass.

Knock it off. Eyes off the rich guy; focus on the normal guy.

"So Darin," Marley said, turning back to him. "I'll see you tonight."

"See you tonight. It was great meeting you."

"You too." He smiled and walked out of her office. Marley glanced at his backside, disappointed to see the baggy khakis didn't do much for him.

That's not the point. He's a nice, blue-collar man who's different from all the rich, egotistical schmucks you've dated. He's perfect.

She hiked up her purse, straightened her posture, and headed out to the lobby to meet Will. He was seated on a heavy wooden bench that bore a plaque with a donor's name. Marley squinted at it. *William Barclay V.*

He looked up as she approached and smiled. Then he followed the direction of her gaze to the plaque. He stopped smiling and shook his head.

"I've asked them four times to take the damn plaque off. Even came in here with a screwdriver once and did it myself. Someone in maintenance put up a new one."

"Why don't you want it there?"

He shrugged. "Why would I?"

"Fair point," Marley said, not entirely sure it was. "If you like, I'll see that it gets removed right away."

Will grinned, his mismatched eyes flashing. "Are you *handling* me, Ms. Cartman?"

"Do you need to be *handled,* Mr. Barclay?" Marley grimaced. "I've gotta stop doing that."

"For a minute there I thought you were flirting with me."

Marley felt her cheeks heat up and fought to keep her voice cool. "Just repeating your language from earlier. *'You're welcome to handle the donors however you see fit'*?"

"Touché, Ms. Cartman. Handle me as you like."

She was distracted by his mismatched eyes, unable to decide whether to fix her gaze on his blue eye or the green one. Both were mesmerizing, but she couldn't seem to focus or take in both at the same time. She bit her lip. "You're the first person I've ever met with two different colored eyes," she blurted.

She did a mental forehead slap, but Will just laughed. "I might not be. A lot of people with heterochromia iridis tend to mask it with colored contact lenses."

"There are a lot of people with... er, whatever you just said?"

"Heterochromia iridis." He grinned. "Not really. But those who have it often hide it with colored lenses."

"You never have?"

"Nope. I was self-conscious about it as a kid, so my sister looked up a list of celebrities with heterochromia iridis. David Bowie, Dan Aykroyd, Michael Flatley, Jane Seymour, and Kiefer Sutherland all have mismatched eyes."

"That's fascinating. I'll have to tell Magoo about that, since he shares your hetero-chlamydia—"

"Hetero*chromia* iridis."

"Right. That too. It's sweet that your sister would go to so much trouble to make you feel more normal."

"That's Bethany. A heart of gold, and the personality you'd get if a drunk sailor mated with a stand-up comedian."

Marley laughed. "Sounds interesting. I'm eager to meet her."

"You probably will tonight. Ready to go?"

"Anytime you are."

Will reached out, and for an instant, Marley thought he

was going to grab her breast. She wasn't sure which she found more startling—the fact that he might, or the fact that her entire body whimpered *yes, please!*

But instead of groping her, Will pointed to the name badge clipped to Marley's blouse. "You'd better stash that. Bed has very strict rules about board members and employees removing their name badges if they leave the building."

"Oh," Marley said, flushing as she looked down and unclipped the badge. "Thanks for letting me know."

"No problem. Bed has a lot of rules."

"I noticed."

Will stood up and gestured toward the door. "After you."

"Thank you." Marley stuffed her name badge in her purse and followed Will toward the door.

"How do you feel about dog hair?"

"In general, or as a breakfast entrée?"

Will laughed. "In general. Or on your clothing, as the case may be. My car is full of it."

"I can live with dog hair on my clothes or on your car seats. As long as you aren't storing cadavers in the backseat, I'm fine riding with you."

"The cadavers are in the trunk."

"Then lead the way."

They walked in companionable silence through the front doors and out into the parking lot. Marley took a deep breath of warm, high desert air. It certainly smelled different here than it did in Portland. The rainy side of the state was all damp earth and crushed grass, but Central Oregon was different. Sun-warmed ponderosa and juniper mingled with the scent of desert sage. Marley had loved it from the time she was a little girl visiting her grandparents here, and she loved it more now.

Will pulled a set of keys out of his pocket as they approached a silver Porsche, and Marley waited for the beep of the door locks.

Instead, Will moved past the Porsche to the passenger side of a gray Volkswagen hatchback. The car was nice enough, but at least ten years old. Will unlocked Marley's door with his key, and Marley wondered if he was being chivalrous or just didn't have power locks.

Chivalrous, she realized, as Will handed her into the passenger seat before flipping the lock on the driver's side and opening his own door. As Marley buckled her seat belt, Will cranked the ignition. The stereo began thumping with the sound of something that sounded strangely like the Go-Go's.

"'We Got the Beat'?" Marley asked with a raised eyebrow. "You weren't joking about the '80s bubblegum pop?"

"My favorite," Will answered, not looking embarrassed at all. He rolled down his window and eased out of the parking lot. "Want your window down?"

Marley had half expected the windows to be the hand-crank variety, so she was surprised to see his hand on the power button.

"Yes, please," she said, and flipped down her sunglasses.

"There's air conditioning, but I always prefer the breeze."

"Me too. Especially here in the high desert where everything smells so good."

"You don't think juniper smells like cat pee?"

Marley laughed. "I never thought about it."

"My ex-wife can't stand the smell of juniper. Thinks it smells like a pack of drunk tomcats got loose and sprayed the town."

"There's a nice visual. Does she live in Central Oregon?"

"My ex-wife? Yes."

Marley watched his face for a reaction, waiting in case the silence prompted him to fill in the blanks. His expression stayed blank, and Will didn't seem to feel the need to fill the silence.

"I imagine that makes it tough," Marley said at last.

Will shrugged. "Tough for her to avoid juniper, for sure. The stuff is everywhere around here. Last Christmas I gave her some body lotion called Juniper Breeze."

Marley digested the information, intrigued by the context clues. Did it say something that he bought Christmas presents for his ex-wife? Did it say something else that he bought a present he knew she wouldn't like? Marley mulled it over, aware she was probably overthinking things.

She was also aware they were both avoiding the very large elephant in the room. Marley cleared her throat. "So when we met at the Humane Society on Monday, and then later at my house when we—"

"Made out like horny teenagers?"

Marley flushed. "Right. Um, I didn't know who you were."

"And I didn't know who you were. Is that what you're driving at?"

"Pretty much."

Will smiled. "The hiring committee gave the board of directors a chance to review the candidates' résumés throughout the process, but I didn't feel a need to be involved. I didn't even know the name of the person they'd hired until you showed up this morning and I connected the dots."

"Right. That makes sense." Marley fidgeted with the notepad in her lap, trying to think of the best way to phrase what she had to say. "Under the circumstances, with you being the president of the board of directors and me—"

"You're thinking a June wedding then?"

"What?"

He grinned at her. "I'm kidding, Marley. You're right. Under the circumstances, it would be a terrible conflict of interest for us to make a habit of swapping spit in your kitchen."

"Yes, exactly." Marley bit her lip, wishing like hell she wasn't disappointed.

"*My* kitchen would be a much better place. The counters are a little higher, and if we get the angle just right—"

"Will!" She smacked him on the shoulder and laughed, enjoying the fizzle of lust that shot through her belly. "I'm trying to be professional here."

"And I admire that. You're right, of course. No more fooling around between the development director and the board chairman."

"It's important to respect company policy," Marley said. "As a new employee, the last thing I need is a scandal or any sort of disciplinary action."

"Relax, Marley. I'm not going to ravage you in the backseat. Or the front seat. Or on the hood. Or—"

"Thank you," Marley said, not feeling particularly thankful.

Will nodded. "So are you worried about be-ribboning the badgers?"

"Maybe a little," she said, relieved by the shift in conversation. "It's my first time handling a donor dinner party that involves wild animals."

"Get used to it. You're more likely to see a porcupine at a Cheez Whiz charity dinner than a tuxedo."

"Cheez Whiz," Marley repeated, smiling a little. "Have you always called it that?"

"No. I started after new management took over a few

years ago and went on a mission to make the place more respectable and classy."

"Not a mission you support?"

"Not when *respectable* means *elitist* and *classy* means *boring*. I'm not a fan of pretentiousness or false airs. My family has supported the organization for years, and the last thing I want is for it to become a stuffy, hoity place that takes itself so seriously that no one gets to enjoy it."

"I see," Marley said, digesting the information. "I can appreciate that. I've worked for a lot of organizations that take themselves too seriously." She shrugged and looked out the window. "On the other hand, sometimes you have to play the part to get the job done."

"Play the part?"

"Go along with other people's rules for the greater good of an organization that serves the community."

Will was quiet, and Marley turned to see him regarding her curiously. "That's an interesting perspective," he said.

Marley couldn't tell from his tone if *interesting* meant *interesting*, or *interesting* meant *you're a fruitcake*, so she shrugged again. "I've been in this business a long time in bigger cities like Portland and Seattle. Things are a little more formal there. Speaking of which, do you have any tips on dress for this evening?"

Will laughed. "You're asking *me* for wardrobe tips?"

"I guess so."

"You're aware I was wearing bedroom slippers when we met."

Marley smiled and fiddled with the door handle. "I'm aware of that."

"Bed has strict rules about hosiery, neckties, wearing sunglasses in public, saying *bless you* when someone sneezes, standing up when a woman enters the room, printing materials for board meetings in fourteen-point type, and using nothing but Riedel stemware to serve wine at board functions."

"Oh," Marley said. "Are Bed's rules written down somewhere?"

"No. You just have to wait to get yelled at when you break one."

Marley nodded and went back to the topic of clothing. "So for tonight. I assume I'll be safe in a little black dress and heels, but if everyone's going to turn up in jeans, I'd like to know in advance."

"That's what I'll be wearing." He glanced over at her. "The jeans, not the little black dress."

"Really?"

"Maybe you're right. I'd look good in a little black dress, and if I had the right heels—"

Marley laughed. "So will most guests be in jeans?"

"Dunno." He took his eyes off the road a moment and studied her. Marley resisted the urge to cross her arms over her chest or ask what he was looking at. She met his gaze and tried not to squirm.

"You seem awfully worried what people think of you," he said at last.

"I beg your pardon?"

He shrugged. "I don't mean that as an insult. Just an observation."

"Because I care what I wear to my first major fund-raiser?"

Will shrugged. "And what kind of music you listen to at home. And which college sports team you favor. And whether you play golf with board members. And whether Bed thinks you can give her mauve rabbits. And—"

"Enough." Marley swallowed hard, trying to keep her

expression impassive. "For your information, a development director *needs* to be focused on pleasing others. On conforming to their expectations. On learning what makes people tick and using that information to—"

"So when you drive out here tonight, you want to look for that tree," Will said, interrupting Marley's diatribe to thrust an arm in front of her and point at the side of the road. "The big juniper on the left with the orange flag attached. See it?"

Marley blinked and stared at Will's arm. Then at the tree. She opened her mouth to say something, but only managed to nod.

Will grinned and drew his arm back, placing both hands back on the wheel. "I'm a master at avoiding conflict," he said. "I prefer to do it with inappropriate humor, but I don't know you well enough yet to make penis jokes."

Marley stared at him, shaken by the turn in conversation. "You're certainly the most irreverent board chairman I've ever worked with."

"I'll take that as a compliment. I see it as my civic duty to keep Cheez Whiz from becoming a boring, stuffy organization filled with entitled rich people and overeducated snobs." He nodded out the window again as he turned off the highway onto a narrow stretch of country road. "Seriously though, this is where you'll turn tonight. From here, it's almost exactly six miles, then another right on a gravel road flanked by a wrought iron livestock fence."

Marley gave up studying Will and looked at the landscape instead. She scanned acres and acres of pasture, flecked with scrubby sagebrush and gnarled, ancient juniper. The sky was a stunning shade of blue flecked with wispy clouds, and a cluster of red-brown cows dotting a field was the only bright splash of color to be seen.

"Wow, Bed is way out here in the middle of nowhere."

"The family has almost sixty acres," Will said. "And the best mountain views you can imagine. Don't miss the sunset tonight."

"I'll try not to."

They drove in silence for a while, Marley sneaking glances at Will every now and then. She thought about his words, turning them over in her brain like weird gumballs in a plastic sphere. When she gave that up, she just looked at him. He was still in his suit from the meeting, but he'd ditched the jacket and tie in the backseat and unbuttoned the top of his shirt. His sleeves were rolled up, and he was drumming his fingers on the steering wheel completely out of sync with the Cyndi Lauper song on the stereo. The coppery highlights in his hair were even more noticeable in the sunlight, and from this angle she could only see his green eye.

"Here we are," Will announced, jarring Marley out of her thoughts.

She stared at the house and blinked. "Holy crap."

Will laughed and opened his car door. "In a manner of speaking."

Marley had seen a lot of huge houses in her line of work, but this place was massive. The architecture was a fascinating mix of Tuscan and Napa, with elaborate stonework and tastefully aged wood. The roof was tile, and the rockwork surrounding the enormous patio was a work of art.

"Those columns are antique," Will said, reaching into the backseat and hefting the case of wine in his arms as Marley studied the handcrafted stonework. "Bed imported them from Italy."

Marley ran her hand over a subtly dressed stucco wall. "The doors are amazing."

"The wood was rescued from an old church in Tuscany."

He shifted the case of wine to one hip and knocked on the door twice—two quick raps—and then walked inside without waiting for anyone to answer. Marley hesitated, not sure whether to follow or stand on the porch like an idiot.

"Are you just going to stand on the porch like an idiot?" Bed yelled from inside the foyer.

"I was considering it," Marley said, then marched in.

The interior of the home was even more impressive, if that was possible. Gorgeous artwork lined the walls, and ornate chandeliers of copper and glass cast pools of golden light on the terra-cotta tile. Marley followed Will through the foyer and into a large room with ornate tile floors and an array of bistro tables covered in mauve and green linen tablecloths.

"I was thinking here for the rabbit cage," Bed said as the two of them approached. She pointed to an open area at the center of the room before folding her arms across her chest.

"Badger cage," Will corrected, setting the wine down in a corner of the room. "We agreed to the badgers, remember?"

"Hmmph," Bed said, but didn't argue.

"I agree, this would be a lovely place," Marley said. "Your guests will be able to admire the animals right when they enter, and the flooring here is much better than carpet would be for… um, well…"

"Shit," Will supplied.

"Right." Marley cleared her throat. "If you don't mind, I'm going to snap a few pictures of the surrounding furnishings and take a few measurements?"

"Knock yourself out," Bed said. "I'm going to go yell at the caterer."

Marley frowned. "Is something wrong with the food?"

"No, I just feel like yelling at him."

Marley nodded and resisted the urge to beat the woman over the head with a statue that looked like a giant penis. She squinted at the statue more closely, trying to figure out what it was supposed to be.

"It's not a giant penis," Will supplied. "The statue. I wasn't sharing personal information. The statue is supposed to be a mushroom."

"Thank you for clarifying."

"Don't mention it."

"Would you mind holding the other end of the tape measure?" Marley asked. "For the floor space, not the giant penis."

Will grinned. "Thank you for clarifying."

They paced off sections of the floor, deciding the best position for the badgers and for the supplementary display of rabbit photos.

"Is it going to be a problem rounding up bunny photos on short notice?" Will asked.

"Nope, Darin has it covered. We were just hammering out the details in my office when you came to get me."

"Funny, I thought he was asking you out."

Marley flushed as she moved the end of the tape to the edge of the wall and squinted at it. "Darin didn't ask me out."

"None of my business. There are no Cheez Whiz rules about dating among staff as long as there's no supervisory relationship or—"

"Or a conflict of interest like there would be between the board chairman and the development director?"

Will grinned. "Exactly. So feel free to go crazy with Darin."

"Maybe I will."

"I wouldn't have pegged Darin as your type."

"No?" Marley struggled to keep her tone breezy. "What's my type?"

Will shrugged and stretched his end of the tape out to the opposite wall. "Tall, dark hair, a lawyer maybe, with a fondness for cognac and sailing."

Marley bit her lip. He'd just described her ex-fiancé to a T, but there was no way she'd admit that.

"Maybe I'm changing my type," Marley said. "It's a woman's prerogative to change her mind. To reinvent herself and develop different desires."

"I'm well aware of that," Will said flatly.

Marley swallowed hard. *Shit.*

She remembered what Susan had told her about Will's ex-wife coming out of the closet and leaving him for his sister. *Talk about changing your type.*

She opened her mouth to apologize, but Will had moved on. "Speaking of penises—"

"We were speaking of penises?"

He nodded toward the giant statue in the foyer. "Stay with me here. But I wasn't talking about Bed's statue. You've had a chance to look at the figurines my Aunt Nancy donated?"

"Yes. They're quite remarkable."

Will laughed. "That's one word for it. Those remarkable penises have been in the family for generations. They're worth quite a bit of money."

"Yes, of course. The Cascade Historical Society and Wildlife Sanctuary is very grateful for the donation."

"Cheez Whiz."

"Right. Very grateful. Obviously we'll rely on the appraisal to make the final determination about the value of the pieces."

"You're on top of it?"

Marley stifled a giggle. "I assure you I am quite on top of the antique phallus collection."

Will laughed and held his end of the tape measure in a corner of the room. "Looks like penis jokes are well within your comfort zone. Good to know."

Marley felt a fizzle of lust snake through her belly and decided to squelch it fast. "Hold the tape right there for a sec." She jotted the numbers in her notebook before walking back toward Will, winding up the tape as she went. "Thanks for your help."

"Don't mention it. I'm sure Bed will be pleased with your frames and ribbons and whatnot."

"I hope so," Marley said. "It's my first event for this job. I really want it to go well."

"It'll go well. They always do."

"You sound pretty sure of yourself."

"I always am."

He smiled, and Marley felt her insides turn to a melted pool of chocolate. Will's mismatched eyes were intent on her face, his smile warm and knowing. Neither of them spoke for a moment, and Marley wasn't even sure she blinked. She felt his fingers brush hers, and she looked down to see they were both still gripping the tape measure.

"Thank you," she said again, and pulled her hand back. She tucked it into her purse right as Bed huffed back into the room.

"Damn caterer doesn't know a canapé from a crudité."

"It's so hard to find good help, isn't it?" Marley asked.

"Hmmph," said Bed.

"I think we're all set here. The ribbons are going to look beautiful, and I think you'll be pleased with the color-coordinated frames on the bunny photos. That was a great idea you had."

"Damn straight," Bed said. "Next time, though, I want the mauve bunnies."

"We'll see what we can do," Marley said, and prayed there wouldn't be a next time.

—∞—

"I assume your car is back at Cheez Whiz?" Will asked as he headed toward the wildlife sanctuary.

"It is, thanks. I'll need to grab it so I can go shopping for frames and ribbons and things before I head back to Bed's to decorate."

"The craft store on Northeast Third will have the best selection of ribbons." He looked at her. "I'm a little embarrassed those words just came out of my mouth."

Marley laughed as Will turned into the parking area. "Thanks again for taking me out there. I never could have found it on my own."

"No sweat. So I'll see you at the party tonight?"

Marley nodded as she opened the car door and hopped out. "I'm looking forward to the badgers."

"Bet you never thought you'd say that about a charity function."

Marley grinned and bent down to peer through the window. Will caught a glimpse down the front of her blouse and felt all the blood leave his brain.

"Thanks again, Will," she said. "I'll see you in a few hours."

He drove away feeling downright cheerful about that. Then he kicked himself. *Hard.*

As the chairman of the board overseeing Cheez Whiz's

financials, Will knew he should be impressed their new fund-raising expert was adept at the sort of sweet talk that made donors open their wallets. Marley had done her job well, schmoozing Bed with promises of ribbons and Photoshopped bunnies. She'd even given Bed credit for the idea.

All things that should impress you, idiot.

But as a guy who'd spent four years married to a woman who'd spent longer than that pretending to be something she wasn't, Will was on edge about Marley's dual personality. Her willingness to tell people whatever they wanted to hear.

She'd flat-out admitted she didn't know if she could deliver the stupid ribbons, the floral arrangements, and the Photoshopped bunnies.

That's a good thing, dumbass. Pictures of mauve bunnies would be ridiculous.

That was true, but he'd watched Marley stand there and say she'd make it happen, knowing full well the Photoshopped bunnies wouldn't become a reality. It was enough to give Will a tense feeling in his shoulders.

Or maybe it was just his worry about Aunt Nancy's donation to Cheez Whiz. The stone *figurines*—come on, they were rock dildos—had been his aunt's pride and joy since her late husband bought them for her at an auction of Pacific Northwest artifacts. She was certain they were worth an insane amount of money. Enough to create a popular traveling exhibit that would fund an entire new wing for Cheez Whiz.

But Will wasn't so sure.

"You worry too much," his sister always told him.

Bethany had a point. He hated when that happened.

He spent the rest of the afternoon trying to keep his

body and brain occupied. He took the dogs for a hike along the river and spent an hour volunteering at the Humane Society. Sorted through some bills, played a game of Angry Birds on his iPhone. At five o'clock, Will changed out of his jeans and into—well, a pair of jeans with fewer holes.

Board meetings were one of the few times he made a concession to playing dress-up, but there was no need at a charity function that featured animals defecating in the foyer. Pulling on a faded T-shirt, he straightened it so the picture of two unicorns humping settled squarely in the middle of his chest. He started to grab his slippers, but remembered Bethany's chiding.

"Sandals," he said aloud, and stuffed his feet into a pair of old Birkenstocks.

He wandered out to the living room where his three dogs were lined up on the sofa like a furry welcoming committee. Rosco, the German shepherd mix, eyed Will with curiosity and thumped his tail on the couch cushions. Polly licked the end of her stubby pug nose and yawned. Omar lay there like a fuzzy blend of boulder and spaniel.

"How do I look?" he asked them.

Rosco cocked one ear and barked. Polly rolled onto her back for a belly rub, while Omar—deaf as a doornail for longer than he'd lived with Will—kept right on sleeping.

"Excellent," Will said, grabbing his keys off the peg by the door. "Don't wait up, guys."

Rosco barked again and chewed a ratty tennis ball, while Omar snored. Polly hopped off the sofa and trotted over to him with a toy mouse in her mouth. She deposited it at his feet and looked up with buggy brown eyes.

"Thanks, girl," Will said as he stooped to pick it up. "It's the perfect hostess gift."

He drove back to Bed's house with the stereo blasting Debbie Gibson, his arm hanging out the window in the evening breeze. He sang along with "Electric Youth," not caring that he was hopelessly out of tune. He pulled up the driveway and hadn't even brought the car to a complete stop when a uniformed valet came running up.

"Sir, if I can have your car keys, sir."

"Absolutely," Will said. "Good idea auctioning it off for charity."

"Sir?"

Will handed him the keys. "Don't forget to charge extra for the dog fur on the seats."

The valet looked relieved to be rid of Will as he maneuvered around the house to the parking area behind the barn. Will took a moment to dust dog fur off the sleeves of his button-down shirt before striding up the walkway.

The front door flew open before he had a chance to knock, and a constipated-looking butler waved Will inside.

"Sir, right this way."

"Thanks," Will said, and moved through the door.

He spotted the badgers right away, looking resplendent—if mildly annoyed—at the end of their mauve and green leashes. Darin was leading them around the perimeter of the room, allowing them to waddle slowly past the tipsy guests. A woman in a red dress clutching a champagne flute bent down and tried to pet Floyd, and Darin casually blocked her assault with a smile and a Cheez Whiz brochure about wildlife.

Will turned toward the badger cages, which were decked out with colorful ribbons woven with sprigs of juniper and tiny wildflowers. Marley had affixed mauve and green bows to the corners of their Plexiglas digging display, anchoring each with a bit of desert sage.

Will studied the décor, then Bed's curtains. Damn if it wasn't a perfect match.

Darin approached with the badgers and pulled a pair of thick leather gloves from his back pocket. "Hey, Will."

"Darin, how's it going?"

"Not bad, not bad," he said as he yanked the gloves on and began laying down treats to urge Frank up the ramp leading to the cage.

"Didn't those gloves used to be brown leather?"

Darin grinned and locked Frank in his cage before reaching for Floyd's leash. "Once upon a time they did. Marley asked if I wouldn't mind coloring them with pink shoe polish for the event. The hostess wanted everything mauve, and Marley said it would look chic."

Darin pronounced it "chick" instead of "sheik," and Will wondered if he was being facetious or just wasn't familiar with the word. Either way, Will fought a twinge of annoyance at the thought of Marley making fashion requests of the wildlife staff.

"Mauve is definitely your color," Will said as Darin latched the cage and slid a piece of carrot through the bars for Floyd.

Darin laughed. "I don't know about that, but Marley said she'd buy me a new pair when this is over. Can't argue with that."

"I don't suppose you can. Any chance you've seen her around anywhere?"

"In the kitchen, I think. She told the hostess she loves antique silverware, so the old lady dragged her down the hall to check out her collection."

"That sounds… not fun."

"My thoughts exactly."

Will looked in on the badgers, who had already settled into their cages and appeared to be on the brink of a good nap. "They seem to be having a good time."

"They fake it well."

"They aren't alone," Will said, then turned and ambled down the hall.

The crowd was thick already, with guests milling about eating expensive hors d'oeuvres and sipping wine. Will said hello to a few people, pausing to shake hands, clap backs, and inquire about the health of peoples' assorted loved ones, pets, and golf games. He continued his slow progression through the house, grateful he'd been here enough times to know the layout of the house.

He rounded the corner into the kitchen and stopped in the doorway. It took him a moment to register details of the scene in front of him: Marley in a low-cut black dress and killer heels, her blond hair pinned up in an elaborate twist. Marley on a stool at the kitchen counter, her beautiful legs crossed with her shin lightly bumping the knee of the woman to her right. Marley with her head thrown back, her pale breasts moving with her laughter. Marley with her hand brushing the arm of the woman to her left in a gesture of… friendship? Shared humor? Something more?

Will realized he was balling his hands into fists and stopped, flexing his fingers gently as he studied the lovely, bare column of her neck.

At last, he took a step into the room. Then another, and another, until he was even with the jovial threesome. He swallowed and pasted on the same stiff smile he'd seen Marley wear just that morning.

"Ms. Cartman, good evening," he said, and watched her turn to greet him. "I see you've met my sister and ex-wife."

Chapter 4

MARLEY TURNED AT THE SOUND OF WILL'S VOICE AND nearly dropped her crystal champagne flute. The ice in his eyes was enough to chill the blueberry tea in her glass.

"Will!" Bethany squealed, grabbing his arm. "Your ears must have been burning just now."

"We were just talking about you," April added in the sweet, almost childlike voice that matched the halo of wispy blond pixie curls around her face. Marley had spent the last twenty minutes resisting the urge to give one of April's cherub cheeks an affectionate pinch. She tore her eyes off April's cheeks and looked at Will's face instead.

He wasn't smiling and didn't seem particularly delighted to have been a topic of conversation.

"We were talking about you in a positive way," Marley interjected. "I promise your sister wasn't telling me about your prom night zit or where you stashed your porn when you were sixteen."

Will smiled a little at that, but his expression was still guarded. His mismatched eyes looked leery, and his jaw clenched tight.

"Ladies," Will said, glancing down at his sister's fingers still affixed to his sleeve. "I trust you're enjoying yourselves?"

"You didn't tell me the new development director was into mountain biking," Bethany practically shouted. "The three of us are going out to Phil's Trail for a ride next weekend."

"You're welcome to join us, Will," April chirped sweetly. "Not this coming Saturday, but the *following* Saturday. We're going to have a lovely time."

"I was unaware Ms. Cartman was an enthusiastic trail rider," Will said, turning to Marley. "I don't believe she included that on her résumé."

Marley smiled and took a sip of her iced tea. "Actually, you're wrong there. I included it under *hobbies*, thinking it was important information to list when applying for a position in the recreation capital of the universe."

Marley uncrossed and re-crossed her legs, and watched Will's eyes drop to her calves. Okay, so she hadn't actually ridden a mountain bike in ten years. She'd only put it on her résumé so she'd sound outdoorsy and well-rounded like everyone else in Central Oregon. She had the legs for the sport, thanks to countless hours on the elliptical machine. She could surely build up the requisite bike seat butt callus in time to hold her own along the trail with these two women.

"Actually, I never saw your résumé," Will said. "I wasn't part of the hiring committee, so I didn't get a chance to review it."

"Would you like me to send a copy to your office?"

Bethany laughed and slugged her brother in the arm. "I like the idea of Will in an office. That's almost as funny as the idea of Will in a tie."

Will smiled, though Marley noticed the smile didn't quite reach his eyes. "I'll have you know I wore a tie just this morning."

April nodded, her blond pixie curls bobbing a little as her head moved. "The blue tie? I always loved your blue tie. Or the gray one. Or even the green was lovely."

Marley was wracking her brain for a suitable subject

change when Bethany beat her to the punch. "Have you seen Aunt Nancy around anywhere?"

Will shook his head. "Not yet. I just got here."

"So you still have time to hide."

Will smiled at that. "I take it she already found you?"

"Within the first five minutes she described a research project on triorchidism, told April her lipstick was too pink, and asked why Marley was drinking on the job."

"Triorchidism?" Marley asked.

"Males with three testes," Bethany supplied.

Will shook his head. "I didn't need to know that."

"Marley's drinking iced tea," April announced, and offered a sympathetic smile. "She brought her own from home, and it's lovely."

Lovely, Marley thought, and considered making a drinking game of April's speech patterns. If everyone drank on the word *lovely*, the whole room would be tipsy in ten minutes. It was a good thing she'd brought her own tea.

Will quirked an eyebrow at Marley and nodded toward her champagne flute. "You travel with iced tea?"

"Blueberry." Marley smiled and took a sip. "Would you like some?"

"Maybe later."

"It smells absolutely lovely," April sang.

Marley nodded at April and tried to imagine this sweet, soft-spoken woman being married to Will. It was a challenge, not only because their personalities seemed so different, but because April's tiny, French-manicured fingers rested lightly on Bethany's knee.

"I'm sure Aunt Nancy was just having a rough evening," Marley offered.

"Nope, she's always a bitch," Bethany said cheerfully. "And she never lets anyone forget she was a sex therapist who authored three bestselling books and did ground-breaking research on deviant sexual behavior. Richer than God, though, so you're going to want to get to know her."

Marley winced, hating the way that sounded. "I'm always eager to meet any of the wildlife sanctuary's supporters."

Bethany eyed her and took a sip of wine. "You're single, Marley?"

"Yes."

"Straight?"

She hesitated, then realized this was a dumb answer to consider fudging in an effort to relate. "Yes, I'm straight."

Bethany nodded. "We should introduce you to Todd Thomas. He's cute, eligible, and rich. He's a plastic surgeon. Not much of a supporter for the wildlife sanctuary, since he tends to donate to medical charities, but I'm sure you could be very persuasive with him."

Will quirked an eyebrow at Marley. "See? Your ability to *handle* donors is legendary."

"The two of you would make a lovely couple," April chirped. "You and Todd, I mean. Not you and Will. Todd is a very nice man. Not that Will isn't a nice man—"

"Actually, I'm not really interested in dating wealthy men right now," Marley said. "But I can certainly talk with Todd about getting involved with Cascade Historical Society and Wildlife Sanctuary."

"Cheez Whiz," Will supplied.

"Not interested in dating wealthy men?" Bethany laughed. "That's a new one."

Marley flushed and glanced from Bethany to April to Will, worried she'd said the wrong thing. "I have nothing against people with money, of course. It's just… well, I'm ready for a change."

"A change?" Bethany asked.

"Something different from most of the men I've worked with or dated or been raised by," she clarified.

"Ah, daddy issues—got it." Bethany nodded. "I hear you, sistah."

"No, I didn't mean—"

"It's okay," April said, giving Marley's knee a sympathetic pat. "We know plenty of perfectly lovely, single men who aren't wealthy."

Marley smiled and glanced over at Will. He was gritting his teeth so hard she heard them clack together.

"You're probably smart," Bethany said. "Most rich men are pricks. Present company excluded, of course." She grinned at her brother, clearly goading him.

"My prick and I thank you for excluding us from the insult," Will replied evenly.

April looked uncomfortable, and Marley wondered if it was the crudeness of the discussion, or the mere mention of her ex-husband's genitalia.

Fortunately, they were all spared from continuing the conversation when Darin approached, leading one of the badgers on a mauve leash. "We're getting ready to start the digging in about twenty minutes."

Will looked at Darin and shrugged. "I really think the badgers would do a better job, but I do have a trowel in my car."

Marley rolled her eyes at Will before turning to smile at Darin. "I'll get everyone's attention in just a few minutes and direct them all into the other room. Does it seem like they're having a good time?"

Darin quirked an eyebrow. "The badgers?"

Will glanced down. "Floyd looks a little depressed, actually. Maybe he prefers Shiraz to Pinot Noir?"

Marley gave Will a playful slug in the arm. "I meant the guests."

"The guests seem to be enjoying themselves," Darin said. "We've already raised some nice funds charging people to have their photo taken with a badger, though I keep having to fend off guests who want to pet them."

Marley hopped off her stool and gave Will a gentle shove. "Why don't you come help me round people up for the badger digging?"

Will slid off his barstool with maddening ease, his mismatched eyes flashing with amusement. "At your service."

—◊◊◊—

Will had lied about one thing—he actually *had* seen a copy of Marley's résumé.

Nowhere in the document had she mentioned a history of assisting big rodents in displacing large quantities of soil.

But as Will watched Marley work the crowd—and the badger—like a champ, he had to admire her ability to leap with ease into new circumstances. Her smile was broad and genuine, and she had easily coaxed the crowd into wagering large sums of money on how long Floyd the badger would take to dig to the bottom of the Plexiglas cube.

"Fourteen-point-two-three seconds!" Marley shouted as Floyd emerged at the bottom of the cube with his tawny fur caked in dirt. Marley dropped the treat in front of him, and he snatched it quickly and sniffed for more. Darin stooped at the base of the badger-sized off-ramp and clipped the leash back onto Floyd's harness as Marley stepped around them and reached for a black notebook on the corner of a table.

"Let's take a look at our list of wagers here," she called as she held the notebook up for the crowd. "It looks like Marcia Arbol had the closest badger bet with fourteen-point-three seconds. Congratulations, Marcia! You've won—"

Will tuned out, not particularly interested in whether Marcia had earned a Cheez Whiz membership or a plaque on a bench as a reward for her thousand-dollar bet on Floyd's digging skills. It never ceased to amaze Will what gimmicks would prompt people to give generously at charity events. As long as other people saw them forking out large sums of cash, people were willing to donate to just about anything.

At least it's for a good cause, he reminded himself. *Stop being a dick.*

It was true; Marley had raised a lot of money for Cheez Whiz tonight. That's what mattered.

What *didn't* matter—at least that's what Will kept telling himself—is that he'd stopped at Cheez Whiz earlier in the day and asked Susan for a copy of Marley's résumé.

He'd tried to act casual, leaning against the file cabinet as Susan rifled through the drawers and explained how the hiring committee had narrowed the field from more than a hundred applicants to the top five finalists, with Marley at the head of the pack.

"You probably recall we gave the board of directors a chance to review the finalists' résumés before we made a decision," Susan said as she pulled out a file and began rifling through the contents.

"I remember that," Will said. "I trusted the hiring

committee's judgment one hundred percent, so I didn't feel a need to review their documents. But now that Ms. Cartman is here, I feel it's in my best interest to make sure I know a bit more about her background."

"Of course, not a problem," Susan said. "Would you like me to make a copy for you?"

Will had agreed, and spent ten minutes in his car afterward studying Marley's background and googling her former employers on his iPhone. He hadn't learned much, except that Marley had been a remarkably busy woman in her fifteen years since college. He'd do a little more digging once he had time to do it properly. He owed it to Cheez Whiz to be thorough.

You owe it to Marley to admit you're checking her out because you're suspicious she fudges facts to please people.

Not true. Well, true that he maybe had some trust issues, but he was just doing his job. And true that he wanted to be sure Marley's references and work history checked out. As chairman of the board of directors, his loyalty was to Cheez Whiz. He didn't owe Marley anything. Hell, he barely knew her.

You're being a suspicious jerk.

True. Very true.

But isn't that exactly what April had said when she'd caught him scrolling through her cell phone a month before their divorce more than four years ago?

Part of him had expected to find a clandestine email from a guy at the gym, or someone she worked with, or maybe even an old boyfriend. *Something* that would explain why his sweet, soft-spoken, eager-to-please wife had grown so distant.

What he'd found had certainly explained things, though

Will could have done without seeing topless photos of his sister. Apparently, the two women had been enjoying more than margaritas on their girls' nights out.

Should have learned your lesson about snooping.

Probably so, Will mused as he drew his attention back to where Marley and Darin stood before the crowd. Marley clapped, her face flushed with excitement, as Darin led Floyd up a little ramp and into his travel cage. Then she turned back to the crowd and beamed. "A round of applause for the badgers, and an extra round for you, our generous donors."

The audience applauded politely while Floyd twitched his nose and picked up a scrap of food Darin dropped in the corner of his enclosure.

"Thanks to all of you," Marley said, "we'll be able to continue our educational programs for schoolchildren throughout the district. We've already made a nice dent in tonight's fund-raising goals, but don't forget to take a look at our silent auction items in the next room. There's a lot of great stuff up for grabs, and another twenty minutes left on the bidding. Remember that all the money goes straight to the Cascade Historical Society and Wildlife Sanctuary."

"Cheez Whiz," Will said under his breath to no one in particular. He slouched against the wall, out of earshot of the donors filtering by with wineglasses in their hands and dollar signs in their eyes. Will studied Marley as she watched Darin latch the badger cage. She leaned close to Darin and spoke into his ear. Darin smiled and said something that made Marley laugh, and Will tried to ignore the jealous twist in his gut. His fingers tightened around the glass he'd filled with the last dregs of her blueberry tea.

He took a sip to wash away the illicit thoughts he'd been having about her.

Fat lot of good that did. The bright berry smell of it just made Will recall the scent of Marley's hair as she'd tossed it over one shoulder and—

"Billy's got a cruuush, Billy's got a cruuush…"

The teasing whisper in his ear caught Will by surprise, and he whirled around to see his sister grinning at him. No one was close enough to hear, but he caught her by the wrist anyway and poked two fingers into her ribs.

"Knock it off or I'll tickle you until you pee," he whispered.

Bethany giggled and straightened her blouse, yanking her arm away from him with ease. She drained the rest of her red wine and set the glass on a bistro table before leaning against the wall beside Will, their shoulders touching slightly.

"Nice to see we've both grown up enough to attend formal charity functions," Bethany said. "We should make armpit noises next."

"Speak for yourself. I was just standing here, minding my own business—"

"—ogling the new development director's tits." Bethany grinned and grabbed the iced-tea glass out of Will's hand. She took a sip and handed it back. "I was doing the same thing."

"You have no idea how disturbing I find it that we have the same taste in women."

"Relax, bro. This one bats for your team. She's all yours."

Will glanced over at Marley in case their voices had carried, but it was clear they hadn't. His sister was crude, but she knew how to be discreet.

"How do you know Marley bats for my team?" He frowned. "And did you know for a long time that April—"

"Liked playing cuddle-the-koala?"

"I don't even know what that means."

"Well—"

"Don't feel you need to explain it."

Bethany grinned. "I knew before April knew, if that's what you're asking. Lesbians who come out of the closet younger like I did tend to have a finely tuned gaydar detector. It helps us spot the ones who are still locked in the closet but trying desperately to claw their way out."

Will bit down the insult that threatened to bubble up any time conversations with his sister took a turn like this. He didn't still love April—not like that—but he didn't like feeling as though he'd held April prisoner. That his sweet, gentle ex had been desperate or miserable. That he'd been a rich, entitled bastard who'd trapped her in a marriage and an identity she didn't really want.

"So you're positive Marley's straight?" Will said, determined to get back to the issue at hand.

"I'd stake my flannel shirt collection on it."

"Have you ever owned a flannel shirt?"

Bethany straightened the plunging neckline of her red silk dress. "I refuse to answer that on the grounds that my lesbian card might be taken away. Seriously, though, Marley seems nice."

"Hmmm."

"Definitely not after you for your money like a lot of women are."

"Hmmm."

"Smart. Outdoorsy. Loves animals."

"Hmmm."

"Fantastic legs. Great hair. Gorgeous t—"

"You can stop there." Will took a sip of his tea and

looked at Bethany. "You're right though. She does have fantastic legs."

"You're welcome to join the three of us when we go mountain biking next weekend."

"No thanks. Sounds like more of a girls' outing."

"If I didn't know you, I'd say your tone sounded a little bitter there, Mr. Barclay." She grinned. "Wait, I *do* know you—we emerged from the same vagina, if I recall correctly."

"And again, thank you for that visual."

"I was talking about *Mom's* vagina, moron. Though now that I think about it—"

"Don't think about it."

Bethany was quiet a moment. "April and I aren't taking Marley out mountain biking to turn her into a big, raging lesbian. In case you were worried about that, I mean. We're just being friendly."

"Okay."

"And for the record, you can't actually turn anyone into a lesbian, raging or otherwise."

"Absolutely."

"That little vein in your temple is twitching again."

"Thanks for noticing."

Bethany grabbed his iced tea and took another sip before handing it back. "You know, Will, you're going to need to get over your trust issues someday."

Will quirked an eyebrow at her. "An odd statement, coming from you."

"Meaning?"

"Meaning one could argue you had something to do with my so-called trust issues." He tried to keep his tone jovial, but probably failed. Bethany just shrugged, not seeming too insulted.

"You probably have a point. Maybe I'll make it my mission to undo the damage. Call it penance or something."

"There's no damage, Bethy. I'm fine." Will paused, choosing his words carefully. "Look, I'm happy for you and April. You know I am, right?"

"Sure."

"But you also know that discovering my wife—"

"—preferred playing tickle-the-tulips?"

"It wasn't the easiest thing in the world, so I'd appreciate it if you could cut me some slack here." He put his arm around Beth's shoulder and pulled her close. She used the opportunity to steal another sip of his tea.

"Duly noted, bro."

Will kissed her forehead. "I love you, you, evil wife-stealing tramp."

"And I love you, you clueless, dick-wielding breeder."

"We're probably due for some intense family therapy."

"Again?" Bethany grinned wider. "Let me go find April. She lives for the group hug."

"I think she's upstairs with Bed's granddaughter watching the *Bambi* DVD again."

Bethany ducked out from under Will's arm. "I'll catch you later. Let me know if you change your mind about joining us for the bike ride."

"Sure."

"And go talk to Marley already. She's single, you're single, she's cute, you're cute, she's straight, you're straight—"

"She hates rich assholes, I'm a rich asshole. She plays loose with the truth to endear herself to people, I have major trust issues. She—"

"Way to keep an open mind, Will."

He grinned. "I'm the most open-minded guy you

know. Didn't I buy you guys that tandem bike as an engagement gift?"

"Thank you, Will."

"And who marched in the pride parade with you wearing a pink tutu?"

"You looked lovely in it."

"And who bought you *The Big Book of Lesbian Sex Positions*?"

"You just liked the pictures. And Aunt Nancy gave it to you." She slugged him in the arm, the same arm Marley had nailed less than an hour ago. What was it with the women in his life wanting to hit him?

"Now go get the girl," Bethany commanded.

Will had no intention of getting the girl, but he also didn't want his sister accusing him of standing around with his thumb up his butt. He took a few steps in Marley's direction, then a few more. The next thing he knew, he was standing right in front of her.

"Nice badger show," he said.

Marley turned and gave him a broad smile. "That's what all the guys say." The smile was her real one, and Will felt pleased he'd already learned to distinguish between the stiff one she reserved for donors and the one she saved for actual pleasure.

Bet you could find ways to see the pleasure smile more often.

"How's your evening going, Will?" she asked. "I take it you caught the badgers' performance?"

"Great. Floyd was particularly impressive."

"Thanks for all your help earlier today," Marley said. "It's always a challenge navigating these new situations and social structures."

Her expression was surprisingly disarmed, and Will felt something inside him twist. "I *am* the king of social rules."

"So I've heard." She started to say something else, but then seemed to change her mind. They stood there for a moment looking at each other, and Will wondered what she was thinking. She opened her mouth again to fill the silence, but Darin's reappearance halted whatever words she'd been about to utter.

"Hey, Will, good to see you again." Darin pulled off his mauve glove and shook Will's hand, even though they'd gone through this ritual at least two other times throughout the evening. Will shook his hand anyway, careful not to be the dickhead who gripped too hard or tried to prove the size of his testicles by the strength of his fingers.

"Darin, nice job with the presentation."

"Thanks, man. Marley did great too, especially considering it was her first show."

"Floyd and Frank get all the credit." Marley smiled at Darin, and Will tried not to feel jealous. "Well, Floyd and Frank and Darin."

"I'm just glad it could do some good for the Cascade Historical Society and Wildlife Sanctuary," Darin said.

"Cheez Whiz," Will supplied.

One corner of Marley's mouth twitched, but she didn't look at Will. "Seriously, I didn't know half that stuff about badgers. They really hunt in packs with coyotes?"

"Absolutely," Darin said. "It's a uniquely symbiotic relationship with the badgers digging out ground squirrels the coyotes can catch for dinner, and the coyotes serving as bodyguards for the badgers. If you're ever interested in a day trip out to the southeastern desert, you might be able to see it sometime."

"Really? Is it rare to see them in the act?"

"Rare, but not unheard of. I know some great places to look."

"Well then, we'll have to make it a date sometime."

"A date. I'd like that."

Darin smiled, and Marley smiled back. Will wondered how long it would take to drown himself in what remained of his iced tea.

It wasn't that their topic was boring, though he liked to think he could come up with wittier banter to engage Marley.

No you couldn't. You'd just play her some Madonna and crack stupid jokes.

Probably true. Will sighed and downed the rest of his iced tea in one swallow. He set his glass on the tray of a passing waiter and gave Darin and Marley a mock salute.

"I'd better go find Aunt Nancy and say hello," Will said.

"Oh, I was hoping to meet her this evening, but I've been tied up with the auctions and the badgers."

"I'll let her know. Actually, there's a good chance she's already gone. She's leading an early morning gymnophobia support group."

"A fear of the gym?"

"A fear of seeing naked bodies."

"I learn something new every day."

"With Aunt Nancy it's not always something you wanted to learn."

"Well, if you see her, let her know how grateful we all are for her generous donation of... of... of *figurines.*"

Will grinned. "Will do. Then I'm heading home to see my dogs."

Marley glanced at her watch and bit her lip. "I was worried about leaving Magoo this long, but luckily my father planned a last-minute visit. He's keeping an eye on him."

"So you and Magoo are hitting it off well?"

"Splendidly," Marley said. "He's always so sweet and happy and excited to see me at the end of the day. I just love having him there to cuddle with, and he always warms my toes in bed."

Will nodded, trying not to picture Marley in bed. Trying not to feel jealous of a dog. "Give him my regards."

Marley hadn't even finished unlocking the front door when she called for her dog, eager to see a friendly face.

"Magoo! It's me, boy! C'mere, Magoo."

From the darkness, Marley heard a familiar snort. "Please tell me someone else named that animal."

"Dad?" Marley pushed the door open and flipped on a light switch.

Her father tugged off a pair of expensive-looking earphones and smiled. He was sitting in the half-dark living room, the glow of his laptop providing the only illumination in the space. Beside him, Magoo was sprawled on his back with his jowls sagging open. Marley's dad was stroking the dog's belly with one hand and typing with the other. At the sight of Marley, Magoo flipped over as gracefully as he could manage and thumped his stubby tail against the sofa cushion.

Marley patted her knees, and Magoo scrambled off the couch, catching himself as he started to tumble. His furry paws flailed, and he skidded to a halt in front of Marley and licked her knee.

Marley bent to scratch his ears, cooing about what a

good dog he was. Magoo flopped onto his side and groaned with pleasure as Marley scratched his belly with French-manicured fingernails.

Her dad watched the whole thing from the sofa, a bemused look on his face. "Your mother was the same way with animals. Giving them goofy names, slobbering all over them, making them piss themselves from the sheer joy of being around her."

"What goofy name did she call you?"

Her dad grinned. "Rumpy-diddle, Schnooky Lumps, or Studly-do-right. I always maintained bladder control, though."

Marley laughed and stood up. "Need a refill on the bourbon?"

"Just a splash. Care to join me?"

"I don't really like bourbon."

"You should learn to. High-end distilled spirits are a great entrée into upscale social circles."

Marley grimaced en route to the kitchen. She paused long enough to toe off her high heels, which she kicked into the corner by the door. She padded into the living room and grabbed her father's glass off the coaster on the end table. Magoo trotted behind her, delighted with the prospect of a trip to the kitchen.

"You look nice, by the way," her dad said.

"Thanks. My first charity event since I started the new job."

"Things go well?"

"Great. Good turnout, very generous donors."

Her dad set the earphones on the arm of the sofa and turned back to his computer as Marley reached the kitchen. A bottle of Basil Hayden's bourbon rested on the counter, and Marley yanked open the freezer and grabbed the requisite number of ice cubes, careful not to make them too big or too small. She hesitated, then grabbed an empty glass for herself.

He's probably right about bourbon and upscale social circles.

"So Dad," she called. "How long are you in town?"

"A week at least, but I'll be traveling to a lot of meetings so I'll mostly be out of your hair. I want to give you plenty of privacy in case you and Curtis need space to work things out."

Marley rolled her eyes and picked up both glasses. "Dad. I'm not getting back with Curtis."

"Never rule out the possibility of reconciliation, Marley."

Marley bit her tongue, resisting the urge to point out that her father had ruled out the possibility of reconciliation with five previous wives when he'd married his sixth last spring. Marriage was not a subject she cared to discuss with her dad.

"So speaking of your mother, have you heard from her lately?"

Speaking of subjects you don't want to discuss with your dad...

"Mom's doing great," Marley said brightly, handing him his glass as she curled herself on the other end of the sofa. She tucked her feet under his legs and took a sip of the bourbon. She made a face.

Luckily, her dad didn't look up from his computer. He took a healthy swig of the bourbon and set it down on the coaster.

"How is she holding up in—"

"Guatemala," Marley interjected. "That's what I've been telling people. It's easier that way. Simpler. I'd appreciate it if you could back me up on that."

Her father frowned. "You aren't still sending her money, are you?"

Marley set her glass down with a thunk, missing her own coaster by a foot. "Dad, can we not talk about this?"

Her father looked up and shrugged. "Whatever you want, honey. You know I'm just concerned about your financial security."

"I appreciate that," Marley said tightly, not appreciating it much at all. "I'm here in Bend for a fresh start, Dad. No one here knows my mother is a criminal, so maybe you could keep that information to yourself?"

Walter raised one hand. "Say no more. So did you meet any men at the charity event?"

"What?"

"Events like that are a great place to meet single people who have their financial priorities in line. It could be a nice way for you to find someone."

Marley sighed, wondering if it was too late to turn the conversation back to her ex-fiancé or her long-lost mother or root canals or *anything* more appealing than this. Magoo hopped up on the couch beside her and rested his head in her lap. She stroked his ears as Magoo began the tedious process of bathing her arm with his tongue.

"I already found the best guy on the planet," Marley said, scratching Magoo beneath the chin. "Magoo is a more likeable guy than anyone I've ever dated."

"I don't doubt it. But wouldn't it be handy to also have a guy who walks upright and can pick up the tab at a restaurant?"

Marley shook her head. "I'm not looking for a rich guy, Dad. I've had enough of that to last a lifetime."

She waited to see if he took that as a personal insult, but

he merely shrugged. "Money comes with perks, Marley. It's a fact of life."

"It comes with drama, too. I was serious the other day when I said I'm done with rich guys. I want to meet someone more blue-collar. Someone more *normal*. Someone with different priorities than the men I've dated before."

Her father raised his eyebrows but said nothing, turning back to his computer. Marley wriggled her toes under his leg, feeling six years old again and eager to please her father with something she'd made out of macaroni and paste.

"There's a very nice wildlife specialist at the museum. Derek." She paused and bit her lip. "I mean *Darin*. Anyway, I might try dating him. He seems like a very nice, normal, down-to-earth guy who probably doesn't have a bank account the size of Texas."

Her dad sighed. "Just be careful, Marley. You know how you can be with money."

The words felt like a knife between the ribs. "How I can be with money," she repeated, digesting the words. "I've built my entire career around money. Around handling donors' contributions with wisdom and aplomb and professionalism."

"And I'm very proud of you, honey." He patted her knee. "It's just a shame things haven't gone as well in your personal life. But if you find a good man who can—"

"You know, Dad, I'm really tired." Marley jumped up, done with the conversation, done with her drink, just *done*. "I think I'm going to turn in for the night."

Her father looked at her and sighed. "I only want what's best for you."

"I know that. We just have a different opinion about what that is."

Her father nodded and took a small sip of his drink. "Good night, sugar. Sleep well."

Marley nodded and bent to kiss him on the cheek. "Thanks for looking out for Magoo all evening."

"No problem. We had a good time watching HBO and licking things around the house."

She managed a small smile. "Sleep well, Dad."

"You too, baby." He put his earbuds back in, and Marley watched him turn up the volume on whatever he'd been listening to when she'd walked in. Probably hip-hop so he could be current on the latest musical trends for his young wife. Marley sighed and turned away, and Magoo hopped down from the sofa to follow her.

Marley padded through the living room, across the foyer, and down the hall toward the bedroom with Magoo trotting after her. She got halfway down the hall when a knock sounded at the door. Magoo barked once, then sat down on his haunches in the foyer and waited to see what exciting thing might be happening.

Marley pivoted on her bare heels and headed for the front door. She gave a fleeting thought to whether it was wise to throw open the door to a stranger at eleven p.m. on a Thursday night, but she was too tired to care.

She unlocked the deadbolt, yanked open the door, and screamed.

Chapter 5

AT THE SOUND OF MARLEY'S SCREAM, WILL DROPPED THE giant pink bunny he'd lugged all the way to her front porch. The massive stuffed rabbit landed with its ear flopped over Will's crotch and its glassy eyes leering gleefully. He shoved the animal's head aside and grinned at Marley, who gaped at him from the doorway.

"Sorry about that," he said. "I take it you weren't expecting company?"

Marley blinked and looked from Will to the bunny and back to Will again. Her hair was tousled and her feet were bare, and Will was certain he'd never seen her look so beautiful.

"I wasn't expecting a four-foot pink rabbit at the door at eleven p.m. on a Thursday night."

"Good point. Giant pink rabbits generally appear on Wednesdays at noon."

"Will, what the hell is this?"

He rested one hand on the rabbit's head and tried to keep his eyes off Marley's cleavage. She was still wearing that black dress with the billowy neckline that gave him small glimpses of her flesh whenever she moved just right. Maybe if she stooped down for a closer look at the rabbit…

"Rabbit," Will said, struggling to direct the blood back into his brain. "That's a very good question, though. One I asked myself at least four times as I drove here with a gargantuan pink rodent in the passenger seat of my car. For the record, she wore a seat belt."

"I'm glad to hear it. But why is the gargantuan pink rodent on my porch?"

"Bed insisted," Will said. "She wanted to make sure you got the message that she was pleased with how you handled the party this evening. She also wanted an extra special way to present you with *this*."

He lifted one of the rabbit's floppy arms, waving it in Marley's direction until she looked down and spotted the envelope safety-pinned to the creature's pink paw. He watched her brows raise quizzically, and she studied the envelope for a moment before looking back at Will.

"That's for me?"

"That's for Cheez Whiz, but Bed wanted to be sure it was delivered to you personally."

Marley licked her lips and bent down to unpin the envelope. The neckline of her dress gaped open, and Will felt himself grow dizzy. He diverted his gaze to a huge bronze statue that looked like a pterodactyl preparing to crash into the wall, and he studied it intently as Marley tore open the envelope.

"Oh my God," she said.

Will looked back at her, relieved to see she was standing at an angle that kept her tempting flesh off display. Her face was pale, and when she raised her eyes to his, they were wide and stunned.

"Is this for real?" she asked.

"I believe so."

"Is she joking?"

"Bed never jokes," Will answered. "I didn't see the amount, but I trust it's either embarrassingly large or she just enrolled you in a jelly-of-the-month club?"

Marley blinked again. "This is more than ten times the

biggest donation of the night. And that's saying something, considering we had some very generous donors this evening."

Will nodded, not particularly surprised. "Bed does love the grand gesture. Hence the ugly pink rabbit." Will looked down at the creature again, then back at Marley. "Do you mind if I bring this inside? I don't want your neighbors to see it. They might get jealous, and before you know it, they'll all expect me to show up on their doorsteps with massive pink stuffed animals."

"Right. Um, how about right here against the wall?"

Marley pointed at a spot in the foyer next to the airsick pterodactyl, and Will bent down and picked up the rabbit. He half-carried, half-dragged it to the wall and propped it up beside the statue. Marley shut the door behind him and turned to study the arrangement. One of the bunny's massive ears flopped over its button eyes, and Will tucked it back along the side of the creature's head. The ear promptly slid back.

Will shrugged. "A word of warning—it has those eyes that look like they're following you no matter where you move. It's kinda creepy."

"Creepy doesn't even begin to describe it."

Magoo trotted over to inspect the new arrival. He sniffed one of the massive feet, then the other. He gave a tentative lick to the fur on the creature's belly, then sneezed. He trotted to the other side and surveyed the animal's massive leg. Hoisting himself up with a grunt, Magoo began to hump it enthusiastically.

"Magoo, stop that!" Marley hissed, giving him a light nudge with her toe.

Magoo was undaunted. He closed his doggie eyes in bliss and readjusted his position. The rabbit bounced pleasantly as the ear flopped back and forth over its beady eye.

Marley grimaced and tried in vain to shoo her dog away. "Magoo, stop it! Go on—*get*."

Magoo ignored her and shifted positions.

"There's no stopping true love," Will said. "Or puppy love. Or in this instance, a strong case of salax."

Marley stopped shooing and looked up at Will. "Salax?"

"It's Latin," he said. "It means lecherous, lustful, lascivious—"

"Horny?"

"Pretty much."

"Why am I not surprised you know the Latin word for horny?"

Will shrugged and looked back at Magoo, who seemed to be picking up speed. "You have to admire the effort. Impressive stamina, Magoo."

Marley frowned and clapped her hands. "Magoo, seriously—stop."

The command fell on deaf ears, though Will had the sense she didn't really mean it. They both stood for a moment, watching as Magoo released his grip on one leg and moved to the other side of the rabbit. With a delighted snort, he heaved himself onto the rabbit's other leg and got back to work.

"I suppose the rabbit should be grateful Magoo is neutered," Marley said. "Did you know rabbits are capable of conceiving starting at three months old, and the average gestation period is thirty-one days?"

"And now I understand where the term 'breeding like rabbits' comes from. Are you always such a font of trivial animal facts?"

Marley shrugged. "Since I accepted this job, I've been doing my best to develop and demonstrate my wildlife knowledge."

"You know Cheez Whiz doesn't require you to be an expert on everything, right?"

Marley flushed and looked back at the rabbit, which was still clenched in Magoo's passionate embrace. "Does the bunny have a name?"

"I'm glad you asked. Bed wanted me to be sure and let you know Pookie is from her personal collection. She has more than 600 rabbits, in case you're wondering."

"None of them living, I hope?"

"Fortunately not. Had she sent a live rabbit, things might be going differently for Magoo."

Marley frowned down at her pet. "I've never had a dog before. Should I… um… make him stop?"

"He isn't hurting anything."

"I didn't get a chance to walk him today, so I guess it's good exercise."

"That's the spirit."

They both looked away from Magoo, and Will felt his gut clench as their eyes met. He didn't blink, and Marley's eyes held his with the same intensity. Something shifted between them, and Will felt the temperature in the room rise at least twenty degrees.

He wasn't sure which of them would speak first, or if he was even capable of speech. He caught the faint scent of blueberries in the air and breathed deeply, filling his lungs with warm air. Marley blinked and touched her fingertips to the base of her throat. An odd gesture, but one that left Will aching to trail his own fingers over that heated patch of flesh.

At last, he found his voice. "It's a good thing we're standing here witnessing one of the least romantic displays imaginable." His voice sounded dark, strained. "Eliminates any urge we might have to repeat the scene from your kitchen."

Marley bit her lip. "Totally."

"A dog humping a giant pink rabbit—definitely a mood killer."

"Of course."

"Not that there was a mood to begin with."

Neither of them looked at Magoo. Their eyes stayed locked together, and Will realized for the first time that Marley's were the most beautiful shade of hazel with flecks of silver. She bit her lip and tucked a strand of blond hair behind one ear.

Will took a fractional step closer, not sure what prompted him to do it.

Okay, he had a pretty good idea.

"It would be a really stupid idea for us to kiss right now," he said.

"Ridiculous."

"There are strict company policies against it."

"Absolutely," Marley breathed. "I can't afford to lose my job."

"It would be highly unprofessional for the board chairman to break such an important rule."

"And I'm avoiding men who have more money than God."

Will took another step closer. "I can't actually vouch for the current balance in the Almighty's bank account."

Marley took a shuddery breath and moved a fraction of an inch closer. "How much do you *really* oversee my position?"

They lunged for each other at the same time, their teeth

colliding in a most unromantic fashion as Magoo grunted and skittered between their ankles.

This shouldn't be hot, Will thought.

But it was.

If their first kiss had been tentative, this one was nothing like it. The intensity of it left Will panting and dizzy, his hands fumbling to touch every inch of her at once. He slid his palms to the sides of her face and he kissed her hard and deep, his tongue tangling with hers. Marley pushed him back against the door and molded her body against his, her lush curves fitting perfectly against his chest. She pressed her body into him, and Will groaned as her hip bone grazed his growing arousal.

Will broke the kiss, panting hard, eager to feel his mouth against other planes of flesh. He kissed his way down her throat, pausing to savor the throb of her pulse against his lips. Her skin was the softest thing he'd ever felt, and she smelled faintly of blueberries. He breathed her in, feeling dizzy all over again. He moved his lips at last, kissing his way across her throat before brushing his mouth against her earlobe. Marley whimpered and gripped his shoulders hard, pressing her body against his, driving Will mad with the gentle pressure of her pelvis against the fly of his jeans.

Steady, steady.

He traced his tongue against the soft skin behind her ear, breathing her in, feeling her gasp against his throat. He slid one hand up and nudged the strap of her dress across her shoulder, exposing two more inches of flesh. He devoured it like a starving man, grazing the bone with his teeth to feel her writhe against him. Marley gasped and dug her nails into his shoulders, urging him on.

God, she feels amazing.

Will slid his hands around her back, his fingers tracing her spine to where her bare flesh disappeared beneath the fabric of the dress. He found the top of the zipper and he hesitated there, waiting for some sign from Marley.

"Ahem."

It wasn't the sign Will had in mind, and the sound definitely hadn't come from the woman in his arms. Will drew back and blinked at the tall, gray-haired stranger standing with arms folded over his chest in the alcove between the foyer and the kitchen. He wasn't holding a shotgun, but he wasn't offering a glass of wine, either.

Will nodded, not entirely sure what etiquette called for in these circumstances.

"Sir," Will said. "Nice evening."

The man said nothing, and Marley whirled around to face him. Will watched her eyes fly wide and her flushed cheeks lose two shades of color.

"Dad!" she gasped. "Um, hey. I forgot… um, did you need something?"

Marley smoothed her hands over her dress, a desperate attempt to brush Will's handprints off the fabric. He said a quick farewell to his dream of seeing the dress puddled on the floor at his feet and took a step away from Marley.

"Sir, it's a pleasure to meet you." He stuck out his hand. "Will Barclay."

The man hesitated a moment, then gave Will's hand a brief shake. "Walter Cartman. I wasn't aware you were expecting company, Marley."

Marley cleared her throat and smoothed down her dress again, and Will tried not to be distracted by the sight of her hands on her body. "It's okay, Dad. Will was just dropping something off. Er, *that*."

She thrust a shaky finger out to point at the giant pink rabbit, and they all stared at it in silence for a few beats. Luckily, Magoo had finished his business and moved on, so the pink rabbit sat looking debauched but blessedly alone.

Walter raised one eyebrow and turned to Will. "A little late to be making house calls with stuffed animals, son."

Marley put a hand on her father's arm and bit her lip. "Don't blame Will, Dad. He's just making the delivery for someone else who insisted—well, it's a long story. Anyway, did you need something?"

Walter gave Will a hard look. A look that said, *The delivery guy has no business pawing my daughter.*

Will couldn't say he blamed the guy. He shoved his hands in his pockets and turned to Marley. "I should probably get going," Will said. "Your dad's right. It's late."

"But—"

"Here, son," Walter said, reaching into his back pocket to retrieve an expensive-looking wallet. "Did Marley tip you already?"

Will cocked his head to one side. "Can't say she did."

"This should cover the delivery," he said, holding the twenty like a switchblade.

Will quirked an eyebrow at Marley, who appeared to have lost her powers of speech. She flushed and gently edged the strap of her dress back into place.

Will glanced back at the twenty, not having much trouble reading between the lines. Daddy dearest was making sure Will knew his place.

No wonder Marley hates rich guys.

"Dad." Marley put a hand on her father's arm, urging him to put the money away. "You don't need to—"

"Thanks, sir," Will said, reaching out to take the bill.

"That's mighty generous of you. I'll try not to spend it all in one place." He stuffed the cash into his pocket. "Marley. It's been a pleasure. I hope you enjoy your giant pink bunny half as much as Magoo did, though perhaps not in the same way."

"Will, wait—"

He smiled and shook his head. "Your dad's right. It's late, and this probably isn't a good idea. Good night, Marley."

He opened the door with some childish, stupid part of him hoping Marley might grab him by the arm and drag him back, ordering her father to leave.

Instead, Will stepped onto the porch and shut the door behind him.

He felt her father's glare following him all the way to his car.

Chapter 6

THE NEXT DAY, MARLEY WAS STILL FLUSTERED FROM HER encounter with Will. She'd always assumed the idea of taking a cold shower was just a romance novel cliché, not something people really did.

But the instant Will's taillights had disappeared down the driveway, she'd turned to give her father a piece of her mind. Walter had already disappeared into the guest suite, so Marley stalked off to the bathroom feeling hot with anger and lust and frustration that only ebbed when she cranked the water as cold as it would go and stood beneath the spray until her teeth chattered.

Why did he kiss me?

Why did he stop kissing me?

Okay, maybe the last question was dumb. It wasn't tough to figure that making out with a woman—no matter how lovely—lost some appeal with the woman's father standing by with his patented you're-not-good-enough-for-her glare.

Still, Will could have stuck around. Or she could have gone after him. Or maybe—

Stop it, she ordered herself. *A rich guy with trust issues who happens to be your supervisor at a company that happens to have strict rules about that sort of thing? Could you possibly pick a worse man?*

Still, she couldn't stop thinking about Will. The way his hands had felt trailing across her bare back. The feel of his breath in her hair. The delicious scrape of stubble on her shoulder.

Her brain was still reeling from that last image as she marched out of her office toward the restroom. As she turned a corner, she slammed straight into a warm wall of khaki beside the bobcat habitat.

"Ooof!" said Marley as Darin Temple caught her by the shoulders.

"Are you okay?" he asked, his eyes searching hers for signs of distress or possibly concussion.

"Fine, fine. Sorry… I should learn to watch where I'm going."

Darin smiled and released her shoulders. "Not a problem. I'm just glad you're okay."

Marley turned and looked at the bobcat, not sure what to say next. The animal was stretched out on a bed of hay, looking more like an oversized, lazy housecat than a dangerous predator.

"She's almost twenty," Darin said. "In the wild, bobcats generally only live to be ten or eleven, but she's had a nice, long life here in captivity."

"It still seems a little sad. She couldn't be released into the wild?"

Darin shook his head. "Some hikers found her wandering in the woods when she was about a year old. She'd been declawed and had some of her teeth removed, so she couldn't hunt. She was starving when they brought her in, but we were able to nurse her back to health and keep her here at the sanctuary."

"Why would someone do that?"

Darin shrugged. "People try to keep wild animals as pets. When they get tired of them, they'll turn them loose without any thought to how the creature might fend for itself after it's been domesticated."

"How awful!"

Darin nodded. "It is. That's one reason we focus so much on education here at the sanctuary. We want to make sure people know the appropriate and inappropriate ways to interact with wildlife." He smiled at her, his brown eyes warm and friendly. "Congratulations on the event last night. I heard how much we raised."

Marley beamed. "We're still waiting for a final tally, but it was a successful fund-raiser."

"That's going to go a long way toward supporting our education and outreach programs."

Marley nodded and tucked a strand of hair behind one ear. "I couldn't have done any of it without you. Seriously, that badger digging fund-raiser was brilliant."

"I'm glad it worked out," he said. "It's always wonderful when we can expose people to native species."

"As opposed to having people expose themselves to native species?" Marley quipped, envisioning a pervert opening his trench coat in front of the bobcat enclosure. Darin looked confused, and Marley did a mental forehead slap for her own awkwardness. "Sorry, silly exhibitionist humor. Speaking of inappropriate ways to interact with wildlife—"

Darin smiled. "I get it. That's funny."

His smile was really quite nice. He had a fair amount of dirt under his fingernails, and his khakis looked soft and well-worn. In a meeting this morning with another wildlife specialist, Marley had asked a few subtle questions about Darin. She'd learned he was thirty-five years old, had a degree in wildlife biology, and had worked at CHSWS for almost seven years. Based on a quick skim through old job postings, Marley had a ballpark idea of his salary range and found it to be gloriously average.

"So, Marley," he said, jarring her from her thoughts. "I was just about to wash up and grab some lunch. Could I interest you in joining me?"

"I'd love that. Do you eat in the café here, or go off-site somewhere?"

"I brown-bag it most days, but I got up too late this morning to pack anything. I know a nice little lunch spot back in town, if you'd like to try that?"

"That sounds wonderful," Marley said.

"I can drive, if you don't mind. Just give me a few minutes to wash up, and then I'll swing around front and pick you up. I'll be in a tan pickup truck."

Tan pickup truck, Marley mused, liking the sound of that. So far, Darin was turning out to be very close to the blue-collar ideal she'd imagined. Educated but not overeducated, handsome but not polished, confident but not cocky, and safely in the mid-zone between *broke* and *rich asshole.*

"I'll see you out there," Marley said, and hustled back to her office to set her paperwork down. She was touching up her lipstick when Will's sister, Bethany, walked by.

"Hey, Marley," she called, halting in the doorway and flashing a grin that looked startlingly like her brother's. "I was just dropping off one more figurine from Aunt Nancy's collection. Apparently she forgot this one."

Bethany reached into her purse and pulled out a large, oblong velvet box. She flipped the top open to reveal an ornately-carved granite phallus. Marley admired the detail, resisting the urge to reach for it.

"It's… um… lovely."

"I suppose so, if you like that sort of thing." Bethany gave her a wicked grin and flipped the box shut, tucking the phallus back in her bag. "April and I really enjoyed meeting you last night. Were you happy with how things went?"

"Definitely. It was a really successful fund-raiser," Marley said. "I enjoyed meeting you and April, too."

Bethany smiled wider, and Marley saw a flash of dimple that looked just like Will's. Bethany stepped closer and lowered her voice to a conspiratorial whisper. "Nothing like a little awkward family dynamic to kick off your first fund-raiser, eh?"

Marley blushed and did her best to shrug. "It didn't seem that awkward, really."

Bethany studied her, probably trying to assess whether she was telling the truth or bullshitting a potential donor. It was hard for Marley to know herself sometimes.

"Sincerely," Marley added. "You and Will and April seem to have a very friendly relationship considering—"

"Considering April left Will to play palm-the-softballs with me?"

"Er—"

"Sorry, that was uncouth." Bethany shrugged. "It's an old habit, I guess. Make a dirty joke to diffuse a potentially awkward situation."

"So that's where Will gets it?" Marley asked.

Bethany cocked her head thoughtfully. "Actually, I think we both got it from our mother."

"Interesting. Where's your mom now?"

"Deschutes Memorial Gardens."

"Is that the retirement community over by the hospital?"

"Nope," Bethany said, snatching a paperclip off the corner of Marley's desk and bending the curves to straighten it. "It's the cemetery off Highway 97 on the north end of town."

"Oh." Marley's hands felt clammy, and she struggled to come up with something kind to say. "I'm so sorry. I didn't realize—"

"It's okay, Marley. Really, it's been a long time."

"Still, I'm really sorry."

"Thank you."

Marley grimaced. "Is this the part where one of us is supposed to make a goofy joke to diffuse a potentially awkward situation?"

"I'll let it slide this time. Aunt Nancy raised Will and me after both our parents died in a car crash. And before you say you're sorry again, it's okay. I've been a bastard orphan lesbian for a long time. I'm used to it."

"In that case, congratulations. You're the most well-adjusted bastard orphan lesbian I've ever met."

Bethany laughed and began to twist the straightened paperclip into a new shape. "I like you. You're a cool chick."

"Thanks. You're a pretty cool chick yourself."

"We still on for mountain biking next weekend?"

"Totally. I'm looking forward to it." Marley glanced at her watch and then nodded to the door. "Whoops, I have to run. I'm supposed to meet someone. Do you need a hand getting that… um, figurine… put in the safe?"

"I see Susan over in her office. I'm sure she can help me." She stepped closer and gave Marley a salacious grin. "So, you have a date?"

"I don't know if I should call it a date, exactly. I'm going to lunch with Darin Temple, the wildlife guy."

"Really?"

"What's wrong?"

Bethany shrugged. "Nothing, I guess. He just doesn't strike me as your type."

"I'm afraid to ask what you think my type would be."

"That's easy," Bethany said with a laugh. "My brother."

Marley fought to keep her expression flat, not sure if she wanted to do a giddy dance or roll her eyes. "Will? I don't really think—"

"Oh, please. Good relationships aren't about thinking. They're about making each other feel good. And no, I'm not just talking about—"

"Playing hide-the-salami?" Marley quipped.

"Exactly." Bethany grinned and set the reshaped paperclip on the corner of the desk. "See you later, Marley."

"You too."

Marley hoisted her purse up on her shoulder and glanced at the paperclip on her desk. Bethany had bent it into the shape of a heart.

Marley hustled out the door, putting a little extra kick in her step in case Darin had been waiting awhile. She walked out the front door of the wildlife sanctuary just as a tan truck pulled up in front of the building. Darin reached over from inside the cab to pop her door open.

"Hey there," he said. "Sorry, it's a bit of a jump up here when you're wearing a skirt."

"Not a problem," she said, hoisting herself up. She deliberately avoided making a wisecrack about flashing her lady bits at the paparazzi, then patted herself on the back for her own restraint. She pulled her door closed and smiled at Darin as she buckled her seat belt.

"Thanks for inviting me to lunch. I've been wondering where the good restaurants are nearby."

"This is a good restaurant, but I won't claim it's fancy."

"I don't need fancy."

"Then this'll be perfect. It's a barbecue joint, so I hope you aren't a vegetarian. If you are, they've got plenty of good salads and a veggie burger that's nice and spicy."

"I love barbecue," Marley said. "The spicier the better. The only thing I can't do is dairy. I'm lactose intolerant."

"We'll skip the cheese fries then."

Darin smiled as he steered the pickup out of the parking lot and onto the highway. "Hopefully we'll beat the lunch rush. The baby back ribs are outstanding, in case you're not sure what to order."

They made idle small talk as Darin drove the short distance to the restaurant. When they arrived, Darin parked the truck and scrambled around to open Marley's door and offered a hand down. Marley studied her hand, waiting for signs of tingling or electric currents, but there was only the pleasant sensation of someone else's flesh touching hers.

Pleasant, she mused. *That's not so bad.*

They strolled inside together, and Marley tried to relax into the idea that they were on a date. Well, not a *date,* exactly, but maybe a prelude to a date. She smiled as Darin pulled her chair out for her before scooting around to the other side and dropping onto the bench seat. He smiled at her and offered a paper menu stained with barbecue sauce. Marley took it and began to peruse, her mouth watering as she read.

"You said the baby back ribs are good?"

"The best."

"How about the fried okra appetizer?"

"I've never had it, but I'm sure it's great. Don't forget to save room for dessert."

Marley looked up as a cheerful blond waitress scampered

over with a notepad. Darin ordered a pulled pork sandwich and a garden salad, while Marley opted for okra and ribs. The waitress hustled away to place the order before hurrying back with two frosty glasses of iced tea with lemon wedges anchored on the side. Marley tugged the wrapper off her straw and stuck it in her drink as she inhaled the heady scent of smoked meat and tangy sauce. Beside them, a giggling couple took turns feeding each other bites of potatoes au gratin. In the far corner, a trio of young men in cycling jerseys and bike shorts argued over the bill.

Marley took a sip of iced tea and smiled at Darin. "So you enjoy working at the wildlife sanctuary?"

"Very much. I've been there just over seven years, and I can't imagine working anywhere else."

"Seems like a great place."

"It is," he agreed as he rolled up the sleeves of his khaki shirt and spread a napkin on his lap. "So what made you leave your job in Portland to come here?"

Marley shrugged and took a sip of her iced tea. "It was time for a change. I got tired of the city scene, and all the formality that comes with doing donor relations in a setting like that. Bend just seems more—"

"Laid-back?"

"Exactly." Marley smiled, hopeful she was giving Darin the right impression. Her style was laid-back and casual, no frills at all. No need for fancy dining or big paychecks or—

"So, Marley." Darin cleared his throat. "What sort of wedding do you want?"

Marley choked on her tea. Darin didn't wait for her to stop sputtering before he spoke again. "I know this might be premature, but I like you, and I think you like me, and if there's a chance this could turn into something, I just think we should know up-front whether our marital ideals are compatible."

Marley wiped her mouth with her napkin and stared at him. "Darin, we just met."

Darin took a sip of his drink before setting it back on the table and reaching for her hand. "Do you have your own house, or would you be comfortable moving into mine?"

"Um—"

"What about kids? I don't really like them, but I'd consider having one or two if—"

"*Darin*," Marley said, staring down at their interlaced fingers. "I haven't even gotten my appetizer yet."

"Mmm, yes, well, that's another thing. Do you generally prefer to order separate appetizers when you dine out with a significant other, or do you prefer to order things that can be split? It's not a cost savings issue so much as a matter of whether you're okay with sharing and—"

"Darin!"

"What?"

Marley pulled her hand back and gripped the edge of the table, resisting the urge to grab him by the shirt collar and give him a shake. "I wasn't even sure this was a date, and you're already naming our future children?"

"Don't be silly. Their names are completely open for discussion." Darin shrugged and took a sip of his tea. He made a face and signaled to the waitress, who came bounding over to the table. "This tastes too fruity. Can I have something else? A Sprite, maybe?"

The waitress hustled away with the offending drink, and Darin turned back to Marley. "Where were we? Oh, right—well, I guess technically this isn't a date. What's the point in dating if two people aren't sure whether there's any long-term potential?"

Marley blinked. "Um, *finding out* if there's long-term potential?"

"Isn't that what we're doing?"

Marley sighed and took a sip of her tea. At least, that's what she tried to do.

She turned her head at exactly the wrong angle, stabbing the straw up her nostril.

"Yeowch!" Marley said, jerking her head back. Seeing Darin's face twist in horror, Marley offered a halfhearted grin and rubbed her nostril.

"Well that was awkward," she said. "For my next trick, I plan to make armpit noises and give the waitress a wedgie."

"My God, Marley. Are you okay? Do you want me to call a doctor or something? Here, take these napkins in case you start bleeding and let me grab you a new straw and—"

"Darin! I'm fine. Chill out, okay?" She put her hand on his arm and pointed at her face with the other hand. "I'm fine, see? Not even bleeding."

"I don't know…" Darin eyed her with concern and handed her another straw. Marley took it and peeled the wrapper off as she leaned back in her chair.

"Look, I'm pretty sure we aren't compatible."

Darin frowned. "Why would you say that?"

Marley sighed and stuck the new straw in her drink. She took a sip, weighing her words carefully. "The guy who's right for me would respond to something like the straw incident by making a joke. You know, something to lighten the mood so I feel less like a doofus."

"I don't understand," Darin said slowly. "You want me to make light of your misery?"

"I'm not miserable, Darin. A little embarrassed, maybe. More embarrassed if you make a big deal of it."

"I see."

Marley couldn't tell from his tone if he was hurt, confused, or genuinely mulling over her words. She touched his arm again, hoping for the latter. "Look, don't feel bad," she said. "I'm pretty sure I'm not your type, either. I hate sharing my food, I make inappropriate jokes all the time, and I snore."

He frowned. "You snore?"

"That was a joke."

"Of course." Darin sighed. "You're right, obviously. We're probably not compatible life-mates."

"True enough."

"No shame in that."

"Absolutely," Marley agreed. "Hey, look—food's ready."

They both turned to watch the waitress pile platters of food on the table. Marley had never been so grateful to see a pile of fried okra, and she pounced on it like a starving dog snatching a roast. Darin stabbed at his salad, looking pensive.

"Sorry to spring all that on you," he said at last. "The stuff about marriage."

"Don't worry about it."

"You're right about us not being compatible. I don't know what I was thinking."

Marley shrugged. "Same thing I was thinking—that it was worth finding out if we're a good match."

"And now that we know we aren't?"

Marley grinned and pushed her okra platter to the middle of the table. "We agree to be friends. And I agree to share my okra."

"Deal," he said, and reached for the platter.

—◦◦◦—

Will strode purposefully through the halls of Cheez Whiz, trying hard to look like a man with important business to tend to.

He knew he really looked like a man hoping to catch a glimpse of the woman he'd groped the night before, but maybe he was overthinking things.

Shaking Marley from his mind, Will turned left toward the wildlife exhibits. As he rounded the corner between the birds of prey exhibit and the small mammal enclosures, he spotted a familiar mane of long, auburn hair. He stepped up to the edge of the fox pen and leaned on the railing.

"I figured 'scooping the fox droppings' was another one of your euphemisms when I got your text this morning," he called to his sister as he surveyed the pen. "I take it you're volunteering?"

Bethany looked over her shoulder and grinned at him. "I offered to help out with cage cleaning a couple times a month. It gives me the satisfaction of knowing I'm not just the unemployed sister of an eccentric millionaire whose wealth ensures neither of us ever has to work a day in our lives."

"Beats the hell out of lunching at the athletic club with the rest of the socialites."

"That it does," she said, spitting hair out of her mouth as she scooped the shovel into a corner and deposited the contents into a big green bucket. "So what brings you here?"

"Just checking on some paperwork."

"Is that a fancy way of saying 'stalking Marley'?"

"Very funny. Bed asked me to drop off a few pledge forms from last night's event."

"Where's the big pink delivery bunny?"

He quirked an eyebrow at her. "I take it you talked to Marley?"

"I have, but that's not how I know." She grinned and scooped up another shovel full of soiled straw. "It's a small town. When your eccentric, wealthy brother is spotted driving through town near midnight on a Thursday with a big pink rabbit strapped into the passenger seat of his car, people tend to talk."

"I'll remember that next time."

"Do. And since you'll surely hear about it anyway, Marley is on a lunch date with Darin Temple."

"Oh?" Will tried to infuse the syllable with perfect nonchalance, but he was pretty sure Bethany knew better.

"I think they went to Baldy's," Bethany added, "in case you want to ride in on your white steed and break the whole thing up."

"My steed is in the shop, and the only thing I want to break up is that big bale of hay in the corner. Is there another shovel around here?"

"Just this one, but I'm almost done. Keep your pants on."

She made a few more scooping motions and then unlatched the gate, handing Will her shovel as she elbowed her way out of the pen with the big green bucket in hand. Will maneuvered around her and stabbed the shovel into the hay bale with more force than necessary. He began flinging it around the pen, sending bits of straw swirling through the air like angry confetti.

Darin Temple? he mulled. *On a date with Marley?*

It figured. The guy was nice, educated, responsible, and had the sort of blue-collar status Marley wanted. He was perfect for her.

Will stabbed the shovel into the hay again and flung a hunk of it to the opposite side of the fox pen.

"You trying to spread that straw or maim it?" Bethany called from the edge of the pen.

"Just getting the job done," Will grunted, trying hard to bite back his own frustration.

"If the job is mutilating an innocent bale of hay, nicely done."

"Thanks."

"So Jeannie told me you asked for a copy of the background check they did when Marley was hired."

Will winced, grateful he had his back to Bethany so she couldn't see his dismay. "Jeannie talks a lot for an HR person who's supposed to exercise discretion."

"I know, isn't it great? So why'd you want Marley's background check?"

"Just doing my due diligence to make sure I know everything there is to know about our new development director. She'll be handling hundreds of thousands of dollars worth of donations each year, and as president of the board of directors supervising that position, it's in everyone's best interest for me to know as much as possible about her background."

"Sure, that sounds good," Bethany mused. "Also, you want to jump her bones."

"Please tell me this conversation is almost over."

"And if you want to jump her bones, then you also need to look for reasons not to trust her. Well played, little brother."

"You can stop any time."

Bethany laughed. "Fine, we're done. And I'm done shoveling. Can you hang here for a sec while I get Maggie and ask her to grab the fox?"

"You just added that to your list of euphemisms, didn't you?"

Bethany tossed a handful of hay at him as she walked past, grinning. "Thanks for the help, Will."

Will sighed and stopped shoveling for a moment, thinking of Marley having lunch at Baldy's with Darin Temple, laughing up at him with those hazel eyes twinkling, dabbing barbecue sauce from the corner of her perfect, kissable mouth. Was she having fun? Was it really his concern?

Will gritted his teeth and stabbed the shovel into the straw again, a whole lot harder than he needed to.

"Thanks so much for taking a look at the figurines," Marley said, pushing through the door to the climate-controlled room at the back of the CHSWS administrative offices. She waved her cousin Kayley ahead of her and pointed toward the largest safe in the corner. "Everything's in there. Just let me find the right key."

Kayley smiled and marched ahead. "I just have to remind you again this isn't an official appraisal," she said, pivoting to survey the area. "You know my area of expertise really isn't... um, well..."

"Ancient sex toys of Pacific Northwest tribes?" Marley shrugged. "As you might imagine, there aren't a lot of experts in the field. The one guy I've managed to track down is working in Connecticut right now and can't come out here for an appraisal until next week. For now, I'll take a non-expert opinion."

"That I'd be happy to give you." Kayley smiled. "I do know Pacific Northwest artifacts. Just not granite giggle-sticks."

"I'm sure you'll find these very impressive," Marley said as she moved toward the safe.

Kayley grabbed her arm and pulled her into a quick hug. "I'm so glad you finally got to move to Bend. You've been talking about it since we were kids."

"And I'm just glad the promise of whitewater rafting and rock climbing is enough to lure you out here a few times a year to visit. It really is good to see you again."

"You too, sweetie."

Marley pulled back and spun the keys around to find the right one. Locating it, she slipped it into the lock for the safe and gave it a firm twist. The door swung open, and Marley blinked into the darkened interior. As her eyes adjusted, she surveyed rows and rows of soft velvet rectangles.

She reached for a larger box near the front and popped the top open. She held it out to her cousin, whose eyes had gone wide with wonder.

"This is the new one the family brought this morning," Marley said. "The rest have been here since right before I started the job. Have you ever seen anything like it?"

Kayley pulled a pair of rimless eyeglasses from her bag and reached for the box. "Is this where I say the detailing is exquisite and the markings are indicative of the Chinook Tribe of the Columbia River Valley, or can I just say that is the biggest rock cock I've ever seen?"

Marley laughed and reached for another box. "You can say whatever you like. Just don't say it in front of the donor. I've had at least a dozen calls from her this week telling me what priceless works of art these are and how she hopes this family heirloom will merit its own special show in the museum."

"Stone skin-serpents of the Pacific tribes—I like it."

Kayley turned the phallus over in her hands before placing it back in the box. "Can I look at the rest?"

"Knock yourself out. Just don't drop anything or Nancy Thomas-Smith will skin me alive. Or diagnose me with some sort of sexual dysfunction—I'm not sure which is worse."

Kayley picked up another box. "I've made a living appraising antiques for ten years, Marley. I'm pretty sure I know how to avoid dropping them."

"Sorry, just being paranoid. This donor seems to be a little bit—"

"Crazy?"

Marley smiled. "I was going to say *challenging,* but I was just being polite."

"No, I'm serious. This chick is crazy if she thinks these things are worth millions." Kayley held up a medium-sized phallus made of granite and pointed to the tip. "Look, I'm not an expert on antique stone beef-wands, but the detailing here is all wrong. These markings right here? I'm not even sure these are Pacific Northwest tribal. They don't look like ancient artifacts."

Marley swallowed hard. "What do they look like?"

"Big rock wankers."

Marley grimaced and picked up another box. She peered inside, assessing the contents with a critical eye. "I don't think 'big rock wankers' are enough to create a traveling exhibit that's guaranteed to make millions for the organization."

Kayley shrugged and picked up another box. "Look, that's just my quick impression. Like I said, this isn't my area of expertise. I may be totally off base here. When did you say the expert appraiser is coming?"

"Next week sometime."

"He'll be able to do some testing and analysis. Maybe he'll discover I'm completely off my rocker. It wouldn't be the first time."

Marley sighed and closed the top of the box she was holding. "If you're right, I don't want to be there when the donor finds out. Or the rest of the staff here. Everyone's counting on these pieces being worth some ungodly amount of money."

"Sorry, cuz." Kayley put her box back in the safe and put an arm around Marley's shoulder. "Let's hope I'm wrong, and I just don't know a concrete cream-stick from a valuable piece of art. Come on, you want to go grab some coffee and chat about boys?"

Marley sighed, feeling deflated. "I have to get back to work, but maybe a glass of wine after work?"

"Can't, I'm going for a hike." Kayley glanced at her watch. "Let's skip the coffee and just talk about boys then. Curtis is officially history?"

Marley nodded as she re-latched the safe and pocketed the key. "Yep. He's called a few times asking if we can work things out, but I'm over it. I'm just done with entitled rich men and their obnoxious egos."

"Speaking of your entitled rich men, how long is your dad in town?"

Marley laughed. "My dad isn't that bad. He's gotten better, anyway."

"What's he doing in Bend?"

"He has some business in the area. He'll be back and forth between here and Portland for the next couple weeks."

"Let me guess—he still thinks you and Curtis are going to work things out?"

"Pretty much." Marley sighed and leaned against the wall, feeling very tired all of a sudden. "It's not that he was so crazy about Curtis as a future son-in-law. I think he just liked the idea of having someone financially stable to take care of me."

"Walter Cartman—always a romantic."

"He can't be doing that bad if he's convinced six women to marry him."

Kayley snorted. "You know as well as I do that's not about romance. That's about dollar signs."

"Right. Which is part of what inspired my new plan."

"What new plan?"

Marley offered a sheepish smile. "I decided I'm going to stop dating guys who are Joe Millionaire and start dating Joe Comfortably-Lower-Middle-Class."

"No shit?"

Marley looked at her cousin, relieved not to see too much judgment in her eyes. Just confusion, and maybe a little curiosity. "I'm thirty-five years old, with a pretty obvious track record of dating well-to-do men who bear a startling resemblance to my father. That hasn't worked out, so I figure it's time to try something new."

"And your *something new* quota couldn't be met dating blondes instead of brunettes or guys who play racquetball instead of tennis?"

Marley shook her head. "I need a bigger change."

"Met anyone promising yet?"

"One guy who fit the bill perfectly except for the small fact that we had nothing in common." Marley shrugged. "Then there's this obnoxious rich guy who happens to be in charge of the board of directors supervising me. Off-limits, but he kisses like a god."

Kayley beamed and grabbed Marley's arm. "Oooh, introduce me to the god if you don't want him."

"You don't want him either. Rampant trust issues, a complicated relationship with his ex-wife, overbearing family—"

"Say no more," Kayley said, though Marley could have said a lot more.

Great sense of humor, gorgeous eyes, good with animals, generous with his loved ones, killer hands...

"Have you heard from your mom?" Kayley asked.

Marley blinked and fought to push thoughts of Will out of her mind. "Mom sent a birthday card last week."

"And instead of including a check, she included a request for a check?"

Marley bit the inside of her cheek and looked away. "Of course not," she lied. "She asked me to give her regards to the family."

Kayley was quiet, and Marley looked over at last to see her cousin studying her sadly. Marley felt the weight of her pity like a lead blanket.

"Do they know?" Kayley asked. "The people you work with here. Have you told them your mother—"

"Went to jail?" Marley winced and lowered her voice. "No. Not that it's anyone's business."

"Of course," Kayley said quickly. "I just wondered how much you'd shared about what happened."

Marley shook her head. "Nothing. I believe in second chances. Everyone deserves that."

"Speaking of that, tell me about this dog you rescued."

Marley smiled, relieved at the subject change. "He's great. Loving and sweet and happy and active."

"Sounds like the perfect man."

"He is. We're going for a hike early tomorrow morning if you want to come along."

"I'll call you," Kayley said, wrapping Marley in a big hug. "Take care of yourself, okay? I worry about you."

Marley hugged her hard, then drew back. "I'm fine." She offered up her best fake smile, the one reserved for contentious donors and disgruntled board members. "Seriously, I'm okay. Thanks so much for taking a look at the figurines."

Kayley smiled back, her grin so genuine Marley's spleen hurt. "Call me if you need anything. Or if you get into any trouble. I mean it this time—no keeping quiet out of shame or embarrassment or—"

"Okay," Marley said, torn between wanting to hug her cousin again and wanting the conversation to be over.

"Promise?"

"I promise," Marley said, crossing her fingers behind her back.

Chapter 7

MARLEY LEFT THE HOUSE AT NOON ON SUNDAY. BY TWO p.m., she couldn't remember the last time her butt had been so sore.

"Want to trade, Magoo?" she called to her dog. "How about you ride the mountain bike and I run alongside?"

Her shaggy companion turned and cocked his head, his tongue lolling out to one side. Magoo barked once before turning back to the trail and trotting ahead. Marley sighed and followed after him, doing her best to ease her aching backside off the bike seat. She couldn't understand it. She'd bought the mountain bike at a secondhand store that morning, deliberately selecting a well-used model so it wouldn't be obvious she was a relative newbie to the sport. She'd purchased a cushy new gel seat in hopes of thwarting the inevitable saddle soreness, but the seat had done little to cushion her aching sit-bones.

Whoever coined the phrase "*it's just like riding a bike*" had never taken a ten-year break from it, Marley decided. This was a lot tougher than she remembered from her early twenties.

Up ahead, Magoo turned and bounded back toward her, impatient for Marley to keep up. His dirty mop fur flopped across his mismatched eyes, and his tongue flopped in front of him like a flattened sausage. His paws were filthy, but his tail had been wagging nonstop since they'd arrived at the head of Phil's Trail.

Marley hadn't been sure at first if it was safe to have Magoo off-leash on a mountain bike trail with their relationship still so new. What if he forgot she'd adopted him and took off sprinting for the hills?

But two things were clear within five minutes on the trail: Magoo was devoted to Marley, and Magoo wasn't much of a sprinter.

"Careful, boy!" Marley yelled as the dog tripped over his own paws and rolled off-trail. He hopped back up, gave himself a cursory shake, gave Marley something that looked curiously like a doggie grin, and took off running again. Ten seconds later, he turned and barked twice.

It sounded a lot like *keep up!*

"I'm trying," Marley called, trying not to sound discouraged. "Keep your shorts on."

"Maybe that's your problem," someone called behind her. "You should wear the bike shorts, not the dog."

Marley turned, clamping her fingers around the hand brake. She spotted Will ten feet behind her and nearly fell off the bike. She slammed her foot into the ground and screeched to a halt, while Will did the same to avoid running over her.

"Will?" Marley said, her voice unexpectedly breathless. "What are you doing out here?"

He adjusted his bike helmet. "Skiing."

"Very funny. I meant—actually, I don't know what I meant." Marley looked down at her dog, who had scampered back at the sound of Will's voice and was now doing a clumsy dance of joy at his feet. Will bent down and scratched the dog's ears, and Magoo flopped onto his side and rolled in the dirt with ecstasy.

Marley couldn't blame him.

"Hey, buddy," Will said as he scratched the dog's belly. "Had any new romantic interludes with giant pink rodents?"

Magoo grunted and licked Will's hand.

"I'm thinking I need to lock the bunny up so Magoo can't sexually assault her anymore," Marley said. "As long as she never comes out of the closet, we should be good."

"That *coming out of the closet* business can put a damper on a relationship," Will agreed.

Marley grimaced. "Sorry. I didn't mean—"

"I know you didn't. I was just making light of a weird situation. Want me to make a joke about your dad tipping me twenty bucks after I groped you in the doorway, or should I make a wisecrack about your date with Darin Temple?"

Marley blinked. "Wow. You don't beat around the bush, do you?" She held up her hand. "Stop right there—that wasn't a lesbian ex-wife joke, for the record."

"See? You're getting the hang of my family's coping mechanism."

Marley laughed. "Not that it's any of your business, but Darin and I aren't compatible. He's a nice guy and all, but—"

"You checked his wallet and he had more than five dollars cash?"

"I'm going to go back to what I said before about this being none of your business."

"Fair enough. Your butt, however, is my business. Or at least I'm going to make it my business. Seriously, you need a good pair of bike shorts."

Marley touched a hand to her left butt cheek and gave it a self-conscious rub. "I'll get on that. And I'll get back on the bike in just a minute, as soon as my sit-bones stop throbbing."

Will laughed. "At least Magoo seems to be having fun."

"For sure. I had no idea he'd enjoy mountain biking this much."

"Which is funny, considering he can't reach the pedals."

"He's still probably a more accomplished cyclist than I am." Marley grimaced. "I've fallen off twice in an hour, and my butt cheeks feel like someone's been beating them with a hammer."

Will's eyes dropped to her derrière, and Marley flushed. Then his eyes dropped lower and Will cocked his head, studying her bike.

"Did you just buy that?"

Marley hesitated, worried she'd blown her cover as an avid outdoorswoman with a fondness for mountain biking. But hell, it's not like she was fooling anyone. It was one thing to exaggerate a little, but Marley didn't have it in her to lie.

"I got it at the secondhand sporting goods store this morning," she said. "I used to have a mountain bike years ago, but I needed a new one now that I've moved here."

Will nodded. "I recognized the frame and that sticker right there. The bike used to belong to a friend of mine." He gave the seat a fond pat, and Marley felt inexplicably embarrassed. "It's a nice bike; you made a good choice."

"Thanks," Marley said. "I'd be a lot happier if I could keep it upright without maiming my tailbone."

"The rocky terrain on this trail is hell on your sit-bones even if you're used to it."

"Are you used to it?"

"I can assure you I have iron-clad testicles and a butt-callus you could bounce a quarter off of."

"Please don't feel you need to show me."

Please do, Marley thought as her mind drifted to the way his hands had roamed over her body last night. The warmth of his lips against her throat, the softness of his breath in her ear.

She couldn't believe she'd just thrown caution to the wind and forgotten her father was in the next room. What would have happened if she'd been home alone? What would have happened if Will had inched down the zipper on her dress and—

"Come on," Will said, nodding toward the trail. "Let me get in front of you and I'll show you a much better section for a beginner."

"I wouldn't say I'm a beginner, exactly. It's just been a while."

"Understood," he said. "But think of it like sex. If it's been more than a couple years, you're a virgin again."

"Oh." Marley fought the blush she felt creeping up her neck and into her cheeks. "In that case, I'm a virgin. At least as far as the bike goes."

"Glad you clarified." Will edged past her on the trail, his arm brushing her rib cage as he moved. Marley gave an involuntary shiver as every nerve in her body snapped to attention.

As soon as he was in front, Will turned around. "Ready?"

Marley hesitated, then bit her lip. "I'm sorry about last night, Will."

"You're going to have to elaborate a little there. You're sorry you neglected to inform me your father was in the next room when I started groping you, or you're sorry about the groping itself?"

"Both, I guess. I mean, we agreed it's a horrible idea for us to be involved."

She heard her voice go up a little at the end of the sentence, making it sound more like a question than a statement. She wasn't sure whether to be annoyed with herself or with Will for her own uncertainty.

"Apology accepted but unnecessary," he said. "After all, I got twenty bucks out of the deal."

"I hope you put it to good use."

"I gave it to the homeless guy I saw pushing a shopping cart full of mannequin parts on my way home."

"I'm glad. Really, Will, I'm sorry if my dad seemed rude. He doesn't like the idea of me dating someone who isn't financially stable. He can be a little judgmental sometimes."

Will cocked his head to one side. "Your dad is judgmental for choosing your potential suitors based on income, but you're okay with doing the same thing?"

Marley felt the heat creep into her cheeks. "It's not the same thing at all."

"No? Your dad rules out poor guys because he thinks they're all wrong for you, and you've ruled out rich guys for the same reason. Just my opinion, but it seems the apple didn't fall too far from the tree."

"You aren't poor," Marley said, knowing she was arguing the wrong point. "And anyway, my ex-fiancé was a jerk."

"A jerk with money," Will added. "And if I'm reading things right, I get the feeling your father and your ex have a few things in common."

"My dad has my best interests at heart," Marley said, wishing it were that simple.

"I'm sure he does. All I'm saying is that two jerks with big bank accounts don't necessarily mean every guy with a few bucks to his name is a raging dickhead. Now are you ready to ride or what?"

He didn't wait for a response, but edged around her on the trail, apparently done with the conversation.

But Marley wasn't quite. She bit her lip. "My father won't stop talking about me getting back together with Curtis." Will turned around, frozen in the act of remounting his bike. Marley shrugged and touched the edge of her helmet self-consciously. "He brought it up over breakfast. Said Curtis has been calling him since I won't answer."

"That's your fian—*ex*-fiancé?"

Marley nodded. "My dad kept offering me his vacation home at the Oregon Coast so Curtis and I can have a romantic beach weekend and work things out."

"It's a lovely time of year at the beach."

"I don't want to go."

Will shrugged. "So don't."

"Easier said than done."

Marley realized her tone had turned bitter, and she tried to soften her voice. "Sorry. I didn't mean to sound bitchy. Tense subject. You know how it can be with exes."

"Sure."

She knew she was baiting him, waiting to see if he'd weigh in with his own ex story. But Will wasn't looking at her anymore. He'd stopped to scratch Magoo's ears.

Of course, he hadn't cycled off down the trail yet. Maybe the conversation was still going.

Marley cleared her throat. "Your ex-wife seems nice."

"She does seem that way, doesn't she?"

Marley cocked her head, curious. "If I'm not mistaken, that was a slightly bitter tone you used there. Glad I'm not the only one sounding bitchy about an ex."

Will looked up from petting Magoo and grinned. "Men don't sound bitchy. We sound *tense*."

"Why do you get to sound tense and I'm stuck being bitchy?"

"It's in the rule book. It's right after the section on the difference between men's and women's magazines."

"Magazines?"

"Yes. Men's magazines feature pictures of naked women. Women's magazines also feature pictures of naked women. This is because the female body is a work of art, and men's bodies are more like a tractor."

"A tractor?" Marley blinked, not thinking about tractors at all. She was thinking of what Will's body had felt like when she'd explored it last night. His chest was hot and coiled with muscle, and his arms were strong and dusted with gingery hair. She recalled the feel of his shoulders beneath her palms, and a tractor was the furthest thing from her mind.

Of course, she'd almost forgotten about the exes. "Nice job diverting my attention from the ex conversation. You almost had me. What did you mean April *seems* nice? Like you're implying she's not really what she seems."

"Is anyone?"

"I like to think I am."

Will grinned. "You like to think you're a seasoned mountain biker too, but I'm not sure that's working out for you. Come on. Let's get moving. There's a section up ahead that's a lot smoother. I think your backside will be much more comfortable there."

"Thank you for your concern about the health and well-being of my butt."

"The pleasure is all mine," Will said, and headed up the trail.

Will liked to think his presence was a salve to Marley's aching butt. Fortunately, he had the good sense not to say that out loud.

"How's your butt?" Will called from up ahead.

"Fine, thanks for asking. How's yours?"

"This is a peculiar line of conversation for two people who've known each other a week."

Marley laughed, and Will glanced over his shoulder to make sure she was doing okay. Beside her, Magoo ran along with his tongue lolling to one side and his oversized paws flailing like hairy toilet plungers. He sure looked happy.

Can you blame the guy? He gets to go home with Marley.

He shook his head, intent on clearing away that line of thought. No way in hell could he consider getting involved with her. Even without the stupid Cheez Whiz corporate policy, dating a chronic people pleaser would be the worst thing he could do. He needed another woman confused about her identity as much as he needed a third nipple.

"Need me to slow down at all?" he called.

"Nope, I'm great. You're right, this trail is way better."

"It's a little flatter and straighter. And there aren't as many—*rock*!"

Will swerved to miss the small, sharp stone in the center of the trail. He said a fast, silent prayer Marley heard his warning, but the loud *Pop!* behind him suggested she wasn't that lucky.

"Dammit," she yelled. "I think I wrecked my tire."

Will turned around and grimaced. He stopped his bike and hopped off, resting it against a large boulder before he trudged back to Marley's side to survey the damage.

"You wrecked more than your tire," he said. "Looks like you bent the frame. I'm sorry, I should have yelled louder to warn you."

"I heard you yell *rock*," she admitted. "I just thought you were commanding me to get down and boogie."

"Remind me to be clearer next time." Will sighed. "I don't recommend riding it like this. Got a repair kit?"

Marley blinked at him. "Does it make me an idiot if I don't?"

"No, but it'll make you pretty tired of pushing your bike. I have a kit for the flat tire, but I'm not sure it'll do you any good. Even with the tire reinflated, your frame looks too bent for riding. You'll wreck it if you try."

"What do I do?" she asked, sounding a little panicked.

"Walk it. Slowly."

Marley bit her lip. "Isn't it going to get dark soon? And aren't there mountain lions out here? The anatomy of their long hind limbs allows them to cover a distance of forty feet in a single leap, and they can jump cliffs up to eighteen feet high."

"Relax, zoo lady. You've got another hour of daylight, and mountain lions don't like blondes. Only brunettes."

"You're making that up."

"How do you know? By the time you get eaten, it'll be too late for you to blame me."

Marley grinned as she turned her bike around and pointed it back down the trail. Will moved back toward his bike and maneuvered it around, falling into step behind her. Magoo whined and switched directions, his floppy ears sliding over his eyes as he turned.

"You don't have to walk with me, Will," Marley said. "You came out here to ride, not to walk your bike around like an idiot."

"Maybe that's exactly why I came out here. I try to do it at least once a week. I call it my idiot bike walk. It's kind of like a cakewalk, but without the cake."

"Highly unsatisfying."

"Not necessarily."

His eyes were on Marley's butt when he said it, and he tried to bring his gaze up before she turned around and caught him.

"Want me to get out my camera phone and snap a photo?"

"What?"

"Of my butt."

"I'll have you know, I was merely assessing you for damage. Butt injuries are nothing to trifle with, you know."

Marley laughed and steered her bike around a large boulder. "I'll try to remember that."

"So how are things going with the appraisal of the family figurines?"

She didn't answer right away, but he watched her shoulders tense. "Fine," she said at last. "I've found an appraiser with expertise on Pacific Northwest tribal erotica."

"I hope it says that on her business card."

"*His* business card. And he won't be able to come out and do the appraisal until next week, so I'm sorry I won't have answers for your family right away."

Will shrugged, which was dumb since she couldn't see him walking behind her. "It makes no difference to me. I just want the whole thing over so my Aunt Nancy can stop talking about it."

"And so she can stop calling me every ten minutes?"

"Aunt Nancy can certainly be persistent," Will said. "Wait 'til you meet her in person."

"I look forward to it."

"You're a terrible liar."

He watched Marley's shoulders tense again and wondered what the hell that was all about. She was quiet for a while after that, and Will wondered what she was thinking. Mulling over her first few days on the job? Plotting strategies for dating blue-collar men? Calculating pi out to the millionth digit?

"How long were you married, Will?"

The question caught him off-guard, and he hesitated for a moment before replying. "Why do you ask?"

"Just curious. I have a hard time picturing you and April as man and wife."

"So do I."

"There's an evasive answer."

Will laughed. "Four years."

"Really?"

"You thought longer or shorter?"

Marley shrugged, and Will watched her ponytail swish across her back with the rocking of her steps. "I guess I thought shorter."

"Good taste and professional decorum is preventing me from making a comment about how it's better to be longer than what's expected."

Marley looked over her shoulder and rolled her eyes at him. "You're really a champ at using humor as a defense mechanism, you know?"

"Absolutely. If it were an Olympic sport, I'd take gold."

"Your sister might give you a run for your money."

"I see you've picked up on the sibling dynamic."

"You two seem close. Surprising, considering—"

"She plays tickle-the-jellybean with my ex-wife?"

Marley halted in the middle of the trail, and Will had to

stop fast to avoid hitting her. "I was going to say considering the eight-year age difference."

Will shrugged. "The age difference was never a big deal."

"And the divorce?"

"I'm over it."

"Are you?"

Her tone was as intense as her expression, and Will felt her eyes boring into his. Something roiled in the pit of his stomach, and he looked away. "Come on, we're almost to the end of the trail. Do you have a bike rack for that?"

"No, actually. I live so close that I just rode the bike here from Dad's condo."

Will hesitated, scratching his chin. "You can't walk it all the way back to your place like that. I've got a rack on my car. Might as well get that to a shop so we can get it fixed up quickly."

"Do you know a good place?"

"Sure, there's one just up the road a ways. We can drop the bike off, and then I'll run you home and collect another twenty from your dad."

"You only get that for keeping your hands off me," she taunted.

Will stole a glance at her backside and thought that was one twenty he'd be happy not to earn.

Will had only himself to blame.

That's what he thought as he watched the Neanderthal bike repair guy wipe the arm of his plaid shirt across his forehead while ogling Marley over the seat of her bike.

"You sure did a number on this baby," he said, tearing his eyes off Marley long enough to point out some of the damage on the bike. "You've dinged up the frame right here, and the rim is bent badly enough it's hitting the brake pads here. And see this spot on the fork where it's a little crooked?"

Marley bit her lip. "Can it be fixed?"

"Sure, we'll just have to order some parts, and it'll take a few days to do the work. You want me to write up an estimate for you?"

"That would be great."

The guy reached past Marley for a pen, brushing his hand against her arm in such an obvious way, Will wanted to grab the letter opener off the counter and poke the guy in the eye.

But Marley just smiled politely and left her arms on the counter. Plaid Neanderthal began jotting numbers on a form, pausing twice to look things up on the computer.

"Have you worked here long?" Marley asked.

"Six years. I actually manage the place, but I still do a lot of the labor myself."

Will stole a glance at Marley. Her eyes were fixed on the guy's tool belt, and she seemed to be assessing him with more care than necessary in choosing a bike repairman.

It's none of your business who she dates, he reminded himself through gritted teeth.

"Have you been biking long?" he asked Marley, glancing up from his form to smile at her.

"Oh, off and on for a while," she replied. "Can't wait to hit the trails hard now that I'm in Bend."

"You're new here?"

"Just moved last week. I can't wait to do more biking!"

There was a faux eagerness in her voice that made Will think of beribboned badger cages and forced enthusiasm for football teams and all the other times Will had caught Marley feigning interest in something for the sake of connecting with someone. The thought annoyed him, and he moved around her to admire a display of bicycle shorts.

"Hey Marley, you probably want to grab a couple pairs of these," he said, nodding at the well-padded backsides. "For all the cycling you're going to be doing?"

She looked at him, then looked down at the counter, and Will felt triumphant and guilty all at once. "I'll add that to my list," she mumbled as Plaid Neanderthal stopped scribbling on his form and looked up.

"Here's what I came up with," he said, pushing the form across the counter and handing it to Marley. "The total bid is down here at the bottom."

Marley squinted at the paper and traced her hand down one column. "That's parts and labor?"

"Yup. All-inclusive."

"Seems fair," she said. "Let's get it done so I can get back out on the trail."

She seemed to be trying for chipper enthusiasm, but there was a distinct note of dread in her voice. Will felt a pang of sympathy, followed by something that felt more like frustration.

If she wants to bruise her ass pretending to be a cycling nut, let her. Why do you care how she wins friends and influences people?

He didn't care. He didn't. Marley's butt—and her habit of feigning interest in things to connect with others—was none of his business.

Plaid Neanderthal brushed his hand against Marley's as he pointed to a few spots on the form. "Be sure to include your phone number right here in case I need to get in touch with you."

His tone was slightly suggestive, and it made Marley look up at him.

It made Will want to take a shower, but Marley's smile seemed genuine. Beautiful. When she flashed her real smile instead of that stiff one she reserved for donors, Will could swear he felt his heart swell in a tight, throbbing ball.

That's not your heart.

"I'm just writing my cell phone here, since I don't have a landline," Marley said as she scribbled on the form, leaning across the counter as she wrote. Plaid Neanderthal didn't even pretend not to look down the front of her shirt. Will wondered if the guy would be ogling her so brazenly if Marley hadn't introduced him earlier as "my colleague, Will."

Colleague? The word sounded like a sneer, even though he knew that's exactly what they were. And their professional relationship was precisely the reason they would *not* be getting involved.

Will looked back at Plaid Neanderthal and considered waving a hand in front of his eyes to distract him from the view down Marley's shirt.

Fine, if Will were being fair—which he didn't much feel like—he could admit he'd stolen the same glimpses any chance he'd gotten since he and Marley met. But seeing this guy doing it so blatantly, hungrily—

"Do I need to sign here?" Marley asked.

"Yup, and right there, too."

"Why is it asking for my address?"

"So we can mail you our quarterly newsletter. It's also in case you want the bike delivered back to your home when the work is complete. We offer that as a complimentary delivery service."

"You can get anything delivered in this town," Will said. "Kibble, bicycles, giant pink rabbits—"

"I think I'll just pick it up when it's ready," Marley said, jotting her father's address before scrawling her signature on the bottom of the form and pushing it across the counter. "Any idea when that might be?"

"I have to check on the parts," Plaid Neanderthal said. "It might take an extra week, maybe longer, if anything's back-ordered. This time of year that's possible. Are you in a big rush to get it back?"

Marley frowned. "Kinda. I'm supposed to go biking next weekend with some new friends."

Will stepped a little closer to Marley, effectively blocking Plaid Neanderthal's view of her curves. "You mean your outing with Bethany and April? Beth has an old bike she could probably let you use. Want me to check?"

"I don't want to impose—"

"It's not a problem. The bike's just sitting in her garage anyway as a backup. Let me shoot her a quick message and see what's up."

Will pulled out his phone and fired off a text to his sister. Marley busted her bike. Can she borrow your extra?

He waited only a few seconds for the reply to pop up. You're with Marley?

Will sighed. Yes. Not WITH Marley, but with Marley.

Whatever. We're home now, so bring her by & grab the bike.

Will stuffed the phone back in his pocket and looked up

to see Marley watching him and Plaid Neanderthal watching Marley.

"All good," Will said. "My sister says we can swing by for the bike on the way home. That way you'll have it all week so you can practice."

"I probably need a rack," Marley said.

"A nice rack is key," said Plaid Neanderthal, staring dazedly at the front of Marley's shirt.

Will cleared his throat and Plaid Neanderthal blinked once, then tore his eyes off Marley. He nodded toward the back of the shop. "We have a lot of models in stock. Let me show you some of our most popular ones."

As Plaid Neanderthal led Marley toward the back of the shop, Will gave some serious thought to backing over him with his car. Instead, he texted his sister.

> Grabbing Marley's rack & heading over in
> 10 minutes.

He'd set up the joke perfectly, so he wasn't surprised by Bethany's quick response.

> You should take longer than that to grab
> Marley's rack.

Will smiled, predictably soothed by the power of a lame joke to keep the awkward feelings at bay.

Chapter 8

WILL PULLED UP IN FRONT OF A MODEST RANCH HOUSE ON Bend's west side and killed the engine. Marley studied the home's exterior, thinking it was exactly the sort of place she imagined April and Bethany living in. There was very little grass in the front yard—xeriscaping, she'd heard it called. The high desert landscape lacked the water that made for lush forests and lawns on the other side of the mountains, so environmentally conscious Central Oregonians landscaped with river rock and drought-resistant native shrubs.

The home was painted a neutral taupe with sunny yellow trim and a red door. An orange cat snoozed in an Adirondack chair adorning the wide front porch, and two gnarled juniper trees hunkered on either side of the driveway.

"Looks like they've got company," Will said.

"What?"

He gestured at the street, where Marley spotted at least a dozen cars parked neatly against the curb. They ran the gamut from glossy BMWs to minivans with car seats in back to Volkswagen busses decorated with political bumper stickers.

"I recognize a few as friends of theirs," Will said. "Beth didn't mention a dinner party, but she and April are always doing something like that. We'll make this quick."

Marley hesitated, not wanting to barge in on a party. "We shouldn't intrude if they have guests. Is this going to be weird?"

"No weirder than any visit to see my sister and my ex-wife."

His voice was even, devoid of the ice she sometimes detected when he referenced the odd dynamic. Still...

"We shouldn't intrude—"

"Marley, she told us to come by. Besides, I know most of their friends. It's really not a big deal to grab the bike and go."

"Think it's okay to leave Magoo in the car?"

At the sound of his name, Magoo leaned over the seat and licked Marley's arm. Will reached out to scratch behind his ears and was rewarded with a healthy slurp across the cheek.

"I'm sure he'll hump the seats, but he's not going to do much damage," Will said. "We've got the windows down and the car's in the shade. He'll be fine."

Magoo licked Marley's hand again, then sneezed. "Are you sure it's okay to just barge in?"

"Come on," Will said, opening the door and stepping out. "It's not barging in if we're invited."

Marley gave Magoo one last pat on the head. She got out of the car and followed Will up to the front porch, self-conscious in her sweaty T-shirt and faded shorts. Her sneakers were caked with trail dust, and she was sure her bowlegged, butt-coddling walk marked her as a rookie cyclist who'd been thoroughly debauched by her bike.

Will knocked on the door while Marley tried to discretely peer though the blinds. She couldn't see anyone, but the eruption of feminine squeals and laughter told her something was happening inside. She hated to interrupt, especially if they were having some sort of formal dinner party. Not the best way to make an impression as a professional fund-raiser in a new town. Maybe they should come back another time.

She touched Will's arm as he reached for the doorbell. "Will, let's just—"

Ding-dong!

Marley jumped as he pressed the bell. She watched him lean casually on the doorframe, a man who'd clearly been here dozens of times before. How weird must it be to pay social visits at the love nest of his ex-wife and sister? She studied Will's face, watching for signs of discomfort. Sensing her eyes on him, he turned and smiled at her.

"How's your butt?" he asked.

"Is this going to be our new greeting? Because I kind of preferred hello."

Will's smile broadened as shrieks of laughter echoed inside the house. At last, the sound of clicky footsteps across a wood floor echoed inside the house. The front door flew open, and Will took a step back as Bethany launched herself at her brother, engulfing him in a big hug.

"Will! Bro! So nice of you to come!"

Will staggered back, not so much hugging his sister as keeping her from toppling into the shrubs. "Bethany! *Sis!* So nice of you to sanitize the front of my shirt with vodka!"

He spit out a mouthful of her hair and gave her a perfunctory squeeze before stepping back. Bethany swayed a little on her feet and gave him a loopy grin.

"I take it you're having a party?" he asked.

She gripped the doorframe and beamed, her blush-tinged cheeks showing a dimple that perfectly matched her brother's.

"Pure Romance! Ohmygod, Will, I'm so glad you're here. And Marley—so great to see you."

"You too, Bethany," Marley declared, stifling the urge to laugh. "You're looking very... *jolly*."

"I sure am!" she slurred, beaming wider. "I can't believe you're here."

"It is a surprise," Will agreed, "considering you told us to come ten minutes ago."

"You said *come*!" Bethany squealed, slugging Will in the shoulder. At least, she seemed to be aiming for his shoulder. She missed, and the punch bounced ineffectively off the decorative wreath by the front door.

Marley studied Will's bemused expression, uncertain what to do. "Um, if this is a bad time—"

"It's a great time!" Bethany announced. "The best time ever! Have you ever had a screaming orgasm?"

"Um, well—"

"It's a drink," April said, stepping up beside Bethany and shooting Marley a sympathetic smile. She placed a hand on Bethany's arm, either a gesture of affection or an attempt to hold her upright. "The screaming orgasm is made with vodka, Bailey's, and Kahlua. It's an absolutely lovely cocktail, if you'd like to try one. Please, come on inside and join us."

Will tossed his keys from one hand to the other. "We aren't staying long. We're just here to grab the bike."

"The bike, right!" Bethany yelped. "Right right right *right-e-o*." Without warning, Bethany grabbed Marley's arm and began towing her inside. "Don't leave, come on— the party's just getting good, and we can grab the bike so you have a place to sit."

"That makes perfect sense," Will said as he followed them into the house.

Marley tried to study the décor as Bethany pulled her

through the entryway and into the living room. The art on the walls consisted of tastefully framed black-and-white photos and a few colorful, abstract paintings. The floors were a high-gloss hickory, and an antique-looking bench was piled high with brightly whimsical throw pillows. April trotted along beside them, looking like a nervous spaniel.

"Welcome to our home," April chirped, stopping to straighten a throw pillow. "Bethany's been… um, enjoying the refreshments a lot this evening. Can I get you something? A cocktail, maybe some water, or a glass of wine? We just opened a lovely chardonnay."

"Water would be nice."

"Lovely!" April said, clapping her hands together as she veered off from their dysfunctional little parade. "I'll be right back. Will, can I get you anything?"

"A bullet between the eyes."

"Ice water!" April called brightly as she disappeared around a corner.

Marley stumbled a little as Bethany tugged her around another corner, and Will caught her elbow to steady her. She looked at him, trying to read his mood.

"We can come back later," she whispered. "If you're not in the mood to deal with a dinner party crowd."

Will quirked an eyebrow at her. "Did you hear what she said about Pure Romance?"

"Pure Romance?"

"They're not having a dinner party, Marley. It's a gathering of women who get together to shop for—"

"Sex toys!" Bethany squealed as she halted abruptly at the entrance of a small, cozy living room. "And lotions and potions and whips and lubes and—"

"Lions and tigers and bears," Will finished, stopping right behind Marley and standing so close she could feel his breath on her neck. Half a dozen women were piled on two over-stuffed leather sofas the color of old saddles, and another eight or nine were lined up on folding chairs scattered around the room. Everyone looked up and regarded the newcomers with curious expressions as Bethany waved an enthusiastic hand.

"Everyone, this is my brother Will and his girl-friend, Marley."

Marley coughed. Behind her, Will either choked or stifled a laugh.

"Bethany, quit being silly," April chided softly as she approached from behind and handed Will and Marley each a glass filled with icy water. "Will is Bethany's brother, and Marley is his colleague, the new director of development at the Cascade Historical Society and Wildlife Sanctuary."

"Cheez Whiz," Will supplied.

"We're colleagues," Marley emphasized. "Not dating. Not even sleeping together or—"

"—or making out in doorways in front of giant pink bunny rabbits," Will added.

There was a long silence from the living room, and Marley gave some serious thought to hiding under the sofa. At the center of the room, a petite brunette wearing a pink-and-black top and the fluffiest ponytail Marley had ever seen beamed at the two of them as she gestured to the table in front of her piled high with pastel merchandise. "Will you be staying for the party?"

Marley gulped and surveyed the products. There were bottles and tubes and booklets and… "Ohmygod," Marley gasped. "Is that what I think it is?"

Will took a sip of his ice water. "There's no safe way

to answer that without knowing the depth of your dirty thoughts or the expanse of your field of vision."

"It's huge," Marley stammered, her eyes fixed on the array of toys lined up like pastel soldiers. She turned to Will and lowered her voice. "What the hell is it with the women in your family and phalluses?"

"Years of therapy, and we still haven't figured that out."

"Were you admiring the Thunder Vibe?" called a voice across the room. Marley turned to see a small brunette hoisting a pale pink object the size of a small car. She held it aloft for everyone to admire, and several woman in the audience tittered appreciatively.

"It's a very popular item," the brunette added. "Waterproof, too."

Marley stared, part of her wanting to glance away, part of her wishing the woman would quit waving it around so she could get a better look.

"Do you need a roof rack to get it home?" Marley asked.

"It's not *that* big," called a busty redhead sitting cross-legged on the closest sofa. She held up the catalog and smiled. "It's six-point-five inches in length and five-point-five inches in circumference. It has multi-speeds, flexible nubbies, and needs two AA batteries."

"My boyfriend has all that," said the woman beside her, hiccupping loudly. "Minus the batteries. And the nubbies. What's a nubby?"

"The average male penis is 5.1 inches in length, so the Thunder Vibe is bigger than average," announced a very pregnant blonde on the other side of the room.

"Male penis?" someone hiccuped. "What's a female penis?"

The woman with the catalog trailed her finger down the

page and smiled thoughtfully. "Oh, and it also has a nylon wrist strap."

"Of course it does," Marley said. "How else could you take it for a walk?"

The women began to pass the Thunder Vibe around the room, and Marley saw Will grimace as it landed in April's lap. She grasped it in one hand, looking cheerful and disturbingly childlike in a pink-and-white sundress patterned with daisies. Her angelic blond curls framed her face, and she smiled at the object before passing it to Marley.

"They make a lot of other models," April said. "And they're throwing in a lovely little hidey bag to store them in."

"Um, thanks," Marley said, and tried to pass the Thunder Vibe to Will.

He jumped back as though threatened by a burning sword. Marley rolled her eyes. "It doesn't have cooties."

"You can't be sure about that."

Marley sighed and handed it to Bethany.

"Ten percent discount on all toys tonight," called the saleswoman.

Will raised his hand. "Can I get a Rubik's Cube and a Cabbage Patch doll?"

Marley elbowed him in the ribs and shot a glance at Bethany. She leaned toward Will and whispered, "About the bike—"

"Okay, ladies!" the woman at the table yelled, clapping her hands. She shot a look at Will and frowned. "And gentleman." Her frown deepened. "Actually, corporate policy says we aren't supposed to have men or children at these events. Only women."

"He doesn't count as a man," Bethany said, smacking Will on the shoulder. "He's my brother. And my partner's ex-wife."

"Ex-husband," April corrected, giving Will an apologetic smile.

"Whatever."

The saleswoman furrowed her brow, apparently trying to figure out how this negated the women-only rule.

"We really should be going," Marley said. "My dog is waiting in the car, and I need to get him home. If you could just show us where the bike is, or maybe it would just be better if we came back—"

"Will!" a voice boomed behind them. Marley jumped, whirling around to see who else had joined the dysfunctional family reunion. A middle-aged woman approached with a tray of neon pink cocktails and a startled expression. It took Marley a moment to realize the expression wasn't so much startled, but rather the result of too many facelifts. Her skin was pulled so tight her forehead looked like it had been ironed. She wore her dark hair in a tight bun, which accentuated her razor-sharp cheekbones. She wasn't smiling, but considering the lack of movement in her face, Marley tried not to take that personally.

The woman looked Marley up and down and sniffed. "Who are you?"

Marley stuck her hand out to shake, then realized her mistake as the woman rolled her eyes at the tray of cocktails.

"Marley Cartman," she said. "I'm just here to borrow a bicycle."

"Are you aware of the effects of handlebar position on female orgasm?" she asked. "A recent study showed that handlebars positioned lower than the bike seat are associated with increased pelvic floor pressure and decreased anterior vaginal wall and labial sensation."

Will cleared his throat. "Aunt Nancy," he said, his tone

somewhere between a sigh and a groan. "Please meet Marley Cartman. Marley, meet Nancy Thomas-Smith, PhD, bestselling author of *Integrated Treatment for Sexual Perversion* and *Orgasm Essentials*."

"You forgot *The Big Book of Bondage: From Playful to Paraphilic*," Nancy said. "That hit the list too."

"*Hit* being the operative word," Will said.

"How lovely you two can finally meet," April said, nodding like a bobblehead. "We were so surprised to learn Aunt Nancy wished to join us this evening."

"Of course I wished to join you," Aunt Nancy said, her tone mocking. "I spent my entire career focusing on sexual health and abnormal psychology. I have a particular interest in all forms of artistic phalluses."

"Artistic," Bethany said, and hiccupped.

Nancy ignored her and leveled a look at Marley. "So you're the Marley Cartman I've been speaking to on the phone."

"Wonderful to finally meet you, ma'am." Marley smiled, but the gesture wasn't returned.

"I do hope you're getting a fair appraisal on the artifacts?"

Marley swallowed hard and nodded. "Of course. We're flying in an expert appraiser to take a look next week."

Nancy sniffed and looked around the room. "I trust you'll find the donation to be quite large."

"Quite large," Marley agreed, ignoring the giant purple phallus making the rounds in her peripheral vision.

"I've already informed my accountant to expect a size-able write-off on this year's taxes, due to the donation," Nancy continued.

Marley's stomach clenched as her cousin's words echoed in her head. Hopefully Kayley's gut assessment was wrong. Hopefully the rock cocks—er, *figurines*—were worth every penny the family expected.

"We'll leave it to the professionals to assess the value," Marley said, "but sometimes the monetary amount is less important than—"

"The monetary amount is *always* important," Nancy snapped. "You haven't been in this business long if you don't know that."

"Right," Marley said. "Of course. Money is the issue, and I'll be certain we get a fair and accurate appraisal just as soon as possible."

Nancy folded her arms over her chest. The tension in the room was so thick Marley could spread it on a bagel. Will stepped forward and took the tray from Aunt Nancy. "I'll just pass these out," he said, and moved around the sofa.

"Pussy," Bethany muttered.

"Where?" asked a petite redhead on the end of the sofa. "Are we already on the page with the handheld Vajayjay and the Lotus Flower?"

Will ignored them as he made the rounds handing drinks to nervous-looking guests. "It's not every day a guy gets to give out screaming orgasms to a dozen women."

One of them reached out and grabbed Will's butt, as another woman passed the Thunder Vibe to her neighbor. That woman turned a switch on the end and smiled.

"Buzzy," she said.

"My husband can't do that."

"Damn shame."

Aunt Nancy cleared her throat, snapping Marley's attention away from the rest of the party. "So how long have you been in this line of work anyway?" Nancy demanded.

Marley swallowed and pasted on her best donor relations

smile. "Well, I've been working in donor development for more than a decade, and—"

"So you're a financial expert then?"

Marley blinked and resisted the urge to take a step back. She focused on smiling harder, on looking for some way to click with Nancy. "I do have a great deal of experience, yes." Marley rubbed her lips together and put an extra note of enthusiasm in her voice. "I'm also a huge fan of vintage jewelry, and I have to say that's a lovely necklace you're wearing. Is it a family heirloom?"

"No. And why are you changing the subject?"

"I wasn't changing the subject. Merely remarking on your exquisite taste in jewelry."

"And I was asking how you got to be a financial wizard."

"I wouldn't say I'm a financial wizard," Marley said, folding her hands in front of her to keep them steady. Or to keep herself from wrapping them around Nancy's neck. "I'd say I'm more of a people person who happens to enjoy working with individuals and corporations who wish to make charitable contributions to worthy causes like—"

"Cheez Whiz," called Will.

"And other charitable entities of that sort," Marley agreed. "I can help them maximize their donations in a way that's mutually beneficial to—"

"So you schmooze rich people for money," Aunt Nancy interrupted. "Not that there's something wrong with that, but let's call a spade a spade."

Marley felt her smile beginning to falter, and she took a shaky breath to calm her nerves. "I can assure you, Ms. Thomas-Smith, I'm quite good at what I do."

"I don't doubt it. So what does your portfolio look like?"

"I beg your pardon?"

Nancy shrugged and took a sip of something Marley assumed was champagne but secretly hoped might be lighter fluid. An untimely death might be the only way to escape this conversation. "If you make a living telling other people what to do with their money, I assume you've handled your own just as wisely."

Marley lifted her chin. "I prefer to keep my personal finances quite separate from my professional life, but I can assure you I'm comfortable. Why do you ask?"

Her voice quavered only a little on those last words, so Marley was pretty sure no one heard. Nancy opened her mouth to reply, but Bethany elbowed Marley in the ribs.

"She's asking because she thinks you're after Will's money," Bethany said. "And not in a donor relations sorta way."

Marley choked back a bubble of laughter, which came out sounding more like a snort. "My only interest in Mr. Barclay's finances is as they pertain to his professional investments in the operations of—"

"Cheez Whiz," Will said, setting the empty drink tray on the counter as he rejoined the group. "Be nice, Aunt Nancy."

"Hmph," she sniffed. "Will's had enough trouble with women in his life. Keep that in mind when you're sniffing around his fire hydrant."

"Will's fire hydrant is safe from me," Marley said, fighting to keep her voice bright and cheerful. "Our connection to one another is purely professional. But I'm sure he appreciates your concern."

"Not especially," Will said, touching Marley's elbow so lightly she wondered if it was by accident. "But I try not to hold it against her."

"The bike's out here in the garage," April called, her

voice high and nervous. "It's got a lovely little basket on the front you can take off when you go trail riding, and if you'll just follow me—"

April started down the hall, and Marley turned to follow with Will right beside her. She looked up at him, careful to keep her voice to a whisper.

"So you and your sister diffuse awkward situations with dirty jokes, and April does it by being ridiculously chipper?"

Will grinned down at her. "You got a better method?"

"How about ruthless smiling?"

"Whatever works."

From the sofa, Bethany called out to April, "You got it, babe? I'll make another round of drinks if you can handle the bike thing."

"Absolutely," April chirped over her shoulder.

"Okay then," Will said, turning back toward the group. "It was lovely meeting all of you. Aunt Nancy—always a pleasure."

"Hmph," said Aunt Nancy.

"A pleasure meeting you, ma'am," Marley said. "I'll keep you posted on the appraisal. And thank you for having us over, Bethany. This has been… well, lovely."

Bethany grinned from her perch on the sofa and squeezed Marley's hand. "Don't mention it. You sure you don't want to order anything? Here, take a catalog in case you change your mind."

She thrust a pink-paged, glossy magazine into Marley's hands, and Marley took it, not sure what else to do.

"Have a great evening," Marley called to everyone, and turned to where April waited by the door to the garage, shifting nervously from one bare foot to the other.

Will followed behind her. "Well, that was fun."

"We should do it again sometime."

"Definitely. A few more visits with my family and you'll be able to get in on our group therapy discount. Watch your step."

Marley marched down three short stairs into the garage and spotted April polishing the bike's handlebars with the hem of her dress.

"It's a little dusty," April sang, "but let me just get it tidied up and it'll be lovely."

"It's a mountain bike," Will said. "If it isn't dusty, you aren't using it correctly."

"Right," April said and stepped back. "I hope it's the right size."

"It looks perfect," Marley said, studying the shiny yellow and white bike that looked brand new. Marley knew very little about bicycles, but she could tell this was a nice one. "Are you sure this is okay? It looks too nice for you to be loaning it to a complete stranger."

April beamed. "You aren't a stranger, Marley. You're our new friend, and friends take care of each other."

"That they do," Will said.

Marley looked at him, surprised to hear the hint of ice back in his voice. Sensing Marley's eyes on him, he offered her a smile that didn't quite reach his eyes and patted the seat of the bike. "What do you think?" he asked.

Marley glanced between April's earnest expression and Will's brittle one, thinking it was no wonder everyone was a walking coping mechanism considering the amount of awkwardness in this family dynamic.

"It's lovely," Marley said, and beamed at them both.

Chapter 9

WILL SURVEYED THE SCENE AS HE PULLED UP MARLEY'S driveway. As much as he hated to admit it, he was keeping a tense watch for expensive-looking cars.

"My dad isn't here," Marley said, reading his thoughts. "He had a business meeting in Burns, so he's staying the night over there."

"There go my plans to earn an extra twenty bucks," he said as he opened his car door and swung himself out. Magoo hopped over the seat and jumped out behind him, padding over to a water dish at the edge of the garage. Marley followed and punched a few numbers on a keypad beside the door. The garage powered open, revealing an interior so spotless you could lick the concrete floor. Not that Will wanted to, but the option was there.

He turned and nodded toward the bike attached to the rack on the back of his Volkswagen.

"You want the bike in the garage, or on your back porch?" he called.

Marley looked up, and Will felt something clench in his chest as her eyes locked with his. Hers skittered away first, studying the interior of the garage.

"Let's put it in the garage. I'll feel better if I know it's locked up."

"From thieves or from Magoo?"

"Both."

Will pulled the bike off the rack as Marley uncoiled

a garden hose off a neat wooden rack beside the house. She dragged the hose over before bending down to tip the slobber-saturated water out of Magoo's dish. It shouldn't have been sexy, but Will still caught himself staring. There was so much to see. Wisps of hair drifting free from her ponytail to frame her face. A shadowy glimpse of curved flesh beneath the neckline of her T-shirt. Her taut backside in those snug cotton shorts.

Stop it, Will commanded himself. *You are not a Neanderthal.*

Yes, he was. The trick was not to act like it.

Magoo pranced around while Marley splashed fresh water into the dish and Will wheeled the bike into the garage. He propped it against the wall and then trudged back to his car and grabbed the box containing Marley's new bike rack. He hefted it out and carried it back toward the garage.

He found Marley standing over Magoo's dish, the hose still splashing water over her bare toes as she studied the Pure Romance catalog she'd gotten from Bethany.

"Need help hooking this to your car?" he asked.

Marley looked up, blinking in surprise as she closed the catalog. "Oh—I almost forgot about that."

"It shouldn't take too long to attach it. Got any tools?"

Marley gave him a sheepish grin and waved the catalog. "Funny you should ask. I was just studying the Jelly Tool Belt."

"Does it have an Allen wrench?"

"That may be the only thing it doesn't have." Marley rolled the catalog up and tucked it under one arm, effectively ending Will's efforts to peer at the pages.

He set down the bike box and nodded back at the Volkswagen. "I've got tools in my car. The real kind, not the ones you'd be embarrassed to have spotted in your luggage by airport security. This shouldn't take more than a few minutes."

"I can't ask you install my bike rack, Will. It's too much trouble."

"You aren't asking me," Will called as he dug his toolbox out of the trunk. "I'm offering. Totally different thing."

"At least let me make you dinner. I could throw something really simple together. Shrimp scampi, maybe, and a salad. I grabbed some fresh bread from Baked, so I can heat that up with garlic butter."

Will grabbed his toolbox and returned to the garage, his stomach already growling. "That sounds amazing."

"How long do you think the bike thing will take?"

Will shrugged. "Twenty minutes, thirty tops."

She smiled, and Will felt his heart twist. "Perfect," she said. "I'll have dinner ready by then. Thanks again, Will."

He stared after her as she retreated into the house, the smell of blueberries drifting after her even though he hadn't seen her drinking any of her iced tea all evening.

He had to admit, the meal sounded incredible. It had been a long time since he'd had a woman feed him. For the first year after they'd divorced, April would bring him food. Some lamb stew here, a plate of cookies there—"*just leftovers, and I happened to be passing by.*"

Will had known the truth. April felt guilty, and when April felt uncomfortable, she turned into a Stepford wife.

She'd spent the last half of their marriage being relentlessly cheerful and efficient. Will had to admit, he'd enjoyed it sometimes. Now he just felt like hell for putting her in a position to feel compelled to fake anything at all.

You should have known she was unhappy, he told

himself. *You should have seen the meatloaf and stiff smiles for the warning signs they were.*

Maybe so. But having Marley cook for him seemed different. More intimate somehow. His mouth watered as he thought about Marley hovering over a steamy pot of noodles, her nimble fingers dropping fat, tender shrimp into the butter. Will sighed and opened his toolbox.

The heady smell of garlic was wafting through the garage door before Will had the last screw tightened. He knocked twice on the door leading from the garage to the condo, then wiped his feet on the doormat and walked inside.

"Marley?" he called, stepping into the foyer where he noticed the giant pink rabbit still occupied copious floor space. "I'm all done out here. Where would you like me to wash up?"

Marley popped her head around the corner of the kitchen, her cheeks flushed from cooking. At least Will assumed it was from cooking. She had that catalog, after all.

"There's a bathroom right around the corner there," Marley said, nodding at the hallway. "First door on the left. Great timing, by the way. The scampi's just about done. I hope you don't mind garlic."

"I'm not a vampire, if that's what you're asking."

"That saves me the trouble of staking you at the dinner table then."

Will trudged through the foyer en route to the bathroom. As he passed the small end table by the door, something buzzed. He looked down at a small basket of keys and coins and saw Marley's phone vibrating on top of the pile. He froze as an incoming text message flashed on the screen.

> Did more research. Rock cocks almost definitely worthless. Call me.

The words flashed up so fast Will didn't have time to register whether he should be reading them. And who the hell was Kayley?

Will stepped away from the phone and moved toward the bathroom. Two waves hit him at once—a wave of guilt for snooping, and a wave of suspicion about the message. It had to be about Aunt Nancy's figurines. But Marley had said she couldn't get them appraised until next week. So what was going on?

There has to be an explanation. Just ask her.

He shook his head as he stepped into the bathroom to scrub his hands.

Great idea. *"So, Marley, I was reading your private text messages and couldn't help noticing—"*

No. Keep your mouth shut and your eyes open.

Will twisted off the taps and ignored the twist of uneasiness in his gut. By the time he returned to the dining room, Marley had the table set and was ladling giant servings of buttery scampi onto plates. "Hang on a sec. Let me clip some parsley from my plant on the back deck."

"Wow," Will said, sitting down to survey the spread. "Is this blueberry iced tea?"

"It is. There's white wine too, if you want it. It's right inside the fridge. Take your pick between the Sauvignon Blanc and the Chardonnay."

Will pulled the wine from the refrigerator and located a corkscrew in the drawer beside the refrigerator. He returned to the table right as Marley dropped a handful of chopped parsley over a steaming plate of pasta and set it on a blue placemat.

Will sat down and spread a green polka-dotted napkin across his lap before uncorking the wine.

"This smells incredible. It *looks* incredible."

"Now we just hope it doesn't taste like cardboard," Marley said as she set down her own plate and took a seat beside Will. "I'm not a great cook, but this is the one thing I make pretty well. I have to go a little light on the butter since I'm lactose intolerant, but parmesan is one of the few cheeses I can handle." She placed a frosty glass of blueberry tea in front of him before picking up the dainty, stemmed wineglass Will had filled with Sauvignon Blanc.

"Cheers," Marley said, and took a sip.

"Cheers."

They clinked glasses, and Will noticed the flush still hadn't left Marley's cheeks. Her hair was pulled into a sloppy knot on top of her head, and damp little curls framed her face. She looked ridiculously beautiful, which was crazy. She was wearing a dirt-smudged T-shirt, for crying out loud. She couldn't be beautiful. She couldn't be trusted, either.

Give her the benefit of the doubt. Stop snooping, stop being suspicious, and eat your damn pasta.

Magoo trotted into the dining room and looked from Marley to Will and back to Marley again. He licked Marley's bare calf twice, then curled himself into a tight donut shape at the base of her chair.

Will set his glass down and took a bite of the pasta. "This is delicious."

"Thank you. It's my go-to easy meal when company drops by."

"I don't cook much myself."

"No? What do you eat?"

He shrugged and speared a fat, pink shrimp with his fork. "Rubber chicken."

"Rubber chicken?"

"At charity functions, local fund-raiser galas, that sort of thing. I attend a lot of them, and no matter how swanky it is, they always seem to serve chicken that's been cooked to the consistency of a superball."

"Rubber chicken. Got it."

"It's not so bad once you get used to it. Sometimes it's actually pretty tasty."

Marley laughed and forked up a mouthful of pasta. "I thought the food at Bed's event was pretty good. I'll have to get the name of that caterer."

"It was April."

He could tell from Marley's expression he'd surprised her. "Your ex-wife is a caterer?"

"Yep. She works out of 900 Wall downtown. Another chef runs the restaurant portion, and April handles the catering side of things."

"Wow. So will she be catering the event your sister hosts next month?"

"Probably. It's good promo for the business, plus April can't ever resist the urge to feed people."

Marley was quiet a moment, and Will wondered what she was pondering. He didn't have to wonder for long.

"Is it weird having so much social interaction with your sister and ex-wife? I mean, given the circumstances—"

"—of my wife leaving me to play snuggle-the-hamster with my sister?" Will took a sip of tea. "No."

Marley's eyes were fixed on his face, waiting for more detail. But Will wasn't interested in offering it. Instead, he picked up the basket of sliced baguette and offered it to her. "More bread?"

Marley shook her head and speared another shrimp. "No

thank you. Sorry to be nosy. It's just odd to me. As soon as my ex-fiancé and I broke things off, that was pretty much it. Aside from a few awkward interactions where we sorted through belongings and decided who got what, we didn't have a whole lot to say to one another."

"Is that a good thing?"

"I think so. And since I moved three hours from Portland, we pretty much eliminated the chance of running into each other on a date or backsliding into post-breakup pity sex." Marley laughed and speared another shrimp. "Of course, without the post-breakup pity sex, I probably should give some serious consideration to the merchandise in Bethany's catalog."

Her eyes flitted to the china hutch behind them, and Will realized she'd set the Pure Romance catalog there. He stared at it a moment, feeling very warm under the collar of his T-shirt. He speared another mouthful of salad and chewed thoughtfully, his eyes still fixed on the glossy pages. He finished chewing and set down his fork, reaching over to snatch the pink and black cover page featuring a photo of a woman looking rosy-cheeked and joyful over the contents of a gift-wrapped box.

Will flipped past the first few pages as Marley dabbed the corner of her mouth with her napkin. "I kinda want to see what all the fuss is about," he said, flipping another page.

"There's something for everyone in there. Especially Aunt Nancy, given her apparent phallus fixation."

"There's a visual I didn't need." Will flipped another page as Marley twirled the tines of her fork in her last puddle of noodles. He stopped flipping and stared at a photograph of a pink lotion tube.

"Coochy?" Will squinted at the page. "They make a product called *Coochy*?"

"I'm afraid to ask what it is."

"Apparently it's a shaving lotion."

"Don't feel you need to explain which body parts it's intended to shave."

Will grinned and flipped another page, pausing to take a bite of garlic bread. He dropped the bread as his eyes landed on the next section of merchandise.

"Wow," he said, picking up the bread again. "I didn't realize there's so much variety."

"Variety in what?" Marley stretched toward him to get a look at the page, and Will resisted the urge to look down the front of her shirt. Instead, he turned back to the page, holding it up so she could see. "Vibrators," he said, flipping to the next page to demonstrate the array of products. "They've got g-spot vibrators, vaginal vibrators, dual-action vibrators, and clitoral stimulators. Which are we shopping for?"

"*We* are not shopping for anything," Marley said, making a grab for the magazine. "Give me that."

Will pulled the catalog back, flipping to the next page. "I love the names for these. Platinum Pete, All-Night Bender, Tongue Tied, Big Bang—"

Marley finally managed to snatch the catalog from his hand, and Will didn't fight to hold on to it. Instead, he enjoyed the warm brush of her bare arm against his.

He wouldn't have blamed her one bit if she'd marched away to stuff the catalog in a drawer, but something must have caught her eye.

"They make a vibrator called the Wild Hare?"

"I saw that one," Will said. "It's the bunny ears."

"Now I know what to get Bed for Christmas." Marley turned the page, seemingly fascinated by the selection. "There's also a Major Hare. She could line them up and march them around her nightstand."

"There's a pleasant thought."

Marley laughed and flipped another page. "You're the one who started this. I don't think I need to tell you this is a wildly inappropriate channel of discussion between two virtual strangers attempting to establish a professional business relationship."

"Who's holding the magazine here?"

"Me, thank you very much. How else would I know about the Diamond Collection?"

"Diamond Collection?"

Marley smacked the page with the back of her hand. "A girl's best friend, apparently. A girl with money to burn, anyway. Look at this."

She held the page out to him, and Will's eyes fixed on the shiny, phallic shape before shifting to the price. He whistled. "For $279, I hope it buys you dinner first."

Marley flipped another page. "We really should stop. This is highly unprofessional."

"Depends on your profession." He peered at the page she'd turned to and raised an eyebrow. "Is the Double Trouble Dual-Bullet C-ring a sex toy or something you'd use to remove paint?"

"Can I close this now?"

"Wait, I'm trying to decide between the Jelly Tool Belt and the Jelly C-ring. Which would be better for bike repairs?"

Marley shook her head and closed the catalog, setting it beside her wineglass. She folded her hands on her placemat and lifted her chin. "We really should stop. Don't you think?"

It was a real question, not a rhetorical one, and Will met her eyes. Her smile was faint, but still in place, and there was something else in her eyes. Curiosity? Intrigue? Desire? He didn't know her well enough to tell, which also meant he didn't know her well enough to do any of the dozens of things he urgently wanted to do with her right now. He held her eyes anyway, since it seemed wiser than holding *her*.

His brain veered dangerously there, imagining Marley in his arms, her bare flesh warm against his fingertips, her hair skimming his naked chest. He imagined burying his face against her neck, smelling blueberries on her skin, tasting the salty sweetness of that soft spot behind her ear.

Stop it! he ordered himself. *You know you can't trust her. She's a neurotic people pleaser with a hidden agenda and a suspicious text message on her phone.*

Will blinked, and his eyes focused on her face again. Her cheeks were flushed, and her hazel eyes held his with an intensity that made all the air leave his lungs.

Just a fling. As long as I don't get attached...

Marley's lips parted, and he felt a surge of lust as her tongue flicked the corner of her mouth. "You're trying to come up with a joke right now, aren't you?" she asked.

"What?"

"To break the awkwardness." Her voice was oddly husky. "Here we are, sitting at my dining room table with a sex toy catalog and a lot of sexual vibes between us, and you're racking your brain to come up with a bad joke to diffuse the tension."

"A good joke would suffice."

"I'm waiting."

Will hesitated, not sure whether she waited for a joke or something else. Maybe she didn't know either.

"Knock knock," he said.

Marley grinned. "Who's there?"

"The guy who wants to strip your clothes off and have his way with you on the table."

Her lips quirked into a smile. "Is that your idea of a punch line or foreplay?"

"Sometimes they're the same thing."

Marley hesitated, then moved her hand a little closer to Will's. "I know we agreed it would be a dumb idea for us to get involved…"

"We did?"

"I think so."

"Right. Remind me again why?"

"Corporate policy strictly forbids it," Marley said, licking her lips. "And I've given up on dating rich guys."

"Right. That."

"And also you have all kinds of crazy trust issues," she added. "Which means I'd be crazy to get involved with you."

"Define *involved*."

Marley moved her hand closer, but still didn't touch him. Will was pretty sure the temperature in the dining room had risen twenty degrees in the last ten minutes. He shifted his eyes to the flutter of pulse in her throat and realized she was breathing harder, her skin more flushed now than it was when she'd emerged from the kitchen with the pasta.

"So anyway," Marley continued as though Will hadn't mentally undressed her a dozen times in the last minute, "we really shouldn't fool around."

"Fool around," Will repeated, choosing to ignore the first part of what she'd said. He was too busy studying her hand now, watching the delicate bones of her fingers drumming the table in a nervous rhythm. He thought about capturing one in his mouth, sucking the tip of it to make her moan and press her body against him. He was starting to feel dizzy now and wondered if there was any blood left in his brain.

"I mean, I know plenty of people get away with some sort of friends-with-benefits arrangement," Marley continued, her voice high and tight now. "But really, I don't think that ever works when—"

"Marley?"

She blinked. "What?"

"Shut up."

Then he made sure it happened. His mouth was on hers before she could protest, and he pulled her out of her chair with more force than necessary. He dragged her onto his lap, and she came willingly, twining her fingers behind his neck.

She made a tiny squeak in the back of her throat as he shifted her weight across his knee, but she didn't move to get away. Will's mouth was on hers, devouring, tasting, probing. Her lips were unbelievably soft and tasted like blueberries and crisp white wine and desire. Marley twisted her fingers in his hair and kissed him back, hard.

They kissed like that for a while—minutes? Hours? Decades?—Will wasn't sure. The one thing he was sure of is that he needed to touch a whole lot more of her soon.

He scooped his hands under her backside, lifting her as he stood. She stiffened in his arms for an instant, but latched her fingers behind his neck, holding on tight.

"Will, you can't pick me up like you're some sort of caveman," she protested.

"A caveman would toss you onto the floor right now and have his way with you. This is my attempt at being a gentleman. Where's your bedroom?"

Marley blinked, then shifted her weight in his arms. "That way." She nodded down the hall, which wasn't much direction, but it was a start.

Will turned and headed down the hall.

Chapter 10

WILLIAM BARCLAY THE FIFTH IS CARRYING ME INTO MY BEDROOM to do naughty things to me.

Marley didn't say the words out loud, but she forced herself to articulate them clearly enough in her brain, gauging how her mind and body would react.

At the moment, her body was screaming, *"Hell yeah!"* while her mind fretted over whether Will might blow out a knee halfway down the hall.

But Will's knees seemed fine, and since neither Marley's brain nor body seemed to be protesting, she tightened her hold around his neck. She pressed her lips against the stubble on his throat, testing his pulse with her tongue. He groaned and dug his fingers into her bare thighs.

"Left or right?" he asked.

"Left. Right. Wait, what?"

"Your bedroom."

"Oh. Turn here. The one with the creepy-looking painting of the eggplant on the wall."

"A handy landmark," he said, but obeyed her direction as Marley licked her way across his throat, her breath hot on his flesh.

"Keep that up and I'm going to drop you," he groaned.

"Take five steps to the bed, *then* drop me."

"Yes, ma'am," he said, and tossed her back onto the feather duvet. He landed on top of her, his lips seeking hers as his palm slid up the side of her body. His fingers were hot, possessive, and Marley whimpered with the pleasure of his touch.

"God, you feel good," he murmured against her mouth.

"Mmm," Marley said, the closest thing she could manage to "*you too*," as she toed off her shoes and wrapped her legs around his back. She gripped him with her thighs, enjoying the hard, hot length of his body pressed against hers.

He kissed his way along the column of her throat, and Marley almost forgot to worry whether her skin was salty from her bike ride. She pressed her sock-footed heels into the back of his legs, pulling him tighter against her, craving more of him still.

She slid her hands down his back and found the hem of his T-shirt. Tunneling her fingers beneath it, she savored the heat of his bare flesh, the strong ridges of his spine. Will kissed her behind one ear and Marley gasped, digging her nails into his shoulder blades.

"You appear to have some rather sensitive nerve endings there, Ms. Cartman," he murmured, his breath warm on her earlobe. "How's the other side?"

"Oh," Marley gasped as Will moved to her left ear. As his lips found that perfect spot, Marley raised her hips and pressed her body tighter against him. She gasped, savoring the delicious weight of his body on hers, delirious from the heat and tingle of his touch.

Marley slid her hands further up his shirt, tracing his bare shoulder blades with her fingertips. His flesh was smooth and hot beneath the heels of her hands, and she pressed into him, feeling the hard coil of muscle. Will shifted slightly, angling his kisses down her shoulder, his lips soft and urgent and so damn good at what they were doing.

Marley wanted more.

"Take your shirt off," she gasped.

Will laughed, his breath warm against her collarbone. "You first."

He sat back on his heels, and Marley wriggled to a seated position, eager to rid herself of the T-shirt so she could touch him again. Will smiled, his mismatched eyes glinting in the faint glow of the hall light.

"I asked first," she pointed out. "Shouldn't I get the first striptease as a courtesy?"

"How do I know you'll follow through on your end of the bargain?"

"Trust issues, much?"

"How about we do it on three?"

She must have looked startled, because Will laughed and grabbed the hem of his shirt. "I don't mean *do it* on three. I promise I have better foreplay skills than that. I just meant—"

Marley whipped her shirt over her head, cutting off whatever his next words would have been. She tossed it across the room and grinned.

"I'm an overachiever," she said.

"Thank God," Will replied, and tugged off his own shirt. "It really isn't fair you're still partly clothed above the waist. Let me help you with this."

He reached for her bra clasp before Marley could decide whether she was ready to remove it. But once Will flicked the clasp with one hand, it felt so damn good to have her breasts bare that she forgot all about any hesitation. Will nudged the straps off her shoulders and Marley gasped as the cool air brushed her breasts.

They didn't stay chilly for long.

"You taste so good," Will murmured as his mouth found her left nipple, teasing it to a stiff peak.

"Don't stop," Marley hissed and buried her fingers in his hair.

"Wasn't planning to," Will murmured in reply, the vibration of his words exquisite on her flesh. Will devoured her with his tongue a while longer, then moved across her rib cage to the other breast.

"So soft," he murmured.

"Will," she hissed through clenched teeth. His hair was baby-fine between her fingers. She caught a faint whiff of sage and wondered what shampoo he used. Will trailed his tongue from one breast to the other, taking his time in the shallow valley between her breasts. When his tongue found her other nipple, Marley arched tightly against him and cried out.

"It seems easy to make you moan," he murmured. "This bodes well for me."

"Should I make it harder?"

"You already are."

She pressed her palms against his bare back, letting her fingertips bump over his ribs, then back up the trail of his spine. She leaned up and kissed his bare shoulder, tasting his flesh with the tip of her tongue. Grazing him with her teeth, Marley pressed softly to feel the hardness of bone beneath his skin. Will moved from her breast back up to her throat as Marley drew back to study him in the dim light of the room.

"You have freckles," she murmured, planting a trail of kisses across his breastbone. "Tons of them."

"If you get bored with this, feel free to play connect-the-dots."

"Don't let me get bored," she said. "I have a Sharpie in my pocket, and I'm not afraid to use it."

"We'd better get rid of your pockets then," Will said, tucking his fingers into the waistband of her shorts.

He slid down her body, moving his mouth down to her naval. He dipped his tongue into it, then circled back up with a hot trail of kisses leading to her ribs. He started to move down again, gripping her waistband with both hands now. Marley raised her hips, inviting him to go ahead and disrobe her.

Will smiled and met her eyes. "This may be the wrong time to ask, but do you have any—"

"Condoms?"

"I was going to say Grey Poupon, but condoms would be handy, too."

Marley nodded. "Medicine cabinet in the guest bath. Should I go grab one?"

"Allow me," Will said, sliding off her. Marley's flesh screamed in frustration, craving his touch again. "I'll be fast."

"Not the best thing to say before sex," she called after him.

He laughed as she watched his bare back retreat, admiring the spray of freckles across his shoulders and the small tattoo of an hourglass between his shoulder blades. She'd have to ask him about that later. Much later. Right now, all she wanted was to kick off her shorts, dig her nails into Will's back, and—

Ding-dong!

Marley frowned and looked at her watch. It was after nine on a Sunday night. What the hell?

Ding-dong!

"Marley?" Will called from the hallway. "You want me to get the door?"

Marley frowned and reached for her T-shirt, not bothering with the bra. At this hour, it wasn't likely a salesman. Her dad wouldn't knock. Maybe she'd left the hose on and a neighbor was stopping by to let her know?

"I'll be right out," Marley called, tugging the shirt over her head. "Would you mind glancing out the window to see who it is?"

She heard the shuffling of feet in the hallway and pictured Will peering through the etched glass panel to the right of the door. He was quiet for a moment, and Marley stopped rustling clothing and listened.

"Will?" she called. "Is it a salesman?"

"That depends. Do salesmen usually kneel on the welcome mat when they're peddling rings?"

Marley leapt off the bed, her ankles tangling in her own discarded bra as she scrambled for the door with her gut clenched in a knot of dread.

Chapter 11

WILL STEPPED BACK AS MARLEY SKIDDED INTO THE foyer looking disheveled and frantic and so beautiful Will's throat ached. She tripped over the giant pink rabbit's leg, but caught herself before Will could reach for her. Her cheeks looked beard burned, and she'd pulled her T-shirt on backwards, but at least she was wearing one.

She definitely wasn't wearing a bra.

Will turned toward the bedroom to find his shirt, but changed his mind as Marley gripped the knob and yanked open the door.

"Curtis," she breathed. "What are you doing?"

The kneeling man blinked up at her, and Will resisted the urge to make a dozen smartass suggestions what a man might be doing on bended knee with a diamond ring in one outstretched hand. It was pretty damn obvious what Curtis was up to. The question was why.

"Marley," Curtis said, thrusting the ring at her in case she'd missed it. "I love you. I miss you. I traded up to get an extra half-carat for you. What do you say, Marley?"

"I think I'm going to throw up."

Judging from Curtis's expression, it wasn't the answer he'd hoped for. Will kinda felt for the guy. He reached out to offer him a hand up, but Curtis turned and frowned.

"Who are you?"

Will withdrew his hand and shrugged. "Bicycle repair guy?"

Curtis narrowed his eyes. "You work without a shirt?"

"It's an extra ten bucks if I work without pants."

Curtis turned back to Marley, effectively dismissing Will as irrelevant. Will couldn't really blame the guy. He stole a glimpse at Marley, who wore a mortified expression and a faint love bite just below her right earlobe.

She glanced at Will and two spots of color appeared on her cheeks.

"Um, so—" she began.

Both men waited, but apparently that was as far as Marley had gotten with her planned retort.

At the sound of toenails clicking across hardwood, Will turned to see Magoo trotting through the foyer with one ear flopped over his blue eye. Spotting the figure kneeling on the doorstep, Magoo put an extra spring in his step and bounded toward Curtis.

Will saw it happening even before Magoo hoisted himself onto Curtis's thigh and twitched his stub-tail with pleasure.

"Magoo, no!" Marley snapped, nudging her dog with her bare foot. "Stop it!"

Magoo began to gyrate, holding Curtis's leg in an amorous grip as his tongue lolled out the side of his mouth.

"Stop!" Marley hissed, nudging him harder this time.

Magoo quickened his rhythm.

Curtis frowned down at the shaggy animal with distaste. "What the—"

"Magoo!" Marley stooped down and grabbed her dog around the middle. She tried to pull him back, but Magoo clenched his front paws around Curtis's leg and gave a whimper of sexual frustration.

Will could relate.

"Let go, Magoo!" Marley leaned down further, squeezing her dog under one arm and prying his paws loose with her free hand. Her T-shirt rode up in back, making it obvious she hadn't bothered donning panties beneath her flimsy cotton shorts. Will forced himself not to stare as he took two big steps back.

"How about I give you three lovebirds a minute alone?" Will said. "I'll just head back out to the garage to, uh, tighten some bolts."

He retreated slowly, stealing one more glance over his shoulder before he reached the garage door. Curtis was still on one knee, and Marley held Magoo in a death grip with both hands. Magoo looked disappointed, while Marley wore the same frozen expression she'd had since opening the door.

Will stepped into the garage and hesitated, wanting to stay within earshot. Curtis certainly didn't look dangerous, though the size of that rock in the engagement ring could make it a formidable weapon if need be. The guy's intentions didn't seem malicious, but Will figured it was wise to stay within earshot.

That proved easier than expected. Though Marley's father's condo was clearly well-constructed, it was evident the builders had scrimped on doors. Either that, or the voices on the other side had risen to a level that permeated solid hickory.

Will heard the sound of a door closing, followed by a soft whimper suggesting Magoo had been locked in a bedroom. He leaned closer, listening for the sound of Marley's footsteps.

"Please get up, Curtis," she said. "I'd prefer to have this conversation with both of us upright."

"Marley, what's going on here?"

"We ended our engagement, Curtis. No offense, but what's going on here isn't your business."

"I think we made a mistake."

"What?"

"I want to give us another shot. I've been talking with your dad, and—"

"This isn't 1850," Marley said. "No modern woman wants a marriage proposal that contains the phrase, 'I've been talking with your dad.'"

"Just look at the ring. The stone is much larger, and if you look right here—"

"I don't want to look right there, Curtis. And I don't want a bigger ring. I just want to go our separate ways like we agreed."

"Marley, be reasonable."

Will shook his head in sympathy. Being married had taught him many things, not the least of which was never to argue using the phrase, *"Be reasonable."*

It was Curtis's turn to learn.

"Ouch, Marley! Cut it out!"

"You don't just show up on my doorstep after a month and start ordering me to be reasonable!"

"Marley, put down the stuffed animal. Why do you have that thing, anyway?"

"It was a *gift*."

"Ouch! Cut it out."

The beating must have subsided, because there was a momentary lapse of silence on the other side of the door. Will stepped closer, not wanting to miss anything.

"We were supposed to get married, Curtis. *Married*! And instead you threw me over for a corner office and granite counters in your kitchen. Who *does* that?"

"I'm sorry, Marley. You're right. Look, I've been think-ing about what you said before you left. About not putting jobs and possessions and material things before the other person. I think I get it now, and I have a proposal. Besides *the* proposal, I mean. And I want to take care of you."

"I want to take care of *myself*," she said.

"Come back to Portland. I'm making enough now that you won't have to work. I can get rid of my condo, and we can get a nice, smaller house in one of the suburbs. Beaverton, maybe. Or Tigard? Come on, Marley, what do you say?"

Marley didn't say anything. Not for a long time. Will frowned at the door, unnerved by the silence. Then he heard the thud of bare feet darting across the wood floor. He jumped back from the garage door, expecting her to come barreling out with a lecture on eavesdropping. Instead, he heard a door slam, and the distinct sound of Marley making good on her earlier promise to throw up.

Will frowned at the door, waiting to hear Curtis come to her rescue. He heard the thud of male footsteps crossing the foyer, followed by the sound of the other man's voice.

"Marley, if we could just sit down and discuss this like adults—"

Fuck this, Will muttered, and he pushed back through the garage door into the foyer. He headed straight for the kitchen, where he reached into the cupboard and pulled down two glasses. He filled one with tap water before pull-ing Marley's pitcher from the fridge and filling the other with blueberry iced tea.

"Excuse me!" Curtis yelled, stepping forward as Will approached the bathroom door. "We're trying to have an adult conversation here—"

"No you aren't," Will said calmly, moving around Curtis. "You're badgering her by calling her unreasonable and bullying her to do what you want, and she's trying to keep from getting puke in her hair. If that's an adult conversation, I'll stick with juvenile ones. Marley?" he called through the door. He didn't wait for a response. "I'm setting a glass of water and a glass of tea beside the door, and I'm going to escort your friend to his car now. If that's not okay, knock twice on the floor and shove your panties under the door."

There was a brief silence, and Will wondered for an instant if he'd overstepped. Then he heard a sound that was either a sob or a giggle. Maybe both.

"Thank you, Will." Her voice was faint, but not shaky.

Will turned and looked at Curtis. "Shall we?"

Curtis sneered. "You're a boy toy. Nothing more. Bicycle repairman? She'll have her fun with you and move on in a week. You're nothing serious."

"That's printed on my business cards. Ready for me to escort you to your car?"

Curtis shook his head and brushed past Will, deliberately bumping him with his shoulder. Will bit back the urge to bump him harder as he turned and followed the other man to the door.

"Have a nice drive," Will called cheerfully.

Curtis slammed the door, and Will flipped the lock behind him, pausing to wave as Curtis stomped toward his Mercedes. Curtis waved back, though only with one finger. Will shrugged it off, thinking it must be frustrating to go through life feeling threatened by the false bravado and obscene hand gestures of other men.

He returned to the hallway outside the bathroom, where

the two glasses on the floor had vanished. The door was closed, so Will knocked softly. "Marley? You okay?"

She didn't reply right away, and Will was torn between retreating to offer her privacy and breaking down the door to make sure she was all right. He was saved the trouble when Marley flipped the lock and opened the door.

"Hey," she said, giving him a faint smile. Her face was pale and a little greenish, and several wisps of hair were plastered against her cheeks.

But she still looked lovely, and Will fought the urge to take her in his arms.

Instead, he cleared his throat. "The next time you utter the phrase, 'I'm going to throw up,' remind me to take you seriously."

Marley laughed—a weak laugh, but still a laugh. "I never joke about vomit."

"Very wise. Bodily function humor is the lowest form of comedy."

"I thought that was puns."

"Puns about bodily functions are even lower. It's like hitting rock bottom and starting to dig."

"I'll try to remember that." Marley turned and picked up the glass of tea off the bathroom counter. She held it up in a mock toast before taking a sip. "Thanks for this." She took a bigger gulp. Lowering the glass, she wiped her mouth with the back of her hand. She smiled again, a little stronger this time. "This isn't really how I imagined the rest of this evening going."

"No? When I set out to seduce you, all I could think was *I sure hope we cap off this evening with a stomach flu and an unwelcome marriage proposal*."

"Probably not a stomach flu. That happens sometimes

when I get really uncomfortable. Or when I eat dairy. Maybe I put too much butter in the pasta."

"And you accused me of having a poor coping mechanism in awkward situations."

She took another sip of tea. "Point well made. Look, Will—"

"Say no more. You want to take your clothes off and pick up where we left off? I'll go grab the condoms."

She put a hand on his chest to stop him, even though he'd made no move to head anywhere. Then she looked at her palm pressed against his bare chest and did a funny little shudder. She drew her hand back, and Will felt the chilly absence of her heat.

"Very funny," she said, tucking her hand behind her back as though he'd burned it. "Under the circumstances, how about we call it a night?"

"Under the circumstances, I'm inclined to agree." He bent and kissed her lightly on the forehead. "Not that I don't find you irresistibly beautiful even after you've been praying to the porcelain gods."

"Thank you. I just—" Marley took a shuddery breath and one step back. "I know we keep agreeing it's a really dumb idea for us to get involved, and then somehow we end up groping each other anyway."

"Funny the way that works."

She smiled, but inched back another half-step. "Seriously, Will. I'm trying to move on with my life. In a different direction, I mean."

Will raised one eyebrow and tilted his head toward the door. "I can assure you I'm a different direction from a guy who believes an extra half-carat is the key to getting in your pants."

"Be that as it may, you're my supervisor and there are rules, and I can't afford to lose this job—"

Will pressed a finger to her lips, silencing her and giving him the urge to kiss her all at once. "I know," he said. "I get it. Dumb idea, unethical, complicated, probably illegal in several states. Don't worry about it. Won't happen again."

"Really?"

Will studied her eyes, not sure whether her tone was hopeful or disappointed. Maybe a little of both.

He nodded and took a step back. "From now on, I'm keeping my hands—and the rest of my body—completely off you."

Wise decision, his conscience insisted. *The last thing you need is another unpredictable female you can't trust.*

He watched her blink slowly, then swallow. Her expression was still unreadable, but Will thought he saw a flicker of hurt in her eyes.

"Good," Marley said. "Hands off. That's good."

Will shrugged. "Unless you beg me to do otherwise. Gotta leave the door open, right?"

Before she could say anything, he reached for the knob and yanked open the front door, stepping out into the cool night air with Marley staring dumbstruck after him.

The next morning, Marley woke to a pounding in her head.

At least she thought it was in her head. It took her a minute to realize it was the front door.

Remembering Will's comment about leaving the door open, Marley yanked on a robe and padded to the front of the condo, not sure whether to feel dread or delight at the prospect of seeing him again so soon. Magoo trotted along behind her, running his wet nose into the back of her bare calf as she stopped to check her hair in the hallway mirror.

She looked down at him. "Sorry, Magoo."

He licked her knee in response, thumping his tail on the floor in an excited drumbeat.

Marley turned back to her reflection, pleased to see her hair looked sexily sleep-tousled instead of like she'd stuck her head in a food processor.

She glanced through the window beside the door, and her pleasure faded a little. It wasn't Will on the doorstep. It wasn't Curtis either, so that was a plus.

She looked down at Magoo. "No humping. Got it?"

Magoo thumped his tail twice on the wood floor and licked Marley's knee.

Marley sighed and flung open the door to greet the bike mechanic she'd met the day before.

"Hey there," she said a little warily.

A slow, sexy smile spread across his face, and Marley's disappointment ebbed a little. He had broad shoulders, great arms, and the spread-legged stance of a man at ease in his own skin. He raised one hand, and for a moment Marley thought he was going to touch her cheek.

Instead, he pulled off his sunglasses to reveal what Marley felt fairly certain fit the textbook definition of "bedroom eyes." They were warm and brown and quite possibly capable of seeing right through her robe.

"Surprise," he said, gesturing behind him to reveal Marley's bicycle. "Turns out I had all the parts in stock. I worked late last night and got it all fixed up for you."

Magoo flopped down at Marley's feet and yawned, seemingly unimpressed.

"Wow," Marley said, reaching out to touch the gearshift. "I don't know what to say. Thank you so much, um—"

"Brian," he said and stuck out his hand. Marley took it, half expecting him to drop a kiss across her knuckles instead of shaking it.

"I'm Marley."

"I know. Your name and address were on the form." He smiled again, still holding her hand. "I know you said you didn't need to have the bike delivered, but I had some other deliveries to make in the neighborhood and I remembered how eager you were to get your hands on it."

"I… I was. Eager. To, um, get my hands on it."

Gawd, Marley, she thought, drawing her hand back at last. *Idiot.*

"Thank you," she said again, grateful she'd stashed April's loaner bike in the garage so it wasn't too obvious she'd already solved her bike dilemma. It was nice to have her own bike, and so quickly.

"I really appreciate this," she said. "What do I owe you for the rush charge and the delivery?"

He gave her a dismissive wave and grinned. "Happy to do it. No extra charge at all."

"Coffee?" she blurted, then hoped he didn't accept. She had to be at work in an hour, and she was still in her robe with several patches of flesh still flushed with Will's beard burn.

At the thought of Will, Marley felt her pulse kick up two notches. She pulled the robe tighter around her body and took a deep breath, pushing Will's face to the back of her brain.

"I'll take a rain check on the coffee," Brian said. "I have three other deliveries to make this morning."

"Of course, I understand. If you wouldn't mind propping it right there against the rail, I'll put it in the garage as soon as I'm dressed."

His eyes dropped to the opening of her robe, and he grinned. "Sorry about showing up so early," he said, not looking the least bit sorry. "I didn't want to miss you before you went to work, and I remembered you really wanted the bike quickly."

"No worries, I needed to be up anyway. Normally I'm up really early—like five or six—but yesterday was kind of a long day and then it was a *really* long night and—"

Stop talking, Marley. Stop talking.

Marley bit her lip and looked at Brian. He wore a plaid flannel shirt with grease on one sleeve and a concert T-shirt underneath. His abs were gym-chiseled beneath the cotton, and the stubble of his goatee looked deliberately manicured. He smiled and Marley couldn't help but notice his teeth looked professionally whitened.

He was definitely not Will. That was a good thing, right?

"Would you like to have dinner sometime?" Marley blurted. "My treat. I mean, as a thank you for fixing my bike so fast."

Brian laughed and ran his fingers through his sun-streaked brown hair. "And here I was trying to think of a good way to ask you out without seeming like a douche-nozzle who only fixes your bike to get a piece." He frowned. "Pardon my language."

"It's okay," Marley interjected, eager to cut him off so she could maintain her lust buzz. "So, dinner then?"

"That would be awesome. Anyplace in particular?"

"I'm new to town. What do you recommend for something casual, maybe a good happy hour or something?"

"Someplace downtown, maybe. 900 Wall has a killer happy hour from four to six. Are you free Friday night?"

"I can make that work."

Brian grinned. "How about I pick you up around five and we'll see how things unfold from there."

"It's a date," Marley said, wondering if it was. She studied Brian again, committing his positive qualities to memory. Manager of a bike shop, athletic, nice smile, bike grease on his knuckles—

"So I'll see you later," he said, putting his sunglasses back on and giving her a wicked grin. He stooped down to scratch Magoo behind the ears. "You too, doggie."

Magoo sniffed Brian's hand and gave it a tentative lick. Then he put his head back down on Marley's bare foot.

Marley watched Brian amble off down her driveway, his practiced swagger showcasing a bike-toned backside. "Thanks again for the rush job on the bike," she called.

"No worries," he called back as he popped open the door on an aging van with the bike shop logo on the side. He turned and winked. "Catch you later."

Marley closed the door and stood there for a moment not moving. It was partly that she didn't have the heart to nudge Magoo's head off her foot, but she also needed a moment to digest things. Had she really just asked Brian out? Was that really a good idea?

"Yes," she told herself.

Magoo lifted his head and pricked one floppy ear.

"Come on, Magoo. Time to take a shower."

Magoo sighed and heaved himself up off the floor. Marley turned and ambled down the hall with Magoo trotting obediently behind her.

When she reached the master bath, she dropped her robe

on the floor. Magoo promptly curled up on it, yawning as he maneuvered his body into the shape of a lumpy donut.

Marley studied her body in the mirror, turning from side to side for a better view. There was no physical evidence of her wild romp with Will. The beard burn had mostly faded, and there were no lasting love bites, no handprints anywhere on her skin.

A good thing, right?

So why could she still feel him everywhere?

With a sigh, Marley turned and twisted the taps off the shower, determined to scrub Will out of her mind and off her body.

"Will is not the man for you," she said out loud, adjusting the water pressure to fine needles of spray.

"No more rich boys," she added. "No supervisors thinly disguised as father figures. No guys with stupid trust issues. Just a nice, normal man for once."

Like Brian.

She smiled at the thought. Brian with his nice smile and grease-flecked knuckles and floppy brown hair. Brian with his bedroom eyes and blue-collar job. She lathered her hair, rinsing and conditioning and scrubbing as she thought about her upcoming date with him.

It was totally worth shaving her legs.

"A good guy," she said aloud with a final flick of her razor. "A normal guy. That's what you need."

"Marley?"

She jumped at the sound of her dad's voice on the other side of the door. His knuckles rapped the wood, and Marley jumped again, banging her knee on the tile soap dish.

"You okay in there?" her father called. "I thought I heard you talking to someone."

Marley sighed and dropped her razor in the soap dish, dipping her leg in the spray for a final rinse. She twisted the tap off with one hand and reached for a towel with the other.

"I'm fine, Dad," she yelled back, dragging the terrycloth over her damp skin. "Just talking to myself. A career pep talk, you know?"

There was a long pause. "Where's Curtis?"

Marley rolled her eyes and wrapped the towel around her head turban-style. She tugged her robe out from under Magoo's body, ignoring her dog's grunt of protest. Pulling the robe on, she belted it around her waist before yanking open the bathroom door.

"Welcome back, Dad. How was your trip?"

"Fine, fine," he said, looking over Marley's head to the interior of the bathroom.

Marley sighed. "Curtis isn't here. Did you put him up to that stupid stunt with the ring?"

Her father's eyes snapped back to her face, and he gave his best look of fake surprise. "Curtis gave you a new ring?"

Marley rolled her eyes. "You know he gave me a new ring. Or at least tried to. I wasn't interested. Not then, not now. It's over between us."

"Maybe if you just give him a chance—"

"I gave him a chance," she interrupted. "I gave him plenty of chances, before I realized he just isn't the right guy for me. Come on, Dad. You of all people should realize what a bad idea it is to marry the wrong person."

Her father sighed. "I just want you happy, Marley. And safe. And well cared for."

"I want those things too. I just don't think I need a man with money to give them to me."

"Fair enough. But if you change your mind, Curtis is still in town. He's staying in the condo over in the Old Mill District."

"I'm not changing my mind. I mean it." Marley cinched her robe tighter around her waist. "Was there something else you needed?"

He nodded and leaned against the door frame. "Just letting you know there's a plumber stopping by in about ten minutes to fix that leak in the kitchen sink."

"A plumber?"

Walter frowned. "Don't get any ideas, Marley. I know you're on this quest to date blue-collar men, but really—"

"I promise not to pounce on the plumber, Dad." She grinned. "Or walk naked through the kitchen pretending I can't find my robe. Or seduce him by asking him to snake my pipes. Or—"

"That's enough." He smiled and shook his head. "What am I going to do with you?"

"You're going to promise not to harass my date when he shows up Friday night."

"Date? It's not with that delivery guy who brought the rabbit, is it?"

Marley sighed. "Not that it's any of your business, but no. I'm going out with a guy who runs a brothel."

"A brothel?"

"It's actually a bike shop. But I thought if I started a little lower on the spectrum, your disdain wouldn't be so pronounced."

Walter folded his arms over his chest. "Marley, I don't know what you're trying to prove with this quest to date low-class men."

"Low-class? What is it with the men in my life suddenly

sounding like Southern gentleman from 1850? You and Curtis could do a historical reenactment."

"Just be careful, Marley. Take things slowly, okay?"

"I will, I promise. Can you throw me that dress over there?"

"If it will prevent you from greeting the plumber naked, then yes."

Her dad turned and grabbed the purple sweater dress off the corner of the dresser. Marley reached for the garment just as she noticed what lurked beneath it. Her father spotted the wallet at the same time she did and picked it up. He looked at Marley and raised one eyebrow.

"Carrying a man's wallet now?"

Marley grimaced. It was definitely a man's wallet, and she was pretty sure she knew whose. The duct tape was a dead giveaway.

"Yes," Marley said, stretching to grab it from him. "Men's wallets are the hot new female accessory of the season."

Her dad nodded at a spot behind the door. "Men's underwear, too?"

Marley started to grimace again, then stopped herself. "Nice try, Dad. He didn't take his underwear off last night."

Her father folded his arms over his chest. "*He*? I thought the wallet was yours. So much for taking things slowly."

"Good-bye, Dad. I have to get ready for work."

He shook his head. "You're the worst liar in the world, Marley."

Marley bit her lip. *Maybe not the worst liar...*

"See you later, Dad."

"Have a good day at work," her dad said, turning away. "Will I see you afterward?"

She shook her head. "I'm heading out with the realtor to

see a few more properties. With any luck, I'll have a new place lined up by the end of the week."

"You know you can stay here as long as you want."

"I know," she said. "But what I want is to move on."

"Fair enough," he said, and closed the door behind him.

———◦◦◦———

Will was in the middle of prying the *William Barclay V* plaque off the bench in the lobby at Cheez Whiz when his sister came flouncing by.

"Destroying furniture again?" she asked, picking up his screwdriver off the end of the bench.

"You say destroying, I say improving," he said.

"Potato, po-tah-toe," she parroted. "Nice hickey on the side of your neck, by the way."

Will reached up and touched the side of his throat, conscious of Bethany's eyes on him. "Where?"

"Nowhere. I just wanted to know if there's the possibility you *could* have a hickey so I have some idea where things stand with you and Marley."

Will dropped his hand and grabbed the screwdriver from his sister. "We're friends," he said, pleased with the certainty in his own voice.

"Sure, whatever you say." Bethany plopped down on the bench and reached out to catch the first screw as Will dropped it. Will caught sight of the small hourglass tattoo on her wrist and felt a sharp twist in his chest. He and Bethany had gotten the matching design years ago to honor their mom, whose favorite soap opera was *Days of Our Lives*. They'd watched it together when Will was small, curled on his mother's lap with Bethany snuggled beside them in her favorite green afghan and a bowl of fresh blueberries tucked between them in a chipped orange bowl.

Like sands through the hourglass…

They'd gotten the ink long after their mother died, but before April had come into their lives. Before everything went to hell and—

"Nice screw." Bethany held it up, turning it from side to side as though admiring the threads. "Speaking of screws, is Marley going to be ordering anything from the Pure Romance catalog?"

"We weren't speaking of screws," he said, grabbing it back from her and tucking it in his pocket. "On the list of conversation topics brothers and sisters should discuss, screws don't even make the top one hundred."

"Party pooper."

"Based on the parties you host, I'm okay with that."

Bethany grinned, the smugness in her expression an indication she knew damn well he wasn't really annoyed. That was the problem with siblings, Will mused. They know you better than anyone has a right to.

"Right," Bethany said. "So which stuff did Marley seem to like best in the catalog?"

"I wouldn't know."

"Of course you would. I know you, Will. There's no way you could resist the urge to use full-color glossy photos of sex toys as a seduction tool. Let me guess—you made your move somewhere between the g-spot vibrators and the anal beads?"

"I'm going to pretend my sister didn't just say the words *anal beads* to me."

"G-spot it is," Bethany said, reaching out to catch the next screw as it fell. "Aunt Nancy spent thirty minutes last night trying to lecture the partygoers on the history of Native American phallic devices. She's seriously obsessed with those stupid figurines."

"How is that new?"

"Don't you think she's gotten worse since she donated them?"

Will shrugged. "Maybe." He hesitated, thinking about the text he'd seen last night on Marley's phone. What if the figurines weren't real? Aunt Nancy had pinned all her hopes on leaving them as her legacy. If something went wrong—

Bethany nudged him with her toe. "For the record, the sexual tension between you and Marley last night was so thick I could use it to bludgeon someone to death."

"This from a woman who was too intoxicated to stand upright."

"Please. I could have been deaf, blind, drunk, and standing on my head with my knee in my armpit and I still would have picked up on the vibes. Speaking of vibes, if Marley wants to order anything—"

"If Marley wants anything, she'll call you herself."

"If Marley wants what?"

Will jumped at the sound of her voice, dropping the last screw from the plaque. He watched it bounce across the slate floor, then spin in a lazy circle near the toe of Marley's high-heeled shoe. He stared for a moment—not at the screw, but at the glorious expanse of leg stretching from the curve of her ankle all the way to the bottom of her toned thigh where it disappeared under her skirt and—

"Need this screw?" she asked.

"What?"

Marley rolled her eyes and bent down to pick it up. Will

caught a glimpse down the front of her blouse and looked away, only to catch sight of Bethany laughing behind her hand. He frowned at his sister and she straightened up, making a visible effort to be an adult.

Bethany drew her hand back and cleared her throat. "We were just talking about last night's party," she said to Marley. "If you want anything from the Pure Romance catalog, give me a shout. The consultant asked me to have all the orders in by tomorrow evening, but we can always submit orders late if you need more time."

"Thank you," Marley said, glancing at Will with a bemused expression. "I did see a few things that caught my interest. Do you know if most of the products come with batteries?"

"Everything comes with batteries," she said, grinning at Will. "So to speak."

Will didn't want to meet Marley's eyes, so he looked down at the bench and began to smooth the wood around the edges of the screw holes. Then he stopped, thinking *wood* and *screw holes* weren't the words he wanted pulsing around in his brain at the moment.

"I'll take a look at the order form on my lunch break and fill it in," Marley said. "So to speak."

"Christ, you two," Will said, shoving the screwdriver in his back pocket so he wouldn't be tempted to gouge out his own eyes. "You've known each other four days and you're already sharing tasteless innuendos and sex toy orders?"

Bethany pretended to look thoughtful. "You think that's better for day five?"

"Day two always seems like the right time for me," Marley said. "That way you know right off the bat if you're going to spend the duration of the friendship apologizing for offending someone."

"I like how you think," Bethany said, then turned to Will. "You know, if we were men, you wouldn't think twice about the fact that we're bonding over crude humor."

"If you were men, you wouldn't be my sister, and this wouldn't be quite so weird," he said.

"So does Pure Romance take credit cards?" Marley asked, and Will looked back at her, pleased to be distracted from the conversation with his sister. "Because I've got this great new wallet, and I'm betting there's a card or two I could use."

She reached into her purse and pulled out an oblong leather wallet marked with two grungy strips of duct tape. Will tried not to let the surprise show on his face as she smiled at him.

"I believe this belongs to you?" she said.

He reached out to take it, deliberately letting his fingers linger an extra moment so he could savor the electric tingle he felt when he touched her. "Thanks. I didn't even notice I'd lost it."

"Spoken like a man who never has to think twice about money," Bethany said, and Will shot her a dirty look.

"Weren't you leaving?" he asked.

"Actually, no. I kinda want to hear how Marley ended up with your wallet."

Marley laughed. "Nothing terribly illicit, I'm afraid," she said, lying so effortlessly it made Will's gut ache. "You must have taken it out of your pocket in the garage when you were working on my bike rack?"

"I'm going to have to remember that," Bethany said. "'Working-on-my-bike-rack' is an excellent euphemism."

Will gave her another look, and Bethany laughed. "Okay, okay… that's my cue to leave. Marley, shoot me a message anytime about the order. Will, call me later about dinner at Aunt Nancy's?"

"Sure."

Bethany wandered off, leaving Will alone with Marley. Well, alone in the Cheez Whiz lobby with several dozen visitors and several birds of prey within a hundred-foot radius.

"Thanks for bringing the wallet by," he said.

"Actually, I didn't realize I'd see you here today. I just put it in my purse so my father wouldn't be tempted to go through it in an effort to assess your net worth."

"If he's judging my net worth by the contents of my wallet, I'm valued at two dollars, a Blockbuster card, and a coupon for a free Egg McMuffin."

"And no condom," she said. "I think we got off easy there."

"We didn't get off at all, if I remember right." Will grinned. "Then again, things got fuzzy after your fiancé showed up."

"*Ex*-fiancé," Marley pointed out. She frowned. "Have you noticed how frequently you and I end up being defined by our exes?"

"How do you mean?"

Marley shrugged. "Everyone wants to refer to Curtis as my fiancé instead of my e*x*-fiancé—including him, I guess. And my father. And the nature of your divorce means you're pretty much resigned to spending the rest of your life attending family gatherings with your ex-wife."

"There's a pleasant thought."

Marley shrugged. "Doesn't make it easy for either of us to break free from past relationships and patterns."

"Is this conversation going to get less depressing at some point?"

Marley smiled. "How about if I tell you my father was the one who found your wallet?"

"Wonderful."

"Incidentally, he's not a fan of me dating the delivery guy."

"We're not dating, and I'm not a delivery guy. You've pleased your father already."

"All in a day's work." Marley rubbed her lips together. It was probably just an effort to evenly distribute her lipstick, but Will couldn't stop thinking about the way her lips had felt pressed against his. About the feel of them trailing across his neck when she—

"So I have a date on Friday with the guy from the bike shop," she blurted.

Will frowned. "The Plaid Neanderthal?"

"What?"

"Nothing." He cleared his throat, not sure why he was surprised. He knew the second the bike guy had asked for her phone number and address that he was plotting to do more than paperwork. Will didn't like to think about that.

"I also have a date with a plumber," Marley said. "Wednesday after work."

Will nodded, trying to keep his expression impassive. "Don't let him sell you any faulty ballcocks."

"What?"

"The ballcock is the mechanism in your toilet tank that keeps water levels normal. If you'd like, I can also make jokes about hardness leakage, discharge heads, and cockhole covers. All plumbing terms that sound filthy but aren't."

"Maybe I should write these down so I have something to talk about on my date."

"Maybe you should stick with discussing sports teams

and favorite restaurants," Will said. "Just be sure you check his wallet first to be sure he doesn't have more than twenty bucks to his name."

Marley sighed. "I'm not the first woman to take money into account when dating someone, Will."

"Of course not," he said. "Shallow hang-ups about money are a universal issue."

She nodded at the screwdriver in his hand. "Says the guy who just pried his own name off a bench so he can keep up the pretense of not having much."

"Touché," Will said, flipping it into the air and catching it before tucking it into his back pocket. "For the record, this is no one's business but mine. It has nothing to do with getting dates or choosing someone to knock boots with."

"And that makes it better?"

"It makes it *different*," Will said, not entirely sure what point he was trying to make. He only knew he didn't want Marley to leave. Not yet. "When it comes to relationships, though, money is always the hang-up."

"You think?"

Will shrugged. "Why did your fiancé—*ex*-fiancé—stay behind in Portland instead of moving here with you?"

"His job."

"Money. A bigger paycheck and a real estate transaction. It all comes down to that."

"Okay, wise guy," Marley said, folding her arms over her chest. "How do we attribute your divorce to money? And don't make a crude lesbian joke using a *coin purse* euphemism."

He laughed, surprising himself with the sudden burst of it. "Why Marley, I had no idea you had such hidden depths of depraved humor."

"There's plenty more you don't know about me," she said, turning away.

He waited until she was out of earshot to mutter the words under his breath.

"That's what I'm afraid of."

Chapter 12

MARLEY TOOK TWO STEPS INTO HER OFFICE AND INSTANTLY fought the urge to take four steps back out the door.

"Marley!"

Susan's voice was urgent, probably because she recognized Marley's urge to flee. The CHSWS director stood and beamed stiffly at Marley, catching her by the arm in what was either a familiar greeting or a means of escape prevention.

"Just the woman we've been waiting for," Susan gushed. "You've met Nancy Thomas-Smith?"

"We just met last night," Marley said, pasting her own donor relations smile in place and taking a step toward the older woman. "So wonderful to see you again, Ms. Thomas-Smith."

Aunt Nancy nodded from her seat in the corner of Marley's office. "I trust you enjoyed the penis party?"

Marley didn't let her smile falter, despite Susan's grimace. "I only regret I couldn't stay more than three minutes," Marley said. "I hope you had a lovely time though."

"Hmph," the old woman grunted. "Let's cut to the chase. I'm a renowned sex therapist with three bestselling books. The fact that these figurines are from my personal collection makes them particularly valuable and highly sought-after by museums around the country. I can't wait around forever for the appraisal, and we need to start moving forward with plans for the traveling exhibit."

"Of course," Marley said. "We're eager as well."

"We've already had a number of inquiries from other museums expressing interest in the figurines if they're part of a large traveling exhibit," Susan said. "If we opt for one-month installments, we should be able to book at least eleven shows a year at different locations. If we go with the forty-thousand-dollar fee we discussed, that's quite a revenue source for the Cascade Historical Society and Wildlife Sanctuary."

"Cheez Whiz," Marley murmured.

"What's that, dear?" Susan asked.

"Nothing." Marley cleared her throat. "We're as excited as you are about the exhibit, Ms. Thomas-Smith. And I know you'd like to see things move forward. But we can't proceed without the formal appraisal."

"And that's scheduled for next Thursday, Marley?" Susan looked hopeful.

"Yes, with one of the foremost experts in the country."

"Hmph," Nancy said. "I'm traveling to New York next Tuesday to meet with my accountant and my attorney. Getting my affairs in order, you understand. Isn't there some way we can hurry this along?"

Susan folded her hands in her lap and turned to Marley. "Marley, you mentioned a few days ago that you have a cousin with some expertise in the area who might be able to give an informal assessment of the value of the figurines. Did she happen to give you any sort of impression of what the pieces are worth?"

Marley clenched her fingers. "Nothing concrete. I really think if we just wait until the formal appraisal is complete, we'll be able to offer a very accurate picture of what the figurines are worth."

Or not worth, Marley thought grimly.

Aunt Nancy sighed. "In that case, I'd like some photographs, please."

"Of course," Susan said. "Just let me put on some lipstick and—"

"Not photographs of *you,*" Nancy snapped. "Photos of the art."

"Certainly," Marley said. "If you'd like, I can have a photographer out here this afternoon to capture some professional images that should meet your need for tax or insurance purposes."

"That won't be necessary," Nancy said. "I've got an iPhone. Doesn't need to be anything snazzy."

"But for tax purposes—"

"This is just for personal use," Nancy interrupted. "The figurines have been in my family for more than fifty years, and they're extremely valuable. I entrusted them to the Cascade Historical Society and Wildlife Sanctuary with the understanding they'd become part of a popular exhibit, but if that's not going to happen expediently—"

"It's going to happen," Marley said, standing up so fast her chair nearly tipped. "It's going to happen very soon, and we're just as excited about it as you are. We just need to make sure the appraisal is done properly."

"Marley, why don't we escort Ms. Thomas-Smith to the safe and let her take the photographs she needs," Susan said. "It's the least we can do in light of such a generous and valuable donation."

"Of course," Marley said. "If you'd like to come with me, I'd be happy to take you to the safe for a look at your… um… at the *figurines.*"

She reached down to offer the older woman a hand up,

but Nancy ignored her, hefting herself out of the seat and onto her feet. Susan stood too, beaming at Marley with a look that said, *Please don't blow this.*

"Follow me," Marley said cheerfully, reaching into her purse for the keys to the safe. She led the little procession through the administrative lobby, down a hall, and into the back room. She fumbled with the keys as Susan and Nancy stood to one side waiting.

"We've all been very excited about the prospect of featuring your figurines as part of a traveling exhibit," Susan prattled. "We've been researching, and while there are many exhibits featuring Native American artifacts, and a number of exhibits featuring Old West erotic artifacts like items from brothels, no one has ever created an exhibit of the sort we'll be able to display with your pieces, Ms. Thomas-Smith."

"Absolutely," Marley said, crossing her fingers that this whole thing didn't blow up in their faces once the appraisal came through. "Our tentative plans would be to keep the figurines on the road for eleven months of the year, and with the revenue generated from the traveling exhibit, create a new wing here at CHSWS devoted to the arts, with a special emphasis on Native American artifacts."

"The Nancy Thomas-Smith Wing," Susan supplied.

"Nancy *Ursula* Thomas-Smith," Nancy added. "The Nancy Ursula Thomas-Smith Arts Center."

Marley bit her lip. "We may want to think twice about making that into an acronym."

Nancy frowned at her. "What's that, dear?"

"Nothing," Susan said quickly. "Marley, do you know how to work the lock?"

"Absolutely," she said, inserting the key into the safe

and turning it. "I was just here the other day showing the pieces to my cousin."

She twisted the handle and popped open the door, allowing light to flood into the small, enclosed space.

For a moment, no one said anything. Marley stood blinking in the cool air, her eyes adjusting to the dimness of the safe's interior and what she saw inside.

Or rather, what she *didn't* see.

It was Susan who spoke first, her stiff smile making her words tight and difficult to understand. "Marley? Did you… um, did you relocate the figurines?"

Marley blinked. She had a brief, panicky thought that if she just closed the door and opened it again, the figurines would reappear. *Poof!* Just like a magic trick.

But magic wasn't going to save her here. Where the hell were the figurines? Her brain clawed for some reasonable explanation.

She turned to face the other two women, trying to keep her panic from showing. She looked at Susan, who pressed her lips together. Then Susan turned to Nancy and smiled.

"I just remembered!" Susan said brightly. "We sent the figurines out to be professionally cleaned. Weren't the cleaners picking them up this morning, Marley?"

Marley blinked, too stunned to respond. *Oh, Christ. Not again.*

Nancy looked at her, and Marley forced her expression into a stiff smile. Forced her mouth to form the words.

"Of course!" Marley said. "The cleaning service. It completely slipped my mind."

Susan nodded and put a hand on Nancy's arm. "I'm so sorry we forgot to inform you, but I'm sure you'll agree it's important to have the figurines looking as polished and perfect as possible for the appraisal."

Nancy frowned. "I suppose."

"It's a crucial part of the process," Marley babbled, wishing like hell she could just crawl into the safe and hide for the rest of the day. Or the rest of the year, depending on how this whole thing shook out.

The old woman was still nodding as she stared into the safe's interior. Marley watched, wondering if she was suspicious, annoyed, or completely convinced of their story.

Not again, not again, Marley's brain chanted, throbbing to the rhythm of the words.

Marley looked at Susan, whose expression was blessedly impassable. Marley turned to Nancy. "I'll call the cleaning service and find out when we'll get the figurines back. And after that, we'll make sure you have some lovely, professional-caliber photographs to cherish for personal use, or to utilize for all your accounting purposes."

"Absolutely," Susan agreed, nodding so hard Marley thought the woman's head might fall off.

Nancy shrugged. "Fine. I suppose that will do."

"I'm sure the figurines will look just *lovely* once they're polished, don't you agree?" Marley said.

"Lovely," Nancy repeated, her tone suggesting the faintest hint of sarcasm. "I have an appointment to get to across town. I'm meeting with a group at the college to discuss my research on foot size and penile length. Would one of you please walk me back to the lobby now?"

"Allow me," Susan said, taking the older woman's arm. "Marley will just stay here to lock up, and I'll show you the way."

"It was wonderful seeing you again, Ms. Thomas-Smith,"

Marley called, projecting an enthusiasm she didn't really feel. "I look forward to working with you again very soon."

"Likewise," Nancy called, and headed out the door with Susan trotting beside her like a nervous mother.

For a moment, Marley just stood there in the storage room listening to the tick of her watch. When she started to feel dizzy, she realized she was holding her breath.

She let it out in a whoosh, wondering what the hell was going on. Where the hell were the figurines? Who could have moved them, and why?

Marley was still standing with the safe gaping open behind her and her arms hanging limply at her sides when Susan scurried back in.

"Oh, God, Marley. What's going on here?"

"I have no idea." She bit her lip. "I take it the figurines aren't really being cleaned?"

"I was just covering."

"That's what I was afraid of."

Not the only thing.

Marley looked back into the safe once more, in case the figurines had magically appeared.

Still empty.

"I have no idea what's going on," Marley said slowly. "I brought my cousin, Kayley, here last Friday to give me her gut impression about the value of the pieces. That was around three in the afternoon. I haven't been in here since."

Susan bit her lip and nodded. "I came in yesterday afternoon to look at the new piece Bethany Barclay brought us the other day."

The tension in Marley's shoulders eased just the tiniest bit.

I wasn't the last one in here. It could be much worse.

"So you have a key, and I have a key. Who else has one?"

"The head of security. Have you met Jimmy yet?"

Marley shook her head, and Susan continued.

"We'll have to introduce you soon. Besides the three of us, there's the checkout copy that's kept at the front desk in Administration."

"Checkout copy?"

"Yes. It's for the curators. They sometimes need access, so they can sign out a key and leave their badges as collateral. We've been doing it that way for years."

"Can we look at the checkout sheet?"

Susan nodded, and Marley closed the door on the safe, careful to lock it tightly.

For all the good it does.

Both of them took off at a quick clip, but Susan put her hand on Marley's arm to stop her. "Wait—slow down."

"Why?" Marley asked.

"We don't want to alarm anyone. Right now, we're the only two who have any idea the figurines are missing."

"You don't think Nancy suspects?"

Susan shook her head. "I think she bought the story about the cleaning. So until we know what's going on, let's try to keep this quiet."

Marley hesitated, then nodded. "You're the boss."

Susan turned and strode out the door. Marley followed right behind her, concentrating on keeping her expression neutral. She wished she could come up with some casual line of conversation to initiate with Susan so they looked more like two colleagues out for a stroll than two panicked women who'd just lost a valuable donation.

"Did you hear one of the porcupines is pregnant?" Susan blurted as they passed the grant writer's desk.

"What?" Marley asked.

"Pokey," Susan said. "She's pregnant again."

"Wow. I didn't realize she was in a relationship."

"Yes, well, she and Spike have had three pups in the last four years, so they've been very good breeders for our program."

"She's done such a nice job keeping her figure." Marley swallowed as her mind scurried into dark corners in search of ways to keep the casual conversation going. "I read recently that baby porcupines are known as porcupettes. They're born with soft quills that get hard within hours and…"

Marley stopped talking, partly because she was thinking about Will, and partly because they'd reached the front desk.

"Thank God, Anna must be in the restroom," Susan murmured. "Look casual and smile. I'll just take a quick glance at the sign-out sheet."

Marley nodded and leaned against the counter, projecting her best look of innocence. There were plenty of employees milling about, but no reason for anyone to be suspicious about two upper-level administrators consulting a notebook at the front desk.

"See anything?" Marley asked under her breath as the older woman flipped open a green notebook.

Susan ran a finger down the page. "Darin Temple was in the storage room yesterday at four p.m. to grab an antique papoose for the display in the west hall, but that would have been a different safe."

"Does the key ring give him access to all of them?"

Susan frowned. "I suppose so. We can at least ask him if he saw anything."

"I wasn't suggesting Darin stole the figurines," Marley said quickly as the two of them turned and retreated to Marley's office. "Or even that the figurines are *stolen*. If anyone really had evil intentions, they wouldn't sign the key out in the first place."

"Of course, you're right. I'll talk to Darin today and see if he noticed anything amiss."

Marley pushed her office door shut, but kept her voice low anyway. "What about the security guy—Jim?"

"Jimmy, yes. I don't want to alert him just yet. There may be nothing at all to worry about."

"Nothing at all," Marley repeated, willing it to be true.

"For now, we keep this quiet. At least until we get more information. We don't want to alarm anyone unnecessarily."

Marley nodded, wondering how long Susan planned to keep the secret. A few hours? A few days? Longer?

She swallowed and glanced toward the door. "I don't want to point out the obvious, but you know the pieces aren't insured, right?" Marley said. "We can't insure them without an appraisal, and without insurance—"

"Don't panic," Susan said, her voice belying an inability to follow her own instructions. "We'll figure this out. In the meantime, we don't want to alarm any employees or donors or, God forbid, not a word to the family members."

A cold shiver chattered up Marley's spine, even though her space heater kept the room at near tropical temperatures. *Will,* she thought. *Will and his stupid trust issues would have a heyday with this one.*

"No family members," Marley repeated. "Okay."

—⁂—

Will kicked his toe through a pile of orange and red leaves as he hurled a soggy tennis ball for Rosco. The dog scrambled after it, skidding to a halt in a cloud of flying leaves and bark chips at the base of a tall ponderosa.

"Good boy, Rosco!" Bethany shouted, clapping her hands as Polly danced around April's heels.

Will stooped to pick up the ball again as Rosco dropped it at his feet. "You don't think there's something a little dysfunctional about going for a walk in the park with my sister, my ex-wife, and my dogs?"

"Shut up, Will," Bethany said, stooping to scratch Polly's ears. The dog gave a cursory tail wag before sprinting off to chase a chipmunk. "This is our time to get to see our niece and nephews. Don't ruin it for us."

Will grinned. "The fact that you refer to my dogs as your niece and nephews? Also a sign of dysfunction, in case you're wondering."

"I wasn't wondering. Were you wondering, April?"

"It's such a lovely day, isn't it?" April said, stooping to pick a sprig of lavender off a shrub beside the walking path. "I adore autumn afternoons like this when the weather's so crisp and cool, but it's still sunny."

Bethany kicked her hiking boot through a pile of leaves and Will felt a pang of fondness for his sister. In spite of everything they'd been through with their parents and Aunt Nancy and April, Will still considered her one of his best friends.

She grabbed his arm, and for a second Will thought it was a sign of mutual fondness. Then she pointed one of her purple-gloved fingers toward a bank of large pine trees. "Is that Marley over there?"

Will felt his whole body lurch pleasantly at the sound

of Marley's name, and it took him a moment to shake the feeling. He looked the direction Bethany was pointing and felt another surge of longing.

Beside him, April smiled. "It sure looks like Marley with that beautiful blond hair and that trim figure. Such a lovely girl."

Will stopped walking and stared, still breathless at the sight of her. He'd spent the last two days trying to avoid her, tending to volunteer duties that kept him away from Cheez Whiz and away from the temptation of *her*.

They'd been right to avoid romantic entanglement, he was sure of it. The last thing he needed in his life right now was a woman with a romantic agenda angled the opposite direction of who he was. A woman with text-messaged secrets and unclear motives and a habit of bending who she was to please the people around her.

You don't need that, he told himself, willing his brain to buy it.

But as he looked at her now across the sprawling park, it was hard to remember. She wore rainbow-patterned mittens and a matching scarf over a fall parka in a shade of green Will knew would bring out the color in her hazel eyes. Her hair fluttered behind her in bright threads of gold, and he could swear he smelled blueberries in the breeze.

His breath caught in his throat, and he fought the urge to sprint for her.

"Who's that guy she's with?" Bethany asked.

April cupped a hand over her eyes to shield against the sun's glare. "And what's that thing she's holding?"

Will was aware of a strange buzz in the back of his brain, the sign that he was losing it once and for all. That the women in his life had driven him to the brink of insanity, where he heard voices in his head and buzzing in his skull and had the faint urge to climb Pilot Butte naked, cover his body in peanut butter, and roll down the side of the cinder cone.

"Earth to Will," Bethany said, jabbing him in the ribs with her elbow.

Will started walking again, his eyes still on Marley. "It's a remote-controlled airplane," he said, relieved to realize the buzzing was coming from the sky and not his skull. "Marley's date is flying it."

The word *date* tasted bitter on his tongue, and Will stared at the man, wondering whether he was the plumber or someone else Marley had decided to go out with. He sized the man up, hating the clench of jealousy in his gut, hating the way the guy's hand lingered on Marley's as he handed the remote control to her.

"Come on," Bethany said, grabbing April by one arm and Will by the other. "Let's stop standing here staring like morons and go say hello."

"I kinda preferred being a moron," Will said, but allowed his sister to tow him toward Marley.

The dogs scampered along beside them, thrilled to be heading off on a new adventure. Rosco dropped his tennis ball and picked up a pinecone, prancing like he'd just discovered the holy grail. Polly scooped up the abandoned ball and bounded ahead before turning back to check on Omar.

"She's such a good girl," April said.

"What?" Will asked, his eyes still fixed on Marley.

"Polly. Your dog? I love how she's always looking out for Omar," April said. "Like she knows he can't hear, so she wants to make sure he doesn't wander off. Such a lovely gesture."

Will nodded, barely hearing her. They were ten feet from Marley now, and Will could see her gloved thumbs working the remote control in her hand.

"Like this?" she asked, blinking up at the burly man beside her in an orange parka.

The man grinned and nodded. "You're doing great. Good call picking the SkyScout. It's a great little plane, isn't it?"

"I love it!" Marley said, her face upturned to watch the small aircraft arc across the sky.

"Hey, guys!" Bethany called. Marley turned at the sound of her voice, her face registering surprise as she spotted Bethany, then April, then Will.

Her eyes lingered longest on Will, and he couldn't help feeling glad about that.

He also couldn't help noticing Marley's date register that detail.

"Watch out!" he said, pulling the remote control out of Marley's hands. "You're going to hit the tree with it."

"What? Oh... sorry about that." Marley looked at the man's hands for a moment as he worked the controls on the plane. Then she turned back to Will. "Josh, I'd like you to meet Bethany, April, and Will Barclay. Guys, this is Josh Johnson."

"Josh Johnson the plumber?" Bethany said. "I see your ads all over town."

"That's me," Josh said proudly, smiling at Bethany before turning his attention back to the model airplane. "I'm also president of the Deschutes Oregon Radio Control Society."

"DORCS," Will said slowly, sounding out the acronym. Josh glared, then looked back at the sky, dismissing Will as insignificant.

Will didn't blame the guy.

Bethany shot Will a warning look before flashing Josh a peacemaker smile. "Cool plane," she said.

"So lovely," April exclaimed, beaming up at the sky.

"Marley thought so, too," Josh said, looking fondly at Marley. "Never met a woman so fascinated by small-scale aviation, but when I told her about this, she was really into it."

Will raised an eyebrow at Marley, who refused to meet his eyes. Or maybe she really was fascinated by remote-controlled airplanes since her gaze was fixed heavenward. He watched her for a moment, trying not to be distracted by the flashes of silver in her eyes.

"Marley certainly has varied interests," Will agreed. "Golf, mountain biking, plastic planes—"

"It's not plastic," Josh said, frowning at Will as he lowered the remote control. "This here's the SkyScout P2GO with a multiplex airframe offering the precision of Hitec electronics in a protected-top mounted outrunner motor with optional ailerons."

"Of course," Will said. "I stand corrected."

"It's a wonder of modern technology," Josh said, still frowning at Will.

"In that case," April said, "is it less likely to break if it hits that tree?"

"What?" Josh snapped his attention back to the sky in time to watch a small yellow plane smack nose-first into the trunk of a massive ponderosa.

"Goddammit!" he screamed, hurling his radio controller to the ground and stomping it under his work boot. He stomped it a few more times before turning to Will. "Look what you made me do."

Will stared at Josh, unsure whether to apologize or to

point out the fact that the person holding the remote control was in charge of the aircraft's flight path. He was saved from making either statement when Marley laid her hand on Josh's shoulder.

"I'm sorry, it's my fault. I didn't mean to distract you with—"

"What's the first rule of radio-controlled aviation?" Josh barked.

Marley blinked. "Um, don't take it too seriously?"

Josh growled, not amused. "Always keep your eye on the sky."

Bethany folded her arms over her chest and leveled a cold stare at Josh. "I need to point out here that the only two people who didn't have their eyes on the sky were you and Will. And since Will wasn't in control of an aircraft at the time, let me go out on a limb here and say the rule doesn't apply to him."

"He distracted me!" sputtered Josh. "With his stupid comments about radio-control aviation and Marley paying attention to you people instead of the job at hand."

Marley grimaced. "You know, maybe the job at hand isn't the right fit for me."

Will pressed his lips together, fighting hard to control the urge to make a hand job joke. It was best to let Marley handle this on her own.

"Fine," Josh huffed, shaking his head. "I'm sorry I overreacted. It's fine. Everything's fine. Let's just go get dinner."

Marley blinked, then forced a smile. "Actually, I'm really tired. I think I'll skip dinner and call it a night."

Josh snorted. "You women and your diets. Fine, we'll skip dinner. Do you want to go catch a movie then? There's that new one about Amelia Earhart. You'll like that, being an aviation fan and all."

"Actually, I think I just want to go home." Marley's voice was still calm, but Will could hear an edge to it.

Josh kicked his remote control again. "But what about your plan? You said you wanted to learn more about remote-control aviation."

"Maybe some other time." Marley wore her donor relations smile like a shield, but her eyes flashed in warning.

Josh scowled. "You broke my goddamn plane for nothing."

Will watched as something snapped in Marley's brain. She crossed her arms over her chest and leveled him with an icy look.

"Actually, *you* broke your goddamn plane," she snapped. "And to be perfectly honest, I'm not interested in continuing a date with a grown man who throws tantrums over a toy. And FYI, that orange coat makes you look like a pylon."

The words hung in the air for a moment, and no one spoke. Beside them, Rosco barked once. Marley looked down at the ground. "A simple 'thank you for the lovely date and have a nice night' would have been better, wouldn't it?"

"Not really," Will said.

Marley looked up at him, and he saw something pleading in her eyes. "Would you mind giving me a ride home?" she asked.

Will looked into those hazel depths and felt something twist in his gut. Part of him wanted to tell her she deserved to stay here with Josh. That this was the inevitable result of feigning interest in something she had no interest in.

But most of him just wanted to take her into his arms and tell her she deserved better.

"Come on, Marley," Bethany said, grabbing her arm. "Let's get out of here."

Marley bit her lip, then looked at Josh. "I'm really sorry about your plane."

Josh gritted his teeth as a vein pulsed in his forehead. He was trying to control his anger, but not doing the best job of it.

"Have a nice life," he snapped in a tone that said he hoped she wouldn't. He bent to pick up the broken pieces of his remote control.

April grabbed Marley's other arm and steered her away. "Lovely to meet you, Josh!" she called over her shoulder.

Will hesitated, then trudged after them feeling like a third wheel. Or was it a fourth wheel?

"Fourth wheels are functional," he muttered. "What the hell am I doing here?"

Bethany turned and grabbed his arm, pulling him into the line beside them. "What are you mumbling about?"

"Nothing," Will said, glancing at Marley. "You okay?"

She nodded and shot him a sheepish look. "Sorry you guys got dragged into that. He seemed like a nice guy when he asked me out."

"Not everyone turns out to be what they seem," Will said.

He watched April wince on the other side of Marley and felt bad. Nothing he was saying was coming out quite right. Beside him, Polly whimpered and dropped a stick at his feet. Will stooped to pick it up, and Bethany let go of his arm.

Will straightened and tossed the stick, then caught up with the girls. "Why don't you let us take you to dinner," Will said. "Since you're missing out on your meal with Josh."

"That's a lovely idea," April said.

"Burgers!" Bethany shouted. "Pilot Butte Drive-in."

Marley laughed, a warm and musical sound that made Will want to keep her laughing forever. "Sure, I'm game. But I'm buying. Seriously, thanks for rescuing me, guys."

"No problem," Will said. "I'm sure you'll find we're much more amicable dates than Josh, though slightly less likely to put out."

"Speak for yourself," Bethany said as she looped her arm through Will's again, pulling him close enough to smell blueberries in Marley's hair.

Marley wasn't sure how things had gone so wrong on her date with Josh, but she was glad about one thing.

"So we saved you from having dinner with the plumber's parents?" Bethany asked, popping a fry into her mouth. "Seriously? The guy was taking you to meet his mom on a first date?"

Marley shrugged and took a bite of her burger. The patty was thick and juicy and tasted like heaven coated in bleu cheese. "His mom was making meatloaf," Marley said. "It seemed like a reasonable idea at the time."

"If that's your idea of reasonable dating behavior, remind me to invite you to help repave my driveway," Will said. "It's romantic, I swear."

"Be nice to her, you two," April said, daintily dipping a fry in a perfectly round pool of ketchup. "She said she's spent most of her adult life dating a different sort of man. She just didn't know what to expect."

Marley felt a rush of gratitude toward April and wondered, not for the first time, what her marriage to Will had been like. Did she regret those years of being someone she wasn't, or did it take a relationship with the absolute wrong person to recognize right when you saw it?

She smiled at April, who smiled back and gestured to Marley's ears. "Those are lovely earrings, Marley. Where did you find them?"

"My mother made them," Marley said, squelching a pang of sadness by popping a tater tot in her mouth. "She used to be a jewelry designer. She owned a jewelry store in Portland for almost twenty years."

"Where does she live now?" Will asked, shifting on the bench seat to lean back into the corner. The movement tipped Marley toward him, and she shivered as she felt her thigh brush his.

"My mom lives in Guatemala," Marley said. "She and my dad divorced years ago."

"How is your dad, anyway?" Will asked, shifting the subject from one subject Marley didn't want to discuss to another she wanted to discuss even less.

"He's fine," she said, and took a bite of her burger.

"How'd he feel about your date with the plumber?" Will asked.

"He didn't send me to my room and ground me, if that's what you're asking."

Will grinned and reached out to steal a tater tot off her plate. "You do seem like you could use a good spanking."

"Time out!" Bethany yelled, waving her arms. "If you two are gonna do it on the table, can I at least move my food out of the way?"

Marley felt heat creep into her cheeks, and April looked equally uncomfortable. She was struggling to come up with a good way to change the subject when a waitress approached the table with four large takeout boxes. She set them on the table in front of Will, who thanked her and handed one to Marley.

"I took the liberty of ordering an extra burger for Magoo," he said. "I hope the bacon cheeseburger is okay. That's what my three are getting."

"Thank you," Marley said, taken aback. "That's very sweet of you."

"I can be sweet when I try."

Across the table, April sipped her diet Coke and smiled at Marley. "How was work for you today, Marley? Are you settling in okay?"

"Work is… well, mostly fine."

Not a word to the family members. Susan's warning echoed in Marley's ears as she reached for the saltshaker.

"I'm settling in really well," Marley amended, adding an extra note of perkiness to her voice. "I really enjoy working with donors."

"Even Aunt Nancy?" Bethany snorted.

Marley felt a chill slither down her spine, and she forced her smile to stay in place. "I get to work with a very diverse group of CHSWS supporters, and Ms. Thomas-Smith certainly keeps me on my toes. I spoke with her today, as a matter-of-fact."

"Did she tell you about the new study she's doing on the long-term health effects of nipple clamps?" Bethany asked.

Marley grimaced. "I tried to change the subject, but she just kept talking."

"Welcome to our childhood," Bethany said, taking a sip of her strawberry milkshake. "I'm having lunch with her tomorrow. She wants me to go with her to New York next week to meet with her attorney."

"New York is lovely this time of year," April said.

Bethany smiled and turned back to Marley. "Is she making you nuts with demands about the rock cocks? Honestly, those things have been her pride and joy for decades. I couldn't believe she finally decided to donate them."

"Wanting to leave a legacy is a lovely gesture," April said. "I admire her for doing it."

"Any word yet on what they're worth?" Will asked.

Marley swallowed hard, wondering if it was a piece of sesame bun or just her conscience lodged in her throat. She looked down at her plate and began to dissect a piece of tomato with her fingernail.

"We're taking our time and making absolutely certain we handle this donation correctly," Marley said, ignoring the twist of guilt that grabbed hold of her small intestine. "Finding the right appraiser, having the figurines properly cleaned and handled—"

"Of course," Will said, shifting again on the bench seat so Marley fell against him. "Because nothing's worse than a granite wanker that's dirty or improperly handled."

Marley flushed and looked up at Will. His mismatched eyes bore into hers, and for a horrifying moment, she worried he knew everything. About her mother, about the lost figurines, about the way she imagined tearing off his shirt and sinking her fingernails into his chest as he devoured her throat with his mouth.

She swallowed and scooted back on the seat. "I have everything handled," she said, knowing nothing could be further from the truth.

Chapter 13

FRIDAY EVENING, MARLEY WAS STANDING BY THE DOOR ten minutes early waiting for Brian to pick her up. She glanced at her watch, not sure why she felt so nervous. True, her date with Josh hadn't gone very well.

But she had high hopes for Brian the bike guy and his delightfully sexy smile.

"What kind of car does he drive?" her father asked, joining her in the foyer and peering out the window.

"A bike," Marley replied with another glance at her watch.

"Is that a joke?"

Marley shrugged. "The restaurant isn't too far away, and Brian lives less than half a mile from here. He offered to pedal his tandem bike over here by himself so we could ride together to dinner."

Admittedly, Marley had been surprised at the suggestion. How many first dates involved both parties riding the same bicycle? But she told herself it was a quaint and charming notion, not to mention practical. This way, no one had to operate a car after a couple glasses of wine.

"Tandem bikes are romantic," Marley told her father, pretty sure that was true.

"So is not fracturing your skull on a first date. Promise you'll be careful, Marley."

"I'll be careful, I promise. See? I have a helmet and everything. I even left my hair down so I don't end up with helmet head."

"Please say this man at least owns a motorized vehicle."

"He owns a motorized vehicle. Now cut it out, Dad. How do I look?"

"Very beautiful," her father said, studying her from head to toe as he took a sip from his glass of bourbon.

"Thank you. I wouldn't normally go for capris and sturdy sandals on a first date, but I've never had a first date on a bike. It's nice to be fun and casual for a change."

Her father sighed. "In my day, a man wouldn't ask a woman out and expect her to dress like she's going hiking."

"I asked *him* out," she informed him. "And I'm paying, too. It's a thank you for a speedy repair on my bike."

Her father frowned. "You're positive this is a date?"

"Yes," said Marley, not entirely certain.

She smiled as Brian came wheeling up the driveway, his magnificent—albeit, hairless—legs pumping the pedals. He braked at the top of the driveway, pulled off his aviator sunglasses, and gave her a slow, sexy smile as she walked down the front steps.

"Marley," he said. "You look hot."

"Thank you," she said, stealing a glance at his legs. "You too."

He laughed. "Looking at my legs?"

Marley flushed. "I just—"

"It's okay. I'm used to it from non-cyclists. Competitive bike racers keep their legs shaved." He turned one calf to the side to give her a better look. "It's a safety thing. Makes wounds easier to clean if you crash and end up with road rash."

Marley strapped on her helmet, delighted by the invitation to stare openly at his legs now. "But competitive bike racers don't shave their arms? Aren't they just as likely to get road rash on an elbow or forearm or something?"

Brian laughed. "Good observation. You're quick, Malory."

"Marley."

"Sorry. See, the truth is, cyclists like to claim they shave their legs for aerodynamics and wound cleaning, but the most likely reason is they just want to show off their toned calves."

"Can't say I blame them. You're a competitive cyclist?"

"I do a few USA Cycling events from time to time, sometimes cyclocross in the winter. Keeps me out of trouble." He flashed a mischievous smile and nodded to the back of the bike. "You ready to roll?"

"Sure. Is there any trick to this? I've never ridden a tandem bike before."

"No trick. If you've ridden a regular bike, you'll be just fine with this. I'll hold it steady and you hop on."

"Got it."

"Let me know if the seat doesn't feel right and I'll adjust it. I went off the measurements for your other bike, so it should be pretty close."

Marley did as instructed, seizing the opportunity to catch her balance once by latching on to Brian's shoulder.

Nice, she thought. *Toned, muscular, nice smile, fun-loving. This could work.*

"Ready?" he called, flashing her another sexy grin.

"Let's roll."

They set off peddling down the street, with Brian calling out warnings about turns and potholes. Marley felt herself start to relax as she studied the scenery and Brian's back-side, bracing herself each time he announced a bump in the road.

Kind, considerate, great ass, Marley mused.

It occurred to her she was spending an awful lot of time categorizing Brian's strengths, talking herself into seeing him as the perfect guy.

He could be the perfect guy.

He turned the bike onto a car-lined downtown street, signaling as he merged into the left lane and pedaled toward a tall brick building. He steered them up a curb and into a glossy red bike rack.

"Here we are," he called, hopping off the bike and holding it steady so Marley could do the same. Marley followed suit, unhooking her helmet as she glanced down at the bike rack. Someone had crocheted duck feet for it, and the effect was whimsical and goofy. Marley hooked her helmet over her arm as Brian locked up the bike. She fluffed her hair, trying to catch a glimpse of her reflection in the restaurant window.

"We've still got plenty of time for happy hour," Brian said, reaching over to tuck the key to the bike lock into the breast pocket of Marley's shirt. She jumped back, surprised, and Brian laughed.

"Hope that's okay. I don't have any pockets."

"Oh. Right, sure. No problem."

"Come on, let's get inside. I recommend the greyhound and the carpaccio if you're ordering off the happy hour menu."

"Sounds good," she said, following him inside as she made a mental note that he'd held the door open for her.

A gentleman, she mused. *With good culinary taste and a frugal sensibility that doesn't sacrifice a quality meal.*

Shut up, Marley.

"What?" Brian asked.

"Nothing."

He grinned down at her and touched her elbow to steer her toward the hostess station. Marley smiled at the familiarity of the gesture, pleased things seemed to be starting off on the right note.

"Hey, Brian!" Marley looked up to see the hostess sidling toward them, thrusting her breasts toward them like cupcakes on a dessert tray. "It's soooooooo good to see you again. How've you been, honey?"

Brian smiled with a hint of a grimace as the hostess grabbed his arm.

"Hey, Shari," he said. "Good to see you."

"Carrie."

"That's what I said." Brian cleared his throat. "We need a table."

Carrie looked at Marley, not even trying to pretend she wasn't performing a head-to-toe appraisal. She sniffed and looked back at Brian. "For how many?"

"Two. A table for two."

"How cozy," Carrie said. "Right this way."

She flounced ahead of them, putting an extra wiggle in her walk for Brian's benefit. Marley resisted the urge to roll her eyes.

Carrie led them to a table next to one of the windows overlooking the sidewalk. "Here you go. You want the happy hour menu, right?"

"That's right."

"Enjoy!" she said, and sashayed off.

Marley watched Carrie go, then turned back to Brian.

He flashed her an apologetic smile. "Sorry about that."

"No problem. Friend of yours?"

"Hmm? Oh, yeah… friend, right. She's a friend."

Marley took a deep breath, chiding herself for feeling jealous. They barely knew each other, and obviously he dated other women—

"Brian!" squealed a female voice.

Marley looked toward the bar, where a muscular-looking blonde in a sundress was hurtling toward them. She had a killer tan, and sandals that laced up her well-toned calves. Marley glanced at Brian, who was drawing out his slow, sexy smile as the woman approached.

"Hey, babe," he called. "Good to see you again. Did you have fun Friday night?"

The woman trailed a finger up Brian's arm and giggled. "I sure did. We'll have to do it again sometime."

Marley looked away, intent on scanning the menu for dairy-free options. *Scallion and tofu fritters, Caesar salad, lamb sausage and rosemary*—

"We'll totally have to do it again," Brian said as Marley kept her eyes on the menu. When he touched her arm, she looked up to see him extending the same sexy smile to her. "Marney, this is my friend Tasha. Tasha, Marney."

Marley frowned. "It's Marley, actually."

"Sasha," the other woman said, and stuck out her hand for Marley to shake.

"Right," said Brian, picking up his menu. "We'd probably better order before happy hour ends. It was good seeing you."

Sasha sniffed and turned on her heel, returning to the bar at the front of the restaurant. Marley watched her go, then returned her gaze to Brian.

"You're a popular guy."

He flashed her his million-dollar smile. "Yeah, I guess so." He squeezed Marley's hand, and she tried to let go of her discomfort. After all, this was a fairly small town, and Brian was bound to have plenty of friends.

She picked up her menu and began studying it again. *Carpaccio, portabello sandwich, peel-and-eat shrimp—*

"Sasha's a cool chick," Brian said.

"Oh?" Marley glanced up from the menu, pleased at Brian's conversational attempt—awkward though it may be. She waited for him to say more, but apparently he was done. "Carrie too?" she prompted.

"What?"

"Carrie. She seemed like a cool chick."

"Oh, right. Yeah, she's cool."

Marley waited for more, but Brian had said all he needed to. Marley lowered her menu. "What makes a cool chick?"

"Huh?"

"Just curious what separates a cool chick from… um, well, an uncool chick."

Brian stared blankly at her for a few beats, then grinned. "We should order."

Marley frowned. "Okay." She looked back at her menu, trying to put her finger on what was so annoying about Brian.

You're just being picky, she told herself, and focused her energy on deciding what she wanted to eat.

French onion soup, stuffed piquillo peppers, oysters on the half-shell—

"Hey, sexy," purred a female voice disturbingly close to Marley's ear. She snapped her gaze up to see a woman with a long dark braid down her back and her coral-manicured fingertips covering Brian's eyes. "Guess who?"

"Um—" Brian said.

"Just start at the beginning of the alphabet," Marley

suggested helpfully, taking a sip of her water. "Alison, Amanda, Amy, Angie—"

"It's Vicki," the woman snapped, giving Marley a dirty look as she uncovered Brian's eyes and put a hand on his shoulder.

"In that case, I'm glad you said something," Marley said. "It would have taken a long time to get to the Vs."

Vicki ignored her and began to stroke her fingers across Brian's bicep. "A bunch of us are getting together Thursday night if you want join us. Barbecue at Jill's house. You remember Jill?"

"Yeah, sure, of course," Brian said, his expression suggesting he had no idea who Jill was. "Jill's great. A really cool girl."

"Awesome, so you'll be there?" Vicki cooed.

"Sure, sure, baby. How about we—"

"Brian!"

Marley resisted the urge to kick Brian under the table as another woman approached. This time it was a petite redhead whose hurried pace made the contents of her T-shirt jiggle pleasantly.

"Baby, so good to see you!" the redhead gushed, draping herself across Brian's lap and bumping Vicki out of the way.

Vicki bumped her right back, and the two women spent the next few seconds jostling each other, making it evident neither was wearing a bra. Brian edged back, giving the ladies more room for their impromptu wrestling match.

"What are you ordering, sweetie?" the redhead cooed to Brian. "I know you love the greyhounds. Hey, let me buy you one."

"He's with someone, you idiot," Vicki said, and Marley

started to thank her. Then Vicki draped herself over Brian's lap, and Marley considered shoving her butter knife up the woman's nostril. Instead, she picked up her menu again.

At least Brian is well-liked, she mused. That said something about him, though it was clear Brian was a bit too well-liked for her taste.

"Have you ordered yet?" the redhead gushed, waving a martini glass so it sloshed on the table in front of them. "You have *got* to try the new drink the bartender's mixing. It's a pad thai martini. Here, try a sip."

She thrust her drink—and her breasts—in Brian's face in an impressive display of agility even Marley had to admire. Brian sputtered a little, but took a sip and nodded.

"Mmm, it's good," Brian said, nodding approvingly. "Rory made that?"

"Uh-huh. Brand new drink he's mixing special tonight."

"Mmm," Brian said, licking his lips. "What did you say that's called?"

"It's a pad thai martini," the redhead announced. "It's made with basil, coconut milk, peanut-infused vodka—"

All the blood drained from Brian's face. He blinked at Marley. "Peanut? Did she say peanut?"

Marley frowned and looked at the drink, then at the redhead. "I think so. That is what you said, right?"

The redhead nodded. "There are also some spices in there. Curry, maybe, and I think some tamarind and—"

"I'm allergic to peanuts," Brian gasped. "Shit, I don't have my EpiPen. Does my throat look red? Is it getting hot in here?"

Marley jumped up, alarmed. She didn't want to date Brian anymore, but she didn't particularly want to see him drop dead on the floor beside their table. She surveyed the restaurant, not entirely sure what to do.

"Doctor!" she yelled. "Is there a doctor in the house? My friend is having an allergic reaction and needs a doctor!"

Brian clutched his throat and made a choking sound. Vicki whacked him three times on the back. The redhead rolled her eyes.

"He's not choking, you idiot. He's having an allergic reaction."

"Does he need mouth-to-mouth?" yelled Carrie the hostess as she bustled back to the table. "I know how to do that."

Brian gagged and clutched his throat.

"Shit," Marley said, and surveyed the rows of gaping diners, none of whom had made a move to assist. "Doctor?" she yelled again.

A man with kind eyes and a white chef's coat hustled over. He looked at Brian, then at Marley. "I already called 911," he said. "Food allergy?"

"Yes, that's what he said. Peanuts, I think."

"Does he use an EpiPen?"

"What's that?" Marley asked.

"A shot of epinedrine. It's common for allergic reactions. Does he carry one of those?"

"I have no idea," Marley said. "We only just met, and—"

"Yes," Brian gasped, nodding frantically and pointing to his thigh.

The chef frowned. "You have your EpiPen with you?"

Brian shook his head and coughed again. "No!" Brian gasped, turning an interesting shade of blue. "At home."

The man held a slender object out to Marley. "It's mine," he said. "I'm allergic to bees, so I always have one with me. I can't give him the shot—liability issues and all—but you can have it."

Marley took it, dumbfounded. "What is it?"

"It's a measured dose of adrenaline designed to treat allergic reactions or the onset of anaphylactic shock."

"What am I supposed to do with it?"

"Shot," Brian gasped. "Stab. Thigh."

Marley stared at him in horror. "I'm supposed to stab you on our first date?"

"It's not as bad as it sounds," the man in the chef's coat said. "He should be able to do it himself, or—"

Brian slumped to the side and began drooling on the redhead's shoulder.

"Eeew!" Vicki squealed, and launched out of her seat. Carrie and the redhead followed, retreating to a safe distance across the restaurant.

"Great girlfriends you've got there," Marley muttered.

Brian snorted, but didn't come to. Marley pressed her fingers to his throat to make sure he still had a pulse. It was steady, and he was still breathing fine, though his neck seemed swollen.

"I can quickly walk you through the steps," the chef said. "My name's Joe, by the way."

"Marley," she choked out. "Okay, I can do this."

"Here, take the EpiPen out of the little safety tube," Joe said. "Good. Don't touch the tip; it's sterile. There's a spring-loaded needle that'll pop through that membrane."

"Wha—what do I do?" Marley stammered.

"Hold it there with the orange tip pointing down toward his outer thigh. Good. Now pull that blue safety release there."

"Okay," Marley said, not sure whether her voice or her hands were shaking harder. "Now what?"

"Stab it into his outer thigh, right through his shorts, and then hold it there for ten seconds."

"Stab," she repeated, coming to terms with the idea.

She started to close her eyes, then thought better of it. She should probably see what she was doing. Brian was still breathing, still drooling, which seemed like good signs.

She held the EpiPen over the spot Joe had indicated. "One, two, three—"

She jammed the device into Brian's outer thigh with a warrior cry that startled her. She held it there, fascinated. "One Mississippi, two Mississippi, three Mississippi—"

"We're in Oregon," Vicki chided from nearby. "Duh."

Marley ignored her and pulled the EpiPen back. She looked up at Joe. "Now what?"

"Generally you want to massage the injection site—"

"I'll do it!" squealed three female voices, as Brian's fan club swarmed the table once more. Marley scooted back, happy to let them take over. She couldn't see Brian's face, but could tell he was stirring amid the cacophony of female voices buzzing around him.

"I'm rubbing, back off!" Vicki yelled.

"No, me!"

"Move it, bitch. You had him last night."

"We should take his shorts off."

"Oooh, he's all smooth. Must've just shaved."

"He always shaves before dates and bike races, duh."

The redhead yanked Vicki's braid, and Carrie pushed her out of the way. Marley took another step back and saw Brian's eyelids flutter. He took in the pile of women surrounding him and gave a slow, lazy smile. He reached out and put a hand on Carrie's butt.

"Hey, baby. What's your name?"

—◈◈◈—

Will was lying on his back on his living room floor surrounded by all three of his dogs. Rosco, the German shepherd mix, picked up a soggy tennis ball and dropped it on Will's abdomen with a splat.

"No more," Will grunted. "We've been fetching for an hour. Aren't you done yet?"

Rosco whined in response, and Polly jumped up to join him, never one to miss an opportunity for whimpering. They began a lovely two-part harmony, and Will felt almost bad that deaf Omar couldn't hear it.

Then again, Omar didn't look distressed. He was hard at work chewing a beef marrowbone Will had given each of the dogs after dinner. Rosco had promptly buried his, while Polly had offered hers to the neighbor's beagle.

Will sighed and turned back to Rosco and Polly.

"You guys, enough with the singing," Will said. "How am I supposed to hear myself think?"

Like he really wanted that. He'd spent the whole day unable to get Marley out of his mind, and it was starting to piss him off.

Marley and her secrets.

Marley and her incessant need to please.

Marley and her beautiful legs.

Marley and her date, he reminded himself, wondering how that was going.

He pictured the Plaid Neanderthal reaching his hand across the table to take Marley's, his grease-speckled knuckles making her shiver with anticipation. Would things heat up between them on a first date? Marley wasn't that kind of girl, was she?

Not that Will had anything against that kind of girl.

Hell, he lived for that kind of girl. Lord knew he was that kind of guy, so he wasn't one to judge.

Still, Marley wouldn't get steamy with a stranger on a first date.

You made out with her in the kitchen the day you met, he reminded himself. *Her father caught you groping each other in the foyer a few days later, and if it weren't for her ex-fiancé showing up on her doorstep the other night—*

"Stop," Will said aloud.

Rosco barked, and Polly perked up her ears. Omar went on chewing his bone.

Will sighed and palmed the soggy tennis ball on his abdomen, barely noticing the dog slobber that squished between his fingers. He had to get his mind off Marley. Off the warm taste of her skin at the base of her throat, her sharp little intake of breath as his fingertips traced the edges of her ribs and slid beneath the lace of her bra. He had to stop thinking about the smell of blueberries and the way her eyes flew wide as he kissed his way between her breasts and—

"Quit whimpering, Rosco," Will ordered. Rosco twitched his ears, and Will wasn't sure whether he was annoyed at the dog for interrupting his fantasy, or at himself for having the fantasy in the first place.

"Sorry, buddy," Will said, and reached out to scratch the big dog under his chin. "You're right. We should definitely fetch again."

Will rolled over and chucked the soggy tennis ball down the hallway. Rosco scrambled after it in a blur of paws and fur, with Polly trailing behind him. Will turned back to Omar.

"It's just you and me for the three minutes it takes them to find that in the laundry hamper," Will said.

Omar went right on chewing his bone. The phone rang, and Will heaved himself up off the ground. He began to hunt for it, locating it in his fruit basket on the third ring.

"Hello?"

"Will, hey—it's April."

"You know, we were married for four years," Will said, stooping to pick up the ball Rosco deposited at his feet. "Even if I didn't have caller ID, don't you think I'd know your voice by now?"

"Right, sorry. Look, Will, there's been an incident here at the restaurant."

Will froze with the ball poised for throwing. Rosco barked once sharply, then fell silent. "Incident? Are you okay?"

"I'm fine. It's Marley."

"Marley?" Will's heart was in his throat. "Did her date do something to her? Is she in trouble or hurt or—"

"Will, stop. I'm trying to tell you." There was a pause, and he knew April was giving him a minute to get a grip. He stayed quiet, though everything in his brain screamed for answers *rightfuckingnow*.

"Marley's fine," April said, and Will waited for his pulse to slow down. It didn't, and April continued. "Her date had an allergic reaction here at the restaurant. He seems okay now, but his *girlfriends*—" April paused at that, waiting for the words to sink in. "His girlfriends want to take him to the hospital as a precaution. That leaves Marley stranded here. She said she could walk, but I'm not sure she knows her way yet, and I guess I could call a cab but—"

"I'm on my way," Will said, and he hung up the phone.

Chapter 14

WILL WAS BREATHLESS AS HE CHARGED THROUGH THE front door at 900 Wall. He scanned the room for Marley, but April caught his eye first, waving to him from her station at the edge of the open kitchen. April pointed to a table near the front of the restaurant, and Will turned to see Marley standing awkwardly beside a cluster of women fawning over a man on a stretcher.

A paramedic swatted one of the women away, but two more circled back like flies, not giving the medics more than a few inches of space.

Marley looked up then, her eyes going wide at the sight of Will. He raised a hand in greeting, before striding slowly toward her.

"Marley," he greeted, then looked down at the Plaid Neanderthal on the stretcher. He had lipstick marks in two different shades on his cheek and forehead, and Will tried to remember if Marley wore lipstick. Pushing the thought from his head, he nodded at Plaid Neanderthal.

"How you feeling, man?"

Plaid Neanderthal gave a lazy smile as a redhead bent over him, fluffing the pillow behind his head. "Good," he said. "Real good."

One of the paramedics snorted and made another attempt at shooing the women away. "Come on, ladies. We're heading to the ambulance now. Out of the way, please."

Will stepped around them and reached Marley's side,

watching her for signs of how she was feeling. Worried over her date's affliction, or embarrassed by the public scene? Will honestly couldn't tell.

"How are you doing?" he asked.

"Will." She blinked, and Will noticed for the hundredth time how many shades of color made up the hazel in her eyes. "What are you doing here?"

"April called. She said you might need a ride. What happened?"

Marley glanced toward the door where the medics were wheeling Plaid Neanderthal out onto the sidewalk. She sighed, then turned back to Will with a shrug. "Peanut allergy. I had to stab him with an EpiPen."

"Penetration is the mark of any good date."

Marley laughed, and Will felt something in his chest go warm and liquid. "Good date," Marley repeated, still laughing. "Remind me again what that is. I haven't had one for a while."

"Did things at least go well before he fell unconscious?"

"A question I never thought I'd be asked after a date." Marley paused. "Not so well, no. But I'd rather not talk about it. Are you really here to give me a ride?"

"That's the plan."

"In a car?"

Will frowned. "As opposed to the sort of ride a gentleman generally shouldn't suggest on a first date?"

"That's not what I meant. Brian brought me here on a tandem bike. I just wanted to make sure you weren't planning to pedal me home on that."

Will raised an eyebrow. "A tandem bike? On a first date?"

"It might be romantic in a certain context."

"I'm sure it would. Well, at least the date is over."

"I'll drink to that." Marley frowned and looked down at

the table, where water glasses sat sweating and a half-eaten slice of bread was soaking in a golden puddle of olive oil. "You know, I never even got a drink. Stupid happy hour is over, and I never got a greyhound."

"Regular price is only a couple bucks more than happy hour," Will pointed out. "Why don't you let me buy you a greyhound?"

Marley shook her head and looked around the restaurant. "I'd kinda like to get out of here, if it's okay with you. Maybe some other time?"

"Sure, no problem. Did you get anything to eat?"

Marley shrugged. "I'll find something at home." She grimaced, then looked down at the table. "Damn. I'll have to go home and deal with my dad trying very, very hard not to say I-told-you-so about the date."

"Dad wasn't a fan of Brian?"

"Not especially."

"Your father might be a better judge of character than I thought." He looked at her, considering. "Tell you what—why don't I make up for your crappy date by making sure you get dinner, a good drink, and great company?"

Marley raised an eyebrow. "Are you asking me out?"

"Are you implying you think I'm great company?"

She laughed. "Or that I think your ego is genuinely that big."

"I can live with that. But it's not a date. Consider this friendly charity."

"Pity with a drink." Marley nodded. "I can go for that."

"Good. Just give me a couple minutes to talk to April."

"I need to run to the restroom anyway. Oh, and I should probably talk to one of Brian's girlfriends about getting his bike key back to him. Shall I meet you out front?"

"It's a date," Will said. "Only it's not a date."

"I'm glad we cleared that up," Marley said, and headed off to the bathroom.

Will watched her go, then strode to the open kitchen where April was sautéing something over an open flame.

His pretty ex-wife looked up with flushed cheeks and smiled. "Everything okay with Marley's date?"

"Seems to be. He was conscious, and the medics didn't seem too worried."

"Marley was a real hero. Not that the guy deserved it. You should have seen him reveling in all the women swooning around him before the allergy attack. I wouldn't have blamed Marley if she'd stuck the EpiPen in his eye and walked out."

Will felt a surge of pride and glanced back toward the restrooms where Marley had disappeared. "Any chance I could get some sort of gourmet dinner for two to go in the next five minutes?"

April smiled. "You happen to be in luck tonight. I just wrapped up an order for a rehearsal dinner and I have a bunch of extras. How about peel-and-eat shrimp with peach curry dipping sauce, heritage beets with goat cheese and arugula, caprese salad with basil and tomato, baby purple potatoes with—"

"I'll take it," Will said. "All of it. I owe you one. Got anything good in the wine cellar to go with all that?"

"I'll throw something in the basket and put the whole thing on your credit card."

"You're the best."

April smiled and got to work packaging up the food. Will watched her work, wondering how many divorced men trusted their ex-wives with their credit card numbers or meal preparation for a date with a new woman.

"It's not a date," Will said aloud.

"I didn't say it was," April said, tucking a white box into a large brown basket and turning toward the walk-in cooler to grab something else. "Can you see if Bethany's double-parked in the alley? I need her help loading the rest of the food into the car for the wedding reception."

"Sure thing," Will said, and ambled out the back door. His sister was idling in the alley, so he motioned her to roll down her window.

"Hey, Will. What are you doing here?"

"Long story. April needs a hand loading up the food."

Bethany hit her hazard lights and popped open the door. "Let me guess—does your long story involve Marley?"

"Why would you think that?"

"Because you have that flushed look you get every time you're around her." Bethany grinned. "It's either that, or you're developing typhoid."

"I'm pretty sure it's typhoid."

Bethany followed him back into the restaurant, and they each made two trips loading food into the back of the station wagon.

"What's in the picnic basket?" Bethany asked on their last run.

April smiled. "Dinner for Will and Marley."

Bethany rolled her eyes at Will. "Typhoid, huh?"

"Highly contagious," Will said, and he pushed past her to take the last box of food to the car.

When he got back to the kitchen, April held out a large wicker basket with a white linen cloth folded over the top. "Here you go, Will. I need the plates and silverware back tomorrow. The wine's tucked in the bottom with a chill sleeve around it. Chardonnay okay?"

"Perfect. Thanks, April. Good luck with the wedding."

Bethany grinned and hoisted a pile of tablecloths off the counter. "Good luck with Marley. By the way, have you talked to Aunt Nancy today?"

"I try to avoid doing that unless someone in the family dies or has a really bad case of stress-induced canker sores."

"Do conniption fits count?" Bethany asked. "Because that's what Nancy's having since Cheez Whiz lost her rock dicks."

Will froze, his hands on April's basket of food. "What did you say?"

"The figurines. They're gone. At least that's what Aunt Nancy thinks." Bethany shrugged. "I guess she went to see them and Marley opened up the safe, but there was nothing inside."

Will realized he was clenching his fists and forced himself to loosen them. "What did Marley say?"

"She and Susan told some story about the figurines being sent out for cleaning, but Nancy isn't buying it. She said the look on Marley's face made it pretty obvious something's up."

Will frowned. "Why do you seem so calm about it?"

"Because I'm sure there's a reasonable explanation. Why don't you ask Marley what it is?"

"Right. Because Marley's always so up-front with me?"

Bethany gave him a look. "I'm glad you're keeping an open mind about this."

"I'll see if she brings it up herself. Let me know if you hear anything new?"

"Will do."

Will strolled out the door with a little less spring in his step than he'd had before. He stood in the sunlight for a few minutes, gathering his thoughts. Maybe he was over-reacting. Maybe the figurines really were being cleaned. Maybe Aunt Nancy misunderstood. Maybe Marley would volunteer details about the whole thing.

Sensing her behind him, Will turned to see Marley emerging onto the sidewalk. Her hair looked slightly less rumpled than it had a few minutes before, though her expression was still guarded. She smoothed her hand down the front of her capris and gave him a weak smile.

"Please say we aren't going anywhere fancy," she said. "I'm dressed for a bike ride and happy hour, not champagne and canapés."

"I don't even know what a canapé is, but it sounds sexual."

"You were married to a chef and you don't know what a canapé is?"

Will grinned. "I lied. I just wanted to say 'sexual' and watch you bite your lip."

Marley laughed and looked at the picnic basket. "That's dinner?"

"No, it's your date's decapitated head. You ready to go?"

"I'm ready to follow you pretty much anywhere if you're willing to feed me."

"Let's start with my car and work from there. Right this way."

He led her down the street to where he was parked in front of the bank. He unlocked her door, then opened the door to the backseat and set the basket on the floor. Marley buckled her seat belt as Will moved around and opened the driver's side door.

She looked up at him as he swung into the car. "Thanks so much for coming to get me, Will. I would have been fine walking, but there's something a little humiliating about going home from a date on foot."

"It's my pleasure," he said. "That's what friends are for, right?"

He let the words and the questions hang there for a moment, gauging her mood. "Friends," she repeated. "Exactly. So where are we going?"

"You'll see in a minute."

Will started the car and steered them onto the parkway and headed south. He kept one eye on the road and one on Marley, who was latching and unlatching and re-latching the clasp on her bike helmet.

"You okay?" he asked.

She hesitated, and Will held his breath. Maybe she'd mention the figurines. Maybe she'd confess to something, and they could get everything out in the open.

Instead, she shook her head. "Bad dates always shake me up a little. Especially ones where someone gets hauled off to the hospital."

"You've had more than one of those?"

"I guess not."

"What's the worst date you've ever had?" Will asked, trying to keep things light. Trying to distract himself from his own mistrust. "Besides any of the ones you've had since you moved to Bend."

"You're eliminating some of the best ones, but okay." She thought about it a moment. "Probably the guy who forgot to mention he was married."

"No kidding?"

"His wife showed up at the restaurant and hit him over the head with a candelabra. It was a pretty good sign things weren't going to work for us."

"Wow. You pick some real winners."

Marley raised an eyebrow at him. "And you're batting a hundred?"

"A thousand," Will said. "The expression is *batting a thousand*."

"Are you dodging the question?"

"Nope, just making sure you don't disparage the game of baseball."

"Because that's the point of this conversation," she said, smiling a little. "What's your worst date?"

Will thought about it as he changed lanes and merged left. "That would be my first date with April."

"Oh?"

"I spit a piece of gristle into my napkin at dinner and forgot about it. When I picked up the napkin five minutes later, the gristle fell into her purse."

"You're kidding."

Will grinned and dodged a pothole in the road. "I tried to dig it out when she went to the bathroom, but she came back and found me rifling through her purse. She accused me of being a pervert and a snoop, and I accused her of being a lunatic for having a concealed handgun in her bag."

Marley snorted. "And you ended up getting married after that?"

"Well, not the same day. We did wait a couple years."

"Hard to believe that didn't work out."

The words hung there for a few beats, and Will opened his mouth to blurt a smartass comment. But Marley leaned closer and put a hand on his.

"I'm sorry, Will. I didn't mean to sound harsh. I sometimes open my mouth without considering if I'm about to say something insensitive."

Will glanced at her hand on his, and he was suddenly a lot more focused on the feel of Marley's fingertips against his knuckles than he was on her commentary about his divorce. Her hand was small but warm, and the way she leaned toward him made the neckline of her top gape open.

"You can open your mouth around me anytime," he said. "For any reason."

"Pervert." Marley gave a small smile and looked out the window. "Anyway, I apologize. I don't want to joke about inappropriate things like divorce or heartache or anything hurtful like—"

"My lesbian ex-wife leaving me to rub-the-wombat's-whiskers with my sister?"

"Right."

"It isn't hurtful. And pretty much the only topics you shouldn't joke about are cancer and dead babies."

"Mother Teresa?"

"No, she's okay. Especially that one about constipation and the two drunk nuns in the parking lot."

Marley snorted. "I'll keep that in mind." She turned away and looked at the road. "We're going to Cheez Whiz."

Her tone was flat—not disappointed, and not enthused. Will wasn't sure what that meant in light of the drama with the figurines, but she volunteered nothing further.

Will turned onto the narrow, winding road that led to the Cheez Whiz property. He wheeled into a space at the front of the lot, noticing there were no other cars around. The fact wasn't lost on Marley.

"Are we allowed to be here when it's closed?" she asked.

"No worries. As long as I disarm the alarm before I break the window, we're all clear."

Marley frowned as Will killed the ignition and turned to

her. "Relax, Marley. I have a key. They gave it to me years ago so I could do after-hours tours with potential donors."

"Seriously?"

"Seriously. I'm usually not here alone, since the curators do a better job telling donors about the animals than I do. But I called Susan earlier and let her know we'd be here tonight."

"When did you talk to Susan?"

If Will hadn't been listening for it, he might not have noticed her voice went an octave higher. He studied her face, looking for signs of guilt. She was looking out the window, not meeting his eyes.

"I called and left a message while you were in the restroom."

"Voice mail?"

"Yep."

She looked at him and smiled. "Hopefully that's enough to keep the police from being summoned."

Will waited for her to say more, but she didn't. Maybe there was nothing to say.

"Come on," he said, popping open his car door. "Let's go inside."

He led the way to the front door, maneuvering around water features teeming with trout and statues of wildlife. When he flipped the cover on the alarm's keypad, he hesitated. Looking up at Marley, he cleared his throat. "Would you mind standing over there for a sec?"

Marley frowned. "Why?"

"I have to punch in the alarm code."

She blinked, then stepped back. "Of course."

Will felt like a jerk, but hell, what was he supposed to do? He adored Marley. Loved spending time with her.

Couldn't wait to get her inside so they could enjoy a gourmet dinner together.

But did he trust her?

"So you don't trust me, huh?" Marley called from where
she'd relocated next to a large, bronze statue of an otter.
"For the record, I have my own key to the building. I just
didn't happen to bring it on my tandem bike date. I have
the key code written down in my wallet, too."

"It's corporate policy," he said. "I'm just following
the rules."

"Absolutely. You strike me as a real by-the-book
kinda guy."

"Is that sarcasm, Ms. Cartman?"

"If I say yes, are you going to refuse to feed me?"

He gave her a tight smile and finished unlocking the
door. "Come on. Dinner's waiting."

If she was annoyed at his mistrust, she didn't show it
as she followed him through the lobby and down the hall
toward the planetarium. He paused at the entrance, used
the keypad to open the door, and led the way through the
dark interior. He found the light switch and flipped on the
illuminated cords running along the aisles.

Marley gasped, turning in circles to admire the ceiling. "I haven't been in here yet. I was talking with Susan
last week about maybe doing some Pink Floyd laser light
shows here later this fall. Not the usual educational fare,
but a good money-maker."

Will nodded and set the picnic basket on the floor as he
made his way to the planetarium's control panel. "Good
money-making is what it's all about," he agreed, punching
buttons on the panel.

"Give it a rest, rich boy," Marley called. "Money-making

for the museum is my job. It's what I'm supposed to do. You can't fault me for that."

"Very true," he agreed, ready to be done with this conversation. "Sit down."

"What?"

"Sit," he commanded. "You're in the way of the light beam, and I don't want to blind you."

Marley dropped into one of the theater chairs, but Will shook his head and pointed to the carpeted area in the middle of the planetarium. "Not there, in the center. Grab that picnic blanket and set it up in that empty spot right there. I'll be down in a sec."

"Aye, aye, cap'n," she said, and grabbed the blanket, along with the basket of food.

Will punched a few more buttons, trying to remember how the planetarium manager had shown him to do it. He'd only fiddled with these controls once before, and that had been part of a board member training session. He'd never expected to come here with a beautiful woman for dinner…

It's not a date, he reminded himself. *She's the new development director, and I'm just offering her a tour of the facilities. Keep this platonic, dammit.*

Annoyed with himself, Will flipped one more switch. With a quick burst of light, a universe of stars began to twirl above them.

Will beamed. "Let there be light."

"Wow," Marley said, looking up at the night sky. "Is that Uranus?"

He stepped down from the control panel. "You set that one up on purpose, didn't you?"

She grinned as Will ambled down the steps to join her on the blanket. "It seemed like a good opportunity."

"Sometimes the easy ones aren't worth taking."

"That's what my father always told me," she said. "So what's in the basket?"

"Keep your pants on, Cartman." Will reached inside and pulled out a stack of neat white boxes, not certain what April had told him was in here. Marley grabbed the first box and popped it open, inhaling deeply.

"Mmmm... baby purple potatoes with garlic and rosemary and fresh chives. Yummy."

Will opened another box and grinned. "This one's got peel-and-eat shrimp with a big cup of April's famous peach curry dipping sauce."

"Oooh, arugula and golden beets," Marley gasped. She plucked out a thin slice of beet and popped it in her mouth, then moaned with bliss. "Where does she get this goat cheese? It's amazing."

Will watched her lick the tip of her finger and felt all the blood leave his head. He looked back at the basket and focused his energy on locating a corkscrew to open the bottle of Chardonnay.

"She tries to buy most of her groceries from local farms, so maybe from the dairy over in Tumalo. I can ask, if you like."

"This is incredible." Marley licked her finger again and beamed at him. "Thank you, Will."

He handed her a wineglass, feeling slightly tipsy already in spite of the fact that he hadn't had a drop. "Gotta give my ex-wife credit—she knows the way to a woman's heart." He took a sip of wine and tilted his head to the side. "Or into her pants."

"Is this supposed to be a seduction meal?"

"Definitely not. For the record, I acknowledge that the

only way I'm getting into your pants is if I break into your house, dig them out of your laundry hamper, and put them on while you're sleeping."

"Thank you for that visual."

He nodded. "Okay, seriously. I know we keep saying we shouldn't hook up, and we keep ending up groping each other anyway. But I mean it. We really need to keep things on a professional level."

"I agree."

He blinked, part of him wishing she hadn't agreed so quickly. But hell, it's what he wanted, wasn't it? He needed to keep his distance. Needed to fight this stupid attraction to a woman he knew—*absolutely knew*—he shouldn't trust.

"So we're just friends," he said, trying to convince himself more than her.

"I've got it, Will." She smiled. "I feel the same way. Now shut up and drink your wine."

He hesitated, then smiled back and lifted a glass. "Here's to abysmal first dates. Without them, we wouldn't have this lovely spread before us."

"I'll drink to that." Marley took a sip, then reached for the bottle. "Wow, this is excellent wine."

"April knows how to pick 'em."

"That she does."

Marley reached for the plates and silverware, divvying them between the two of them. She moved between all of the takeout boxes, loading her plate with small helpings of everything. At last, she grasped her fork in one hand and grinned at him. "Bon appétit!"

"Bon appétit," he echoed, shifting to grab the box of shrimp. His knee brushed Marley's, and he resisted the urge to pull back. After all, they were friends. It shouldn't be a big deal to brush knees with a friend over dinner, right?

They ate in silence for a while, pausing every few minutes to refill a plate or remark on the stars overhead. Will tried to keep his eyes off Marley's mouth, his mind off her habit of licking the corners of her mouth or touching the point of her tongue to her fingertips, tasting every last drizzle of sauce.

As Will poured them each a second glass of wine, Marley leaned back on her arms and looked at the pinprick stars on the planetarium ceiling. She sighed and reached for her glass.

"There's something I have to tell you, Will."

"Oh?"

He tried to keep his tone nonchalant, but Will felt his pulse kick up a notch. She had something to confess. Something about the figurines? About her past? The words thrummed in his mind, pulsing with the beat of his heart and the memory of April's confession four years ago.

I have something to tell you.

"I have a date."

Will wasn't sure if the sinking in his gut was due to Marley's lack of confession, or the fact that she hadn't given up on her stupid plan to land a blue-collar man.

"Who is it this time?"

"One of the chefs from 900 Wall. I wanted to tell you because I thought that might be weird since he works with April and—"

"The fact that he works with April is not what makes it weird," Will said, still reeling a bit from the confession that wasn't. "The fact that you're seeking out men to date based on how much you think they make is making it weird."

"So you don't object to me going out with Joe?"

Will shrugged, figuring it was a more appropriate gesture than waving his arms and screaming with fury. "Knock yourself out."

She watched him for a moment, probably expecting him to say more. Will studied her back, grateful she wasn't a mind reader. Marley was the first to look away.

"Let's see if there's any dessert in here," she said, rummaging in the picnic basket. "Oooh! Little lemon tartlets! April thought of everything." She grinned at Will. "Wonder if there's whipped cream in here too."

She rummaged back in the basket and came up with a small foil pouch. She squinted at the writing, frowning. "Whipped? Is this a dessert topping?"

Will reached out and took it from her, studying the fine print on the side. "In a manner of speaking, yes." He handed the foil packet to her. "Creamy lubricant from Pure Romance. I wouldn't put this on my tartlet if I were you."

"Unless *tartlet* is a euphemism." Marley grinned. "April really did think of everything."

"That would be Bethany, not April."

"What?"

"She was there helping April pack up for an event. I knew I shouldn't have left her alone with the basket."

Marley grinned and studied the packet. "It's vanilla flavor. Maybe it would go with the tartlet after all."

Will laughed and lay back on the blanket, folding his hands over his stomach. He hoped he looked like a guy relaxing after a good meal and enjoying the stars on the planetarium ceiling, but he knew he probably just looked like a guy trying not to leer at a beautiful woman holding a packet of flavored sex lube. He couldn't look at her. That was his undoing every time.

"Please tell me you aren't really thinking of putting a sexual lubricant on your dessert," he said.

She grinned, and Will tensed as he felt her shift a little closer. "Tempting, but I think I'll save it. Who knows? Maybe things will work out with my next date."

Will felt something twist in his gut and wished for another sip of wine. Probably not an option while lying on his back, and he didn't want to sit up and risk the urge to touch her. He had to keep fighting this. It was the only way to hold on to his sanity.

"A chef, huh?" Will said. "I hope you double-checked to make sure he's a lower-paid sous chef and not one of those well-paid executive chefs."

"Very funny," Marley said.

Will turned his head to see her studying him. Her hazel eyes flashed under the lights from the planetarium's twinkling ceiling, and her hair was rumpled. Probably from the bike helmet, but it looked more like she'd just rolled out of bed, which was a thought he really didn't want bouncing around in his brain.

He felt an unwelcome surge of lust and looked away, annoyed by his traitorous libido.

"Word of advice," Will said. "Don't break out the sex lube before you've finished your first drink. A guy might get the wrong idea."

"Or the right one."

There was a note of flirtation in her voice, and every nerve in Will's body began to tingle. He fought the urge to look at her, to touch her, to take her in his arms and—

"I'm sure you and the chef and your packet of

vanilla-flavored sex lube will have a lovely time then," Will said. "Joe the chef is a lucky guy."

Will started to sit up, needing that damn drink of wine. Needing to put some distance between them. But Marley reached out and pressed her hand to his chest, pinning him in place.

Will turned to face her and felt everything inside him dissolve. Every ounce of strength he had, every fiber of his brain that screamed *Don't trust her!* liquefied in an instant.

Again.

"Lucky," she repeated, her eyes flashing something besides the planetarium stars now. Her hand was still on his chest, and Will swallowed hard as Marley grinned and leaned closer. "Want me to show you *lucky*?"

Chapter 15

DO NOT USE THIS MAN TO BOOST YOUR CONFIDENCE AFTER A bad date.

Do not use this man to boost your confidence after a bad date.

Do not use this man to boost your confidence after a bad date.

Marley imagined herself writing the phrase on a classroom chalkboard over and over and over again until she got it through her thick skull and just sat back to enjoy a platonic picnic dinner.

She started to draw her hand back—to tell Will she'd made a mistake and didn't really mean it, and by the way, could he please pass the rest of the shrimp?

Then she thought about confessing everything—about the missing figurines, about her mother's criminal past, about what happened years ago that shook her confidence in her career and life and everything she thought she believed in.

But the way he was looking at her now with one blue eye and one green eye fixed on her face in a sexy dare, all she wanted to do was lunge for him.

"Ooof!" he said as Marley pounced, thrusting her breasts against his chest and her lips to his. She kissed him hard, pressing her whole body against him as she slid her fingers up to twine in his hair.

She wouldn't have blamed him a bit if he'd thrown her

off and sat up, reminding her they'd just agreed five minutes ago that anything beyond a platonic relationship was a bad, bad idea.

But this felt good—so good—and Will was kissing her back now, his tongue moving into her mouth and making her dizzy with desire. He slid one hand up her rib cage beneath her T-shirt, moving more quickly than he had the other times they'd found themselves entwined and breathing heavy despite their intentions not to. He broke the kiss for an instant, drawing back to grin at her.

"I figure if I get your top off fast this time, I might have a chance to get you naked before some inevitable interruption breaks up our party," he said.

Markey smiled too. "Allow me."

She sat back, still on top of him and pinning him in place with her knees on either side of his hips. She tried to think of the sexiest way to pull the top off, but then remembered it was a goddamn T-shirt and her hair was a mess and she was on the floor of her workplace and dammit, she wanted him right now.

She yanked the shirt over her head and felt her earring pop off with it. To hell with it; she could find it later. She threw the shirt toward the closest chair, then twisted her arm behind her back to unhook her bra.

"I can help with that," he said. He slid his hands up her spine and found the clasp, his fingers making quick work of the task. He parted the hook and grinned up at her before moving his hands to her shoulders. Marley shivered as he pushed the straps down her arms, then gave a good tug to make the whole garment fall away.

He held the bra up by one finger, twisting it around in

the light to admire it. "Black lace for a bike ride?" he asked as he tossed it toward her fallen T-shirt.

"Isn't that exactly when you'd want nice underwear? In case you end up in the ER having your clothes cut off of you."

Will grinned as he reached up to cup her breasts, and Marley leaned into his hands, savoring the warmth of his palms.

"I've never understood that," he said. "Why would you care what the emergency room staff thinks of you when you're bleeding to death?"

"Appearances are important," she said, and she felt him tense as she leaned down to kiss him again. For a moment, she thought he might call the whole thing off.

But then his hands moved softly up her rib cage, his thumbs trailing over her nipples. Marley tightened her knees around his hips, pressing herself against him. She could feel him hard, solid at the apex of her thighs, and she ground against him, wanting to feel more of him but not wanting to break the kiss.

She was still mulling her options when Will pushed himself up on the heels of his hands, then slid one hand up to palm her shoulder.

"What are you—"

"Trading spots," he said, gripping her waist and flipping her effortlessly onto her back. He used his knees to shove hers apart, wedging his hips into the space between her thighs. Marley gasped, both from the exquisite weight of him and from the sudden closeness of his face.

His eyes were inches from hers, and she stopped thinking about whether to focus on the green one or the blue one and just drank him in. They stayed frozen like that for a few beats, his breath ruffling her hair, her heart slamming so hard against her ribs that she was sure he moved with the beat of it. Then he leaned forward and breathed warm against her neck.

Every nerve in her body snapped to attention and screamed, *Hell yes!*

"Oh Christ," Marley said, and clenched her legs tight around him.

He dragged his teeth across the humming nerves along her throat. "You have the most sensitive neck I've ever touched." He breathed into the hollow behind her ear. "I could do this for hours."

She bucked against him, her pelvis rising to press against the hardness behind his fly. He laughed, his chest vibrating her bare breasts as he dipped his tongue into the hollow of her throat and slid one hand up her side. Marley writhed again, powerless to stop her body from responding to the heat of his breath, the nip of his teeth.

Just when she thought she couldn't take any more, he drew back, propping himself on the heels of his hands. Marley whimpered and tried to pull him back down, but Will laughed and slid down her body. His lips moved across her breasts, drawing one nipple into the warmth of his mouth. She gasped and he swirled his tongue around the left one, leaving her dizzy with heat and liquid and the sheer pleasure of it all.

He moved across her rib cage to brush his tongue over the other nipple, leaving Marley panting and clutching at the back of his head.

Will moved lower, kissing his way down her abdomen. He lingered at her belly button, trailing his lips over the smooth hollow before moving left to the upper edge of her hip bone. His fingers found the waistband of her capris, and he hesitated there, content to plant long, slow, lingering kisses in an uneven trail just above her belt line. He moved to her right hip, his tongue tracing the rounded bone, then the smooth slope of flesh trailing across her belly.

Marley felt her hips rise by instinct, a silent plea for more. Will clutched the button of her capris with one hand and leaned up, looking into her eyes. He was breathing heavy now too, and Marley felt heady with her own power.

I did that. I turned him on like that.

Will grinned and looked at her waistband. "Once I slide down this zipper, there's no going back."

She licked her lips and looked into his eyes. "You mean you won't take no for an answer?"

"No, I mean there's a thread stuck in the zipper. Once I get it down, I don't think I can get it back up."

Marley laughed and angled up to kiss him. Then she slid a hand to the front of his jeans, gripping the firm, hard length of him through the denim. "You don't strike me as a guy who's having any difficulty getting it up."

"You have that effect on me."

Marley shivered with desire and with the pleasure of knowing he wanted her. Brian and his bevy of doting women could go to hell, while she soaked up every ounce of pleasure Will could pour on her.

She moved her fingers under the hem of his shirt, tugging the rumpled cotton up over his back. She traced the muscular wings of his shoulder blades, then dragged the shirt higher, tugging to get it off him. He angled back, taking over before Marley ripped his head off with her enthusiasm. Will yanked his T-shirt off the rest of the way, tossing it behind him. Marley watched it land on their growing pile of clothes, the cups of her bra splayed out on either side of his gray cotton.

"It's starting to look like a yard sale over there," he said. "All we need is a couple old ladies haggling over the price of your shoes."

"I'm still wearing my shoes."

"Better fix that," he said, and leaned back to tug them off.

His fingers traced the delicate pads of her toes as he pried off one sandal, then the other. He tossed them toward the rest of the clothing, the left shoe making a loud clang as it hit the aisle seat.

Will leaned down again, still propped on the heels of his hands, occupying the space above her. Marley wanted to feel more of him, to savor his weight on her chest. She slid her palms up his back and cupped his shoulder blades, pulling him down to her.

"Kiss me again," she breathed.

He did, his mouth slow and soft and deliberate as he made her dizzy with his lips and tongue and teeth and hands and—

"I want the rest of my clothes off," she gasped, breaking the kiss. "And yours. All of it. Now. Everything."

Will laughed and shifted to his side. "Yes, ma'am," he said, and trailed his hand down her belly to the button at the top of her capris. "Any last requests before I ravage you?"

Marley tried to think of something clever to say, her breath coming hard and fast and her brain so fogged with desire that she was having trouble remembering her own name. She opened her mouth to beg him to just fuck her. To take her hard and fast and—

"Security! Freeze!"

Or that.

Will jerked his arm back, sliding it instinctively over her breasts to cover them. Marley blinked against the sudden rush of harsh light flooding the planetarium and the jarring absence of Will's breath on her throat.

She squinted toward the door, trying to make out the shape of the intruder. She saw the silhouette of a man—a tall man—brandishing a gun.

"Freeze!" he yelled again as Marley flailed an arm out to the side, reaching for her shirt. She got Will's shirt instead, but pulled it to her anyway. She covered her breasts, then drew the shirt up over half her face for good measure. The light in the planetarium was dim, but there was no sense taking the risk of being recognized topless in her new workplace.

"Jimmy, it's me," Will said. "Put the Taser away. Nothing's happening here." He looked down at Marley. "Besides the obvious."

"Mr. Barclay?" The man in the doorway took a few steps into the planetarium, lowering his weapon as he moved. "Is that you?"

"The one and only," Will agreed. "Though not entirely alone."

"What are you—? Oh."

Apparently realizing Will was in the company of another human—not to mention partly disrobed—the security guard took two steps back. "Um, I didn't realize… that is, I wasn't aware you'd be entertaining any donors this evening, Mr. Barclay."

"Fund-raising can be a challenge in this economy," Will said. "Sometimes you have to go beyond the normal scope of things."

Will pressed his pelvis against Marley's, and she let out a little squeak of alarm. Or arousal—they were sort of the same. Marley fought the urge to wriggle her hand out and wave or offer a handshake. It was clear the man didn't know who she was, and probably best to keep it that way.

"I'm very sorry," Jimmy said, taking another step back. "I got a call that something tripped one of the internal alarms. Thought one of the coyotes might've gotten out of their pen again."

"Right," Will said. "In a manner of speaking—"

Marley jerked her knee up, threatening a swift jab to the groin. Will pressed his body harder against hers, pinning her in place.

"Thanks, Jimmy," Will said. "For being so diligent about security. On behalf of the entire Cheez Whiz organization, I want to say how much we appreciate your service."

"Right. Okay then, I'm going to leave you now to... um—"

"Raise funds for the organization."

"Yes. Of course. You get on that."

"I intend to."

"Good night, Mr. Barclay."

"Good night, Jim."

Marley winced as the door slammed shut behind the guard. She pushed hard against Will's chest, sitting up and fumbling her arms into his shirt. She could find hers in a minute. She reached back toward the pile and felt around for her bra, a little dizzy from the stars and heat and the unexpected burst of adrenaline. She managed to latch one finger in her bra strap and dragged the black lace to her.

"Do you ever get the sense the universe is conspiring against us?" she asked. "It doesn't seem possible that two people could be interrupted this many times in the quest to remove each other's clothing."

Will grinned and reached out to nudge the bra away. "Maybe we're being tested."

"Maybe we're being told this isn't a good idea." Marley leaned out further and tugged the bra back. "Hadn't we already concluded that on our own?"

Will's arms were longer, so he reached for the bra again. "Are we going to play tug-o-war with your underwear all night, or are you going to get naked?"

"I am not going to get naked." Marley tugged the bra back more forcefully this time. "Even if I weren't seriously freaked out by this curse, there's no way in hell I'm taking off any more clothes with Officer Jimmy out there angling for a peek. Does this place have security cameras?"

"Only in high-security areas. The planetarium isn't one of them."

"Do you think he saw me?"

"Never mind that. Did you hear what he said about the coyotes?"

Marley rolled her eyes. "Coyotes getting out of their cages are the least of my worries right now. I'm a little concerned about my job. And how did Jimmy know you weren't in here assaulting me against my will?"

"You had your legs wrapped around my waist and you were panting at me to fuck you. I think most folks would interpret that as consent."

"Fine. Can you hand me my shirt?"

Will grinned and reached for it. "Are we trading? Your shirt for my shirt, or weren't you planning to give that one back?"

Marley glanced down at Will's shirt wrapped around her

torso, and felt a funny pang of longing. A stupidly sentimental part of her wanted to keep it. To go to bed with it tucked beside her pillow so she could fall asleep breathing in the scent of him.

"Pink isn't your color," she said, and tugged her shirt out of his hands. "And we should probably go home now, don't you think?"

"We haven't had dessert," he pointed out. "I don't mean that as a euphemism. Seriously, how many of those lemon tarts are in the basket?"

Marley rolled away and pulled his shirt off, tossing it to him as she pulled her own T-shirt over her head. She realized too late she'd pulled it on inside out, but decided she didn't care. Spending even three more seconds topless in Will's company could be deadly. She turned and dug her hand into the basket. She came up with two lemon tarts and held one out to him.

"Tart?"

"Tramp? Trollop? Hussy?"

She thrust the dessert at him as she brought her own to her mouth. "Joke all you want, funny guy. I got the last dessert."

Marley bit into the pastry, her heart still racing with lust and terror and a million other emotions she couldn't name.

It's a good thing you got interrupted again, her conscience told her. *Besides all the other reasons not to get involved, you're now hiding the fact that you've lost his family heirlooms.*

"Bad tart?" Will asked.

Marley blinked at him. "What?"

"You got very frowny all of a sudden. Either you don't like the tart, or it's something I did."

"Just thinking about your aunt's figurines." Her own honesty surprised her, as did Will's response.

"Any chance we could take a look at them while we're here?"

Marley felt all the blood drain from her face. "What for?"

Will shrugged. "There was one figurine in particular that Bethany always liked. I've been thinking if it wouldn't ruin the collection to remove one piece, I'd like to buy it back for her birthday."

"I'd love to, but the pieces are being cleaned right now. Some other time?"

Will was studying her so intensely, Marley had to fight the urge to look away. At last, he nodded. "Some other time then."

—⁂—

The drive home was a quiet one. Will wasn't sure whether to blame the post-meal stupor, the awkwardness of another near-miss hookup, or something else entirely.

It's the something else that has you worried.

He'd seen Marley's face when he'd asked about the figurines. He didn't doubt there was something to what Aunt Nancy told Bethany about the empty safe. But what was going on? And what role did Marley play in it?

"Here we are," Will said as he pulled up the driveway of the condo. "I'd offer to do the gentlemanly thing and walk you to the door, but my intentions aren't gentlemanly and I'd hope to get a lot further than the door."

Marley smiled. "I appreciate your honesty."

"I'm nothing if not honest."

Marley didn't respond, and Will stole a look at her. He'd been baiting her with the comment, and the way she bit her lip now told him he'd hit a nerve.

"You okay?" he asked.

"Just preoccupied about work."

"Anything you want to talk about?"

"Not really."

Okay then…

Will sighed and pulled the e-brake. Not volunteering information isn't the same as lying, he reminded himself.

Tell that to any guy who's ever discovered his wife enjoys playing tickle-the-lint-trap more than batter-dip-the-corndog.

Will glanced at Marley again and said a silent prayer of thanks she couldn't read minds. "So are you still planning to go mountain biking with April and Bethany next weekend?" he asked.

Marley looked at her hands and sighed. "I'd like to, but…"

She let the words hang there for a moment, leaving Will to fill in the blank on his own.

"But you actually hate biking and would sooner saw off your own arm with a rusty bread knife than get on a bicycle again anytime this century?" he guessed.

Marley laughed and looked out the window. "I want to like biking, but my last two experiences haven't gone so great. Maybe I'm not cut out for it."

"Once you get past the butt bruising, the busted frame, the expensive repairs, the bad dates with bike repair guys, and being stuck at a restaurant with a locked-up tandem bike and no way home, it's really quite an enjoyable hobby."

"It's sounding a lot less fun the more we talk about it."

Will cleared his throat, then hesitated. "You know, Marley, you don't always have to base all your decisions on what you think other people want you to like."

She turned to look at him, her eyes narrowed almost

imperceptibly, and Will felt the temperature drop inside the Volkswagen. "Thanks for the armchair psychiatry. That's enlightening, coming from a guy who can't have an emotional conversation without cracking penis jokes."

"That's unfair," Will said. "I like to think I made a broad range of sex jokes encompassing all manner of genitalia."

Marley sighed. "Look, there's no point in psychoanalyzing one another. We're both a little fucked up. At least we're being honest about it."

"Honest. There's that word again."

She folded her arms over her chest. "Is there something you're trying to say?"

Will hesitated, then shrugged. "Not really. You?"

"Nope. You want to have a discussion about your trust issues now, or can we just call it a night?"

"Tempting, but I'll pass."

"Okay then." Marley reached for the door handle. "Thank you for the amazing dinner, Will. It was a hundred times better than my real date turned out to be."

He smiled. "My pleasure."

"Be sure to thank April for the food. It was wonderful."

"I'll let her know."

Marley's hand was still on the door handle, but she hadn't pulled it yet. He waited, giving her a chance to fill in the silence. To come clean with whatever secrets she might be hiding.

"Good night, Will."

"Good night. Tell Magoo hello for me. And tell your dad—well, on second thought, it's probably best if your dad thinks you spent the evening with Plaid Neanderthal."

"Or with a roving gang of pedophiles and crack dealers." She grinned. "Take care, Will."

"You too."

She hesitated again, then leaned toward him. For an instant, Will thought she might be angling for a passionate embrace. He was willing and able and starting to reach for her when Marley's lips landed on the edge of his jaw.

The kiss was so soft, so gentle that Will ached from the sweetness of it. When she drew back, her cheeks were flushed. He ached to reach for her again—just to feel her lips on his skin one more time—but Marley pulled the car door open and stepped out.

"Good night, Will. Thanks again."

"Sweet dreams."

She closed the car door softly behind her. She was halfway up the driveway when the front door of the condo flew open. Magoo came scampering out, his fuzzy paws an excited blur as he scrambled toward his mistress. Will smiled as Marley dropped to her knees and began to scratch behind the dog's ears.

"Good boy! Such a good boy! What a very good—"

Marley froze. Will watched her whole body go stiff, and the profile of her smile vanished so swiftly it might not have been there at all. Her eyes were fixed on a spot at the edge of the porch, and Will followed her gaze, expecting to see her father or maybe Curtis waiting at the front door.

Instead, a middle-aged woman with frizzy blond hair stood at the edge of the front step, a timid smile tugging the corners of her mouth. Will watched as the woman opened her arms wide and called to Marley.

"Baby. Sweetie. It's so good to see you. It's been so long!"

Will looked back at Marley, who was still frozen on her

knees in the middle of the concrete driveway. She blinked at the woman, then turned slowly to face Will.

Her expression was somewhere between dumbfounded and terrified, and Will half expected Marley to run back to the car and order him to drive away fast in a hail of gunfire. Will reached for the car keys in the ignition, not sure whether to rev the engine and leave or jump out to come to Marley's aid.

Marley stood up, her face pale with shock. She brushed her hair out of her eyes as the woman walked toward her, arms outstretched.

"Mom," Marley said, and turned to look at Will again.

Chapter 16

HALF OF MARLEY'S BRAIN WAS TELEGRAPHING A MESSAGE to her mother to go back into the condo and wait a few minutes to let her dumbfounded daughter collect her thoughts.

The other half of her brain was telepathically ordering Will to stay in the car and drive far, far away as fast as possible.

Apparently, Marley needed to work on her powers of thought transference.

"Who is this darling young man?" Judy called as she clasped Marley in a giant bear hug and rocked back and forth while peering over her daughter's shoulder. She drew back and nodded toward the car, where Will still sat looking uncertain. "Marley, why don't you invite your date inside so we can get to know him better?"

"He's not my date," Marley protested, wrestling one hand free from her mom's embrace to wave farewell to Will. Maybe that signal would be enough to let him know he needed to hit the road.

"Nonsense. Your father said you were out on a date with a bicycle mechanic, and I've been waiting all evening to get a look at him. At least invite him in for a quick hello."

"Mom, he's not—"

But Judy was already prying open the door of Will's Volkswagen, not willing to take no for an answer. Will raised one eyebrow at Marley as Judy grabbed him by the arm and towed him out of the driver's seat. "It's so nice to meet the lucky young man who caught the eye of my baby," Judy said, wrapping her arms around Will for a hug.

Will kept his focus on Marley, a question in his eyes. Marley wished like hell she had the answer to that question and a lot of others. For starters, how the hell had her mother gotten out of jail?

Please don't let her say anything, she thought. *Not now. Now while Will's here.*

Sensing Judy was about to release Will from her hug, Marley forced herself to walk down the driveway to stand beside her mother.

"Will, this is my mom, Judy Cartman. Mom, this is Will Barclay."

Judy drew back to study Will, looking like a maniacal produce inspector who'd squeezed too many bananas. "So you're a bike mechanic," Judy said. "I think that's just wonderful. Marley's always been afraid of bicycling, so it's delightful to see her branching out and—"

"Will isn't the bike mechanic, Mom." Marley shot Will an apologetic look as she pried her mother off him. "Will is a friend who came to rescue me when my date with the bike mechanic didn't work out."

Will nodded and took a step back. "Ma'am. Pleasure to meet you."

"Well that's just wonderful!" Judy gushed, appraising Will with even more enthusiasm than before. "A real knight in shining armor, coming to Marley's rescue like that. It's so nice to know she has someone taking care of her."

Marley gritted her teeth, wishing the ground would swallow up one of them—her, Judy, Will—it didn't actually matter at this point.

"I'd rather take care of myself," Marley said. The second the words were out of her mouth, she felt like a petulant toddler.

Judy shook her head and put an arm around Marley's shoulders. "You're always taking care of other people, sweetie. Isn't it nice sometimes to let someone else step up to the plate for you?"

She smiled knowingly before releasing Marley, who had a serious urge to snatch Will's car keys and make an emergency getaway in his Volkswagen.

Before she could act on it, Judy grabbed Will by the hand and began pulling him toward the condo. "Come on inside, you two. Your father and I were just sitting down for a drink and catching up on old times. I couldn't believe he got married again—can you believe it? How many times is that now—four, five?"

"Six," Marley said, dragging her feet as she followed behind and prayed for a nuclear disaster. Will looked over his shoulder at her, offering a sympathetic look.

"Ms. Cartman," Will began, "I don't want to interrupt your family reunion, especially if it's been a while since you and Marley have seen each other."

"Nonsense," Judy said, pushing him into the condo's foyer as Marley followed meekly behind. "What better way to catch up with my daughter than by meeting one of the young men she's been keeping company with here in Bend?"

Marley could think of at least three dozen appropriate ways to catch up with an estranged daughter that didn't involve hijacking a date that wasn't actually a date.

"Mom, I think Will has someplace he needs to be."

"Oh, this will only take a second," Judy said. "Have a seat right over there, son. Can I get you a glass of wine?"

Marley's dad looked up from the other end of the couch and watched the peculiar procession filing into the condo. He frowned as his eyes fixed on Will.

"You?"

Will stuck his hand out. "Pleasure to see you again, sir."

Magoo danced happily around Marley's ankles, unaware he was witnessing the world's most awkward family reunion. Marley's jailbird mom, the ex-husband who abandoned her, and the daughter with a whole closet full of secrets.

Marley shot another look at Will and wished he could be anyplace else. He caught her gaze and smiled. Marley returned the smile without thinking, as a teaspoon of dread leaked out of her psyche. She sighed and trudged after her mother.

"So, Mom," Marley said, trying to keep her voice from shaking. "It's been, what? Five, six years?"

"Something like that, dear. Will, honey, would you like red wine, white wine, or bourbon?"

"That's *my* bourbon," Marley's dad objected from the couch.

"None for me, thank you," Will said, settling on the opposite end of the sofa and resting his hands on his knees. He looked like a man preparing to see a tawdry made-for-TV movie, which wasn't too far off the mark. Marley couldn't decide whether she wanted to hit him or kiss him, so she settled for offering him a drink he might actually like.

"I'm having blueberry iced tea," she announced as she pulled two glasses from the cupboard. "Will?"

"Yes, please."

Once they were all seated in the living room with

sweating glasses in their hands, Judy beamed at Will. "So you're having intimate relations with my daughter?"

Marley choked on her tea. "Mom!"

Her father frowned at his ex-wife. "He's what?"

"Oh, pish." Judy smiled and took a sip of her wine. "It's obvious from looking at you two that you're on intimate terms. I think it's lovely. The art of lovemaking is a wonderful and beautiful thing, and in the confines of a committed relationship—"

"Mom, please stop." Marley took a sip of her iced tea as Magoo jumped onto the couch beside her and curled himself in a protective donut around her feet.

Judy ignored her daughter, keeping her focus on their guest. "So Will, if you aren't the bike mechanic, what is it you do for a living?"

Will twisted his glass around in one hand but didn't take a drink. "A little of this, a little of that."

Marley and her father rolled their eyes in tandem.

"He's a deliveryman," Walter said.

"He's a millionaire," Marley said.

Father and daughter glowered at each other. Judy went right on beaming.

"Millionaire deliveryman?" she said. "Well, yes, I suppose if you own stock in UPS or Fed Ex or—"

"Mom, Will doesn't like discussing his career or finances with strangers." She looked at Will, whose expression was unreadable. "Or with anyone."

Marley's mother fluttered a hand to her chest in feigned surprise. Or maybe the surprise was real. It was possible, considering how oblivious Judy could be in social situations. What the hell was she doing here, anyway? She wasn't due to be released for six more months. But maybe the parole hearing had gone better than expected. The state's prison system was overcrowded, and Judy was a good candidate for early release.

Will cleared his throat. "It's lovely to finally meet you, Ms. Cartman. I can see where Marley gets her beautiful smile."

"Please, call me Judy," she said, settling back a little into the leather armchair she'd selected. Walter watched, seemingly perplexed to see his first ex-wife making herself at home in his condo.

"So Will," Judy began again. "I understand from my ex-husband that Marley has been making an effort to date men whose value is measured in the content of their character rather than the content of their wallet. Where do you fit into the plan?"

Marley opened her mouth to say... well, she really wasn't sure what to say. But Will beat her to it.

"I don't actually fit into the plan at all," Will said. "I do volunteer work for several organizations Marley's been involved with, so we became acquainted in a professional capacity. We also interact socially from time to time."

"Oh, volunteer work." Judy smiled. "That's so nice. Very important to be charitable, don't you think, Marley?"

"Absolutely," Marley said for lack of anything better to say.

Judy turned back to Will. "It's important to us as her parents that Marley have friends with the utmost moral standards and strength of character. Tell me, Will, have you been married before?"

"*Mother*," Marley hissed, gripping the arm of her chair.

"Divorced, actually," Will said. "Four years now."

Marley's father scowled. "Divorced? I don't know how I feel about that."

Marley resisted the urge to punch her father in the shoulder.

"But with the volunteer work," Judy argued, "he's clearly an upstanding citizen."

Walter looked at Will. "Have you ever been delinquent on an account, declared bankruptcy, or been refused credit for any reason?"

"Oh, please," Judy scoffed, taking another sip of wine. "You're forgetting the more important questions, like police records, college education, political affiliation, whether he conforms to a vegan lifestyle—"

"Stop it, you two!" Marley snapped, setting her glass down hard on an end table and looking from one parent to the other. "Listen to yourselves. A serial philanderer and a convicted criminal giving lectures about moral standards and the sanctity of marriage. Dad thinks I should be dating for financial stability, and Mom thinks I should be dating for a Nobel Peace Prize, but neither of you seems to think I should be dating for *me*."

There was a long silence as Walter and Judy looked at their daughter as though she'd grown a third ear. Will took a sip of blueberry tea but said nothing. Marley released her grip on the arms of her chair and closed her eyes.

"A simple *please stop harassing the houseguest* would have been better," Marley muttered through gritted teeth.

"Not really," Will said.

———

Will knew he'd never admit it to anyone, but the moment Marley came unhinged in front of her parents?

Sexiest. Thing. Ever.

Of course, she was still hunched on the sofa with her face in her hands, so the lusty appeal was subdued. Seeing her like that made him want to take her in his arms and tell her everything would be okay, but he knew that wasn't the right move. With both parents demanding she find someone to take care of her, the last thing she wanted was him swaggering up to the plate.

But he couldn't just sit there while Walter and Judy looked at her as though she'd just piddled on the sofa. Even Magoo seemed distraught as he tucked his stub-tail between his legs and buried his nose under Marley's arm.

Will stood up, gripping his iced tea in one hand. "Marley, would it be possible to get a to-go cup?"

Marley pried her hands from her eyes and blinked up at him. "What?"

The sight of those hazel eyes brimming with guilt and embarrassment nearly unhinged him, and he forgot for a moment what he intended to say.

"I love your blueberry tea, but I really do need to head to another engagement," Will said. "Is there any chance I could put this in some sort of container to take with me?"

Lame, Barclay. Very lame.

But Marley stood up, her legs looking a little shaky as she trudged toward the kitchen. "Sure, no problem. Would a recycled water bottle be okay?"

"Perfect." Will followed after her, with Walter and Judy still frowning with confusion from their perches in the living room.

Good, Will thought. *Give them some time to consider the folly of dictating their grown daughter's love life.*

As soon as they were out of earshot, Will leaned against the stove and smiled at Marley. "Fun times with the family."

Marley sighed and stood on tiptoe to reach an upper cupboard. "It's a long story."

"I have time."

"I thought you had to be somewhere."

"I lied."

"You're not the only one."

Will studied the side of her face, wondering if that was another slip of the tongue or just an expression.

Marley turned to face him, a plastic water bottle in one hand and a resigned look on her face. "My father is on his sixth wife. My mother has a criminal history. Suffice it to say, I don't have the best role models for integrity and marital longevity."

"At least they seem to want the best for you. Their methods are a little heavy-handed, but they mean well."

Marley sighed and grabbed the full glass of tea from his hand. "And that's why I feel awful, and why I probably need to go back out there right now and apologize."

"Maybe not right now," Will said, leaning against the counter. "You weren't so far off base in your lecture. A little harsh maybe, but not uncalled for."

"I'm a horrible daughter."

Will raised an eyebrow. "Is there more to this story?"

Marley shrugged and began to pour Will's tea into the wide-mouth bottle "There's always more to a story, isn't there?"

"Evasive much?"

"It's just—" Marley frowned and screwed the lid onto the bottle. "Never mind. I wish you hadn't been here just now."

The fragrance of blueberry tea was making him a little dizzy, as was Marley's roundabout reasoning. What the hell was she talking about?

"Marley, is there something you want to tell me?"

She looked at him a little sadly. Then she looked down at the kitchen counter, her fingers gripped around the bottle of tea.

"I think I made a mistake."

She said the words so softly, Will almost didn't hear her. He took a step closer, wondering what she was on the verge of confessing.

"Marley?"

She looked up at him, and Will saw a faint shimmer of tears in her hazel eyes. "My plan to date men based on their income, or lack thereof," Marley said. "I think I need to give it a rest."

Will nodded, waiting for her to continue. There had to be more to her confession, but he knew he couldn't drag it out of her. Marley sighed and looked away.

"There are jerks with money and jerks without money, and maybe I'm just not very good at figuring out who's who," she said.

"There a few decent guys in the other camps too, you know. Nice guys with money, nice guys with none."

"True. I guess between tonight's abysmal date and listening to my dad just now, maybe I've figured out a few things about judging men based on their money."

Will nodded, then reached out to touch her arm. "So at least you've learned something. That's all part of the process, right?"

Marley sighed again, still not meeting his eyes. "Right."

She didn't say anything else, and Will wasn't sure how much longer he should stand here in this kitchen waiting for the other shoe to drop. She'd already admitted her mistake about dating. What more did he want from her?

The truth. All of it, whatever that happened to be.

"Marley? Is there something else you wanted to tell me?"

She looked back at him, her eyes still glittery. She shook her head and held his gaze. "There are a lot of things I should tell you. Unfortunately, that isn't an option right now."

She handed him his bottle of tea. Then she stood on tiptoe to kiss his cheek—the opposite one she'd kissed earlier in the car, not that he was keeping track. "Good night, Will."

―――♒――――

The next morning, Marley reported to work with a heavy feeling in her gut. It was a Saturday, not a scheduled workday for administrative staff, but Marley couldn't stay away. Maybe there was a chance she could find the figurines tucked in some forgotten corner. Maybe she could find them and tuck them back in the safe and banish the sick feeling in the pit of her gut.

The feeling didn't improve much when she trudged past Susan's office to see her boss deep in conversation with a man sporting a gun-shaped bulge beneath his sport coat. Susan's door was closed, but Marley could see them through the small window in the door. As Marley passed by, Susan waved frantically, summoning Marley inside.

"Close the door behind you, Marley," Susan said, turning back to her gun-toting guest. "I'd like you to meet Detective Doug Parker. Mr. Parker, this is our development director, Marley Cartman."

The man stuck out his hand, and Marley caught a glimpse of the contents of his shoulder holster. A shiver chattered up her spine.

"Detective," Marley repeated, looking at Susan. "I

thought you didn't want to involve police until we had time to research things internally."

"Detective Parker is a private investigator, and I've asked him to keep things strictly confidential," Susan said. "Until we know what's going on, there's no point in alarming local law enforcement or the media."

"Or the family," Marley said, her words more a question than a statement.

"Exactly," Susan said. "Detective Parker was just getting ready to share any findings he's encountered since I retained him yesterday."

"Yes, of course," Detective Parker said. "Ms. Cartman, it's a pleasure to meet you."

"Marley, please."

"Marley. Yes, well, as I mentioned to Susan, there was a small security breach last night that we believe is unrelated to the investigation, but worth noting nonetheless."

Marley looked at Susan. She was pretty sure she knew more about the security breach than these two, but she wanted to hear it from the boss.

"Will Barclay was entertaining a donor in the planetarium last night," Susan said, the emphasis on *entertaining a donor* making her meaning clear. "Not terribly unusual, though the nature of the entertainment, coupled with the fact that he's related to Nancy Thomas-Smith, is worth noting."

Marley swallowed hard, wondering if she should volunteer the fact that she knew damn well what sort of entertaining Will had been doing in the planetarium. She decided to keep her mouth shut and listen. Detective Parker's eyes were on her face, and Marley fought to keep her expression impassive, wondering if he already knew.

"We checked to be certain Mr. Barclay didn't have access to the safe," Detective Parker said. "His passcode wouldn't work for the administrative offices, so we feel fairly certain he's not involved."

"Good," Marley said. "I'm glad to hear that."

The detective nodded and continued. "I've been conducting background checks on staff and board members as a starting point to the investigation."

Marley frowned. "Doesn't everyone already have background checks as part of the hiring process?"

"The checks I'm performing are much more thorough," he said. "It's probably unnecessary, but it could be useful in determining if anyone connected to the organization has a history that might be relevant to the investigation."

"Relevant?" Hearing her own voice, Marley was relieved to realize she'd kept the squeak out of it.

"Theft, fraud, forgery—that sort of thing," the detective replied. "Like I said, it's likely not necessary, but we'd like to begin by focusing on the possibility this was an inside job."

Marley looked at Susan. "Is that what you're thinking? Someone on staff?"

Susan sighed. "It's certainly possible, though I can't for the life of me come up with a motive. It's not like it would be a simple process to steal and fence more than fifty stone phalluses."

"An excellent point," Detective Parker said. "Though you'd be surprised what unscrupulous individuals can get away with. Overseas jobs, underground collectors—there are plenty of people who'll pay a lot of money to own unique pieces of art."

Marley nodded numbly, her brain still processing the

notion of a thorough background check. "Susan probably already showed you the records of who's checked out the safe key recently?"

"She did, and while I plan to look into it, I believe it's highly improbable a thief would sign out a key before stealing artifacts from a locked safe."

Susan reached across the desk and touched Marley's hand. "It makes more sense for me to talk directly with staff members who recently signed out the key just to find out if they saw anything or noticed something unusual."

"Darin Temple?" Marley asked.

Susan nodded. "I spoke with Darin yesterday, but he was accessing a completely different vault. He didn't go anywhere near our safe."

"And he didn't see anything that seemed off?"

Susan shook her head. "I didn't want to badger him too much and risk raising suspicion, but I didn't get the sense he had anything to share."

Marley turned back to the detective. "What about fingerprints?"

"I'm heading in there to dust for them shortly," Detective Parker said. "Would you mind if I take your prints quickly, just so we can rule out employees who have legal access?"

"Of course," Marley said, her gut twisting in a giant knot.

The detective smiled and began unpacking tools from a briefcase on the desk in front of him. "Won't take more than a couple minutes, and then we'll let you get back to work." He set a black inkpad next to Susan's stapler and cleared his throat. "I know we all share the common goal of getting this solved quickly and fairly so we can recover the artifacts without alerting donors or community members. I want you to know I intend to exercise the utmost discretion."

Marley frowned at the barely-concealed outline of his firearm. "Is the gun really necessary?"

He smiled and patted the outside of his jacket. "I'm licensed to carry a concealed weapon. It's sometimes necessary in my line of work."

"Sure," Marley muttered. "I can see how administrative offices and cages of birds and skunks might require self-defense."

"The most dangerous places are often the ones you feel safest," he replied, flipping open the top on an ink pad.

Marley blinked. *Don't I know it.*

Susan cleared her throat, looking to bring attention back to the task at hand. "I think the important thing here is that we not panic."

Marley nodded, trying hard to smile. "Too late for that," she said as she held out her hand for the detective.

"I spent several hours with Susan last night picking her brain for details on the case," he said as he began taking her prints. "But I'd like a chance to interview you separately, Marley."

"Certainly," she said. "My office is right across the hall."

"I have to finish up some things here first, but I was thinking maybe lunch."

"Lunch?"

"Maybe someplace private where I could ask questions, get to know you a little better."

Marley wasn't sure they were still talking about the investigation.

He's attractive. He's polite. He probably has an average salary.

And Marley knew beyond a shadow of a doubt that if she went on one more date with one more man who wasn't what she truly wanted, she was going to go insane.

"You're free at lunch, aren't you, Marley?" Susan said. "It might be vital to the investigation."

Doug smiled at her expectantly, and Marley sighed.

"How about the café here at Cheez Whiz?" she offered.

"Cheez Whiz?"

"The Cascade Historical Society and Wildlife Sanctuary," Marley said. "It's still pretty warm outside for September, and there's a nice bank of quiet tables where no one's likely to bother us. We can watch the skunks wrestle while we eat lunch."

"I'll even lock my gun in the car if it makes you feel better."

"Perfect," Susan said and smiled.

Not really, thought Marley, but she refrained from saying so.

Chapter 17

WILL OFFERED HIS ARM TO AUNT NANCY AS THEY strolled out the front door of the downtown branch of Bank of the Cascades. She ignored it and marched ahead of him, pushing her way through the heavy glass doors of the lobby.

"Was it really necessary to ask the bank manager what he thinks about when he masturbates?" Will called after her.

"It's for a legitimate research project," she huffed, hitching her purse higher on her shoulder.

"You asked him to show you porn videos stored on his iPhone."

"He didn't have to do it. Besides, I thanked him politely for being open on a Saturday. That was professional."

"Good point," Will said. "So is there anyplace else you need me to chauffer you to while we're out?"

Nancy hitched her purse again as she marched ahead. "Lunch. And none of that frou-frou crap April's always making with pomegranate seed au gratin over tender filets of duck and puréed fennel or whatever the hell that is. I want a *real* meal. A hamburger."

Will quickened his pace to catch up with her. He knew damn well his aunt's doctor had put her on a low-cholesterol diet, but far be it from him to remind her. "Pilot Butte Drive-In?" he suggested. "You like their strawberry shakes."

"I like the burgers better at the Cascade Historical

Society and Wildlife Sanctuary," she said, stopping in front of the car and turning to look at him. "Besides, they have those little tater tots in the shape of animals."

"Can't argue with that," he said as he unlocked her door and handed her inside. "Are you sure you're not just asking to go there so you can stalk the staff and make inappropriate phallic references?"

She reached for her seat belt and yanked it across her ample bosom. "Isn't that the reason you'd want to go?"

"Probably," he said, and headed around to the driver's side.

As he put the car in gear, Nancy began fiddling with parts of the car. She flipped the visor up and down, picked pennies out of the ashtray, and changed the dial on the radio.

"Are you nervous about something, Aunt Nancy?"

She slammed the glove box shut and scowled. "Those figurines are worth a great deal of money."

"Of course they are," Will agreed.

"Your uncle—God rest his soul—gave them to me before he passed."

"God rest his soul," Will agreed, thinking the request from the Almighty was probably a good idea, considering the circumstances of Uncle Albert's demise. He'd had a heart attack in a brothel in Thailand, leaving his massive fortune—not to mention the rock cocks—to his grieving widow.

"We'll have lunch at Cheez Whiz then," Will said as he turned onto the highway and headed south. "Maybe you'll be able to talk to someone who can put your mind at ease."

As he pulled into the parking lot, Will felt a flutter of excitement as he spotted Marley's car. It was a Saturday, so there was no reason at all she should be at work. The fact that she was made him both excited and suspicious.

"What are you looking for?" Nancy snapped.

"A parking spot."

"There are three hundred empty ones over there. What else are you looking for?"

"The development director's car," Will admitted. "I have a question I need to ask her."

"Is the question 'Are you interested in Nyotaimori?'"

"I'm relieved to have no idea what that means."

"It's the sexual practice of eating sushi off the body of a nude woman."

Will shook his head, trying not to picture Marley with a crab roll in her belly button. "Did you miss the part where I said I was relieved not to know what it was?"

"It's my job to educate you," she said. "I take that seriously."

"I kinda wish you wouldn't," Will said as he angled his car into the parking spot closest to Marley's. "Can we please just go inside and have a nice lunch without asking inappropriate sex questions of any patrons or staff?"

Nancy sighed and unhooked her seat belt. "You know, it's considered unethical to interfere with the research project of a renowned sex therapist."

"I'll take my chances with being unethical," Will said as he flipped the door locks and came around to help Nancy out of the car.

He didn't give her the option to take his arm this time, instead grabbing hers as he led her up the cobblestone walkway. He pretended to study a sign advertising the new butterfly exhibit, but he knew what he was really scanning for. A glimpse of Marley scurrying down the hall with papers in her arm or laughing with one of the curators or bending down to pet the tortoise in the desert wildlife display or—

"Did you hear a word I just said?" Nancy asked.

"What?"

"I said I'd like to go check to see if the figurines are back from being *cleaned*."

Her emphasis on the word made it clear she doubted what Marley had told her.

That makes two of us.

"It's lunch hour on a Saturday, Aunt Nancy," Will said. "Why don't we give everyone a break for now?"

"Hmph," she said, but allowed Will to pull her in the direction of the café.

The indoor seating area was packed with bookish-looking college students and families with wailing children. Will got in line behind a frazzled-looking mother balancing a toddler on one hip as she recited the menu to a school-aged girl.

"I only eat *organic* corndogs," the older child whined.

The toddler screamed and reached for a fistful of ketchup packets from the dispenser.

Will turned to Aunt Nancy. "Let me know what you want, and I'll order for you so you can go sit down."

"Cheeseburger with those animal-shaped tater tots and a small garden salad."

"Coming right up," Will said as he took a step forward in line. "Pick where you want to sit and I'll come find you."

The line moved slowly, and by the time Will ordered their food and walked away with a well-loaded tray, he'd lost sight of Aunt Nancy. He couldn't find her anywhere in the café, so he pushed through a side door leading to the outdoor patio.

There were only three people seated outside—his aunt, Marley, and a dark-haired stranger sitting a little too close to Marley. Aunt Nancy was chatting animatedly about something, waving a napkin around for emphasis. But Marley looked up as he approached, and Will watched as she fixed her stiff smile in place.

"Will, what a pleasant surprise," she said as Will reached the table with the tray gripped hard in his hands. "What brings you here?"

"You mean besides a fervent desire to eat tater tots shaped like hedgehogs?"

"Sounds like a good reason to me."

Still smiling, Marley turned to the man seated beside her. "Will, this is Det—this is my friend Doug Parker. Doug, this is William Barclay and his aunt, Nancy Thomas-Smith."

"Pleasure to meet you," the man said, extending his hand as he gave Marley a knowing look.

Will rested his tray on the edge of the table and returned the guy's handshake. Marley looked down at her cobb salad, suddenly very interested in a slice of hardboiled egg. Will watched her, trying to get a read on the dynamic at play. This wasn't a date, was it? Hadn't Marley said she was through with that?

Will broke the handshake and started to pick up his tray. One thing was obvious—Doug and Marley didn't want company. "Come on, Aunt Nancy. There's an empty table over there."

"So Mr. Parker," Aunt Nancy said, leaning back in her chair with no intention of leaving just yet. "I'm doing a research study on paraphilia. Do you have any stories you'd like to share with me?"

Will gripped the edge of his tray so hard he thought it might snap in two. "Aunt Nancy, I really don't think—"

"Paraphilia?" Doug asked, dabbing his mouth with his napkin. "I'm sorry, I'm not familiar with that term."

"*The Diagnostic and Statistical Manual of Mental Disorders* classifies paraphilia as an Axis II disorder," Nancy explained. "Paraphilia involves distressing and repetitive sexual fantasies, urges, behaviors, or—"

"That's enough, Aunt Nancy," Will said. "I'm having distressing and repetitive urges right now, but they aren't sexual in nature."

Not entirely true, he admitted, fighting the urge to look at Marley. Her smile made the very slight shift from plastic to real, and Will felt his heart clench tight in his chest. How was it humanly possible to simultaneously mistrust and desire a woman this much?

Nancy *hrmphed* and turned to Marley. "So how's the cleaning coming along with my figurines?"

"Figurines?" Doug asked as he speared a cherry tomato on the edge of his plate.

"I donated some very valuable Native American artifacts to the organization," Nancy said. "I came by to check on them the other day, but Ms. Cartman here informed me they're being cleaned."

"Yes, well, I can imagine cleanliness would be important," Doug said. "Can you tell me about these artifacts?"

Will loosened his grip on the tray, listening a little more intently to the conversation now.

"They're ancient Native American artifacts from the Chinook Tribe of the Columbia River Valley," Aunt Nancy said. "Sexual aids crafted from—"

"I'm sorry, did you say sexual aids?"

"That's right," Aunt Nancy replied. "Commonly known as dildos."

Marley choked on her salad, and Will resisted the urge to whack her on the back.

"I see," Doug replied, spearing another cherry tomato. "That sounds fascinating. How did you acquire these artifacts?"

"My late husband—God rest his soul—bought them for me as a wedding gift. They're extremely valuable."

"I can imagine. I'd love to know more." Doug chewed his tomato before glancing at Marley. "You were right—this salad is excellent."

"The dressing is surprisingly good, isn't it?"

Will cleared his throat. "I'm sorry, were the two of you on a date?"

"Yes!" Marley said a little too quickly. "A date. That's right. Doug and I are on a lunch date." She looked at Doug, who was still studying Aunt Nancy.

Then she looked at Will. Her hazel eyes were bright and electric with something Will couldn't quite read. Tension? Lust? She blinked, and Will watched her lips part softly. He ached to kiss them. To touch her again.

He expected her to look away, to turn her attention back to her date and dismiss Will like she had every right to.

But instead, she gave him a small, desperate smile.

Get me out of here, she mouthed.

Will's heart pulsed thickly in his chest.

He was torn between the urge to tell her off for her stupid plan of dating men based on the size of their wallets and the urge to pull her body against his and order her to never look at another man again.

Marley shifted in her seat, and Will caught the scent

of blueberries and saw the warm light flash in her golden hair.

Something besides his heart pulsed.

He turned to Aunt Nancy. "How long do you think you can talk about paraphilia and Native American sex toys?"

"At least six hours without taking a break."

Will stood up and shoved the tray in front of his aunt. "Enjoy your lunch," he said, then nodded at Doug. "You enjoy learning everything you've ever wanted to know about bizarre sex acts. Marley, you're coming with me."

He extended a hand and watched her hesitate, deciding whether to take it or whether to stick around and finish out her date.

She put her hand in his and let Will pull her to her feet.

Chapter 18

THEY'D DRIVEN FIVE MILES BEFORE WILL LET GO OF HER hand to turn onto a gravel road. Marley could still feel her fingers tingling even after he drew away.

"You haven't asked where we're going," he said, glancing over at her.

Marley smiled, leaning back against the seat and thinking that just five minutes in Will's company left her feeling more relaxed and happy than an hour with any other man. Why had she not noticed that on all her other dates? How had she missed the fact that every neuron in her body seemed to breathe better when she was near him?

Frankly, she didn't care where he took her.

She peered through the windshield as he made a sharp turn toward the river. "Are you driving me into the woods to leave me for dead?"

Will was quiet a moment, both hands gripping hard on the steering wheel as he arced the car around a sharp corner and into a deserted clearing in the trees. He made another turn, transporting them deeper into the trees.

"I'm taking you into the woods to tear your clothes off and make love to you on a blanket at the edge of the river."

Marley's heart stopped. Her toes curled inside her shoes, and she had a distinct sensation that her body was melting. "Oh," she breathed. "Okay."

"Okay?" Will pulled the car onto the shoulder of the dirt road and turned to look at her. "Was that consent, or an indication that you think I'm joking because half the words out of my mouth are inappropriate sex jokes?"

"Yes."

"Yes?"

Marley swallowed, dizzy with the intensity in his eyes. "I'm covering both my bases."

"What?"

"If you're joking, I want you to know I appreciate the humor." She took a breath, wondering how the temperature had risen twenty degrees despite the air conditioning in the Volkswagen. "And if you're serious, it's consent."

Will nodded and put the car in park. "I'm serious. For once. I'm tired of seeing you go out on dates with other men and knowing not one of them is right for you."

"And you're right for me?" She didn't really expect an answer. Frankly, she didn't care, since all her nerves were singing in harmony, *Hell, yes.*

"Hell, yes," Will said, and pried his hands off the wheel. "I can make you smile for real and I can make you laugh and I'm dying to see what else I can make you do."

Marley's stomach did a flip, and it was all she could do not to melt into a slobbering puddle on the floor of his car. She folded her hands in her lap, worried she'd lunge for him if she didn't. "Okay."

Will held up one hand. "I realize the following phrase should never be uttered by a man hoping to have sex in the next ten minutes, but I need to text my ex-wife and my sister."

Marley blinked. "Right now?"

"Someone has to go get Aunt Nancy. Or rescue your date, as the case may be. Two seconds."

Will pulled out his phone and began typing furiously.

Marley tried to decide whether to be annoyed or pleased, and decided life was too short not to pick pleasure. Besides, she could see over Will's shoulder that he'd mistyped half the words. This was a man distracted, and Marley liked being that distraction.

Will shoved his phone back in his pocket, and Marley grinned at him. "Got a blanket?"

Will nodded and turned to pop open his car door. Marley's hands were shaking so hard that by the time she got her door open, Will had managed to open the trunk, grab a thick quilt, and make it around to Marley's side of the car before her shaky legs made her fall on her ass.

"Need a hand?" he asked.

"Thank you," she said, and let him pull her out of the seat.

"This way," he said, and led her down a short trail before veering sharply to the right.

"Don't the rules of hiking say you're supposed to stay on the trail?" Marley asked, wiggling her fingers a little in Will's grip.

"Yes, but the rules of outdoor sex say it's wise not to give your fellow hikers a peep show."

"I'll have to read that book."

Will stopped so abruptly that Marley smacked into the back of him. She stepped back and gasped as she realized they were at the fringe of a lovely little clearing overlooking the river.

"Beautiful," she said, gazing down at the ripples in the water.

"Yes," said Will, and Marley looked up to see him gazing down at her.

Her heart wedged in her throat as her mouth went dry

from lust and heat, and she lost the ability to think of anything clever to say.

She licked her lips. "Should we spread it out?"

"What?"

Marley grinned. "The blanket. Should we lay it on the ground?"

Will laughed and took a few steps back. He shook the blanket out, and Marley caught the edge of it, her hands barely cooperating. She gripped the corners of the quilt and pulled it to the ground, careful to avoid the pointy rock she knew she didn't want poking her in the small of her back. She watched him kick his shoes off and use them to anchor opposite corners of the blanket.

So thorough.

"Are we really going to do this?" she asked, her voice quivering a little. "I mean, we keep saying it's a bad idea for all these reasons and—"

"And I can't remember a single one of them right now." Will pulled her into his arms, crushing her pleasantly against his chest. "At least I'm trying very hard not to. How about you?"

Marley looked into those mismatched eyes and shivered with desire. "Yes. I mean no. I mean y—"

"Good."

Then he kissed her. He was gentle at first, testing. Giving her one last out if she wanted it.

She didn't. Marley kissed him back hard and deep. She drew back for one breathless moment and looked him in the eye. "Did I ever tell you I studied Jiu Jitsu?"

Will quirked an eyebrow. "I think you just trumped me for the weirdest pre-sex comment. Or is this another one of those pseudo hobbies for winning friends and influencing people—"

"I really know Jiu Jitsu," Marley said, bear-hugging him from the side. "Which is how I know how to do this."

She locked her hands around him just above his hip. Shifting her weight behind him, she slid her left foot parallel with his and stuck her butt out, pulling them both to the ground. He toppled easily, probably more from surprise than from any real martial arts prowess on Marley's part. She dropped to the side of him, cushioning his fall with her thigh.

Will landed on his back and rolled to face her, laughing. "Remind me not to doubt you again."

"Gladly."

The ground beneath them was softer than she'd expected, cushioned with pine needles and fallen leaves. Will slid an arm around her shoulder, pulling her tight against them and making the space between them vanish. His lips found hers again, and he kissed her harder this time, giving no chance for her to protest.

Not that she had any intention of doing that. She wanted him badly. She ached with it, her back arching to press her pelvis against the hard length of him. He broke the kiss, and Marley leaned back, panting.

"You're sure no one's going to find us here?" she asked.

"Not sure at all. There's a very real possibility some hiker could trip over our legs at any moment."

"As long as we're prepared," she said, as she untucked his T-shirt.

Will began to kiss his way down her neck, lingering in the hollow of her throat as Marley gasped and writhed and went dizzy with sensation. His fingers slid to the opening of her shirt.

"Buttons," he said. "Much easier to remove than a

pullover. Clearly you thought of my convenience when you got dressed this morning."

"Absolutely," Marley breathed, moving against him as his fingers undid the buttons one by one. "When I put my clothes on for a long Saturday at the office, the first thing I considered was the prospect I'd end up naked in the woods with you on my lunch break."

"Thoughtful of you."

Will kept flicking buttons open, planting soft kisses on each patch of newly exposed flesh. By the time he undid the last one, Marley was gasping with need.

"Please," she panted.

"Please what?" he asked, his Adam's apple vibrating against her hip bone.

"Please take me."

Will laughed. "We've waited thirteen days, four hours, and fifty-six minutes," he said, slipping his hand around her back to unhook her bra. "We can wait a few more minutes for me to fully undress you."

"Is full undressing really necessary?" Marley grinned. "Because I can just hike up my skirt, slip my panties off to the side, and—"

He silenced her with another kiss as his fingers deftly flicked open her bra clasp. Marley moaned with the release of pressure, feeling more build up inside her as Will moved from her mouth down her collarbone and over. He drew her nipple into his mouth and Marley sucked in a breath, arching against him to savor the feel of his tongue against her.

She felt a rock digging into one hip bone, so she shifted her weight, rolling so she was on top of Will. He rolled with her, his mouth not losing contact with her breast for even an instant.

"That's talent," she said aloud, startled by her own words.

"I try," he murmured, releasing one nipple and moving toward the other. "For my next act, I plan to juggle flaming watermelons."

"If that's one of your sister's euphemisms, I'm game."

Will laughed and swirled his tongue around her nipple, making her gasp. She gripped his shoulders, certain she'd topple over if she let go. Will's hands slid around her back, fumbling for the zipper on her skirt. He tugged it down, and Marley shivered a little as the chilly forest air hit her bare skin.

"This is wrong," she breathed.

Will's lips froze against her bare belly. "If you're coming up with another reason to stop this, I'm throwing you in the river right now with a rock tied to your ankle."

Marley laughed. "As erotic as I find your death threats, that's not what I meant. I just think it's wrong that you're still wearing all your clothes and I'm half-naked."

"You're totally right. You should be completely naked by now. I'm losing my touch."

Will angled up and flipped her on her back. Marley gasped, amazed by both the maneuver and the fact that he'd managed to avoid impaling her on the rock. Before she could catch her breath, he was tugging her skirt down over her hips, pulling her panties with it and leaving her bare beneath the trees with the scent of juniper and river water in the air and a faint coat of dust on her skin.

She'd never felt so sexy.

Marley reached up and grabbed the hem of his T-shirt. "You weren't as considerate with the buttons," she said. "Either I can chew through this, or you can help me—"

Will yanked the shirt over his head, making his coppery

hair stand up with static electricity. Marley laughed and grabbed his belt buckle with both hands. As she began to unfasten it, Will explored her flesh with his hands. His palms made a slow journey over her hips, her belly, the juncture of her thighs…

"Please!" she gasped as his fingers slipped into her, making her buck and arch against the heel of his hand.

"So soft," he murmured into her hair as Marley finished tugging his buckle free and jerked open his button fly.

"Not the adjective I was thinking," Marley said as her fingers circled the smooth length of him.

Will made a hissing sound between his teeth as she began to stroke him, softly at first, then with more pressure. His fingers were still inside her, and Marley struggled to keep her rhythm as she lost her mind to the dizzying heat of his touch. He was throbbing in her palm, so smooth and hard all at once. Marley ached to take more of him, to feel every inch of him against her, inside her.

"Please tell me you have a condom," she whispered.

"I always bring condoms when I take my elderly aunt to the bank."

She stopped stroking and blinked up at him, hoping like hell he was kidding. Or serious—the two things were confused in her mind with him. Will's mismatched eyes flashed with mischief.

"I'm serious, though it's actually the other way around," he said. "Aunt Nancy's the one who brings the condoms. She considers it her duty to keep me well-stocked."

"And to think my elderly aunt just gives me peppermints." Marley slid her hands down his shaft once more. "So how long are we going to fondle each other before we're too turned on from the petting and just fuck each other's brains out?"

"Subtlety is not your forte, Ms. Cartman."

"I have plenty of other fortes, Mr. Barclay."

"I can't wait to see some of them."

"Allow me to show you."

She slid her hands to each side of his hips and shoved his jeans down, moving them out of the way. She was glad now he'd had the foresight to toe his shoes off earlier. It made it much easier for her to push his jeans off, enjoying the ripple of muscle as he kicked them off the rest of the way. His boxer briefs went with them, tangled somewhere in the legs of the denim.

"Not wasting any time with gradual undressing this time," she breathed, sliding a hand around to stroke his bare backside as he lay back down beside her.

"Hell no. If I don't keep my hands on you at all times, I'm afraid you'll run."

"I'm not running," she said, and leaned up to kiss him. "Not this time."

They lay side by side like that for a while, kissing, touching, stroking, gasping. When Marley was dizzy and panting and certain she was going to explode at any second, Will reached into the pocket of his jeans.

"Need help with that?" Marley asked, watching as he tore open the condom wrapper.

"Nope," he said, kissing her as he rolled the condom on and rolled onto her in one fluid move.

Marley gasped from the hot, solid weight of him and the force he used to push her legs apart with his hips. He hesitated for an instant, giving her one last moment to say no.

"Yes," she whispered, and twined her legs around him.

She pressed her heels into the back of his thighs and arched up, drawing him inside her in one slick motion.

They both gasped at once from the shock and heat and pleasure of it. He began to move, slowly at first, giving her time to catch her breath and adjust to the rhythm. Her thighs were still clenched tight around him, drawing him inside her as she savored the flex and release of muscle, the soft scrape of his leg hair against her bare inner thighs.

His breath was soft against her throat, and his gentle gasps of pleasure made her dizzy. He drew back to find her lips, to kiss her soft and deep. Marley kissed him back, drawing her nails down his back as he quickened the pace of his movements.

He opened his eyes and smiled down at her, his mismatched irises sparkling in the dappled light of the forest. Marley smiled back, trying to remember if she'd ever felt such a strong urge to grin like an idiot during sex.

"I think this is the longest you've ever gone without cracking a joke," she whispered as he thrust into her, his rhythm quickening again as Marley arched to feel him.

He grinned wider. "I save the jokes for awkward moments. So far, there haven't been any."

"It's still early."

He thrust into her again, deeper this time, harder. She could feel her thighs starting to quiver, her body tensing around him as a gentle hum started in her brain and throbbed outward. Marley cried out as the pleasure surged into a new dimension, one where sounds and smells and sights went blurry around her and the only thing left was this sensation, this dizzying, throbbing, all-consuming sensation.

"You're close," Will murmured against her throat.

A statement, not a question, but she nodded anyway as he thrust deeper into her, quickening his pace again. Marley could feel her breath coming harder, her heartbeat slamming hard against her ribs. Or was that his heart? They were intertwined now, just one solid mass of raw sensation and pleasure and—

"Oh, God!" Marley cried out, bucking against him as the first wave hit her. She screamed and clutched a fist-ful of the blanket, her fingers clawing the pine needles beneath it. She closed her eyes and gave in to the sen-sation, feeling wave after wave of it crashing against her. Will moved into her again and Marley matched him thrust for thrust, twining her legs around him to contain the sensation.

He was only a few beats behind her, and she knew the instant he'd tipped over the edge. His body tensed, and he gripped her shoulders hard as he drove into her again. Marley screamed again, both from her own pleasure and the awareness of his. She opened her eyes, surprised to see his open too, flashing with bliss and something deeper. He smiled and drove into her again, slowing now that both of them were drifting back down to earth, washed in waves of gratification as the river surged beside them and wind tickled the pine needles above.

As soon as she caught her breath, she arched up to kiss his shoulder.

"Well that was different."

Will rolled to his side, pulling her with him to snuggle tight against his chest. "I hope Bambi didn't see that. It'll scar him for life."

Marley giggled and buried her nose in his chest. "So what's next on the outdoor sex agenda—hunting or gathering?"

Will tightened his arms around her and nuzzled her hair. "How about you build a shelter while I go kill a bison?"

"Deal," Marley said, and sighed with bliss.

Chapter 19

WILL DROVE SLOWLY BACK TO CHEEZ WHIZ WITH ONE hand on the wheel and one hand on Marley. He really should have both hands on Marley. Ostentatious displays of wealth annoyed him, but maybe if he had a car with a driver, he could keep both hands on her at all times.

"What are you thinking?" Marley asked, reaching over to squeeze his knee.

"Thinking about fondling you," he admitted. "All the time, as much as possible."

"Sign me up for that," she said, grinning. She was quiet a moment, and Will looked over to see her looking thoughtful. "What do you mean by *all the time*?"

"Well, I do like to go to the restroom alone, and I'm not sure you'd be allowed in the locker room at my gym, but other than that—"

"I didn't mean literally," Marley said, gripping the door handle as Will took the corner to Cheez Whiz a little too sharply. "I guess I just wondered if this was a misguided workplace fling we're going to pretend never happened, or if it's something a little more serious."

"Definitely not serious," Will said, glancing at her again. Her expression was impassive, but he thought he saw a flicker of hurt in her eyes.

"Oh. Right, sure, of course."

"I'm rarely serious," Will said. "But if you can tolerate

a committed romantic relationship filled with bad jokes and good sex, I'm your man."

Marley laughed. "Relationship," she repeated, trying the word on for size. "Is that even possible, given the circumstances?"

"Do you want it to be?"

"Kind of," she admitted.

She looked out the window again, her hand still on the door like she was poised to jump from the moving vehicle if the conversation took a wrong turn. She cleared her throat. "What about the fact that you oversee the board that oversees my position and the strict rule about—"

"I'll step down," Will said so abruptly Marley whipped her head around and stared at him. "I've been on the board for years, so someone else can have a turn. Or I'll talk with Susan about the conflict. Hell, maybe I can work to change the rule. Really, Marley, it's not as big a deal as we've probably been making it. The obstacles to us having a relationship aren't that serious."

She was quiet again, and Will stole another look at her. She was still flushed from their lovemaking, and the faint scent of juniper clung to her clothes. He reached over and plucked a pine needle from her hair.

"My turn now," he said. "What are *you* thinking?"

She didn't answer right away, and her gaze was still fixed out the window. "Just thinking about work. There's a lot going on right now, and I want to do a good job."

"Is that why you were working on a Saturday?"

She shrugged. "Pretty much."

"In that case, I'll drop you at the front door instead of your car," he said, pulling the Volkswagen into the loading zone. "Can I call you later?"

"Definitely. I have this wine and cheese tasting event with a handful of donors at four, but I should be home by about six."

He braked in front of Cheez Whiz and unbuckled his seat belt. Leaning toward her, he cupped her chin in his hand and kissed her softly on the lips. "I hope to do that again very soon."

She smiled, and Will waited for it to reach her eyes. "Me too," she said.

She kissed him again, longer this time, and they were both breathing quickly when they broke apart. "I'll talk to you tonight."

"Looking forward to it," Will said.

She got out of the car and closed the door gently behind her. He watched her walk away, enjoying the sway of her hips as she disappeared into the building. *So beautiful*, he thought.

He was going to need to call Susan right away. To let her know he was either resigning his position on the board, or to demand they change the rule. One way or another, he had to make this work.

He glanced at his phone before pulling away and saw two text messages from Bethany. He scrolled through them and saw she'd asked him to drop by their house on the way home so she could give him some sample packs of doggie treats she'd gotten at the Humane Society. He buckled his seat belt again and headed that way, rolling down the windows to breathe in the scent of river water and sun-baked ponderosa pines.

No matter what happens, that scent will always remind me of Marley.

He shook his head, trying to get a hold of himself.

They'd only known each other a couple weeks, and here he was using words like *always* and *relationship* and considering giving up his position on the board. Surely he was rushing things.

But it didn't feel like it. This thing with Marley—it was the first time since his divorce that Will had really thought about a future with someone. Not just *someone*. A future with Marley.

He pulled up in front of April and Bethany's house and killed the engine. There was an extra spring in his step as he hustled up the walkway and banged on the front door.

"Hey, Will!" Bethany said as she flung the door open. "Just in time to play Monopoly."

"Try greeting me with, 'You're just in time to have an appendectomy on the kitchen table,' and I'll be more likely to come in."

"Come on." She grabbed him by the arm and dragged him inside, towing him into the living room. "Aunt Nancy is here, and we think she's cheating."

"Aunt Nancy always cheats at Monopoly. You don't need me to tell you that."

"No, but we need you to distract her so we can cheat, too."

"The moral code in this family leaves something to be desired," he said, but followed her to the living room anyway. April and Nancy looked up as they entered.

"Will, it's so lovely to see you," April said, smiling sweetly as she picked up a pair of dice.

Aunt Nancy grunted and used her elbow to knock a game piece into her lap. "You missed a good conversation at lunch today," she said. "Doug Parker and I discussed the fine points of agalmatophilia."

"I can only imagine," Will said, trying not to.

"That's the sexual attraction to a statue, doll, or mannequin," Bethany supplied. "In case you were wondering."

"I wasn't."

Aunt Nancy shook her head and palmed an orange $500 bill, sliding it into her lap while April's head was turned. "It's a good thing you got Marley away from that Doug character," she said. "Did you know he was married?"

Will frowned. "Married?"

"He slipped once and mentioned a wife," she said. "He tried to cover it up, but I heard. Do you think Marley knows?"

Bethany frowned and looked at Will. "Marley was on a date with a married man? That doesn't sound like her."

April picked up the dice and shook her head. "I'm sure there's some mistake. Marley's such a lovely person. There's no way she'd knowingly engage in an extramarital affair."

Will rolled his eyes. "Because what kind of person would do something like that?"

April flushed and looked away, and Will felt bad. Bethany just slugged him in the shoulder.

"We're immoral, lust-driven bitches," Bethany said cheerfully. "Marley isn't."

"Pity, that," Will said. "Look, I don't think it matters right now. I doubt she's going to see him again."

"I don't know," Aunt Nancy said, stealing a hotel from April's pile. "Before I left, he said he was seeing Marley again tomorrow."

"Seeing Marley, or *seeing* Marley?" Bethany asked, planting her hands on her hips as Aunt Nancy plucked two plastic hotel properties off the edge of the board and slid them up the sleeve of her dress.

"You know, in some families, words mean exactly what you think they mean and no one speaks in code," Will said. "We should try it sometime."

"Those families sound boring," Bethany said. "We're definitely not boring."

"Can't argue with that."

April frowned and looked up at Will. "Do you think it's possible Marley is dating a man who's trying to hide the fact that he's married?"

"No."

Aunt Nancy grunted. "So you think she's dating him knowing full well he's married?"

Will threw his hands up in exasperation. "No. Look, I don't think she's dating him at all. Not seriously, anyway. But if it makes you all happy, I can call Pete and have him check the guy out."

Bethany grinned. "I love that you have a friend in the FBI. If I were straight, I'd totally date him."

"I'll be sure to tell him," Will said, eager to flee the premises. "I'll give him a call tonight, okay? Not that I think it's necessary, but at this point it's worth it just to get you all off my back."

"That's the spirit," Bethany said.

"Whatever. I know how you all love Marley."

"Not the way *you* love Marley," Bethany said, grinning. "So are you going to stay and play?"

Will shook his head, already making a beeline for the door. "By the time Aunt Nancy's done, there won't be any game pieces left anyway. Besides, I need to get home and walk the dogs."

Bethany grinned. "Is that what the kids are calling it these days?"

Will tried not to laugh, but failed. He tossed his keys in one hand and made a move toward the door. "Where are those dog treats?"

"They're on the kitchen counter," Bethany said. "Just grab them on your way out."

"Thanks, ladies." Will waved to April and Aunt Nancy, who waved back and refocused on the game board. Bethany gave him another smack on the shoulder before marching back toward the coffee table to take her place between April and Nancy.

Will drove home the short way, driving along back roads and cozy neighborhoods. He was eager to see his dogs and even more eager for six thirty to roll around so he could call Marley. Maybe she'd be free for dinner, or maybe—

Will's phone rang as he pulled into his driveway.

"Hello?"

"Hey, Will," Bethany said, and Will felt a tinge of disappointment at hearing his sister's voice instead of Marley's.

Will tugged his keys out of the ignition and pressed the phone to his ear. "I know we're close, but don't you think conversing every five minutes is taking it a little too far?"

"Shut up, Will. Look, I just wanted to tell you not to forget to check into that Doug guy, okay?"

Will shifted the phone to his other ear and opened his car door. "Why are you so concerned?"

"Because we care about Marley. If some dirtbag is screwing around with her, she deserves to know."

"I'm sure she'd appreciate your concern."

"It's not just me. Aunt Nancy seems worried too. She insisted on looking in Doug's car before we left."

"Aunt Nancy broke into his car?"

"She didn't break in," Bethany insisted. "Just peered through the windows a little."

"And?"

"And she saw a gun. A least she thought she did."

"A gun?" Will tried to keep the alarm out of his voice.

"It was sticking out just a little bit under a blanket on the floorboards in back, so we can't be sure."

"We?"

"I might've been peering too."

Will sighed, grateful at least that he hadn't been called to bail his sister and his aunt out of jail for breaking into cars in the Cheez Whiz parking lot.

"Look," Bethany said. "I'm sure it's nothing, but just check, okay? Call Pete right away."

"That was my plan," Will said. "I'm heading inside to do it right now."

"Thanks, Will," Bethany said and hung up.

Will stuffed his phone back in his pocket and headed to his front door, stepping back to allow all three dogs a chance to bowl him over with their enthusiasm. "Hey, girl," he said, scratching Polly behind the ears before bending down to rub Omar's belly. Rosco dropped a soggy tennis ball at Will's feet and gave him a hopeful look.

"Give me five minutes, okay, guys? I just need to make a call."

The dogs trotted off, appeased by any word that sounded like *ball*. Will moved inside and set his keys down before pulling out his phone again. He scrolled through contacts until he found Pete's number. His friend picked up on the second ring.

"Yo, Will!" he shouted into the phone. "Long time, no see!"

"Howya doing, Pete?" Will said, rummaging through the basket by the door to find the dogs' leashes. "You coming out here to mountain bike before the snow starts flying?"

"I'm hoping to. Janice and the kids want to wait 'til ski season opens, but I always think this is the best time of year to visit Bend. So what can I do for you, man?"

"If it's not too much trouble, I was hoping you could check someone out for me."

Pete laughed. "Running with gangsters and thugs out there in the high desert?"

"Pretty much," Will said, pulling a Frisbee off the top shelf of the hall closet. "It's probably no big deal, but a friend of mine went on a date with a guy who seemed a little shady. Bethany and April will feel better if we have him checked out."

"Anything for Bethy and April. Give me his info."

Will rattled off what he knew about Doug, then hesitated. There was something else he wanted to ask, but his conscience was standing in the corner of his mind with crossed arms and a disdainful expression.

Don't be a jerk with trust issues.

Will cleared his throat. "While you're at it, could you check out one more person?"

"Sure, what's his name?"

"Her name," Will said, ignoring the stabs of guilt that felt like pinpricks in his spleen. "Marley Cartman."

"Marley Cartman. Got it. What are we looking for here?"

"I don't know," Will said, balling his fist around Rosco's leash. "Just being paranoid, I guess."

"Ah, I see. New girlfriend of yours?"

"Something like that."

"Say no more, my man. Can I call you back in about an hour?"

Will nodded and grabbed a handful of dog doo bags from a basket in the foyer. "Sure. Thanks for doing this. I owe you one."

"No worries. Catchya soon."

Will hung up the phone, feeling like a jerk. Why was he snooping into Marley's life?

Because you're a suspicious jerk with trust issues, his conscience suggested.

His conscience had a point. But didn't it cancel things out that he was going out of his way to figure out if a guy she might be dating had secrets?

You know she isn't dating him, his conscience argued. *Not after this afternoon, anyway.*

"Come on, guys," Will called to the dogs, herding them out the front door. "Let's go to the dog park."

He'd been gone a little over an hour when his phone rang. Will glanced at the readout, disappointed once more to see it wasn't Marley. So what if she wasn't off work yet? He wanted to hear her voice. To make her laugh, to make her moan, to make her—

"Hey, Pete," Will said. "What's up?"

"Got some good dirt for you this time, buddy," Pete said. "You owe me for this one."

"Dirt on Doug Parker?"

"Doug Parker, sure. The guy's a private investigator, married with a couple kids. But that's not what I meant."

Will stopped walking, and the dogs looked up at him with questioning eyes. Polly yapped once, but Will barely heard her over the roar of dread in his brain.

"What did you mean?" he asked slowly, wishing like hell he didn't have to hear the answer.

"This Marley Cartman, man," Pete said. "Wait'll you hear what I've got on her."

—∿—

Marley arrived back at the condo exhausted and mildly queasy. She kicked her shoes into a corner of the foyer as Magoo came running over, furry paws flailing. Marley bent to pet him and felt her stomach lurch. She dropped to her knees, mostly to make it easier to pet Magoo, but also because it put her a few inches closer to the garbage can in case the queasiness took a turn for the worse.

"Hey, buddy," she said, scratching her dog's ears as his stubby tail thrummed the ground. "Remind me why I agreed to go to a cheese tasting event when I'm lactose intolerant?"

Magoo licked her knee before flopping onto his back and looking up at Marley with pleading eyes. She began rubbing his belly as her own rumbled in warning.

"Because I'm an idiot," she told Magoo. "That's the answer to the question about the cheese party. I'm an idiot who agrees to go to a wine and cheese tasting because she thinks that's what's expected of the director of development for a major organization. How pathetic is that?"

Magoo refrained from voicing an opinion, but he did turn his head to the side so he could lick Marley's ankle. After about four minutes of belly rubbing, he rolled to his feet again and trotted off toward the kitchen. Marley plucked her phone out of her purse and glanced at it, disappointed to see Will hadn't called yet. True, it was only six twenty-five, and she'd said she'd be home by six thirty, but some clingy, needy part of her wished he was as eager as she was to talk again.

She smiled, flashing back to their romp in the woods that afternoon. She could still smell pine needles under her fingernails, still felt the scrape of his whiskers on her breasts. How long before she could touch him again?

Marley flipped the phone off and stood up, heading toward the kitchen where Magoo had gone.

"Dad?" Marley called, trailing a finger over the granite countertop. "Mom? Anyone here?"

She rounded the corner into the kitchen and spotted a note on the counter in her father's handwriting.

> *Marley: Your mom and I are watching the sunset.*
> *Don't wait up.*

"Great," Marley muttered, staring at the note for a few more seconds. Magoo's head snapped up, and Marley set the note back on the counter with a sigh. "It's possible my father is courting my mother," she told the dog. "Despite the fact that he already has another wife."

Magoo licked her left ankle, then moved to the right. Marley sighed. "If they get married again, would that make her his seventh wife, or his first wife squared?"

Magoo cocked his head to the side, then barked twice and trotted toward the living room. Marley watched him go, wondering what he'd decided to lick this time. Then she realized someone was knocking at the door. She padded after her dog, hoping there'd be something on the other side of the door that one of them might wish to hump.

She was smiling as she flung open the door to see Will. He wasn't smiling.

Not at all.

"Will?" she asked, taking a step back. "What's wrong?"

He folded his arms over his chest. "Is there anything you want to share with me, Marley?"

Marley winced at his tone as panic rose up her throat like bile. She took another step back and decided to try a page from his book. "I take it you're not asking me to share a cup of sugar, a roll of toilet paper, or a jar of Grey Poupon?"

Will shook his head, not cracking even the tiniest smile. Marley felt her gut curl into a tight ball as she pondered the fact that this was the first time she'd seen Will not in the mood to joke. Part of her wanted to shut the door in his face and open it back up to see the regular old Will standing there grinning and making jokes about sex in the woods.

Part of her knew why he'd come. And part of her was ready to get this over with. She was tired of hiding.

"Why don't you come in?"

He hesitated, then stepped into the foyer as Marley closed the door behind him and tried to pretend her hands weren't shaking.

When Will turned to face her, his expression was flat. Only his eyes betrayed his emotions, flashing with mismatched shades of anger.

"So," Will said, his voice disturbingly calm. "Was there some point you planned to tell the board of directors that you spent more than a year under investigation for fraud at your last job?"

Marley waited for the words to hit her like a punch to the gut. But she'd been braced for them, knew they were coming. The only thing she felt was a strange sense of relief this was finally on the table. She said nothing, waiting for Will to continue.

She knew there was more.

"There's also the fact that you declared bankruptcy and did a short sale on a home you owned in Portland. Relevant info for someone whose job is handling other people's money, don't you think?"

She swallowed, folded her arms over her chest, and licked her lips. "No."

"No?"

"No," she said calmly, measuring her words before she spoke them for once. "I don't think it's relevant. I wasn't aware we were required to exchange financial records before exchanging bodily fluids."

Will's eyes went wide for an instant, but he recovered quickly. "This isn't about me, Marley. It's about professionalism and integrity and trustworthiness and—"

"And the fact that you have enough trust issues for an entire football team of jilted lovers. The hell it's not about you."

Will blinked, clearly not expecting her to fight back. "Okay then, let's make it more about me. Care to tell me about the private investigator who's looking into how you managed to lose my aunt's valuable antiques?"

Marley gasped and took a step back. She hadn't seen that one coming. "I didn't lose them."

"No? They were trusted to you, weren't they?"

"They were trusted to the Cascade Historical Society and Wildlife Sanctuary," she said slowly, waiting for him to jump in with *Cheez Whiz.*

Will just shook his head. "You were in charge, Marley. You were the one tasked with getting the appraisal. You were the one—"

"Oh, spare me, Will," Marley snapped, her attempts at

a cool exterior cracking like a bad ice sculpture. "This has nothing to do with financial records or fraud or even your aunt's stupid sculptures which I *did not lose*, by the way. This is about you looking for reasons to mistrust anyone you're involved with so you don't get blindsided again. Congratulations, Will. Job well done."

She didn't mean to shout, but she realized her voice had risen at least six decibels by the time she hit the end of the sentence.

Which is probably why she didn't hear her parents.

"Marley?" her mother called from the kitchen. "What are you shouting about, dear? We heard you from all the way on the back porch. Such a pleasant sunset this evening."

Marley turned to see them marching into the foyer. Her mom wore ridiculously high heels, and her father clutched a glass of bourbon. His look of concern darkened as his eyes landed on Will.

"You again," Walter said, not sounding pleased about that.

"Marley, sweetie." Her mother planted a kiss on her cheek, engulfing Marley in a cloud of perfume. "What were you yelling about, dear?"

Marley closed her eyes and counted to ten, feeling her stomach roil. She wasn't sure whether to blame the cheese, the confrontation with Will, or the presence of her parents, but she suspected the combination of those things wasn't doing her any favors.

When Marley opened her eyes again, Will was handing her something.

"Here," he said, thrusting it into her palm. "Take these."

She blinked and looked down at her hand. Pink tablets wrapped in plastic? "Did you just give me Pepto Bismol?"

"Now there's a thoughtful gentleman," Judy said, beaming at Will.

Marley blinked at the tablets again, then looked at Will. "You show up on my doorstep to call me a fraud, a liar, and a thief, and then offer me Pepto Bismol?"

Walter cleared his throat. "It is the leading medicine offering fast relief for heartburn, nausea, indigestion, upset stomach, diarrhea—"

"Dad, please," Marley said, closing her fist around the tablets. Then she thought better of it and tore open the little plastic wrapper, chomping the chalky pink forms into minty dust. She couldn't decide whether to feel grateful or annoyed, but settled for saying nothing as she chewed.

"I assumed they'd come in handy," Will said coolly. "Since you just spent the evening at a cheese tasting event because you're more concerned with making friends than you are with making sure you don't puke your guts out from lactose intolerance."

Marley shook her head, her gratitude receding as quickly as it had washed over her. "Was that another accusation? Because I'm losing count now. Let's see, you called me financially irresponsible, a fraud, a thief, and someone who's overly concerned with winning friends and influencing people."

"I always said you'd make a great politician," her father said, clapping her on the shoulder. "We're proud of you, honey."

"Dad, please," Marley said, turning to glare at him. "Normal parents would give their daughter some privacy to fight with her lover. Mine regard it as a spectator sport."

"Lover?" Judy asked, perking up. "Honey, I didn't realize things had gotten serious between you two."

"Oh, don't worry, Mom," Marley said, turning back to Will. "There's very little risk of Will being serious about anything, ever."

Will folded his arms over his chest. "I'm pretty serious now."

"Well so am I. And not that this is any of your business, but yes—I declared bankruptcy. So did one-point-five million other Americans. I lost my job, Will. It happens. I've paid my dues and am working to move past it, and I don't feel it has any reflection on my ability to do the job I was hired to do here."

"But you lied—"

"I didn't lie. Nowhere on my employment application did it ask about bankruptcy. I just didn't volunteer the information."

"The application asked about fraud charges though, didn't it?"

Marley swallowed. She glanced at her mother, then her father, then back to Will. She opened her mouth to tell him to butt out, but her mom laid a hand on her shoulder.

"Stop protecting me, dear," Judy said. "That's what got you into trouble in the first place."

"Mom, don't—"

"Well, if he's going to come here all in a tizzy, he at least needs to hear the facts."

Will frowned. "Tizzy?"

Marley frowned. "Facts?"

Judy shook her head and looked at Will. "I ran a jewelry store in Portland for many years. Every now and then I'd contribute items to charity auctions. I got the tax write-off, and the non-profit group got the proceeds. But times got tight and, well—"

"She scammed them," Walter finished, folding his arms

over his chest and adopting a stance that mirrored Will's. "Made a bunch of fake jewelry and pretended it was the real deal."

"Scammed is such an ugly word," Judy said. "But I did donate a necklace I claimed was appraised at half a million dollars to a charity Marley was doing donor relations for, and when the buyer had it appraised—"

"He discovered it was fake," Walter finished. "And so was half the other jewelry she'd been selling that year."

Will stared at them, not saying a word. "But you were at the center of the investigation," he said to Marley. "According to my source—"

"You're right, I was," Marley said. "I'm the one who accepted Mom's donation, and I'm the one who failed to have it appraised at the outset. My fault."

Judy touched her daughter's arm. "I thought no one would know…"

"I should have known better," Marley said, pulling her arm away. Magoo whimpered softly at her feet, and Marley rubbed her shin against his side as she blinked back tears. It had taken her years to come to terms with this. *Years.* And Will thought he could just waltz in here and—

"So you covered it up?" Will asked.

"No," Marley said softly. "I turned her in."

She watched his face for a reaction, saw those mismatched eyes flash with surprise. *Good,* she thought, not sure why it mattered.

"Judy went to jail," Walter said, stepping up behind Marley and putting a hand on her shoulder. "And Marley was asked to resign from her job. Better than being fired, but willingly leaving a job means no unemployment benefits."

"And with no unemployment benefits and no job prospects," Marley began.

"Bankruptcy," Walter finished. "I would have helped her out if I'd known, but I was living in Japan for business that year, and Marley was too ashamed to say anything."

Marley shook her head, the shame apparent even now after all these years. "I sent my own mother to jail," Marley said. "I turned her in. I put her behind bars. So I guess you're right, Will."

Will blinked. "What?"

"About trusting people. Maybe it's best not to trust anyone at all, not even the people closest to you. Don't trust anyone *ever*—isn't that your motto?"

"Wait a minute—"

"No, Will. I'm done with this conversation. And I'm done with you, too. You can show yourself out. Congratulations on being right."

She turned away and walked slowly, deliberately down the hall, hoping like hell he couldn't see her shoulders shaking.

———

"If I'm right, why do I feel like such a dickhead?" Will asked.

Polly barked once, and Rosco followed suit. Will felt comforted by the reply, even though he knew it was merely because he gripped their tennis ball in one hand. He chucked it down the hall and watched the dogs scramble after it.

He looked down at Omar, who was rolled on his back with all four paws flailed in the air. Will rubbed the dog's belly and sighed.

"You notice she still never addressed what happened

to Aunt Nancy's donation," Will said. "She may have explained the finances and the fraud, but she clearly avoided the subject of the missing rock dicks."

Omar looked at Will, then licked his own nose and closed his eyes. Will rubbed his belly some more. "I know you're deaf, but sometimes I swear you're the best listener I know."

How had the confrontation with Marley gone so completely wrong? He'd gone in feeling self-righteous, determined to prove—

To prove what?

"To prove you can't trust her," he said aloud, feeling vindicated and stupid all at once.

Just hours ago he'd held her in his arms, certain they had a future together, certain he'd found someone who could make him laugh and smile and feel good all over. And when he'd discovered she might not be that at all—

"I was right," he said to Omar, moving up to scratch the dog's thick chest. "About not trusting her in the first place."

Omar opened his eyes and blinked.

That'll keep you warm at night.

"Are you communicating with me through telepathy?" Will asked the dog.

Omar was spared from having to answer when the doorbell rang. Polly and Rosco ran barking into the foyer, and Will stood up, feeling a flare of hope it might be Marley.

Stupid, he thought, but walked quickly anyway.

He opened the door and blinked against the glare of the porch light. She took a step forward, her hair blowing across her face and a miserable look on her face.

"Will, there's something I need to tell you."

Chapter 20

WILL STARED AT APRIL FOR A FEW MOMENTS, HER WORDS ringing oddly in his ears.

"I have something to tell you," she repeated, perhaps assuming he'd gone deaf. "May I come in?"

Will stood still, not sure he wanted to step aside and let her in. Hearing his ex-wife's problems was the last thing he needed right now. "You know, last time you started a conversation with *I have something to tell you,* you informed me you'd been walking-the-unicorn with my sister."

April sighed. "Please let's not start things off on that note. There's something very important I need to share."

"By all means," Will said, waving her in. The dogs leapt and bounded and pounced all over her with joy. April scratched their ears two at a time, stooping to kiss Polly on the snout.

"Such a lovely little doggie," she said as Rosco dropped his ball on April's foot.

Will stood watching her, ready to scream with frustration he knew had very little to do with his ex-wife. At last, she straightened up and looked around the living room. "I don't suppose I could trouble you for a cup of tea? It turned chilly out there this evening."

"April, why are you here?"

She shook her head. "You know, you used to be much better with foreplay."

Will blinked, taken aback by her words. He couldn't

recall ever hearing his sweet, kind ex-wife ever making a dirty joke in her life.

"I see Bethany has been rubbing off on you." He closed his eyes, wincing at his own innuendo. "That wasn't a sex joke, I swear."

"People change, Will," she said, brushing past him. He opened his eyes again and watched her walk toward the kitchen.

He didn't know what to say to that, so he moved toward the kitchen and pulled the teakettle off the back burner. He filled it with water, then reached into the cupboard for tea bags.

"Is that Marley's blueberry tea?" she asked.

The sound of her name made Will's gut clench, but he focused on preparing the tea, on not reacting to her name. "I ordered some online after I saw who makes it," he said. "Bought a whole case."

"Do you love her?"

Will dropped the mug on the counter, and it clattered noisily but didn't break. Rosco barked and clicked into the kitchen to sniff the dropped tea bag on the floor. April stepped around Will and stooped to pick it up, tossing it in the trash before turning back to face him.

"I was going to use that," Will said. "Five-second rule."

"Answer the question, Will. Do you love Marley?"

"Didn't you just show up on my porch saying you had an announcement? How'd we get from there to me serving you tea and answering questions about my love life?"

April sighed and leaned against the kitchen counter. "Marley just called Aunt Nancy to say she'd lost the family figurines. Said she felt horrible about it, but that she wanted the family to know, and she's handing in her resignation at the Cascade Historical Society and Wildlife Sanctuary. Effective immediately."

There was a faint buzzing in Will's head. He leaned against the counter, feeling dizzy. "She what?"

"You heard me, Will," April said, folding her arms over her chest in a way that was reminiscent of every fight they'd ever had. "And you probably already knew most of that. In fact, I'm guessing the reason Marley called is that you accused her of losing the figurines. And I'm guessing you accused her because you love her, and if you love someone, you're on the lookout for how they might fail you or betray your trust or—"

"Cut to the chase, April," he snapped, feeling each of her words like a punch to the gut. "I don't understand what you're getting at."

"I think you do, Will."

He sighed. "How did I become the bad guy here? Marley's the one who lost the figurines."

"Marley didn't lose the figurines. They were stolen."

"How the hell do you know that?"

"Because I stole them."

Will blinked. "Come again?"

"This is where I refrain from making the filthy joke you and Bethany would make about *coming*," she said. "I stole the figurines."

The teakettle began to scream and Will jumped. He pushed it off the burner, but didn't pick it up. Somehow, making tea didn't seem right in the moment. "You have a knack for shock value, April."

"I'm not trying to shock you. I'm trying to explain why I did it."

"I'm waiting."

She sighed. "I know those figurines have been Aunt Nancy's pride and joy for years, and that she assumed they were worth a lot of money. Remember when she asked me to help get her will in order a few years ago?"

"No."

"Well, she did. So I had a number of her valuables appraised."

"Including the figurines."

"Of course." She hesitated, choosing her words with caution. "The pieces aren't real Native American artifacts, Will. They're just contemporary art made to look rustic. At most, they're about fifty years old and not worth very much at all."

"I'm still not seeing what this has to do with your sudden urge to become a thief."

April shook her head, looking at him as though he was a very dense child. "I wanted to protect Nancy. I was as surprised as you were when Nancy suddenly decided to donate them. I knew she'd find out they weren't real, and it would just break her heart. I couldn't let that happen."

"And you didn't think having them *stolen* would break her heart?"

"Not as much as learning something she loved, something she treasured, something she held dear and believed in with all her heart wasn't what she thought it was." April's voice had risen to a soft shout, and she fell silent now, waiting for the words to sink in. "You can understand that, can't you?"

There was a faint buzzing in Will's ears. It was the sound of his brain trying to wrap itself around what his ex-wife was saying. "How—"

"I figured out where the spare key is kept in the

administration office," she said. "When I was catering that event last week, I snuck in and grabbed the key and carried the figurines out in my empty catering carts."

Will said nothing. He wasn't sure what to say. April watched him for a moment, then stepped over to the stove and grabbed the teakettle. She turned and filled both their mugs, then dropped a blueberry tea bag into each. She rummaged in the cupboard and found a jar of honey, stirring some into her tea before setting it to steep.

Will stayed silent the whole time, still too stunned to move.

"Say something, Will."

"I don't like honey in my tea."

April smiled, but pushed the mug toward him anyway. "Try it and see. Sometimes tastes change."

"Is that another lesson I'm supposed to follow?"

April sighed. "Will, when you and I got married, I really didn't know I preferred—"

"Sipping-the-mango-nectar?" Will grimaced. "I don't even know what that means."

"I didn't know I was a lesbian. Not for certain. And you didn't know that about me either."

"Obviously."

"So stop beating yourself up."

He frowned. "Excuse me?"

"Stop feeling guilty for holding me prisoner. For making me be someone I wasn't. You didn't do that to me. People are complicated. They have different sides, different things they like or don't like. Preferences change, or maybe they were always there but they reveal themselves at inconvenient times."

Will blinked down at his mug, wondering if he'd been

too hard on Marley, too hard on April, too hard on himself. He picked up his mug, blowing into the steam and breathing in the scent of blueberries and home and Marley.

"Say something, Will," April said, her voice pleading.

Will took a sip of tea and set the mug down. "I like the honey after all," he said. "And that wasn't a euphemism."

April smiled and blew on her tea before taking a sip. "It's very good."

Will waited for her to call it *lovely,* to offer him the sweet, reassuring smile that told him everything would be okay even when they both knew it wouldn't.

Instead, April gave him a wicked grin. "It's fucking great tea."

Will laughed and took a sip of his own. "So what happens now with the figurines? Is Aunt Nancy having a conniption?"

April shook her head. "You know what's funny? I don't think she was that surprised."

"Really?"

"Deep down, I think she already knew."

Will nodded. "Me too."

He waited for her to ask whether he was talking about the figurines or their marriage. It was the same answer either way.

Instead, April smiled and touched his arm. "You know the number one lesson I've learned from watching you with Bethany?"

"How to make crude jokes to diffuse awkward situations?"

"That's number two."

"Poop jokes are low-class."

"Shut up, Will." She shook her head. "The number one thing you've taught me is the value of forgiveness and unconditional love."

"Hmph," Will said, because he couldn't think of anything else to say.

"Aunt Nancy will forgive me eventually," she said. "Just like you and Marley will forgive each other."

She reached out and took the tea mug out of his hand, then gave him a gentle shove on the back. "Now get to it."

Chapter 21

MARLEY STOOD IN THE DIM LIGHT OF THE OTTER DISPLAY at Cheez Whiz and stared into the blue-green water of the tank. It was ten p.m., but Bridget the otter was hard at work making laps in the tank.

"Are you sure you won't change your mind, Marley?" Susan asked, turning away from the display and stepping close enough to touch Marley's arm.

Marley nodded and looked at her boss. "Those figurines went missing on my watch. It's only a matter of time until that becomes public knowledge. In light of what I just told you about my last job, I think it's in everyone's best interest if I just go quietly."

"But the private detective might find—"

"It doesn't matter." Marley swallowed hard and looked back at the tank. "I'll know that valuable artifacts went missing while I was in charge of them, and that's not okay."

Susan nodded and looked back at the water. "I appreciate you letting me know right away."

Marley shrugged. "I'm glad you were still here at work. I wanted to let you know in person. This seemed like the right place."

They both watched Bridget some more. Had it been just two weeks ago when they'd stood here preparing for the first board meeting? It seemed like a lifetime ago.

The door opened behind them, and Bed walked in. She

wore a deep frown and a diamond-studded rabbit pin on the lapel of her jacket.

"This better be good, young lady," Bed snapped, striding over to Marley. "You know how far it is for me to drive into town, and at this hour—"

"I'm resigning," Marley interrupted, drawing herself up straight.

"I beg your pardon?"

"I'm resigning from my position. Effective immediately."

The silence hung there for a moment, and Marley let it. No more jumping in to fill it for the sake of making someone more comfortable. No more stupid chatter about mauve rabbits and feigned interest in golf.

"And another thing," Marley said, folding her arms over her chest. "Your ironclad rules about dress codes and dating between board members and employees? They're stupid."

Bed drew herself up in a huff. "Young lady—"

"Don't *young lady* me. The way you treat people is disrespectful and patronizing. No one's had the balls to say it to you before because you're richer than God, but I'm through kissing ass. And I'm done here too."

Bed's mouth hung open, and Marley had a serious urge to toss in one of the dead fish Susan brought for Bridget the otter. Susan touched Marley's arm. Marley wasn't sure if it was a silent show of support or a move to escort a disgraced employee to the door.

She never found out. The door burst open again, and all three women turned to stare.

"Stop!"

Will marched through the doorway, a crazed look in his mismatched eyes and his jacket buttoned crooked. His gaze landed on Marley, and his expression softened. He stood there for a moment just looking at her. Then he strode forward, grabbing her by the hand.

"I don't accept," Will said.

Marley blinked. "I beg your pardon?"

"I don't accept your resignation." He looked at Susan, nodding. "As chairman of the board of directors, it's my job to oversee the director of development, correct?"

Susan took a step back. "Well, technically, yes. But—"

"Then I don't accept Marley's resignation."

"Will," Susan began. "I'm not sure you understand everything going on here. There are a lot of factors at play, and Ms. Cartman is capable of making her own decisions."

"She's done here," Bed snapped. "Good riddance, I say."

"She's not quitting," Will said. "Not without all the information, she's not. Marley didn't lose those figurines. I know where they are, and I know Marley had nothing to do with their disappearance. But that doesn't matter right now. What matters is that Marley knows she's wanted and needed and we desperately, urgently don't want her to go."

Marley stared at him, too stunned to form any coherent thoughts. When she opened her mouth, she had no idea what might come out. "Are you speaking on behalf of the board of directors or yourself?"

"He's not speaking for me," Bed snapped.

"Shut up, Bed," he said. "With all due respect. Until I either resign my position on the board, or grow a pair and fight you on all your stupid rules, I'm speaking as both a board chairman and a man who is wildly, madly, completely in love with you."

Bed frowned. "But we have nothing in common."

Will sighed. "Not you. *Ms. Cartman*. With Marley,

dammit." He turned to Marley and took a careful step toward her. "Marley, I love you. *I love you.*"

Susan blinked, then put her hand on Bed's shoulder. "Maybe we should wait outside."

"Absolutely not!" Bed barked.

Susan fixed her eyes on Bed with a glare so intense, even Marley shuddered.

"Right now," Susan said, her voice terrifyingly chilly.

Bed's eyes widened, but she gave a nod of assent. The two of them marched away, and Marley watched their backs retreating. When they were out of earshot, Marley turned back to Will.

"What the hell?" Marley asked, too stunned to come up with anything more coherent.

He grabbed both her hands. "Marley, you were right. I do have trust issues. I can't promise they'll go away, but I can promise I'll do my damndest to believe in you. To believe in *us*. Please say you'll stay."

Marley looked down at their intertwined fingers. She stared at them for seconds—maybe minutes—thinking about Will and laughter and love and everything else they'd shared. She looked back up into his mismatched eyes.

"Did you know that otters hold hands?" she asked.

"What?"

She squeezed his hands hard and blinked in the dim light. "To keep from drifting apart. They do it when they sleep, so they'll stay together even if the water gets rough."

Will nodded and squeezed her hands in return. "After four years of my sister's wordplay, I have to say that's the best metaphor I've ever heard."

"I'm learning to stand up for myself," she said. "To

not base my decisions on what I think other people want from me."

"And I'm learning to trust," Will said. Marley raised an eyebrow, and Will shrugged. "I'm a slow learner."

Marley laughed, and Will squeezed her hand. "Seriously, I need to be better about giving you the benefit of the doubt. About realizing part of what makes you good at your job is your ability to read people and figure out what they need to hear. That isn't such a bad thing."

Marley smiled and looked back in the otter enclosure. "I can't claim I'll always know exactly who I am and that I won't shift my interests from time to time. I can't promise I won't sometimes be a flake, even if I try hard to make choices for myself instead of based on what I think other people want. But I can promise you'll always recognize me, one way or another."

"You're hard to miss."

Marley grinned wider, looking into his eyes. "Scientists did a study on sheep where they showed them pictures of other sheep and gave them a reward if they moved toward a certain picture. After a while, the sheep learned to pick the same sheep's face eighty percent of the time and could remember an image for up to two years."

Will grinned and pulled her close. "I'm planning for longer than two years."

Marley angled her head up to kiss him. "Me too."

"I love you."

"I love you too."

"Baaah."

"Baaah," she said, and kissed him.

Acknowledgments

While the Cascade Historical Society and Wildlife Sanctuary (Cheez Whiz!) bears some resemblance to the Museum of the Rockies in Bozeman, Montana, and to the High Desert Museum in Bend, Oregon, those organizations are infinitely more professional and well-organized. A million thanks to Cathy Carroll and Melissa Hochschild for allowing me to pick your brains about the inner-workings of such establishments, and for not laughing when I decided a historical society/wildlife sanctuary was a great setting for romance. You ladies are class acts.

Much appreciation to the entire Visit Bend team for the endless support, and for not freaking out when I decided to set a story in the very town we're all tasked with marketing.

Thank you to Judah McAuley for the penis research, and to our respective spouses for knowing that's not as filthy as it sounds. Thank you to Errica Liekos for the photos of stone dildos. That's exactly as filthy as it sounds.

I'm grateful to Malin for giving me April, along with the encouragement to write a lesbian relationship that's wacky, loving, a little risqué, and no big deal.

Huge thanks to Elyse Douglas of Douglas Fine Jewelry Design for indulging my questions about how to get thrown in jail for selling fake jewelry, and for making my lunch hours brighter with your lovely, sparkly creations. I'm also grateful to Jamie Flanagan for being the savviest, sexiest Pure Romance consultant on the planet.

A million hugs and sloppy smooches to my amazing critique partners, Linda Brundage, Cynthia Reese, and Linda Grimes, as well as my terrific beta readers, Larie Borden, Bridget McGinn, and Minta Powelson. I couldn't do this without your eagle eyes and utter fearlessness when it comes to pointing out when I've managed to wedge my head up my butt again.

Thank you to Jessica Corra for being my sounding board and co-pilot in navigating the unexpected terrain of post-divorce authorhood and the weird, wonderful world of single fathers and their offspring. We've gotta write that book someday.

Thanks to the Bend Book Bitches, my RWA chaptermates, and the readers of my blog, *Don't Pet Me, I'm Writing*, for unwavering support and book love.

Thanks to Deb Werksman, Danielle Dresser, Todd Stocke, and everyone else on the Sourcebooks team for being so fabulous. You guys rock!

I am eternally grateful to Michelle Wolfson, the best agent and support system any writer could hope for. Without you, I'd still be hunkered under my desk rocking back and forth drinking wine and cursing.

Thank you to my parents, Dixie and David Fenske, for every butt pat, pep talk, good laugh, or genetically shared brain cell. I owe everything to you guys. Thanks also to my baby brother, Aaron "Russ" Fenske, and his lovely bride, Carlie Fenske, for always being so genuinely eager to read my books.

Thanks to Cedar and Violet for being the most amazing little people on the planet, and a daily source of joy, laughter, and fart jokes.

And thank you to Craig for being the best reason I can imagine to write a book about finding love where you least expect it.

About the Author

Tawna Fenske traveled a career path that took her from newspaper reporter to English teacher in Venezuela to marketing geek to PR manager for her city's tourism bureau. An avid globetrotter and social media fiend, Tawna is the author of the popular blog *Don't Pet Me, I'm Writing* and a member of Romance Writers of America. She lives with her gentleman friend in Bend, Oregon, where she'll invent any excuse to hike, bike, snowshoe, float the river, or sip wine on her back deck. She's published several romantic comedies with Sourcebooks, including *Making Waves* and *Believe It or Not*, as well as the interactive fiction caper *Getting Dumped* with Coliloquy and the novella *Eat, Play, Lust* with Entangled Publishing.